THE KIND GHOSTS

She sleeps on soft, last breaths; but no ghost looms
Out of the stillness of her palace wall,
Her wall of boys on boys and dooms on dooms.

She dreams of golden gardens and sweet glooms,
Not marvelling why her roses never fall
Nor what red mouths were torn to make their blooms.

The shades keep down which well might roam her hall.
Quiet their blood lies in her crimson rooms
And she is not afraid of their footfall.

They move not from her tapestries, their pall,
Nor pace her terraces, their hecatombs,
Lest aught she be disturbed, or grieved at all.

WILFRED OWEN
JULY 30, 1918

One

MAY 1924, LONDON

I followed my brother across a plateau where a bitter wind howled and the sky flashed. A sudden glare revealed churned earth and a monstrous coil of metal. My brother marched ahead, immaculate in his cap and pressed uniform. I tried to keep up but floundered thigh-deep in mud. Though I thrashed and scrabbled, there was nothing to hold on to, neither root nor rock.

At last I wrenched a foot free but James was now yards ahead, far beyond my reach. I clutched at my thigh with both hands and hauled until it was released and I could crawl forward. The front of my night-gown was a sheet of freezing sludge.

"Jamie."

He trod lightly, springing from one dry patch to another. The sky flickered again, and this time I saw a man fallen like a puppet on the wire, back arched, legs splayed. And in the next flash there was another boy, perhaps fifty yards ahead, waving. Tears made runnels down his filthy cheeks, his mouth gaped, and the lower half of his body was a mash of blood and bone.

I faltered again. "James," I cried, through lips clogged with mud, "come back," but he didn't hear me. His arms were extended toward the boy.

The sky roared. Above a shudder of gunfire came the earsplitting whizz and crack of a shell. I yelled again, "James," but my voice was drowned by an explosion that swiped my brother off his feet, plucked him upward, and crucified him against a violent flare of light.

He thumped back to earth.

Silence.

He was facedown, one arm torn away at the shoulder. When he raised his head, I saw that the side of his face had been blown off and an eyeball dangled by a thread in the space where his right cheek should have been.

He looked at me with his good eye, a chip of ice.

"It's me, Jamie. Don't you know me?"

The eye went on staring.

"I'll be there in a minute, Jamie. One minute. Please wait . . ."

The mud held me fast and the night thundered again. If only I could reach him, hold his face to my breast. Then he would be covered up and made warm, healed. In a shattering racket of shellfire I fought the grip of mud that dragged me deeper, deeper, away from James, and filled my mouth, nostrils, and eyes.

Another pause, this time prolonged. I was hot, breathless, shaking, my eyelashes wet. Moonlight shone through the thin bedroom curtains. My skirt and jacket hung ghostly on the wardrobe door, my heap of underclothes shimmered.

From two floors down came a knock on the front door.

I fumbled for my watch, carried it to the window, found it was two thirty-five. Though I yearned to be back inside the dream—this time I had so nearly reached my brother—already my hands were struggling with the sleeves of my dressing gown, my feet had pushed into their slippers.

The landing was quiet. Thank heavens nobody else had heard the knocking, no sign even of Prudence, jowls aquiver, hairnet remorselessly pinned to thinning hair. Stairs groaned underfoot. My hand, still trembling from the dream, skimmed the banister; and my heel caught on the last stair rod. In the hall the trapped smells of the house fluttered like moths: dinners, rose water, endurance.

Knock, knock, knock-knock. "Oh, please be quiet," I muttered. A seepage of yellow from the lamp outside oozed through the fanlight and fell across the hats on the hall stand—James's boater, Father's trilby—and the silvery haze of looking glass. I grasped the latch, my jaw tightened to conceal whatever emotion, other than outrage (surely permissible in the circumstances), might be thrust upon me.

A child of about six stood on the doorstep under the spread beams of light, his face upturned; a neat, rectangular brow, shadowed eyes, lower lip drooping with sleeplessness. My body sagged so that I clung to the doorframe for support. Dear God, James, stepped from my dream, whole, a child again. In a moment his clenched fist would unfurl to reveal the best, the shiniest, the weightiest marble.

My voice was a thread. "No. No, it can't be."

"Forgive us if we woke you," came a voice from farther down the steps and dimly I registered a transatlantic twang. "Evelyn, is it? I would have known you anywhere. You are so like your brother and he described you so fondly, your hair especially."

A woman's head appeared level with the child's shoulder, her face bony and neat-featured, with a pointed chin. Despite her confident words she seemed high-strung as a cat; the sinews in her neck were taut and her eyes too wide-open. Extending a small, gloved hand, she said: "I'm Meredith Duffy, and this is my boy Edmund. Perhaps we should not have woken you but the boat got in very late and though I thought of looking for a hotel, in the end I decided to come right on here."

I stared at the exhausted boy, who swayed slightly. "James," I murmured. "Jamie."

"Yes, he really is so like his father, it's uncanny. I'm hoping that you might have some photographs of James when he was a child so we can compare father and son at the same age." She took yet another step toward me and I noted a trim ankle beneath a daring hemline. Behind her on the pavement was a collection of neat though shabby traveling bags. "Oh, this isn't *all*," she exclaimed, "I have another trunk and assorted boxes, I'm afraid, but we couldn't manage them in the cab. They'll send them on tomorrow morning."

Mother and child were like a tide coming in over the steps and across the threshold. "I absolutely do not understand," I said.

The woman gasped and put her hand to her mouth. "Don't say you never got my letter. Oh, the post from Canada is so unreliable. I expect it will arrive tomorrow, just when we don't need it. No wonder you're surprised to see me. I must admit I was puzzled that nobody was there to meet us off the boat, but now I understand completely."

"But don't you see," I said, still blocking the way, "I have no idea who you are."

She frowned. "But you must. I'm Meredith and Edmund here is my son, your brother's child."

The boy's prominent eyes were fixed on my face, occasionally losing focus as his eyelids fluttered. Brown knees stuck out from beneath flannel shorts: my brother, at precisely the height when, if I knelt, his head was level with mine as he gripped me with monkey arms and legs. We used to call it *a cling*. But here, on the step, in the small hours of Monday, May 19, 1924, with the dream of the real James still fresh, this other child was unreachably out of time.

"I didn't know James had a son," I said.

"Well, surely you must have done. Unless . . . don't tell me your father kept it from you all this while."

"My father died last year." The boy's hair, I noted, sprouted up at the crown in a backward quiff; his lower lip was moist and full.

"Ah, that explains a great deal. I'm sorry. I would so like Edmund to have known his grandpa. But listen, I must get this child to bed. We don't mind where we sleep," Meredith was saying. "After the ship we're just so grateful not to be afloat, on *waves*. A sofa and a blanket would do."

Surrendering, I leaned forward to take the child's hand—I knew that it would feel warm and a little sticky in mine—but he hung his head and held back, so instead I picked up the luggage. Now I was terrified lest he disappear, but mother and child came tripping into the house hand in hand, she with just her little purse hanging from a chain over her shoulder while I struggled with a cluster of bags. "We must be very quiet," I whispered. "I don't want anyone else to be woken."

We crept upstairs, past James's hat and blazer on the hall stand, the urn of dried flowers on the half-landing, the sleepers on the first floor and the gallery of Victorian Giffords above the dado, to my own landing, where the door to James's bedroom was kept tight shut, but in the spare room next door, where a couple of empty beds lay flat as boards covered by camberwick bedspreads. I took armfuls of mothball-smelling blankets from a linen chest and starched sheets from the airing cupboard, but when we set to work I was put to shame: Meredith was an expert bed-maker, who could create angular corners and shake a pillow dead-center in its case first time, whereas I hadn't made a bed since Girton.

I showed them the bathroom but told them not to flush the lavatory at this hour. Meredith only gave me a preoccupied smile and it was clear that I was now expendable. She was lifting the child's shirt over his head; I glimpsed pale, smooth skin, the little disks of nipple and navel, the fragile collarbone. My boy, how I would have kissed him between neck and shoulder.

They ought to be fed, I realized, and crept down to the kitchen for something suitable. A hot drink was impossible, as it would mean re-lighting the stove, beyond me at the best of times. In the end I took up cold milk and cookies; by the time I'd climbed three flights of stairs, there was no light under their door—they must already be asleep—so

I went back to bed and lay, picturing the boy tucked up under the white sheet, his palm beneath his cheek. In a little while he would turn onto his back and throw his arm across the pillow.

The house seemed to sag under the weight of these new arrivals. Rigid as an effigy, I relived the last half-hour: the dream of James, the child on the doorstep, James's child. As dawn thinned the darkness, I tried to work it out. James had written regularly, right up to a fortnight before his death, and never mentioned this woman Meredith. I thought he confided everything in me. Was it possible that he had time, in the midst of war, to conduct a love affair? Had my father really known? Why had nothing been said? And what did this woman, now installed with her son in the spare room, want from us?

℀

At six o'clock, abandoning any attempt to sleep, I got up. Above me, on the attic floor, our maids Min and Rose (collectively known as *the girls*, though both approached sixty) were astir. The light, reflected off the white tiles in the bathroom, was pitiless when I risked a glance in the mirror. The Canadian woman, Meredith, had been lying; I was nothing like my clear-eyed brother. My thirty-year-old face was all hollows and angles, my gaze haunted.

Fumbling with the small buttons of my blouse, I tried to decide how best to alert the household to our visitors' arrival. The process would be a tedious one and I was bound to be held responsible for the shock. The maids were straightforward; they must simply be told that for the time being there were two extra mouths to feed (without additional housekeeping money). Grandmother (maternal), nearly deaf and partially blind, would be agog with interest but slow to comprehend the complexities of the situation. Prudence, Father's elder sister, would have a hundred remarks and accusations. And Mother would weep.

But she, after all, was Father's widow and nominal head of the family. James was her son and Edmund her grandson. It was Monday morning and I was due to leave the house at eight. There was nothing for it but to break the news at once, so I went down to the kitchen, had Rose make a pot of tea, and carried it up to Mother's bedroom myself.

She had the infuriating habit, blamed by Prudence on poor circulation and lack of exercise, of being cold even in the height of summer. At any rate, I found her sound asleep under a winter quilt, the room a fug of sleeping female flesh and lavender. As I swept back the curtains, she raised herself on one arm, gray-brown hair falling away onto the pillow, hand shielding her eyes. In her youth, when a soft chin, melting eyes, and tight lacing were all the rage, Mother had been considered a great beauty. Now in her mid-fifties, she was too thin and her lips drooped at either end as if with the weight of abandoned hope. "What is happening? What's the time?"

"I've brought tea because I need you to wake up properly so I can talk to you. You'll need to be very strong, Mother, and prepare yourself for a great surprise." I perched on the edge of the bed, allowed her a sip of tea, and then removed the cup and saucer because I was afraid her hand would jolt. "We have a visitor whose name is Meredith. She has come with a small boy called Edmund who she claims is James's son. From what I can gather, she and James had a love affair during the war. There now, that's all I know. Would you like more tea or will you spill it?"

I had seen her receive shocking tidings before, of course, and knew she did not manage it well. On this occasion, she fell back on the pillow, arms rigid on either side, shut her eyes, and took gasping breaths while I studied the greasy smear made by the milk on the surface of her tea and wondered if I might have been less brutal. But I was irritated by these dramatics, which were all too predictable and ensured that the rest of us felt we had to protect her from bearing responsibility.

Mother now covered her face with both hands and moaned: "I can't believe it. I can't . . ."

I had always disliked her bedroom, which as a child I regarded as a distastefully private place where I was summoned for little chats while Mother put up her hair or fastened her corsets. At dead center, on a strip of Turkish rug, stood a round table covered by a lace-trimmed cloth, upon which a writing box with brass fittings was placed, like a reliquary. This was the repository of James's school reports, his letters, and the appalling telegram. On the mantel were twin oval photograph frames, one containing a picture of James aged thirteen when he started at Westminster; the other my father in his prime, dressed in top hat and tails, his belly round and his smile hearty between beard and mustache. Father, before James's death, had been powerful and noisy, with a glint in his eye that spoke of a hunger to earn, own, conquer. The only photograph of me was relegated to a side table. Aged twelve years, I had been decked out in a frothy gown and ringlets for a studio portrait in which my mutinous eyes and thrusting jaw were strikingly at odds with the soft curls and girlish throat.

"They woke me at about three," I told the prostrate figure in the bed, "so I put them in the spare room. I've asked Rose to grill extra toast when they get up. I'm about to leave for the office, but I expect our visitors will sleep late and then they could go for a walk or something, which will keep them occupied until I get home."

Mother's round eyes opened. "Oh, no, no, no you can't leave me."

"I must, I'm afraid."

"But you can't ask me to deal with them on my own, Evelyn. I can't take in what you're saying. A boy? James's son? But how can we believe them? They might be impostors. What proof is there?"

"The child is unmistakably James's son, I would say. You've only to take one look at him to know that. Meredith says she was in correspondence with Father, but lately of course he didn't reply. Do you know anything about all this?"

Mother's eyelid gave the merest flicker as she shrank down under the quilt. She had known of the boy's existence and kept it from me; that much was clear. The knowledge diminished my sympathy still further. "Well, I am going to work now. Be prepared for the fact that Edmund is so like James, it's as if James were a child again." The image shimmered between us, prompted by the miniature Jameses that hung from ribbons in the alcove by her bed: baby James in a bonnet on her knee; James the schoolboy in cap and overtight tie; James in cricket whites. For a moment, I thought I would reach her; I ached for her to recognize that I suffered too, that I had been struck by the savage disjunction between one child and another.

Instead she wept. "Ah, no, don't leave me, oh, Evelyn, what shall I tell Mother and Prudence? How could you be so cruel?"

"I can because I must. I am needed elsewhere." I ran swiftly downstairs to the hall, where Min was passing through with a breakfast tray, bottom lip caught between her teeth as a sign that she was suppressing comment with difficulty. "Please make sure that our visitors have everything they need, Min. I forgot to give them towels last night."

Then I rammed on my hat, skewered it with a pin, buckled the belt of my jacket, and seized my briefcase and gloves. As I set off into a warm, blowing morning, I thought: Thank God, I have my work.

Two

Male *Giffords had been lawyers* for generations. Our house in Clivedon Hall Gardens, Maida Vale, was adorned by portraits (bad oils or stiff daguerreotypes) of gentlemen with the same demanding eyes and fob watch as my father; each, in his turn, a luminary of the firm Gifford & Aldridge. When James and I were children, sometimes, as a treat, we were taken to visit Father's office in Holborn, where James, as young as three, was placed in Father's chair from whence he beamed at a procession of admirers, his plump hands pummeling the arms and his cheeks bulging with toffee supplied by the elderly Mr. Aldridge, who promised to teach young Master Gifford all about property law, the moment he was old enough.

Since nobody else was interested in my future, I plotted it myself. Hurdle number one was to get myself sent to a decent school. Mother deplored the idea but Father, more indulgent, said it would keep me amused, so each morning I went by omnibus to St. Paul's in Hammersmith. On the way, from my perch on the top deck, I glimpsed other lives, less ordered and opulent than my own. At twelve, I was introduced to a bowdlerized version of *The Merchant of Venice* and fell in love with Portia, who contrived to be wayward, clever, and successful, all qualities I wished to have (I was resigned to being without beauty and thought I didn't care for wealth). Later we studied the French Revolution and found that the likes of Robespierre, with the compelling sea green eyes (same color as my own), had also trained as a lawyer. The law, it seemed to me, was my destiny. I discovered that though the British Law Society stood firm against women lawyers ("If there's one calling in the world for which women are conspicuously unfitted . . ."), my legally qualified sisters were allowed to practice in the United States, in Canada, India, France, and Denmark. Surely it was just a matter of time.

James was on my side. "The main argument is: tradition dictates that women should not be lawyers and the law is governed by tradition. Just wait and see, Evie. Tradition is usually overturned in the end by historical imperative. One day you and I will be partners in a firm called Gifford & Gifford. And we won't deal with property, like Father, we'll deal with crime and family law. We'll speak for those least able to stand up for themselves."

But when I finished school in June of 1911, Mother put her foot down and said my gadding-about days were over. She had me fitted with stays and rustling silk petticoats and hooked me into high-necked muslin day dresses and revealing evening frocks with tiers of lace in the skirt. Meanwhile, I fumed and fretted at the wasted time spent piling up my hair, filing my nails, changing for tea, and talking to stupid women in the drawing room where I wasn't even permitted to read a newspaper. Whenever I dared, I pleaded headache, stomachache, fatigue, faintness, anything to escape to my room, where I had squirreled away books and files borrowed from a clerk in Father's firm. With my sharp elbows resting on the dressing table, I made careful notes in a series of red exercise books.

When war was declared, James was seventeen. Gripping him by the lapels, I butted him playfully in the chest. "Oh, how terrible it must be, poor Jamie, to have a choice. Save the country or go to Wadham. Poor, poor little James Gifford, which shall he do?"

"Father says I have no choice. He says fighting for one's country is the greatest glory a man can hope for. He says he wishes he were me."

"But you might die. Has Father thought of that?"

I had spoken flippantly—at that time, the war was not *real* to me—and I was stricken by the dread in his aquamarine eyes. But he went to war and I signed on for work at the censorship office. And afterward, when it was all over, I thought well at least I can work, at least that is left to me. When I pleaded to be sent to Girton, Father was too deep in mourning to refuse.

In 1922 the Law Society at last opened its doors to women. But as I soon realized, passing exams was only half the battle, because who, given the choice, would employ a female? The handful of females I knew who qualified with me and actually found employment had usually done so by family connections. Though I applied to perhaps thirty firms in search of articles, none would look at me. In the end, I disguised my name and college on the application letter by writing *E. Gifford, graduate of Cambridge*, but the shock when I appeared in person wearing a four-year-old gray wool two-piece with drooping pockets in the jacket and a skirt ending three inches above my ankles was always too much. Interviews rarely lasted more than ten minutes. Nobody wanted a woman, however she was clothed. "We must give priority," said the pinstriped legal gentlemen who deigned to give me an interview, "to the poor fellows back from the trenches. And in any case, my dear young lady, the law is no place for a woman. What would your father. . . ?"

As they well knew, my father would rather have employed a criminal half-wit than me, provided he was male. It was one thing to give your headstrong daughter an education, quite another to let her into your office. So I filled my time in those tense and dreary months of unemployment (during which I had to put up with a nightly chorus of lamentation from Mother and Aunt Prudence that I would even dream of becoming a lawyer) reading the *Law Society Journal* and applying for clerkships. Most mornings were spent observing in courts across London. A couple of afternoons a week I volunteered at Toynbee Hall, a settlement in the East End that offered education, cultural activities, and advice, including legal help for those who couldn't afford a lawyer. Occasionally, at Toynbee, there'd been a burst of joyous camaraderie with other students past and present: Appelbe, the MP Clement Atlee, and Carrie Morrison, a friend from Girton with whom I became an expert in the law concerning rent arrears, employment rights, and death duties. On the whole, though, it was a lonely time, haunted by the knowledge that it should have been James, not me; that if James were alive, his path would have been smoothed by a combination of his own talents and Father's connections. The obstructive legal world became in my mind associated with guilt.

But at Toynbee I made a vital though tenuous connection. A name that Carrie mentioned often as a champion of the poor was Daniel Breen, and one day, from the public benches of Bow Street Magistrates' Court, I witnessed a performance by this famous Mr. Breen himself.

The defendant was a woman in threadbare overalls, disheveled after a night in the cells. From her appearance, one would judge that she could not have afforded a cup of tea let alone a solicitor to speak for her, and yet she was represented by a smartly dressed, snapping-eyed lawyer who berated the police for imprisoning a woman overnight merely because she had stolen a secondhand scarf from a dealer in the Old Kent Road. "*Secondhand,*" he said, glowering at the bench, and I noted that his vowels were not quite as polished as my own, "worth a farthing at most, I'd say. Of course the police were only doing their duty in arresting her, we can't have an *honest* secondhand clothes' dealer stripped of his assets" (a raised eyebrow, a glint in the eye inviting the bench to share the joke), "but what's wrong with a caution? Admittedly my client has numerous previous convictions for like offenses, but the temperature yesterday afternoon was below freezing, and she has only the clothes she stands up in. Small wonder she was tempted by a scrap of moth-eaten wool. If I were addressing a less-experienced bench, I might despair, but you, Your Worships, with your considerable knowledge of these types of cases, will seek not just to punish but to reform. Now I have found her a place in a hostel for. . . ."

Breen thereby alternately hectored and flattered the magistrates until they were so full of compassion and largesse that the defendant, who had appeared dozens of times in the courts and was surely due for a lengthy spell of imprisonment, was given half a crown from the poor box and sentenced to a night in the cells, deemed to have been already served.

Afterward, I pursued Breen, who scurried out of court so fast that I could scarcely keep up with him: "I was wondering, sir, do you need a clerk?" He stood stock-still and regarded me with his head on one side, like a blackbird. "I heard your name mentioned at Toynbee Hall and I have been looking out for you. I'm a bachelor of law and I need to be given a chance. Nobody will take me, because I am a woman. But you, sir, I think you might."

His best features were his fiery eyes and exceptionally fine skin, otherwise he was unremarkable-looking, perhaps forty years old, blunt-nosed, balding but with a frizz of wild hair above his ears, and barely an inch taller than me. "You know nothing about me."

"I know you by reputation. My friend Carrie Morrison speaks very highly of you. And I saw you in court today. I guessed you would listen to me at least."

"Put it in writing. I can't stop now." And he was off, clapping his trilby low on his brow as he hurried down the courtroom steps. But I had noted a flash of interest and knew he wouldn't forget me, so I found out his address from an usher and within an hour had written my letter.

Later, I discovered that my application to Breen could hardly have failed, given that the source of his immense energy was a passion for proving everyone else wrong. It was therefore a characteristically Machiavellian move to take on a female. The fact that I had been turned down by dozens of firms with partners educated at private school and Oxbridge rather than grammar school and London, like himself, inflamed him further.

However, his championing of my cause had not so far extended beyond accepting one hundred and fifty pounds by way of a fee (a crippling amount that drained the entire fund my father had set aside for my dowry) and allocating me sad and unsavory cases usually involving women in marital difficulties; a mountain of paperwork, such as the copying out of wills and writs; and a very unpleasant space in which to conduct my business.

⚭

Breen & Balcombe occupied the ground floor and basement of a sixty-year-old terraced house in Arbery Street off the Euston Road. My so-called office was in what was once the basement kitchen. No sunlight had ever shone there, and the room was still equipped with a greasy stove and a wooden rack on a pulley for drying laundry, which I sometimes employed as an extra shelf for documents. Over the past twenty or so years, the old kitchen had become the last resting place for files, so that I worked in a gloomy nest of paper and cardboard harboring a host of black beetles.

Aside from Breen and his partner, Theo Wolfe (the Balcombe half of the partnership was never mentioned and, I believe, had died out several generations back), the only other employee was Miss Drake, the secretary, a thin-haired woman who had perfected the art of speaking without moving her lips, and who viewed me as an upstart traitor to her sex and therefore contrived not to communicate directly with me at all. On my first morning, Miss Drake, instructed to give me a guided tour of the premises, had done so without once looking me in the eye and had ended by showing me a cupboard in the kitchen, housing a stinky mop and stiffened dusters, as if to suggest that my true vocation actually resided there.

Nevertheless, when I pushed open the street door and descended to my fusty office, I usually felt relieved to be out of reach of the clinging tentacles of home. Even on the Monday my nephew exploded into my life, when part of me longed to run back and reassure myself that the boy really was asleep with his mother in the spare room, I was glad not to be a part of the inevitably tortuous conversation between the females of Clivedon Hall Gardens and the interloper Meredith over the toast and marmalade. Though the events of the past twelve hours hung about my consciousness like black drapes and my eyes stung with lack of sleep, I tucked my chair up close to my pitted desk, dipped my pen, pulled closer a spike holding a pile of bills awaiting payment, and began writing the first of a series of polite but firm reminders.

So, James had fathered a son. James, my lovely, soft-haired young brother had embarked on a love affair. (I scrunched up a page spoiled by too many errors and hid it in my pocket—among Breen's many pet hates was wastage of paper.) James was so careful, so intact. James deliberated every action before embarking upon it. James, as my father always said after a whiskey or two, would have made a wonderful lawyer because he relished order. (Another sheet of paper wasted.)

The telephone rang in Miss Drake's office on the floor above. She liked to maintain the myth that her fingers were worked to the bone, so never answered until the ninth or tenth bell, and my nerves jangled as the vibrations trilled along my thin ceiling. In the end I moved to answer it myself and was halfway up the basement stairs before she at last picked up the receiver. "Breen and Balcombe . . . Mr. Breen is not expected back from his holidays until later today . . . Mr. Wolfe is at a meeting . . ."

Long silence as a voice spoke on the other end of the line.

"Well, there is no one else here," drawled Miss Drake then added, after a significant pause: "unless you're prepared to have Miss Gifford . . . Articled clerk . . . I presume she's qualified . . . Yes, you heard correctly, she is female. Capable of taking notes, I believe . . . Well, if you're sure . . . Yes, I can leave her a message. If you want . . ."

Five minutes later, a typewritten note was pushed under my door. *Telephone Shoreditch Police Station. 447. A lawyer is needed. Case of kidnapping.*

I was still novice enough to be awed by the responsibility of representing a client, and that Monday in particular, my nerves jumping with the impact of Meredith's arrival, I would almost rather have stayed hidden in my basement. On the other hand, I could not help marveling, as I clapped on my hat, that Evelyn Gifford had been called on to deal with a crime so sensational.

At the police station, I braced myself for the tedious business of convincing the duty officer that I was indeed a qualified advocate. "But you're a woman." His pink-rimmed eyes were insolent.

"I believe the secretary at Breen and Balcombe mentioned that I would be attending the case."

"I've never seen a woman lawyer before. Are you sure you'll be of use?"

"I presume you know Mr. Breen? He trusts me completely."

"It was Mr. Breen the prisoner was after, as you were told back at the office."

"Mr. Breen is away."

The officer raised his brows, made a note in his ledger, and allowed me through the smoky back office to the narrow flight of steps leading to the cells. In the lobby, a plump jailer manned a small desk, his stomach so vast that his short arms could barely reach to write in the ledger. "So you're the lady they said was coming from Breen and Balcombe. Well, madam, I hope you're ready for this."

Hauling himself up, he led me to the last cell in the row, where he opened the wicket and showed me a woman called Leah Marchant, dressed in an assortment of skirts, blouses, and shawls, feet shoved into men's shoes, hair falling about her face, complexion dead-white, and eyes red with weeping. She stood with her back to the wall opposite the door.

"Please open the door," I said.

"She's not fit to be let out, I warn you."

"I cannot speak to a client through bars."

"On your head be it."

When the door was thrown open, Leah Marchant stared at me for a moment. I tried to smile into her eyes, to offer my hand as Breen would have done, but too late I sensed her implacable rage. Springing forward with a kind of grinding roar, she fell on me with such force that I was driven back against the jailer and felt the full weight of her chest on mine and the flailing of her muscular arms across my head and shoulders. She tore at my jacket collar, then my hat, which went flying despite the pin, allowing her to grab a fistful of hair so that I yelped with pain. Her breath was damp and fumy with alcohol. "Fuck off. Fuck off an' all. Give me my fuckin' baby. Where is he now? Give him back, you whore. An't you got no babies of your own?"

The noise in so confined a space was ear-piercing; the woman clung like a cat, and I ducked my head just in time to avoid her fingernails, which fortunately scraped my cheek rather than my eye. I was rescued by the jailer, who tore her off me and dumped her back in the cell. "Maybe come back later when she's calmed down," he said. "Or fetch Mr. Breen. She insisted she would only see Mr. Breen. It's probably because you're a lady."

"Did she say how she knew Mr. Breen?" I fumbled in my briefcase for a handkerchief to staunch a trickle of blood.

"Met him once years ago when she was charring for some couple in Marylebone. He was a regular visitor to the house, and kind to her. She's never forgotten his name, apparently. Begged us to have him fetched here."

I sat bolt upright on a bench, prodded a strand of hair back into its coil, put my hat on, and pressed the handkerchief to my torn cheek. My first battle wound, I thought grimly.

The jailer disappeared, so I was alone with the locked door separating me from the woman in the cell, her fury palpating through the walls. After ten minutes or so, it was still quiet on the other side of the door, so I went to the jailer and asked if I might approach Leah Marchant again. When we peeked through the wicket, she was sitting on the bed with her head in her hands. "I am here to help you, Mrs. Marchant," I called. "The police asked me to come. I am a lawyer. I work with Mr. Breen."

"I don't want you. I want Mr. Breen."

"Mr. Breen is away, I'm afraid. He'll be back tomorrow. So can I help until then?"

"Fuck off. I don't need no 'elp. I want my baby."

"*Your* baby? But you are charged with kidnapping."

"My baby. My baby. Mine. Mine," she sobbed.

"Mrs. Marchant, if you would only calm down and tell me . . ."

"Don't tell me to be calm. I won't be calm no more."

"I am here to listen. I'll not go away until you've told me the whole story."

"I'm not tellin' you nothing."

"Very well. But I shall sit here and wait, nonetheless."

I seemed to have won the jailer over, because a few minutes later he set a tray on the bench beside me and handed me a sheaf of papers. "A sup of tea might soften her up," he said. "It's a terrible case. They've brought down the notes at last. Her own baby. It was put with a foster mother and she couldn't get it back by legal means so she snatched it while it was left outside a butcher's. Bet you've never come across anything like this before."

So I read the notes and sipped my tea. Then I called through the wicket: "Mrs. Marchant. Please let me help you."

This time she said nothing at all, so the jailer opened the door and passed in an enamel mug of tea. I then sat beside her on the bed while he leaned on the door frame. "I gather that Charlie is your own baby, Mrs. Marchant, who has been placed with a foster mother. And your two daughters are in a children's home, is that right?" She took a slurp of tea and ran the back of her hand across her eyes. "Can you tell me why the children are in a home, Mrs. Marchant?"

"Because I took them there. I used to pass it when I worked the buses and I thought it looked like a kind place. I had nothing to give them to eat. I'd borrowed till I couldn't borrow no more. I thought if I gave them up for a bit, I could get work. Nights. Anything."

"Is your husband alive, Mrs. Marchant?"

Mirthless laugh. "Gone to sea."

"Does he send you money?"

This, apparently, was an inappropriate question. The mug went flying across the cell, hit the wall, ricocheted against Mrs. Marchant's foot, and was given a kick for good measure.

I sprang up; the jailer picked up the mug, ushered me out, and slammed the door behind us. "That's quite enough for one day," he said.

Three

It was *six-thirty before I* reached home in Clivedon Hall Gardens, but my step slowed when I came to our railings where the Monday smell of reheated roast crept up from the basement. As on every other evening, I climbed the steps reluctantly and my hand faltered as I inserted the key in the lock. And yes, here it came, the familiar tremor of apprehension because now, as always, would begin the series of events that had brought the telegram telling us James was dead.

∽

On November 21, 1917, I arrived home just after half past seven, chilled by freezing smog and sore-eyed from too much close reading at the censorship office. I stuffed my gloves in a pocket, hung my hat and coat on the stand, gave James's panama a flick for good luck, and threw open the drawing room door. Grandmother urged me to sit by the fire and Mother poured tea as they plied me with questions about my journey and workmates, taking care not to delve further; my task of reading hundreds of postcards a day was grindingly humdrum but they were impressed because it was top secret. Mother said she had been busy at the church hall, packing relief parcels for war widows and orphans. She was wearing a gauzy evening blouse under a long, bottle-green cardigan knitted by Grandmother, whose sight was much better in those days, and fastened at the bosom by two iridescent mother-of-pearl buttons.

We were fragile still from the news a month ago that James had been injured, and we treated each other with great care as if we were all convalescing from a dangerous illness. There was a slight air of self-congratulation among us, because we had come safely through a crisis and thought we had behaved well. At one point, we'd been informed that James's injuries were so severe he would be sent home, then that he was being treated in a military hospital and would soon return to the front. All in all, it has been a tumultuous time, but we had ended by convincing ourselves that he was now immune from harm. Surely nobody could have two brushes with death in quick succession?

I leaned toward the fire, took hold of the toasting fork, and wondered if it was too near supper to ring for a couple of slices of bread. My mouth watered at the prospect of buttered toast. There was a knock on the front door.

I threw down the fork and crossed the drawing room, calling over my shoulder: "I suspect it's Father, forgotten his key. How many times must we tell him the girls hate being disturbed when they're in the midst of mashing potatoes . . . ?" Then I was in the hall, my hand was on the latch, and, all unsuspecting, I threw open the door.

The telegram was succeeded, a couple of weeks later, by a letter from James's company commander: . . . *sad duty to give you details of how Captain Gifford died . . . climbed from the trench in full view of enemy snipers in order to rescue one of his men trapped in deep mud . . . exceptional courage . . . Mentioned in dispatches . . .*

I was not satisfied. The picture was too vague, the choice James had made too extreme. In my mind, I roamed across a sea of mud searching for him, unconvinced that he was dead.

I wrote letters to everyone I could think of, and in the end got the truth from an officer friend of James, invalided home after Christmas.

The story I heard was that one of Gifford's men, or rather a boy not yet eigh-
teen, had been wounded on no-man's-land and was crying out. It was a frosty
night and therefore murderously clear, but in the end Gifford simply climbed
out of the trench and clambered the hundred yards or so to the boy. Miss Gif-
ford, you ask me specifically about his injuries, you tell me not to spare you. He
lost an eye and was severely wounded in the right shoulder. He was still alive
when they finally reached him the next night, and died when they tried to
move him.

Night after night, after reading the letter, I stood in the fusty gloom
of the dugout, listened to the boy crying in the mud, and tried to fathom
my brother's decision to step outside and die. What absurd, feckless,
reprehensible courage. I used every possible argument to change his
mind but out he went time after time, under a clear sky. Try as I might,
I could not preserve him.

When I showed the letter to my father, he said we should keep the
details to ourselves. Meanwhile, Grandmother shrank into a corner of
the sofa and knitted sock after sock, Mother took to her bed, Father the
bottle, and I continued as usual. But two months after James's death, on
the last Sunday of January, I found myself with an unexpected opportunity to be alone. The girls were to spend the afternoon with an ancient
aunt in Tooting, and we had been invited to lunch with Prudence, who
at that time was still living in Buckinghamshire. As soon as the trip was
mooted, I knew I wouldn't go ("Mother, I'm under the weather. Please
explain to Father. The time of the month . . ."), even though I had an
inkling of what would happen once the house was empty.

And how right I was. The instant they'd driven away and I had
closed the front door, the absolute quiet surged back and I was alone
with James's hat and summer blazer. Limp as a puppet, I waited to be
engulfed.

I was seized by anguish that twisted my guts so that I choked and
retched and slumped down to the brick-red and yellow tiles of the hall

floor, voiceless and gaping. The only words that formed in my mind were, I want him back. I saw him, instead of the smart youth of the photographs, lying in a swamp of gore and mud with his shoulder blown off and an eyeball hanging from its bloody socket.

When I got up at last to wash my face, I was a hundred years old.

But by the time my parents and grandmother came back, I was composed. Rose served us hot milk, which we drank together before bed (Father's laced with a stiff whiskey). They reported that Prudence's hens weren't laying, presumably the time of year, and that her cottage was always ridiculously chilly, because though Father ensured she was well provided for, she *would not* spend money on creature comforts (this from Mother). I sipped my milk, jolted by an occasional shuddering breath, and realized with an unexpected pang of regret that my opportunity for mourning was over.

☙

Those memories never went away: each time I returned to the house, back they all came, the toasting fork, the telegram, the frantic letter-writing, the prostration on the hall floor. But on the evening after Meredith's arrival and the interview with Leah Marchant, I was distracted the instant I stepped through the front door, because a well-traveled trunk had arrived, along with various other items of luggage stacked in front of the potted fern, including a hatbox with racy stripes. Even before I'd removed my hat, Mother shot out of the drawing room, gripped me by the wrist, ushered me inside, and closed the door.

Everything was much as ever; Prudence was seated at the writing desk with her back to the room in a posture of frigid restraint, and Grandmother perched at the very far end of the sofa, holding her crochet to the dim light that filtered through thick lace curtains. There was no sign of our visitors.

"She's still here," whispered Mother, hands on hips.

"Of course. She would be."

"For heaven's sake, Evelyn, what have you done to your face?"

"It's nothing."

Mother looked baffled but continued: "Well, anyway, she's un-packed."

"She must wear clean clothes, I suppose."

"She left the boy with us for hours while she went out. She said we needed to be better acquainted with him though I can hardly bear to look at him. He's so like . . ." She dabbed her eyes and added: "We couldn't think what to give him for lunch. Prudence said the girls couldn't be expected to provide different meals for a child. If we had a house full of servants like before the war, but we're so overstretched . . ."

"Didn't you ask Edmund what he'd like?" I asked, eager to prevent a well-rehearsed complaint about the servants.

"He was very vague, just said, 'No tomatoes,' and you know it's mean of me but I thought, *she's* told him to say that because James—oh my darling boy—never liked tomatoes and she wants us to believe in him. In the end Rose boiled an egg. I couldn't go to bridge and leave him with Mother and Prudence, it wouldn't have been fair."

"Well, I should think not."

Prudence suddenly turned around, pen suspended midair. She had a habit of staring very hard when she spoke, and her light gray eyes were full of disapproval beneath drooping lids so that she resembled, at times, a basset hound. Her voice was too loud for the dimensions of the room. "I said he ought to eat tomatoes. Boys should eat plenty of fruit and vegetables."

"It was the way his mother just left him without even saying where she was going or asking if we minded. I can't *stand* her," said Mother. "And as for the letter she's supposed to have sent telling us she was coming, I've seen no sign of that."

"Where is Meredith now?"

"Upstairs somewhere with the boy."

"I'll go to her."

"Be very careful what you say. She makes no bones about it, she's short of money. She wants the boy to have an education and she wants to live here, in this house, presumably rent-free. Oh, good God, I wish your father were alive."

But it was Father who landed us in this situation, I thought. Mother's habit of idolizing the dead (as she had the living) was infuriating, especially as the full extent of Father's failure to insure his family against unpleasant shocks had come to light. "Since there is no question that Edmund is James's son," I said, "we must take some responsibility for him, as I'm sure Father would have wished."

Mother would not meet my eye. "She might want a lot of money—which we don't have. It's one thing to believe we're related to the boy, but can we be sure she's really the mother?"

"You've presumably had plenty of opportunity to question her."

"She tells me that she was a nurse in the hospital to which he was sent when he was wounded but what does that prove? He can't have been there long. A couple of weeks later he was . . ."

"What else did she say about James?"

Mother flinched. Over the years, his name, like *Jesus*, had become a word almost too sacred to form. A shiver trembled across the muffled surfaces of the drawing room, the layers of wool and lace and linen among which we women moved with slippered feet, the arrangements of dead birds and foliage under glass domes, the china figures, the photograph frames; James in his rugby shirt, James as a fat baby in a perambulator.

"Some questions one cannot simply ask," said Prudence.

"Did Father never speak about it to either of you? He obviously knew of Edmund's existence."

Silence. I had placed Prudence in a dilemma that she managed by pressing her shapely lips together and folding her hands. If she admitted Father had confided in her, she would be guilty of having withheld vital information from me. If she hadn't known about Edmund, her position as Father's chief adviser, adopted since her arrival in the house in 1919, would be diminished. She therefore wished me to believe that of course Father had confided in her but had bound her to secrecy. In fact, I suspected she hadn't been told.

Mother put her hand to her forehead in a gesture that in prewar days she'd used to great effect in Christmas charades but was now usually a precursor to tears. "He might have mentioned something. It was all too terrible, so soon after James was killed. You can't expect me to remember . . ."

"You must remember, Mother. If Father made her promises, we should honor them."

"Oh, he would never have done that. He was much too careful."

Grandmother now made one of her unexpectedly apposite interventions into the conversation. "He's a nice little boy. I like him."

"Mrs. Melville was very patient with him, weren't you, dear," enunciated Prudence, "showed him all your cards and buttons."

I hovered for a moment longer by the window, clutching my elbows, head down, then, braced to meet Meredith and the boy again, took the stairs two at a time. But when I reached the second floor, I was shocked to see that the door to James's room was flung wide open so that light from its unshuttered window poured onto the landing, a light made mellow as it soaked color from the deep red curtains, the crimson and green and blue in his rug, the faded red of his bedspread. I hesitated for a moment, then took another step. Usually this room was visited only by Mother, who made a daily pilgrimage. Until today, James, had he miraculously returned, would have found nothing changed: his books in order, his shirts and socks folded neatly in the drawers, the seam of wallpaper near his pillow peeled where he had picked at it during a bout of measles, his plaid slippers still thrust under the bed.

This sudden violation of hallowed territory took my breath away: the sash was thrown up so that noises from the street burst in, the quilt was rumpled, and James's childhood books tossed about on the carpet. Mother and son sat on the bed, passing my brother's kaleidoscope between them, as if unsure what it was. Edmund's legs were swinging and Meredith was wearing a light green frock that left her round arms and slender ankles visible. It seemed to me that James's room had been reconstituted, its dull, breathless parts raked over to reveal their shiny sides, like glowing coals.

Meredith's eyes, when she glanced up and saw me, were abnormally large in her kittenish face and bright with relief. I could not help recognizing the dreary day she must have spent in our house among hostile women, and I softened a little, despite this desecration.

"Well, hello there, Evelyn," she exclaimed and, leaping off the bed, seized my wrists, raised herself on tiptoe, and kissed my cheek. "You look very hot. And oh my Lord, what happened to your face?"

"Nothing, it's nothing."

"It looks to me like a very nasty scratch." Her cool fingertips touched the wound inflicted by Leah and I smelled the floral perfume she must have dabbed on her wrist. "I have some lotion in my room. Let me fetch it."

"Please. Leave it. Oh, be careful with that, James was very fond of it." The boy was shaking the kaleidoscope and holding it to his ear. "Bring it to the window and you'll see better how it works."

I took it from him, put it to my eye, and glimpsed the chips of colored glass re-forming into patterns I could no longer bear to see. When Edmund stood shyly beside me, I covered his left eye with my palm and told him to look into the tube. "I see colors," he cried. "I see them change. Mommy, won't you take a look at this?"

His tousled head was waist-high to me and he had a distinctive fragrance like fresh greens. He was all green, in fact, just as James had been. His eyelashes fluttered against my hand and I noted, as he twisted the kaleidoscope, that his fingernails were grubby and needed cutting. Until he was eleven, I had been James's nail-cutter, after that fingers and toes were his own responsibility and I was wordlessly excluded from yet another intimate ritual. The back of Edmund's head from crown to nape was so endearingly steep-angled that I had to resist the urge to cup it in my hand.

Meredith gripped her son's shoulder and dropped a kiss on his hair. Then, her hip leaning into him, she took the kaleidoscope and peered through it. My heart gave a lurch of recognition because there, prominently displayed on her middle finger, was a silver signet ring engraved with James's initials, JHG, bought by me for his eighteenth birthday on the day before he went away. The trip to the shop was still vivid in my mind, the glass cases of engagement rings winking their hard eyes, James turning his smooth, slim hand back and forth to admire the new ring. "Are you sure it's not too girlish?"

"You must have something to remind you of me. I'll drop straight out of your head otherwise."

"Absolutely, you're right. I'd never think of you again."

I couldn't help myself; I reached out and touched the ring on Meredith's finger. "I always assumed it must have been buried with him."

She pulled it off and dropped it into my palm with such alacrity that I realized the exposure of the ring had been quite deliberate. It had been fitted with a clip because it was too big for her. I wanted to close my fist around it and hold it to my breast, this fragment of my brother, but she slipped it back on her finger. "Actually I wear it for Edmund's sake, as a reminder of his father." Then she added briskly: "I am so grateful for your kindness last night, by the way. I admire the way you took it all in your stride."

"Hardly. As you probably realize, it's just so extraordinary for us to meet you both."

I told them supper would be served in five minutes, then left them in possession of my brother's bedroom because I couldn't bear to linger another moment. In my own room, I locked the door. My face, pale except for an inch-long gash on the cheek, stared back from the dressing-table mirror. "Where *did* you get that chin?" Mother used to ask. Her own was soft, with a shallow dimple, a *lady's* chin. Mine, she said, was a feature of my intractability, like my mass of untamable hair. "James has all the looks," Mother would add, "the best of both families; your father's intellectual brow and good nose, my mouth and cheekbones. One day he will break hearts."

There were snippets of James in my room too, the hopelessly inappropriate gifts he'd bought me with his pocket money: a powder puff, a small china doll, a notebook too small to write in. And a tin box of letters kept in my bottom drawer alongside winter cardigans: letters from boarding school, from the seaside when he visited a friend, from France.

Snatching the pins from my hair, I dragged at the tangles with my fingers. Meredith's hair was cut so short that the pink tips of her ears and twisty little earrings were exposed. With savage sweeps of the brush, I set to work, coiling and jabbing until my hair was neat and prim as a Victorian governess's. I had longed and longed for James to come back but not like this, under the wing of a spiky little Canadian with guileless eyes and flawless teeth. What had she taken away from me, in exchange for the gift of her son?

ତ୭

Monday dinner was cold roast made over as a pie or fricassee. We stood behind our chairs, Mother at the head of the table, Grandmother at the foot, Prudence on one side, I the other, awaiting our visitors. The electric light did nothing to soften that somber room with its maroon flocked paper and Gothic furniture, including a sideboard hefty as a church coffer. Despite the plainness of the food, the table was laid with exquisite care; white damask cloth, second-best oak mats, napkins in polished silver rings, bone-handled cutlery, including cheese knives though there was never a cheese course. The girls loved any job that harked back to our family's glory days.

At last we heard light footfall on the stairs and mother and child appeared, very spruce with combed hair, Meredith wearing a glittering jet necklace. She had changed into a crushed-velvet evening dress with a draped neckline and wrap-over skirt, and looked dainty as a fashion plate. The rest of us wore evening blouses tucked into our serviceable skirts.

"Oh, good Lord, I hope we haven't kept you waiting," she cried.

Edmund took one look at the empty places beside or opposite Prudence, seized his mother's hand, and wailed: "I want to sit next to Mommy."

We weren't used to howling children and Prudence glowered at him.

"He's not normally shy," said Meredith. "I expect he's still tired from the journey."

"Of course, I'll sit next to Prudence," I said, moving around the table. We then all watched as our visitors sat down without saying grace and unfolded their napkins. Behind Grandmother's head, in full view of Meredith, was the large, framed photograph of James in army uniform with just a hint in his frank eyes that he couldn't entirely take all this seriously: the uniform, the war, his rank as officer. Perhaps only I noticed the shake of Meredith's head when she glimpsed him. After that, she seized her spoon and worked her way ravenously through a bowl of tepid mushroom soup. Meanwhile I was conscious of a tussle within Prudence between piety and good manners. The latter won, though after she was seated she folded her hands in her lap and mouthed a quick prayer.

With her spoon suspended between bowl and mouth, Meredith

asked brightly: "So, tell me, Aunt Prudence—do you mind my calling you that, you are Edmund's great-aunty, after all—how long did you say you have been living in this house?"

Prudence, whose neck was supported by the dozen or so rows of pin tucks in her collar, drew her elbows ever more tightly against her sides and made a great show of laying down her spoon and dabbing her lips before speaking. "Five years."

"And before that?" asked Meredith.

"Before that," I intervened, sensing that antagonism had already sprung up between the two women, "Prudence was still living in Buckinghamshire. After the war, when money was short, it became uneconomical to keep up both this house and her cottage, so she let the cottage and moved in with us. We were—are—very grateful for her company."

"Well, it seems a very convenient arrangement for you all. And you," Meredith added, addressing Grandmother, "Mrs. Melville, have you ever lived in the country?"

Grandmother didn't hear the question until I had repeated it three times. "Certainly not. It would be far too quiet for me."

"Grandmother has always loved London," I said. "She knows it intimately. She used to be an actress, you know, before she was married, so she's performed in some of its great theaters." Mother sniffed; we should not be disclosing our somewhat disreputable family history to a stranger. Nonetheless, I plowed on: "And she marched through most of London's streets, before the war."

"Did you, Mrs. Melville? What was your cause? Personally, I have always been a very keen suffragist."

But Prudence interrupted. Laying down her spoon, she leaned across the table and hissed: "It was a great sacrifice for me, leaving the country."

"I'm sure it was."

"I had a cottage with half an acre. I kept chickens. I was known by everyone in the village. My brother, Edmund's grandfather, had been more than generous in supporting me, but after the war I knew that the family finances could not sustain two establishments." This was presumably a scarcely veiled reminder to Meredith that Gifford money was tight and that she too ought to show some consideration. "When I left, a special service of thanksgiving was held in the church. I was given a eulogy—it can only be described as such—for my services to the congregation. I'd taught Sunday school for nearly forty years. I supervised the flowers. And there was a tribute to James because he was my nephew and a great favorite."

Meredith, who had been staring wide-eyed during this outburst, laid down her spoon. "Do you know, I'm hoping the next course will be served soon. This boy is so sleepy his head is almost hitting the bowl. And yet he must eat, I don't believe he's had a proper meal since we left Toronto, and although you've tried with your soup, haven't you, Edmund, mushrooms are not his favorite."

"I'm afraid we're not used to fussy eaters," said Mother with a nervous glance at Prudence.

"Oh, now, it's only that he's never cared for soup."

"Canada must be a very profligate country, if small boys are allowed to dictate the menu," observed Prudence.

"He's bound to like the fricassee," said Mother. "Rose always manages to come up with something very tasty."

But I was never to discover what Edmund thought of Rose's fricassee, because at that moment the final drama of that momentous day began to unfold. There was a commotion in the hall, the door burst open, Min's red face appeared, full of self-importance, and I was summoned outside. There in our hall was Mr. Breen, of all people, hat in hands, eyes ablaze with excitement, though I noted that he wasn't so preoccupied that his glance failed to take in Meredith's trunk, the potted fern, or the half-dozen men's umbrellas in the coat stand.

"I've been called out," he said in the casual tones he adopted when most agitated, "to Buckinghamshire where an old acquaintance of mine, an insurance clerk, has been arrested on suspicion of murder. You must come. Wolfe is out of town and I may need someone to take notes. Besides, you won't get many other opportunities like this. On with your hat and off we go."

Four

I sat beside Breen in the cab, too stunned to do more than watch the familiar villas and terraces of Kilburn roll by. Though the sky was overcast, the streets were brightened by trees newly in full leaf. We stop-started past shuttered shop windows and locked yard gates, overtook omnibuses and horse-drawn carts, then ground to a halt behind a delivery lorry. On the pavements, a straggle of tradesmen and office clerks in crumpled suits and trilbies headed home. When we set off again at last, the horizon beyond the cab window began to expand, walls were replaced by fences, fences by hedgerows bordering lush suburban gardens, houses by farmland.

The moment we had cleared London traffic, Breen opened his briefcase and worked through a mountain of mail accumulated during his holiday, filing the contents into different categories to be examined the next day by Miss Drake, who would cut out and save every square inch of blank paper; the rest she would consign either to the stove or to the buff folders of clients' papers.

But despite the intensity with which Breen seemed to peruse each document, I sensed he was so fired up that if we had to stop at another crossroad he would surely leap from the cab and run ahead to let other traffic know that this was an emergency, we were in a rush. It seemed to me I could smell the Highlands on him, a whiff of heather and soft rain that clung to his wiry hair and the fibers of his clothes. I, on the other hand, was feeling ever more displaced, unable to comprehend how I had been wrenched suddenly from the dining room at Clivedon Hall Gardens to the inside of a cab with Mr. Breen, and still reeling from the shock of seeing my dead brother's mistress and child eating soup in our dining room.

"Did you have a pleasant holiday, Mr. Breen?" I asked, in some vague hope that if I observed the niceties, the evening might not slip even further out of control.

His head snapped up. "*Pleasant*. What kind of a tepid word is *pleasant*? But yes, I had a good holiday, thank you. I walked, I strode out. I breathed pure air. You should try it sometime." He addressed me, as he often addressed a bench, with biting irony. I thought that he must be referring obliquely to the crowded hall at Clivedon Hall Gardens.

Yet, despite his uninviting mood, opportunities for a tête-à-tête with Breen were so rare that I thought I should not waste this chance. "Sir, I'd like to speak to you about a case that will be in court tomorrow, a woman called Leah Marchant, accused of kidnapping her own child. She wanted you to represent her because years ago, when she was a servant, you were kind to her."

As I'd anticipated, Breen found this flattering portrait of himself irresistible. "You say she *was* a servant. What is she now?"

"Abandoned by her husband who's a sailor—he was last seen more than two years ago. She's now destitute. Accused of child abduction although the baby was her own. After Christmas, according to her notes, she was faced with starvation, having fraudulently claimed poor relief—she was earning a few shillings a week and hadn't declared it. When the relief was withdrawn she surrendered the children, two little girls and a baby of one year, voluntarily to the care of a children's home. Then she worked for a month or two and scrabbled together enough money to provide for them. But the home refuses to hand them back, on the grounds that she is not a fit parent; they say she drinks, that there is no father or other family members offering financial or moral help, and that she therefore has no means to support the children in the long term."

"So this kidnap?"

"Mrs. Marchant discovered the address of the baby's foster mother and followed her until the perambulator was left outside a butcher's shop. Then she simply plucked the baby out and ran off. She only held him in her arms for about two minutes before she was captured."

Breen picked up a letter, studied it with an extravagantly furrowed brow, then thrust it aside. "Well, certainly she should have bail if it was her own child. She's hardly a threat to the public at large."

"The police say there's every danger she'll go after him again. They say she's in a poor mental state. There's no surety and she's as good as homeless."

"What do you mean, *as good as*?"

"It's what the police say."

"Never go by what the police say. She's either homeless or not. Have you tried to find her a hostel?"

"I haven't had . . ."

"We can't have our clients languishing in prison unnecessarily. It's highly unlikely that a reasonable judge will ultimately imprison her for the offense of kidnapping her own child. She must have bail."

"There is no certainty that she'll be able to get him back legally. That's why I don't think the court will grant bail. I've studied the 1891 act which gives the courts the right not to grant custody to unfit parents . . ."

"At this moment I'm not interested in legal rights. The woman must be got off this ridiculous charge. We'll go to court in the morning and have her bailed. Then you can put her in touch with some organization that will help her to earn money while we write to the prosecution. Good Lord, Miss Gifford, I took you on because I thought you'd be resourceful—I didn't expect you to fall at the first hurdle. What about your friends at Toynbee? Miss Morrison. Have you talked to her? I'm sure she'll have some ideas."

"Yes, I could consult . . ."

"Well, do consult. Explore every avenue. Think through and around the problem, Miss Gifford. Use your contacts, limited though they be. I thought you women were good at talking. Nurture your acquaintances, you never know when you might need them. The accused man in this case of murder, Wheeler, for example, is an old acquaintance of mine and suddenly he needs me, all right. We were brought up more or less around the corner from each other, attended the same elementary school. The victim is his wife, shot in the breast at close range. Apparently they were on a *picnic*." He spoke this last word with utter incredulity, as he might have said *a high wire*, and certainly I could not imagine the purposeful Mr. Breen, for whom the outdoors was territory to be mapped and traversed, indulging in anything so purely frivolous as a picnic. "Such a stroke of luck that when I got off the train at Kings Cross I thought I'd just call in at the office to pick up my post. And then, while I was there, this telephone call came about Stephen Wheeler. Of all people. The least offensive soul in the world. At school he was one of those stolid children who never stepped out of line."

"What proof is there that he did it?"

"His army revolver and gloves were found buried near the body. There is a match between the bullet that killed her and his gun. That's all I know."

He resumed his reading and I was left to watch the deepening countryside; a timber-framed farmhouse, a shaggy haystack, and hedgerows blowsy with cow parsley. At the police station we swept through a cluster of onlookers, including a couple of reporters with notebooks, and spoke to the officer on the desk who was breathless with self-importance. In a few minutes we were ushered through to a cramped back office where the investigating sergeant sat behind a heap of papers, taking sips from a mug of tea.

"Wheeler's not speaking," he told us. "If only he'd help himself. He was full of words yesterday morning, apparently, when he came here to report her missing. But since we've arrested him, nothing except your name and details, Mr. Breen. I was hoping I'd have a full statement by now."

"I'm very pleased he's said nothing. As far as I'm concerned a client shows excellent sense in refusing to speak except in the presence of his lawyer. May we see him at once?"

Wheeler was slumped in his cell with his head in his hands. He was a stocky, soft-fleshed man of around forty with a surprisingly heavy beard for an insurance clerk, and ungainly hands, the heels of which he ground into his eye sockets so that I could not help wondering what image he attempted to blot out.

Breen was transformed when with a client; the hurry went out of him and his voice grew tender. But with Stephen Wheeler not even these strategies were successful. His head sank ever further and he wouldn't speak. My notebook and pencil were redundant.

Only once, when Breen asked, "Tell me, Stephen, about the last time you saw your wife," did he look up and allow us to see the expression of utter hopelessness in his swimming eyes. Then his head went down again.

After quarter of an hour or so, Wheeler was handcuffed between two policemen and escorted down a little corridor to a stifling interview room where space was so limited that I, being the most insignificant person present, had to stand with one foot in the passage. And there, beneath the grimy light of a single bulb, Wheeler was subjected to question after question, none of which he answered, not even to give his name or date of birth. By the time he was charged with murder, his head was so low that he might have been asleep except that occasionally a tear fell into his lap or he ran his sleeve under his nose.

An hour later, we left the police station with nothing achieved but an agreement that Breen would represent Wheeler when he appeared at Amersham Magistrates' Court in the morning—which meant that, unless Wolfe rematerialized in time, I would have to deal with Leah Marchant's bail proceedings single-handed.

What we did have, however, was a duplicate résumé of Wheeler's war record and a copy of the police statement, which Breen passed me a page at a time so that I could read them, at great cost to my equilibrium, as the taxicab lurched back toward London.

Five

Stephen Anthony Wheeler

DOB: September 14, 1888

Occupation: insurance clerk

2nd Battalion London Rifles

Rifleman S. A. Wheeler: 289351 2/5 London Regiment

Trained Haywards Heath, Crowborough, Jarris Brook

Served Trenches of Ploegsteert Sector

Invalided (gas poisoning): 2nd Battle of Ypres, April 23, 1915

Spell at Birkenhead: recruiting duties

Promoted: lance corporal, August 1915

Loos: September 25, 1915

Commended (Military Medal): Somme (Gommecourt), July 1, 1916

Promotion: corporal, November 1916

Commended (Bar to the Medal): Cambrai 1917

Commended (Bar to the Medal): March 21, 1918 (wounded)

Light duties, London.

The alleged facts of the Wheeler murder case were as follows:

On Sunday, May 18, 1924, at about seven-thirty in the morning, Police Constable Scrivener, asleep with his wife in Chesham's police house, was roused by a violent knocking on the door. There in the porch was the defendant, Stephen Wheeler (a clerk working for Imperial Insurance), disheveled and out of breath, holding on to a bicycle. He told PC Scrivener that his wife of three weeks, Stella, aged twenty-two years (formerly a waitress at a Lyons tea shop in Regent Street, Central

London), had gone missing, and that he'd last seen her at about one-thirty the previous afternoon when they had sat together on the hill above the church, eating corned-beef-and-pickle sandwiches.

As he spoke of the picnic, Wheeler had sobbed uncontrollably. "I wish I'd stayed with her," he said, "but I had a thirst on me and fancied a beer. We had an argument, she said she didn't want to go to a dirty pub but I may as well and she wasn't bothered if I did so I said I'd just go down for a quick one and be back up, and I left her lying on the blanket in the shade."

Wheeler had duly gone down to the Queen's Head, where the landlord was somewhat lax about opening hours, so that it was nearly half past three when Wheeler, having drunk no more than a couple of pints, finally returned to the picnic spot to find the blanket and the basket exactly where he'd left them, but no sign of Stella apart from her hat.

Wheeler was not overly worried at first. In fact, he thought his wife must have wandered off for a little stroll, so he lay down and had a nap. When he woke an hour or so later, with a blistering headache due to the shade having moved and exposed his forehead to the full heat of the sun, she still wasn't back, so he roamed about the hillside and nearby woodland, calling her name. Next he ran back to the town to see if he'd somehow missed her and she'd gone shopping on Chesham High Street. When he returned to the picnic spot, at about six, he reluctantly decided that she must have taken it upon herself to go home without him.

So he packed up the rug, the sandwich wrappers, and the hat, and made his lonely way back through town to Chesham Station, where he first waited forty minutes for the little steam shuttle to return from Chalfont and Latimer, then took another train back to Harrow-on-the-Hill, from whence he had to walk a mile or so to his home in Wealdstone. As he approached the house, his spirits rose because he thought Stella was bound to be in, but to his despair he found the door locked with the spare key still in its place under a loose brick in the backyard.

At this point, he had no idea what to do next. Though he had known Stella since she was a child—she was some fourteen years his junior—the couple were too recently wed for him to understand all her moods, and he thought perhaps she had been so offended by his departure for a beer that she had taken it upon herself to go home to her mother. So the exhausted man set off again, this time by bicycle to Acton. But when he got to his in-laws, he found no Stella. Afraid of alarming her parents, he told them that he happened to be passing after a day's fishing trip with the chaps from work. Though they offered him a mug of cocoa and cheese on toast, he said he must get back.

Even then, at midnight, he still hoped that when he turned the corner of the street he would see lights burning, but the house was in darkness.

Next morning, after a sleepless night, he got up at dawn and bicycled back to Chesham. First he went to the picnic site. A light rain had fallen but otherwise the area was as he remembered, the grass still crushed from the weight of their bodies on the blanket. Convinced now that something terrible had happened to Stella, he ran down the hill and hammered on the door of the police house, hence a note made in the incident book at seven-thirty a.m. on Sunday, May 18.

Officer Scrivener said he would report the woman missing, and as soon as possible summon a couple of men from Amersham station to take a look at the picnic site—it being Sunday, of course, there would only be a skeleton staff. While registering Wheeler's distress, Scrivener had the distinct impression that there were marital difficulties between husband and wife—Wheeler had seemed nervous when describing his last conversation with his wife. However, when Scrivener suggested that Stella might have perhaps run away, Wheeler had become agitated and insisted that she would do nothing of the kind and that he trusted her with his life. When asked what he intended to do next, Wheeler said that he would have another look around the hillside and Chesham town, then return home and hope that Stella would turn up there.

It was not known how Wheeler spent the rest of Sunday, but in the meantime a couple of policemen went up the hill and had a look about but found nothing suspicious. The search was duly logged in the incident book. However, on Monday morning, a dog walker let her mongrel, Caspar, off its leash in woodland about three quarters of a mile from the Wheeler picnic spot. The dog disappeared for several minutes deep into the trees and failed to reemerge. When its owner went after it, calling its name, it suddenly sprang out with a woman's shoe in its mouth. Urged on by the dog's insistent yapping, the intrepid owner investigated further and discovered that the shoe had been attached to the foot of a young woman buried under a few inches of leaf mold and a pile of bracken. She'd been shot in the heart at close range. Later, a pair of army gloves and a revolver, again lightly covered with soil, were found nearby. The police, after rapid checks on Stephen Wheeler, discovered that he was an ex–army man. They therefore went immediately to his house to arrest him. He was not at home, but Scrivener had made a note of Wheeler's occupation and place of work. Unlikely though it seemed that a man whose new wife had disappeared would choose to go to the office as usual, when they reached Imperial Insurance in Farringdon, there was Wheeler, at his desk. He was duly arrested on suspicion of murder. Wheeler's colleagues viewed the proceedings with disbelief, their consternation shared by the management, including the company director, Sir David Hardynge, who happened to be in the building and was hastily alerted.

୧୨୦

Having read the statement, I rolled down the window and took gasps of the evening air in an effort to cure motion sickness. Breen, unusually, was completely still until we turned into Clivedon Hall Gardens. As I stepped from the cab, he said: "Don't you be making too harsh or quick a judgment of Stephen Wheeler."

"I had no intention . . ."

"He was a good person when I knew him. Heaven knows what the war did to him. I only drove ambulances for a couple of years and still came home with my nerves shot to pieces. Wheeler stuck it out almost for the duration. You keep an open mind until we find out the truth."

"My mind is open, Mr. Breen."

"Good, make sure it stays that way."

A light had been left burning in the porch, but the rest of the house was in darkness. However, when I opened the door of my own room, I was startled by the sight of Meredith perched on the windowsill, in moonlight, knees to her chest, wearing a flowing robe drawn tight at the waist, her eyes huge and dark. "I thought I'd wait up for you. Did you see him? Did you see the murderer?"

I switched on the bedside light, flustered, even annoyed by her intrusion into my room. "I saw our client, Stephen Wheeler. He's not been found guilty of murder yet."

"What was he like?"

"Sad. Very."

"What will happen next?"

"In the morning he'll be brought to court. He won't be granted bail. Then, when the police are ready, he'll be arraigned—he'll have the indictment read."

"The indictment?"

"Charge. Then, if he pleads not guilty, a trial date will be fixed."

"And what will you do in the meantime?"

"I'll probably have nothing else to do with the case, except perhaps to shadow Mr. Breen."

"It's all so exciting. You are lucky."

"I suppose I am. Wheeler isn't, though."

She studied me for a moment, then asked: "And tomorrow. What are you doing tomorrow?"

"Tomorrow I shall be working as usual."

"I should like the opportunity to talk to you alone, away from this house. Might I buy you lunch?"

"I'm afraid I never take a lunch break."

"But just this once, surely. I passed a department store on the bus today, Peter Jones, I'll bet that has a restaurant. What do you say? One o'clock?"

Elfin in her flowing robe, head to one side, eyes fixed pleadingly on me, she was a strange addition to my bedroom. After all, it was rather touching that she'd stayed up for me. In any case I was too tired to argue, and at that moment, lunch in a department store seemed an exceptionally unreal prospect. It was now nearly twenty-four hours since I had slept, and in the midst of yearning for my bed and dreading the next morning's court appearance on behalf of Leah Marchant, I found myself agreeing to meet Meredith punctually at one.

Six

The following *morning I traveled* to Shoreditch to represent Leah Marchant. Once more I visited her in the cells, once more she refused to cooperate with me because I was not Mr. Breen. Half an hour later, her case was called into court and she was brought up to the dock cuffed to a woman jailer, looking even more disheveled than the previous afternoon, with pins dangling from her hair and her eyes puffy. Her case was sufficiently unusual to have attracted a straggle of spectators in the public benches and I was conscious of a frisson of interest as I took my place in an advocates' pew, facing the bench.

Months spent observing from the public galleries had made me familiar with magistrates' courts; the smell of polish, freshly mixed ink, and the clash of body odors, defendants brought up from the cells with only hands and face washed, magistrates and lawyers scented with hair oil and shaving soap, the dim light filtering through windows set high up lest a prisoner be tempted to jump dock, the somewhat languid atmosphere generated by the constant to-ing and fro-ing of ushers, the swinging of the court doors and the inattention of lawyers lolling about waiting for their own cases to be called. Today the bench was occupied by a single stipendiary magistrate, whom I judged to be in his late sixties. The clerk, meanwhile, was a round little fellow with owlish spectacles through which he appeared to see very little.

Leah Marchant was told to identify herself and it was established that she was Leah Joan Marchant, born May 4, 1896, aged twenty-eight, address 9 Caractacus Court, Haggerston.

"Leah Joan Marchant, you are charged with the offense of child abduction; namely that on Monday, May 19, 1924, you unlawfully and without reasonable excuse snatched a baby, Charles Marchant, aged sixteen months, who had been left in his perambulator by his foster carer outside a butcher's shop. . . . And you are represented, Mrs. Marchant, by, ah. . . ?"

The usher handed up a slip of paper on which was written my name: *Miss E. Gifford, Breen & Balcombe.* As I rose to my feet, my knees shook under the mercifully heavy fabric of my skirt. This was, after all, only the third time I'd addressed a bench, the first being to request the extension of a liquor license in a church hall, the second, under the eagle eye of Mr. Breen, to ask for an adjournment for prosecution papers to be served in a case of stealing a loaf of bread. The court went very still when I said in a voice that sounded surprisingly confident but unquestionably feminine: "I appear for Mrs. Marchant, Your Worship."

There was a murmur of surprise and I was aware that the court doors had creaked open to admit another observer. The clerk's myopic eyes crinkled into an unconvincing smile. "So, you are Miss Gifford and you represent the defendant. Are we now ready for a plea to be taken, Miss Gifford?"

"Not yet," I said. "The case is a complex one, as you are probably aware, because it involves Mrs. Marchant's own child. Might my client be seated?"

The magistrate, a trim, precisely spoken individual with very white teeth, gave me a long stare. "Remind me again in what capacity you are appearing in court, Miss er . . ."

"My name is Miss Gifford. I am Mrs. Marchant's legal representative."

"Working for which firm?"

"Breen and Balcombe."

"Ah, Breen. Now all becomes clear. And where is Mr. Breen today?"

"Is this relevant, Your Worship? I am here to represent . . ."

"Are you *qualified*, Miss, er . . ."

The clerk jumped up and held a whispered conversation with the magistrate. There followed a guffaw of laughter, raised eyebrows, then a deep sigh from the bench. "Well, madam lawyer, do proceed and tell us on what grounds you are asking for an adjournment."

"As I've said, this is not a straightforward case, Your Worship. The defendant is accused of taking her own child. I am asking for one week's adjournment so that all the facts can be made known to the defense."

"And what will you do with all these facts, when they are known?"

"They may affect the plea, Your Worship."

"I see. Or is it that Mr. Breen, who clearly believes this court is so lowly that it can be used as the playground in which ladies may conduct a flirtation with the law, is just a little too busy to appear before us in person today, so is adopting one of his notorious stalling tactics?"

"Your Worship, this is an unusual case. There is no question that my client attempted to take her baby but her motives, her understanding of what she was doing, must be fully explored before we can enter a plea."

Another whispered conversation ensued. "Very well," said the magistrate as if humoring a spoiled child, "I'll adjourn the case for one week, after which pleas will be taken. I presume, Miss Gifford, you don't intend asking for bail today because I warn you that you'd be wasting your time."

By now the palms of my hands were ice-cold, my forehead hot. The audience in the public gallery was tittering. "With respect, Your Worship . . ."

"No, with respect to you, Miss Gifford, I have given you quite enough of my time. There is no question of bail. You tell your Mr. Breen that if he wants bail for his clients, he should come to court himself."

"Your Worship, you cannot refuse bail on the grounds that you don't approve of the person representing the defendant. That is unlawful, should . . ."

The clerk rose to his feet and said smoothly: "Your Worship, police bail was refused on the grounds that the woman, in her desperate state, was likely to attempt to take the child again."

"Quite so. I'll remand the prisoner in custody for . . ."

"At least let me speak for my client," I cried.

"When have I ever been able to prevent a woman from speaking, if she has a mind to?" asked the magistrate, quirking an eyebrow at the spectators in the public gallery, who roared with laughter.

"I should like it to be put on the court record that my client was not given a fair hearing today, but that comments prejudicial to her case were made in open court such as: *I presume you're not asking for bail because you'd be wasting your time . . .*"

There was now silence in the courtroom as the magistrate twiddled his thumbs. I glanced at Leah Marchant, who had thrown back her head and was looking at the cracks in the ceiling as if utterly disassociated from the proceedings.

"Ah," said the magistrate at last, "I'm glad that your determination to teach us how to do our job extends not only to me but to the learned justices' clerk who has, let me see, is it thirty years' experience in his current position? What a relief that a young lady has joined the ranks of advocates so that we may all learn how to proceed. You may take the prisoner down." And he snapped his fingers at the jailer.

Gathering my papers and briefcase, I headed for the door, which the usher made an elaborate play of opening for me, then bowing from the waist. In the foyer a group of lawyers went quiet and fixed me with cold stares before resuming their conversation. I went down to the cells to see Leah but was told she didn't want to speak to me.

All this time I had been biting back tears. I thought at last I could escape this scene of humiliation, but as I ran down the courthouse steps, I heard someone call my name and then a hand fell lightly on my arm. Startled, I glimpsed long fingers, shapely nails, a starched cuff under a pinstriped sleeve. "Miss Gifford," a cultivated voice murmured in my ear, "admirably done. We absolutely cannot allow behavior of that kind by these little magisterial despots."

A stranger's face was inclined very close to mine, amused eyes, youthful lips under a glossy mustache, deep forehead, a scent of cologne. "One tip, if I might be so bold. Your worst crime is not that you're a lady—though that's bad enough, as I'm sure you're aware—but that you interrupted the magistrate. My advice: never interrupt a magistrate or judge, whatever nonsense they speak. Makes them mad. Hear them out, agree, ignore. That's the trick."

I withdrew my arm: "Thank you, but I don't believe I asked for advice," and I marched away thinking that to be patronized by a smooth-tongued barrister was the final straw.

༺༻

I arrived in Sloane Square with ten minutes to spare; Meredith, on the other hand, was nearly quarter of an hour late, which at least gave me the opportunity to gather my wits. It seemed to me, after the utter debacle of the Marchant hearing, that I had no choice but to offer my resignation. It was one thing to harbor an ambition to be a lawyer, quite another to see clients suffer as a result.

Having made this self-sacrificial and momentous decision, I wanted to act on it at once and grew irritated by Meredith's lateness. Punctuality was one of the absolutes by which we lived in Clivedon Hall Gardens. When she appeared at last, decked out in a lilac frock with a three-layered frilled skirt and matching hat, she apologized profusely, saying she'd got herself all mixed up with the omnibuses. Seizing my hands as if we were sisters or best friends, she kissed me on both cheeks. This collision of flesh, the waft of perfume, her "Oh, it is such a joy to see you," threw me off balance after the hostility of the courtroom, and for the second time in an hour I felt tears pricking.

As we entered the store, she bestowed a dazzling smile on the doorman, who snapped to attention.

"Where is Edmund?" I asked.

"Your grandmother is keeping him company. They have found a shared interest in collecting things: your brother's stamp collection, her albums of theater programs, Edmund's foreign coins, the few I allowed him to bring, her box of buttons, out they have all come."

"Grandmother will enjoy that."

Meredith paused beside a counter of white fluff, glanced winsomely at a shop assistant, and flung a stole around her neck. "What do you think? Do you like it?" She drew up her shoulders and snuggled her face into the fur, which settled so fetchingly against her pale skin and auburn hair that other customers paused to watch. "You try it, go on, Evelyn."

"I'd rather not."

"Well, how about this pink scarf? I should like to buy you something. I should like to see you in a *color*."

"I have plenty of clothes, thank you." But the next moment I was maneuvered in front of a mirror and faced with a reflection of myself unexpectedly transformed by a wisp of pink chiffon. My jaw and complexion were softened and the harsh lines of my jacket broken by the drift of silk.

"You see. I knew it would suit you. Those wonderful bones need something delicate to show them at their best. Oh, do say you'll wear it."

"But it's so expensive. I wear dark clothes for work, as you see, so it would be wasted. We should go upstairs, I have very little time and we may not get a table." I put the scarf firmly aside; it was so frivolous, so costly, nearly half a week's housekeeping, and yet so lovely that I yearned to touch it again.

In the restaurant Meredith made circumstances adapt to her requirements with startling ease. Although there was no empty table, she persuaded the waitress to look about for a couple of ladies who might be leaving soon. "We don't want a nasty tucked-away table—we want one with a view," she said, and in a few minutes we were facing each other across a fresh cloth. "Now we have the best table," said Meredith, "don't you think? We can see everyone. But tell me what you've been doing this morning. I want to know every last detail."

"I represented a defendant who was remanded in custody."

"But how marvelous. You mean you actually stood up in a court full of people? I wish I'd been there."

"I'm very glad you weren't."

"Why so?"

"I'm not well received in court, as a woman."

"Well, of course not. How would you expect it to be otherwise? Back home in Canada the argument is largely won but there are still those who refuse to regard women as *persons*, and since only *persons* can be lawyers . . ."

"We're envious of the progress women have made as lawyers across the Atlantic."

"I heard Annie Langstaff speak at a University Women's Club lecture when she demolished the argument about separate spheres. Quite brilliant."

"If only we didn't have to get involved with such arguments. If only we could prove ourselves by the quality of our work. I simply want to be left in peace."

"Or do you mean isolation?" She gave my arm a little squeeze as if to soften this last, rather disturbing remark, fell back in her chair, and smiled at the waitress, who made a maternal fuss setting our table with milk jug, tea strainer, napkins, and cutlery.

Meredith now sat with her chin cupped in her hand, gazing about like a wondering child, her big, dark-lashed eyes (did she use some form of makeup and, if so, whatever would Prudence say?) fixing first on one diner then the next with such intensity that occasionally she attracted a shy glance or smile. I saw the restaurant mostly in monochrome: waitresses in black dresses, silver cutlery and condiments, white napkins and aprons. Only Meredith, in her lilac dress, was brightly tinted at that moment. An artful curl peeped out on either side of her hat and I sensed that everything she did was planned, including her spontaneity.

"I expect you're dying to ask me questions," she said, knotting her fingers under her chin like a Kate Greenaway illustration.

"I'm sure you'll tell me exactly as much or as little as you want." She had ordered a ham salad, I a poached egg as the cheapest choice on the menu. It turned out to be tepid and I thought anxiously of the cost of this meal compared to my usual lunch of a cheese sandwich brought from home.

"No, no. I don't want to foist information on you," she said, sprinkling oil on her lettuce. "After all, there may be some things you don't wish to hear."

"What troubles me most is that I didn't know of Edmund's existence before yesterday."

"That must have been your father's choice. I admit I thought it odd that Edmund never heard from his aunty Evelyn or indeed his grandmother."

"When did you tell Father about Edmund?"

"Let me see. I would have written to your father in the early spring of 1918 to let him know I was coming to London, and why. We met for luncheon in a very smart hotel—or so I thought at the time—called Brown's, though I remember the beef was tough. I was pregnant, of course, and a fastidious eater. That's when we reached our agreement. He thought it best that I return to my family in Canada but he promised I would have a monthly allowance. For a while he sent me regular checks, then more erratically, until about eighteen months ago they dried up completely. I wrote but got no answer."

"When Father died last April he left us in very poor financial circumstances."

"But as I had Edmund, in the end I had no choice but to come here and throw myself on your mercy. To be truthful, Evelyn, these years have not been easy. Can you imagine how your family might have reacted if you'd appeared back home six months pregnant by an unknown and incidentally dead serviceman? My family was far from pleased, I can tell you. They are Roman Catholics living in a small village outside Toronto. Everyone talked. Relations between me and my parents post–Edmund's arrival have not been easy, especially since the money from England dried up. And I was surrounded by siblings and cousins who had done the right thing—got married, even been widowed, some of them—as opposed to bearing a child out of wedlock. Besides, nursing in the war had given me a taste for independence. I felt stifled at home and once I thought of traveling to London I couldn't resist, so here I am."

"But weren't you taking an enormous risk, coming all this way and not knowing how you'd be received?"

"I didn't think so. I'd met your father, and James of course, so I knew the type of family you were. I expected you to be charitable."

Was there just a hint of irony in that word, *charitable*? I noted that she had not said *welcoming* or even *merciful*. Apparently she'd got the measure of us already.

Around us, lady diners wagged their heads so that their collective feathers waved and bobbed; from the next table came a trill of laughter as a couple of young women leaned their heads together over a cigarette lighter and the air was warmly scented with food and perfume and smoke. "When I went through Father's papers after his death," I said, "I found nothing about you and Edmund, otherwise of course I would have written." How typical of Father to have kept this secret from me. He would simply not have deemed it my business, unless he chose to make it so. But it must have been on his mind as he sat late at his club or, on the rare occasions he dined at home, in lonely splendor at the end of the dining room table while we ladies yawned over tea in the drawing room, watching the door. "Did you have a formal contract of any kind? I need to know what is due to you."

"I see what you're thinking," Meredith said after a pause, "you think that I may be an impostor of some kind, posing as Edmund's mother. Well, I have this ring. And your father was convinced right away. He was very generous. But then I think he had to be, don't you? After all, there's Edmund."

You think I am an impostor. The expression cut me deeply, that she had so crudely given voice to such an idea. But then perhaps I was shocked because her judgment was so unerringly accurate. I wanted Edmund to be real, but not Meredith. Until now James had been the shining heroic boy, entirely ours, a young brother grown so tall he could hook me under his arm and rest his chin in my hair, whose great feet thundered on the stairs, who used to burst into my bedroom and project himself head-first across my bed, saying, "I swear I will throttle Father if he tells me one more time I'm throwing away any prospect of success if I don't go into partnership with him." I thought I knew him, inside and out. Even when he died, he was still mine; sometimes it felt as if the best part of me had followed him down to that cold, still place he'd found.

"Perhaps, if you don't mind, you should tell me a little of what happened between you and James," I said stiffly. "You were a nurse and he was your patient."

"That's it. I was posted for a while to a hospital near the Belgian border. Men not so badly wounded were sent back to us to be patched up and returned to the front. James, as you probably knew, sustained a severe injury to his upper arm. He was with us about three weeks." She was watching me across the rim of her teacup, which she held daintily, as if it were wafer thin. "A week or so after he'd been sent back, I heard he was dead."

She was so much closer to him than I, had more recent knowledge. It was as if a new fragment of my brother was being dangled before me. "Three weeks," I murmured, "you knew him for just three weeks."

"That's all. A lot can happen in three weeks, in a war."

I reached for my briefcase, finding this last, softly spoken remark, too intimate to bear. "You said you wanted to talk to me alone," I said. "Was there something else, before I go?"

"Evelyn, I want you to be on my side. I want a life here. You have achieved so much. Will you help me do the same? And I want to see Edmund settled in a school. He must have at least as good an education as his father's, don't you think?"

James's old school? The idea was clearly impossible—we would never afford it and they would surely not accept Edmund (the word *bastard* flashed through my mind and I felt a protective pang of indignation on his behalf). But it also dawned on me that Meredith was regarding her stay at Clivedon Hall Gardens not as a visit but as a permanent arrangement. Things were moving much too fast.

"We'll talk again. Now I must get back. I have so much to do."

She caught my hand. "You work far too hard. Really you do. I should like to see you have a little fun. How would it be if you came to the seaside with me and Edmund one Saturday? I feel as if he must catch up on his English heritage and surely a trip to the beach must be part of that?"

"Thank you for asking, but I'm afraid I have to work on Saturdays. I am very behind, as I've said."

She seemed to have forgotten her offer to pay for lunch and made no effort to reach into her handbag. In just one hour I had squandered nearly a fortnight's spending money.

Seven

When I reached *Arbery Street*, I found the door to Breen &
Balcombe's ajar and could hear even at a distance that Breen
was in one of his rages. ". . . And where is that blasted boy?" I heard him
shout. Muted reply from Miss Drake.

I crept into the hall, thinking that I would retreat to my basement
office, write up the Leah Marchant notes, and prepare a letter of resignation. Breen's office door was wide open. "The partnership will be
bankrupt," he yelled as a pile of papers was slapped down on the desk,
"nobody has earned a penny since I left for my holiday—my first break
in six years, note, but the moment I turn my back . . . Where is Gifford,
what excuse has she for deserting a sinking ship?"

"She appears to be taking a very long lunch break," observed Miss
Drake slyly.

"I'm here," I said quietly.

What had formerly been the front parlor of a family house was now
Breen's office; sunlit, dusty, and furnished with ancient Victorian pieces
passed down through generations of Breens & Balcombes. The room
had a maverick quality and could change as fast as its owner's moods.
Sometimes the shelves of ancient tomes and box files seemed to dominate, creating a fusty, legalistic atmosphere, but on other days, such as
winter afternoons when there was a fire in the hearth and Breen was

happily engaged in dashing off one of his devastating tirades against the police or governmental department responsible for victimizing one of his clients, the room was inviting as a Christmas card. Today the desk was littered with ledgers and a window was open, causing a fluttering and billowing of documents and curtains so that it was as if Breen were onboard ship, surging through a backlog of paperwork. Miss Drake sat demurely in an upright chair, notepad at the ready, striped blouse crisply pressed.

"Ah, Miss Gifford, I've been searching for last month's invoices. Where are they?" said Breen, as if genuinely bemused.

"I placed them in the tray as usual."

"These?" He held up a few wisps of paper. "They come to ten shillings and nine pence. Hardly any of your ragtag clients pays a bean, Miss Gifford, you have turned this partnership into a charitable institution." There was no point protesting that my clients were allocated by Breen himself; best allow the storm to pass over. "What about your new case—Marchant—I suppose it's too much to expect that you managed to get her bail?"

"If I may, sir, I'd like to talk to you in private about Mrs. Marchant." I glanced at Miss Drake, who hung over her notepad, feet firmly planted in anticipation of witnessing a delicious row.

"You can tell me on the way. We're going out. I've been waiting for you. We're off to Wheeler's house to collect a few personal items for his use while in prison. I need a female eye—see if you can notice anything the police might have missed."

"Mr. Breen, there is so much . . . I must talk to you. . . ."

He gave me a piercing stare: "If you'll excuse us, Miss Drake."

Miss Drake displayed an excess of feeling by a reduction in expression rather than the reverse. Gathering up her things, she gave Breen a tightly professional smile and closed the door sharply behind her.

After she'd gone, I said, "Mr. Breen, I should like to offer my resignation with immediate effect," but even to my own ears I sounded melo-dramatic, a trait that Breen could not abide in others.

He flung down his pen and I was conscious of a slight movement of floorboards in the passage outside the door. "It's for me to dismiss you, not for you to resign," and he picked up the next document to signal that the conversation was at an end.

"I am doing damage. This morning, in the case of Leah Marchant, I made us all look ridiculous, the defendant, myself, even you, because I am associated with you. She is charged with a very serious offense and must have proper representation."

"She's got it."

"No. She won't even look at me, let alone trust me."

"Is that your only complaint? Stephen Wheeler won't speak to me but that doesn't mean I'm going to drop his case."

"The magistrate made such a fool of me there was no point even trying to argue for bail. Sir, it's you she needs, though I warn you she's got no money whatever to pay your fees. Don't you think she's disad-vantaged enough without me representing her?"

"You found her, you keep her. And as for the fees, I've no doubt we can twist the arm of some journalist or other to pay us a few bob for the exclusive rights to her story." He glanced at his watch. "I said we'd be at the Wheeler house at four."

❧

I felt better. How could I not, when I was marching along dusty pave-ments in the wake of Mr. Breen while above us clouds passed swiftly over the sun so that one moment there was dense shade, the next vibrant heat? As our train puffed its way out of Euston, I told myself that a thousand ladies, at this moment fidgeting over afternoon tea trays, would give their eyeteeth to be Evelyn Gifford, articled clerk. My own face was reflected in the dirty windowpane; *wonderful bones*, Meredith had said.

And as we passed through Queen's Park and Willesden amid grubby factories and terraces clustered together with their backs to the railway line, I glimpsed the lives of other women. Prudence said that when and how people hung their washing was a sure indicator of breeding and it was certainly the case that, it being Tuesday, only gray remnants of laundry remained in certain backyards. I saw a woman sitting on a step as she minded a clutch of children and poultry, and another washing her scullery window.

During the journey, Breen immersed himself in back copies of the *Times Law Reports* but occasionally favored me with a spurt of information, the most momentous being that Stephen Wheeler had not entered a plea (or indeed uttered any other words) that morning in court when the charge was read out, and that committal proceedings were already under way. The police regarded the case as cut-and-dried and expected it to be heard at the Aylesbury Assizes in July. After all, the circumstantial evidence fitted: Wheeler and his wife had been alone on the hill above the church for several hours, the weapon and gloves were his. The police had even fixed on a motive, outlined scornfully by Breen. A fortnight before he was married, Wheeler had taken out life insurance for himself and his wife to the tune of ten thousand pounds each. "The police call this suspicious," said Breen, "but what man, cautious by nature and working in an insurance office, would not be tempted by his company's special rates for employees? His wife was not earning—she'd been a waitress at Lyons but of course stopped working when she was married. He was wise to take out insurance, I'd suggest."

"An insurance company wouldn't pay out in a case where there had been such obvious foul play," I said. "How could Wheeler hope to get away with it?"

"Exactly my thought. Wheeler, as I recall, was hardly the brightest boy in the class, but he wasn't a complete idiot. The police, of course, have come up with a theory. They say it was purely by chance that Stella Wheeler's body was found—after all, it took a particularly tenacious dog owner to unearth it. They say that it was probably Wheeler's intention to go back, remove the gun and gloves, and rebury her more thoroughly, having raised the hue and cry to make it seem as if she was genuinely missing."

"Has Wheeler said anything about all this?"

"Wheeler is still not speaking. He weeps and shakes his head and turns his face to the wall. I suspect he's in shock though the prosecution will say it looks like guilt. I'm very concerned about the health both of his body and mind. Next time I visit I shall take a decent doctor with me."

"Given the gun and the gloves, and Wheeler's silence, isn't it likely the police are right and that he did kill her? Who else would it be?"

Breen raised the newspaper higher to shut me out. "At this moment I have no idea. And it could indeed be Wheeler although I make a point of never believing a client of mine is guilty until he tells me so himself or a jury decides for me. But unless we take action, that man will be in and out of the dock and hung by the neck before anyone has time to get near the truth of the matter."

∾

In Wealdstone we walked along streets milling with children released from school. Girls sat cross-legged in a circle on the curb with their summer frocks pulled up over bony knees, intent on a game of fives despite being in the midst of a crowded football match in which a dozen or so boys kicked a battered leather ball from gutter to gutter. A baby howled in its pram and waved frantic fists; a couple of toddlers earnestly collected a pile of cinders while their mothers leaned together, deep in conversation. I heard the name *Mrs. Wheeler* and realized that by now news of Stella's death would be on everyone's lips.

As we neared the Wheelers' street, we discovered that the atmosphere was indeed charged. Although it was a balmy suburban afternoon, there was a distinct frisson of excitement and, as strangers, we were watched with more than usual interest. At the coal merchant's on the High Street we turned left and then immediately right onto Byron Street, which consisted of two rows of terraced houses, a chosen few, including number 7, distinguished by the fact that they had bay windows on the ground floor. Later, as I built a mental image of Stella Wheeler, I realized that having that superior bay window would have meant a great deal to her.

A policeman waited on the doorstep, very hot and self-conscious, surrounded by a small crowd clamoring for information. Though Stephen Wheeler had paid a deposit on this house a couple of months before his marriage, its faded paintwork suggested that it had not been much cared for since. Even before I set foot across the threshold, Prudence's strictures on the art of good housekeeping (until now, largely ignored) were playing on my mind. Stella Wheeler had not been an ideal housewife; her front step had collected more than a couple of days' litter and her net curtains were grimy.

The policeman removed his hat, revealing a rash of pimples on his youthful forehead, and let us into a narrow hall. Pushier members of the crowd had to be discouraged from clustering in after us. There was a strong smell of damp, even in midsummer, and the linoleum on the floor was so well-trodden that in places the pattern was worn away. Though the house had been shut up for only a couple of days, there was a hopeless quality in the stale air as if even the bricks and mortar knew that the Wheelers were not coming back.

Prudence would have had a field day; there was grit along the skirting and dado, torn wallpaper, and grease marks around the door handles.

The front parlor was bleakly furnished with a couple of ugly chairs, probably passed on by relatives of the newly married pair, and the hearth was ornamented by unlovely china, a floral vase with a yellow rim and base, and a matching ashtray.

The back room was a little more inviting. On the dresser, a dainty tea set was arranged with great precision, its gilt-edged cups polished, its saucers stood on their sides to show off their pattern. Inside the milk jug was a little card with a printed bouquet of flowers at one corner: *On Your Wedding Day. From All Your Friends at Lyons.* In the scullery beyond, preparations for the picnic were still evident (more proof of Stella's slovenliness); it looked as if mice had got at the heel of a loaf of bread, and a pickle jar had been left open, attracting the attention of flies.

I had rarely felt as uncomfortable as I did then, on the verge of those other, ruined lives. And the stillness of the air, the way in which everything was suspended at the moment that the couple had set forth to catch the Metropolitan Line train to Chesham, the knife flung across the bread board and a dishcloth trailing on the side of the sink half in and half out of scummy washing-up water, reminded me of how time becomes warped in moments of trauma, so that physical surroundings are out of step with the lives that inhabit them. I remembered how Clivedon Hall Gardens, at the instant that I flung wide the front door and saw an envelope in the hand of a telegraph boy, had become frozen in time, so that it was not until the next morning that the toasting fork was hung back on its hook in the hearth or the tea tray carried down to the kitchen. Until then, Grandmother's crochet remained in a heap on the floor, my coat and hat flung untidily across the hall stand, my satchel on the bottom stair.

I was reminded of this, fleetingly, at sight of Stella Wheeler's little scullery with its half dozen or so flies buzzing at the window. She had presumably expected, as she left the house for a picnic, to return and continue where she had left off.

"The prisoner's things will be upstairs in the cupboard," said the policeman, suddenly officious. "I was told nothing else should be disturbed." We climbed the stairs with their strip of diamond-patterned carpet and found two rooms, the back pitifully unused, with a spare bed covered by a blanket and a few incongruous household items, including a brand-new cast-iron boot-scraper in the form of a hedgehog, and a pitcher and basin in pink ceramic. I edged past a heap of packing cases and a chair with a broken cane seat, to peer out of the window onto a little backyard containing a privy, a shed, and a couple of pots planted with dying geraniums. Beyond and on either side were more backyards, in one of which a trio of women stood with folded arms, staring up at me. My appearance at the window would presumably cause yet more sensation in the neighborhood.

As we left that bleak little room, I saw a picture propped face to the wall. Expecting a wedding portrait—I had seen none so far—I turned it around, but it was, in fact, a photograph of two soldiers, one scarcely more than a child, full-lipped and with a pimple between his brows, the other a beardless Stephen Wheeler. Then as now, Wheeler's eyes were his best feature, steady and solemn. Both men had signed their names underneath: *Paul Christopher Fox. Stephen Anthony Wheeler.* I thought it the saddest thing in the house, not the photograph itself but the fact that it had been set aside.

We went through to the front bedroom and here at last the figure of Stella Wheeler became more vivid to me. I understood that though she loathed housework, a great deal of time had been lavished on her own appearance. This room was entirely hers; there was no sign that she was married even, other than the man's plaid dressing gown hanging on the back of the door. The bed was covered in a patchwork quilt, worked in shades of pink, and the surface of the dressing table spread with lace mats, upon which were arranged bottles, brushes, and pots of lotion. A flighty satin nightdress was folded on the left-hand pillow, great care having been taken to smooth it flat and keep the elaborate embroidery on the bodice exposed, and fluffy pink slippers of the kind also favored by Meredith peeped from under the chair by the dressing table.

Fortunately, there was hardly room for the policeman to enter—he had obviously been instructed to keep us in his sights—so instead he had to stoop under the lintel and crane to see what was going on as Breen made a great show of slamming drawers and throwing open wardrobe doors in search of Wheeler's underwear. Meanwhile, I did as I had been instructed and attempted to uncover Stella's secrets, which included a drawer full of surprisingly expensive-looking undergarments (all far more glamorous than my own): a bust flattener, a flesh-colored rubber girdle, a white *broderie anglaise* petticoat, satin knickers with fine lace trim, meticulously rolled silk stockings (I had one pair, Stella three). The dressing table had a shelf under the mirror and two small additional drawers on either side. One contained a few items of costume jewelry, the other her sponge bag, which smelled of damp toothbrush. Presumably, in the absence of a bathroom, Stella carried this bag down to the scullery each morning and night.

"So have you got everything?" asked the policeman.

"That's it," said Breen, "handkerchiefs, underwear. Good. Do you want to check them over, Officer? Anything else catch your eye that you think the poor man might need, Miss Gifford?"

I had found nothing startling; everything fitted the portrait I had been building of a youthful wife with a taste for finery and not much interest in her domestic surroundings. When I glanced inside the wardrobe, I thought the allocation of space very telling, Stella's pastel frocks and coats occupied two-thirds of the rail while Stephen's two suits were crushed at one end. But as we waited for the policeman to make a note in his book of the items we'd removed, I took another look at the sponge bag, it being the most personal item in the room. It contained toothbrush and paste, face cream, tweezers, rouge, a lipstick. Nothing else.

Except that there was a tear in the oilskin lining, and slipped inside, between the inner and outer shell, was a scrap of paper, folded very small and of poor quality. I felt a little stab of excitement, thinking this might be it, whatever it was we were looking for, but when I smoothed it out, I found that it was just a cloakroom ticket, number 437.

∾

When I returned that evening, late again, to Clivedon Hall Gardens, the aura of the Wheeler house and its abandoned contents still clung about me and mingled with those other, more powerful images of my own loss. But as I unlocked the front door, all other thought was driven from my head by the sound of music—*jazz,* of all things—coming from the drawing room, and then the trill of Meredith's laughter. As I hung up my hat, I was amused to catch myself patting my hair into place at the mirror. Just because Meredith said she admired you at lunchtime, I told myself, suddenly you've grown vain. Then I pushed open the drawing room door.

Meredith sat in Grandmother's usual place at the end of the sofa by the open French window, the curtain blowing against her shoulder and a glass of what looked like whiskey in her hand as she mouthed the words of the song. Prudence was at the writing desk, as if to disassociate herself. A whole clutch of unwritten rules were being broken: no strong alcoholic beverage to be drunk by women unless in extreme circumstances such as Christmas, influenza, or a death; no music in the drawing room where, since James's death, the piano had been shut up tight.

Another unwritten rule of postwar Clivedon Hall Gardens: no discussion of relations between the sexes, unless in the pages of an Ethel M. Dell novel sneaked up to her bedroom by Prudence and discovered quite by chance one day when Min brought it to me, supposing it must be mine. It had got caught up in a mound of sheets taken down to be laundered. After reading the first page and the last, I was never able to view Prudence in quite the same light again. *You are the prince of my heart—for ever. I love you as—as I never thought it was humanly possible to love.*

Poor Prudence, had there been a prince of her heart? Did she have, beneath that rigid corset, a needy, romantic side? James would have loved to know that Prudence read Ethel M. Dell beneath the covers—he and I would have succumbed to fits of laughter, but alone I was more compassionate. When she was occupied downstairs, I returned the book to her room and slipped it into her dressing-gown pocket. Now I imagined from the set of her shoulders that she was yearning toward the music as she yearned toward the sentiments of Ethel M. Dell, but would not let herself weaken.

Mother, on the other hand, was weeping, and after another moment I understood why.

Edmund was dancing with Grandmother; she barely a head taller than him, her little feet in their buttoned shoes occasionally tangling with his, her half-blind eyes gazing over the top of his head as they held each other by the hand and upper arm. The little boy was too young to be self-conscious about dancing with an old lady, and allowed himself to be maneuvered back and forth in a cross between a waltz and something much more modern, Grandmother's approximation to jazz. She was utterly absorbed, leaning into the music, grinning, whisking her small partner from foot to foot, swinging him back and forth to the limits of her stiff limbs.

And as for Edmund, no wonder Mother was weeping. He was dressed quaintly in pale blue trousers and a loose cotton shirt with a girlishly rounded collar, and his brows were drawn together by the concentration required to keep in step. And in this expression, posture, determination, he was James, our little man, returned to us as his beloved six-year-old self. But at the same time he was patently not James, and therefore not ours. I caught Meredith's eyes across the rim of her tumbler and saw that they were soft with love.

When the gramophone wound down, the record was left fizzing on the turntable. Nobody spoke until Mother said, wiping her eyes, "Well, I understand that you and Meredith are taking the boy to the seaside next Saturday, Evelyn. I'm very surprised you've managed to find the time given that the other day you said you couldn't spare me two hours to come with me to St. Mark's fete."

The spell was broken; Grandmother sank into a chair, Prudence took up her pen, and Edmund retreated to his mother's knee. I said nothing, since if I did I was bound to give offense to someone.

Eight

On Thursday morning, *obedient to Mr. Breen,* I trekked across London to investigate Leah Marchant's former lodgings in a tenement off Gosset Street in Haggerston, half a mile or so from my old stamping ground of Toynbee Hall in Commercial Street. Alighting from the second omnibus, I was pursued by swarms of ill-clad children, some of whom shouted abuse after I had emptied my purse of coppers and said I had nothing else to give them. Despite all my good intentions, I never could quite overcome my fear of the poor. I wanted to help but didn't know how to cross the divide or stop myself recoiling from the dirt and brashness of even those innocent children. Perhaps there was more than a streak of Aunt Prudence in me. According to her, there were no ills that could not be righted by hard work. To compensate, I tried to engage one little girl in a conversation about school. "Can't go to school," she said, "till Ma gets me shoes."

One little boy winked so naughtily that I couldn't resist giving him sixpence though it nearly started a riot among the rest. Edmund was responsible for this flash of generosity; since his arrival, I'd developed a renewed susceptibility to small boys with shapely heads and inquisitive eyes.

Meanwhile, the sun blazed remorselessly down and the smell of privies was in places overwhelming. But when I reached number 9 Caractacus

Court, I found that its front step was much better scrubbed than the late Mrs. Wheeler's and the woman who answered the door was wearing a clean pinafore, her hair neatly controlled by a dozen or so grips. Her manner, however, was hostile. "Are you an 'ealth visitor?"

"No. Most definitely not. No."

"Then what are you?"

"My name is Miss Gifford. I am here on business to do with Mrs. Leah Marchant. Is it Mrs. Sanders? Mrs. Marchant gave the police this address and said that a Mrs. Sanders was her landlady."

Impasse. The woman didn't move a muscle. She had tired eyes and a forlorn mouth, and behind her was a dank cave of a hallway. Meanwhile, from floors above came the racket of children's voices. "I'm a lawyer," I added desperately.

The woman's expression changed from suspicion to cynical amusement. "You and 'oo else?"

"I'm acting on Mrs. Leah Marchant's behalf. As you perhaps know she is in trouble, arrested on a charge of kidnapping. We need to find her a bail address, so I want to know, is there still a room available for her here?"

Mrs. Sanders acknowledged this speech with an infinitesimal shifting of weight. "She 'asn't paid no rent for months. I'm not obliged to keep 'er a room."

"Are her things still here?"

"They might be."

"May I go up and look?"

"At what?"

"As I said, we need to find accommodation for Mrs. Marchant. I want to see if her old room is suitable and if not, to collect her things."

"You're takin' nothin'. Like I say, she owes me rent."

"I'm sure we might come to an agreement if you would show me her room."

At last, after scrutinizing papers headed "Breen & Balcombe" with a good show of actually being able to read them, Mrs. Sanders said: "Well, I suppose I can't stop you. Third floor, door on the right. I'll unlock it for you."

The house was similar in plan to Clivedon Hall Gardens, but whereas noise in the Gifford establishment was muffled by fabrics and the weight of furniture, this house, bare-boarded and uncurtained, echoed like a drum and the stair rail shook under my hand. From behind a half-closed door on a first-floor landing, a baby yelled, there was a sharp slap, then a woman's raised voice and a bellow of outrage from the child. The higher we climbed, the hotter and more rank the atmosphere became, saturated with the smell of old cooking and damp clothes. At last we reached a door, horribly splintered at the bottom, presumably by somebody's boot, which Mrs. Sanders unlocked with a key selected from a set worthy of Holloway.

Fortunately, my weeks among the insect life in the basement of Breen & Balcombe had prepared me for the scuffling that followed our intrusion into the room. There was one single bed, from which all the blankets had been stripped, leaving a mattress horribly stained with what looked like blood and worse. The only other furniture was a table covered with newspapers, assorted broken chairs, an empty hearth, and a dented kettle. Arranged on shelves were various bits of crockery, and poked behind the mantel was a photograph of a young man wearing a sailor's uniform and a rakish smile, Mr. Marchant, perhaps. I disliked him on sight: light hair, prominent ears, a swanky way of cocking his head to one side and looking boldly into the lens.

There were very few signs of the children, except for a couple of indefinable garments hanging from the bed frame, the remains of a slate, and a worn-out packing case from which poked the earless head of a teddy bear. The window was high, small, and greasy, and a moth was trapped behind the glass.

"Thing is," said Mrs. Sanders suddenly, "I'm 'er friend. I've got a loyalty to 'er. We was on the trams together. We knoo we'd be turned off at the end of the war and rather than go back into service she takes the first man that comes along: *'im*. How could she live with 'is boozin' and whatnot? Turns out 'e's even worse than I first thought. Comes back once in a blue moon wantin' money, gets 'er pregnant, disappears. 'Aven't seen him for more'n two years. And if 'e were to crop up it would be the same as before, the drinkin' and the draggin' 'er down with 'im. Another baby on the way. She can't resist, soft as putty when 'e's about. But when 'e's gone she sobers up, gets a grip of 'erself."

"Would you have her back to live here?" I asked quite calmly, though all this talk of children impetuously conceived was painfully close to home.

"I'd 'ave 'er back. Trouble is, the authorities would be down on me like a ton of bricks if she brought the children 'ere. The minute you get that lot involved everything gets inspected and before you know it you're in all kinds of trouble."

"If the rent was paid and a little extra given you, could the room be painted and furnished? Might there even be other, adjoining rooms? We could try and find her somewhere else but if you're her friend and she was happy here . . ."

"Who would pay the rent?"

"I don't know yet. We'd see."

"If the rent was paid that would be a start. But I can't 'ave her goin' out all day and leavin' them kids again. The oldest is not six and she left her mindin' the baby. It worried me to death. I couldn't always be bringing them down to me."

"Might you even, if necessary, be prepared to come to court and vouch for her good character?"

She gave me another expressionless stare. "If it got 'er out of prison, I would 'ave to."

As we went downstairs, I wondered whether I ought to offer payment, but when I took out my purse Mrs. Sanders waved her hand angrily and ushered me out of the door.

ℭ

I was far too hot, my spirits were depressed by my clumsy departure from Caractacus Court—it seemed to me that Mrs. Sanders's respect once lost would be difficult to regain—and I was a little unsure of my direction. My plan was to call at Toynbee Hall to see my friend Carrie Morrison, as Mr. Breen had suggested, and ask her opinion of the Leah Marchant case. Carrie would do me good, she would never allow herself to become mired by the kind of emotional sludge in which I currently wallowed. Her private and professional lives were bound to be kept firmly apart and there was a chance she would know, through her close connection with Toynbee, of the best help available to a woman in Leah's position.

In another five minutes, I found myself in Commercial Road and there ahead of me, in that long, rackety road crammed with shops and traffic, was a familiar clump of greenery and, set in a high wall, a plaque engraved with the words TOYNBEE HALL. From the open doors came music, a Brahms quartet, and I realized that a Thursday lunchtime concert must be in progress.

Had it not been for Meredith, I might have shunned the music altogether, abandoned the idea of seeing Carrie and gone back to the office, but a door in my soul, closed for years, had been pushed ajar by the sight of Grandmother and Edmund dancing in the drawing room. So I marched up the path beside a patch of struggling lawn to the hall where sunlight flooded the lobby, a soft draft blew along the floor, and ahead, through another doorway, the little auditorium was crammed with chairs.

The woman on the door recognized me from the old days. Waving aside my offer of payment, she pointed to a vacant seat at the end of a row where I let my hands fall into my lap, closed my eyes, and gave myself up to the torrent of music. From the street outside, beneath the rumble of carts, came the distant clatter of Spitalfields Market, barely quarter of a mile away. I knew, without opening my eyes, that light would be splintered into shards of color by the stained-glass arch of each window and that the audience would consist largely of unemployed laborers and clerks in collarless shirts and frayed waistcoats, but that among them would be plainly dressed young men, university-educated, the latest batch of idealists come to help out at the settlement.

Of course, it was foolish of me to have ventured inside; quite apart from the music, merely being in that place rubbed me raw, because the smells of beeswax, bodies, books, and soup were redolent of the months of near despair when I was looking for work. And then the music took me deeper still into the past. Perhaps I had known it would, and that was why I couldn't keep away. The previous night, when I watched Grandmother and Edmund dancing, and Meredith so absorbed by love for her boy, I had wanted to feel something deeply too. I thought I could take the risk; surely, enough time had gone by. So I let myself be touched, for a moment, by the rusty emotions generated by two stillborn love affairs.

Peter Shaw and I had first exchanged friendly words when I visited Father's office before the war. Decked out in picture hats and swishing skirts, Mother and I were supposed to dispense charm and encouragement to junior employees at bimonthly tea parties. Mother was an expert; I slouched in my upright chair and envied the young men their enthusiasm. But Peter always looked out for me and drew me into conversation if he could. His eyes were a melting brown and his gaze clung to mine and made a little rip in my composure. I lay awake at night, replaying snippets of conversation in search of inner meaning and dreaming him up an aura, toffee-brown like his eyes. After the Christmas party in 1914, which, as usual, took place in the drawing room at Clivedon Hall Gardens, with the carpets rolled up, furniture pushed back, candlelight, sherry, music (one of the senior partners had a limited repertoire on the violin), we stepped outside together into the smoky, late-afternoon air and ran away, panting and giggling, I in my party dress and thin shoes, until we came to the shelter of a canal bridge, where he kissed me until my mind popped with shock and fear and delight.

But what a wasted opportunity that kiss had been. I couldn't concentrate for wondering: Yes, but do I really love Peter Shaw, or is it just that he's available at this moment and going away in the new year? If I'd known that his might be the only kiss that would ever be granted me, I'd have drawn him into the darkness, abandoned my Clivedon Hall Gardens principles altogether, and let him make love to me à la Ethel M. Dell. Because as soon as he went away, even before he got himself shot or shelled or whatever it was that provoked the word *missing* on the telegram home, in my imagination he became taller, bolder, more beautiful, an ideal boy, in fact, with Byronic hair and features, full of wit.

So the music was an opportunity to lose myself again to his touch, to snatch more forbidden moments in the shadow of the bridge, to remember his three letters, each of which closed with the phrase *You have been on my mind* (into which I read a restrained but passionate yearning), to smell his alien young male scent, to feel his fingertip play secretly along the veins on the underside of my wrist as we sat side by side at the Clivedon Hall Gardens dining table on the night before he went away.

The second affair, nearly four years later, when I was twenty-five, had been more tortured still. It was enough to recall a bowl of red glass cupped in the hand of a uniformed man to feel my blood shudder with the anticipated shock of lovemaking.

The music ended and I opened my dazed eyes to find that I was being scrutinized from across the room by a man I recognized but couldn't at first place. Then I remembered that he was the barrister who had caught hold of me in the foyer of Shoreditch Magistrates' Court after the humiliation of Leah Marchant's bail proceedings and advised me not to interrupt a magistrate. Not wishing to be reminded of that morning, I looked hastily for Carrie but, seeing no sign of her, headed for the door.

"Miss Gifford."

Surely I had been mistaken; he would not bother to follow me into Commercial Road and was hardly likely to have remembered my name. But though I didn't pause, he called again and actually came abreast of me. "Miss Gifford."

I shielded my eyes from the sun to look into his face as he offered his hand. "Nicholas Thorne," he said. "Last time we met, I'm afraid there was no time for introductions—do you remember—Marlborough Street Police Court or some other godforsaken hole?"

You don't deceive me, I thought as I withdrew my hand from his clasp, you remember exactly where we met. I walked on, wondering what on earth he wanted with me.

"Did you enjoy the concert, Miss Gifford?" he asked, falling into step beside me.

"Very much."

"Although I think you missed all but the last piece. I saw you come in toward the end. Such a shame. We had Gluck, and Handel's G Minor sonata. Do you know that particular work? It happens to be one of my favorites. I've not seen you at the Toynbee concerts—is this a first for you? It's like old times for me, quite a nostalgia trip because I was here just after the war offering a bit of legal advice and a spot of lecturing in psychology and French. Sanest thing I'd done for years, it seemed to me."

There were many reasons for my reluctance to be drawn into conversation with him, the foremost being that I could see no reason why he would wish to talk other than to bait me. I had encountered plenty of embryonic barristers at Cambridge and recognized the educated drawl, disarming smile, and acute memory. Yet he was such a gentleman in the way he maneuvered to ensure that he was on the outside of the sidewalk, and his smile was so engaging—barely a muscle was disturbed in his lip or cheek but his eyes were warm—that I could not be completely immune. He was a beautiful, intact, youngish man and therefore a rarity indeed. And of course I was still in the grip of the wretched music.

At last I said: "I used to go to Toynbee Hall last year. I worked on the poor man's law scheme too."

"Actually I assumed you once used to frequent Toynbee."

"Why?"

"You work for Breen. Everybody knows the work Breen did at Toynbee. There was bound to be a connection. Did you enjoy your work there, Miss Gifford?"

"It gave me a degree of purpose. Unlike you, I suspect, I worked there not out of altruism but of necessity. Nobody else would take me. It was the only way I could gain any experience in the law at all."

"Has it been a very rough ride for you, Miss Gifford? Do you know, I'm absolutely fascinated. A couple of ladies have recently been called to the bar, possibly you're acquainted with them, Williams and Normanton. Such stalwarts. So fierce and determined. One has to admire them, one really does. Look I'm absolutely parched, I know of a cracking little tea shop near here, would you mind, could you bear to take tea with me? You probably won't believe this but I have been hoping to run into you these past couple of days."

I was so startled I actually stopped dead. "I'm afraid I have to get back to the office."

He threw back his head and laughed. "Tea, Miss Gifford, is all I'm suggesting. Ten minutes of your time. Don't look so horrified."

But I had grown hotter still, this time with anger. I knew his game all right—Let's charm the frightful bluestocking Miss Gifford into pouring out her little would-be legal heart and then cut her down to size: *I've often wondered, Miss Gifford, perhaps you'd give me your opinion— do you think that tokenism is better than nothing at all? How does it feel to be* a token, *Miss Gifford?*

A cart had slipped a sack of coal and the smell of dust was stifling. Before I knew it, Thorne had seized my case. "You are absolutely white as a sheet. It is rotten of me to have kept you in this broiling sun. I think you'll find the place I have in mind is rather cool and it will barely take you a step out of your way."

He strode along, swinging my case, and short of wrenching it out of his hand what could I do but trot beside him as he scattered remarks like a bird-feeder dispensing corn? ". . . Extraordinary friendships forged at Toynbee . . . missed your Breen by a couple of years but knew of him by reputation . . . opportunity to share one's education with those who . . ." We reached the café, where the door stood open and inside the edges of checked tablecloths were ruffled by an electric ceiling fan. He chose a corner table and took my jacket, held back a chair for me, and folded himself into another—his long legs would not fit under the table. "The truth is I was very impressed when I saw you in court the other day. Less impressed by the magistrate, I might add, who I thought treated you appallingly. For the first time, when I heard you pleading for your client, I saw the case for women in court. I realized there might be sympathy between women in trouble and a woman lawyer."

An urn hissed behind the counter while an offhand woman in a flowered overall came forward to take the order. I gathered my wits. "No," I said firmly.

"Miss Gifford?"

"That's not why I trained, to help just women. No, I wish to serve all people. I don't want to become part of some lesser branch of the law, as I think has happened to some extent with women in medicine."

"I didn't mean *lesser*."

"I think you probably did. I have heard the argument before, numerous times. Would you consider yourself to be an effective barrister if you were only allowed to practice with one half of the population?"

"You have a point, Miss Gifford, but you must allow me to take one step at a time. Before I met you I had an entirely different viewpoint; I didn't see the need for lady lawyers at all." He paused to bestow a smile on the waitress as she set out the cups, ran his fingers through his damp hair to slick it back from his forehead, and rested his arm along the table. "I couldn't imagine doing battle with a lady across the floor of a courtroom. It would be like sparring with my mother or fiancée, something that as a well-brought-up young man I simply couldn't do."

"Forgive me, but I believe that to be a wholly unconvincing argument. Are you suggesting that gentlemen politicians will find themselves unable to argue with female members of Parliament and councilors? Are you telling me you never argued with your sister? What you mean, I believe, is that women aren't worth arguing with because they'll never be able to withstand your mental and verbal dexterity."

His laugh had the most perverse effect on me, like a finger drawn across my breastbone. "I don't have a sister, Miss Gifford, so I can't answer the first part of your argument. And later I'll examine my conscience and judge whether you have in fact found me out with the second."

Everything about him was leisurely, as if there was a lag between thought and deed, so that his smile dawned at the back of his eye and at last, after the lapse of a second or so, reached the corner of his lip. It was the same with his gestures. When at one point he hitched up his trouser leg, the movement was a slow lifting of first hand, then knee.

He removed the teapot lid, stirred, took the strainer, and poured the tea expertly. As he handed me a cup, he glanced into my face and must have seen my absorption, because he raised an eyebrow: "Do you not approve of my method, Miss Gifford? I have a Lancashire grandmother who taught us to put the milk in last."

"I'm sure it will be very good tea."

"Thing is, I'd better come clean. It was a stroke of luck meeting you. I'd been due to pay a visit to Breen and Balcombe on behalf of a client of mine who happens to employ a client of yours, Stephen Wheeler. I've been asked to keep a friendly eye on the case, see if there was anything we could do to help out. So when I saw you today . . ."

"Stephen Wheeler is Mr. Breen's client, not mine."

"But Mr. Breen wasn't in Toynbee Hall and you were, so I thought I'd have a word. Fact is, Miss Gifford, my client, Sir David Hardynge, is concerned for the reputation of his company. It's all over the press that Wheeler killed his wife for the insurance payout, which we find hard to believe."

"You can hardly expect me to . . ."

"Of course, you can't discuss the case, but I wanted to offer my assistance, should it be required. Obviously I can't represent Wheeler, due to a conflict of interest. I am very closely connected to Hardynge, served with his son—friends since boyhood, in fact—engaged to his daughter, actually, but if I can advise . . ."

"Thank you. I shall tell Mr. Breen about this conversation. And now, if you'll excuse me . . ." I pushed my cup aside.

"You seem taken aback. Perhaps I've handled this badly. I'm simply speaking on behalf of a concerned employer. Hardynge cares for all his men, particularly those who served in the war, to whom he shows almost paternal indulgence. He telephoned me on the afternoon of Wheeler's arrest, asked me what could be done. All in all I'd say he's a most enlightened employer, would do anything for Wheeler."

"I don't doubt Sir David Hardynge's good intentions and I'm sure Mr. Breen will be most grateful." I signaled to the waitress to bring my jacket, then, without pausing to fasten the buttons or adjust my hat, picked up my case and held out my hand. "Thank you for the tea, Mr. Thorne."

"I'll give you my card."

"Thank you. As I've said, any correspondence should be with Mr. Breen."

"Miss Gifford . . ." Instead of releasing my hand, he held it within his own. "You look upset. What is it? Please don't dash away."

"I must, I'm afraid. As I've said, I feel it's quite inappropriate to discuss the Wheeler case further."

"Then we'll talk of other things."

"Really, no, thank you."

I left him at the table, one hand in his pocket as he reached for change, a bemused smile on his face but otherwise unruffled.

I, on the other hand, walked away at a great speed, muttering to myself: What were you thinking of? You made an utter fool of yourself. Why else would he want to buy you tea except to gain information? Engaged to Sir David Hardynge's daughter. Fool. Fool. And you thought he was impressed, attracted to you, even. Yes you did, that's why you're upset. You thought he'd singled you out.

☙

In our last week at Girton, one of our sternest lecturers, a woman in her fifties dressed in the regulation soft-collared blouse, belted cardigan, and ankle-length skirt, had proposed the motion in a debate titled "The Future, My Dear, Must Perforce Be Female." Until Miss Lang spoke, the atmosphere had been lighthearted. Examinations were over and we were about to graduate. Our only objection to the debate was that the subject was so tediously familiar it could hold no surprises. But we had overlooked the fact that Miss Lang had no qualms about uttering the unutterable.

"You are the first generation of young women that has ever faced a future in which you will not depend on men. This will give you extraordinary freedom and extraordinary responsibility." We smiled and nodded, of course, and felt rather proud and excited. "For most of you this will not be a choice but a fact of life. We are missing nearly a million men and these, as you are painfully aware, were your contemporaries. I don't want to dwell on the agony of loss, not a woman among us is unmarked. But I would argue that you are the lucky ones, because all of you have brains and some of you a private income. Pity the poor girls who have neither. I urge you, my dear young ladies, don't waste your youth seeking out a husband who in all probability is lying in an unmarked grave somewhere in northern France. Instead, seize the opportunity of your single status to change the world."

I had always hated prophetic statements; I suspected the ones that struck home were the ones we knew in our hearts to be true. We'd read the statistics and the evidence lay in the empty bedrooms in our family homes, the widows' weeds in church, the cripples on the street corners, the newly built war memorials. But I can't have been alone in thinking: It may be true for some but it won't apply to me.

Because of that debate, the last week at Cambridge was tainted. Until then we had been studying because that was the path we'd chosen. We regarded ourselves as exceptionally clever girls with an insatiable appetite to prove ourselves capable of all that our brothers could do and more. We looked down on our mothers and their friends and neighbors, the ladies in the grand houses and the housewives in their terraces, because we thought their lives hollow. Most of us envisaged that we would have a career, yes, but we wanted to be loved as well.

And now this wretched Miss Lang had said that we wouldn't marry.

"This is it, girls, the years of expectation are over. We are sisters, and on our sisters and ourselves we must rely or we shall face a future filled with pointless yearning."

So while some of us went into medicine, teaching, or research, Carrie Morrison and I entered the law, where, ironically enough, we met nothing but men: the aged, the avuncular, the damaged, the very youthful, the very fortunate, the very quick-footed. But on the whole these men wanted nothing to do with us. While they were fighting, they had yearned for their civilized chambers, offices, and courtrooms, and what most of them had hoped was that on their return nothing would be changed. We women were the symbol of an outcome they hadn't looked for. They certainly would never have considered *marrying* a dowdy legal woman when they had the pick of soft-skinned girls in translucent frocks, who would grace their hearths and refrain from asking awkward questions.

The fact was that until Edmund turned up on my doorstep and Thorne touched my arm in the foyer of Shoreditch Magistrate Court, I had convinced myself that the one thing I really did not need in my life was a man. I had no intention of sacrificing years of hard work for the sake of a sickly, lascivious, fortune-hunting, or cradle-snatching type, such as Mother occasionally insinuated my way after church. I thought I was immune. I don't believe I even saw Breen and Wolfe as men so much as accessible outposts of the law. And then Edmund turned up and I wanted a child, and Thorne poured my tea, adjusted the cup on the saucer, glanced at me with unexpected deliberation, and I wanted a lover.

Nine

Before leaving *Clivedon Hall Gardens* for our trip to Eastbourne, we were cautioned to take umbrellas, spare woolens, gabardines, even the address of a distant cousin of Prudence's who lived in Polegate and might be persuaded to put us up should we be stranded for the night.

"*Stranded!*" exclaimed Meredith.

"You never know with trains," said Prudence, "they can be extremely unreliable," and it was as if each locomotive had a wicked will of its own.

"If we're stranded," said Meredith, "we shall bivouac on the beach. Wouldn't that be something, Edmund?"

So I found myself on yet another unaccustomed journey, steaming through blousy late-May fields, first Surrey, then Sussex. It was hard to leave behind the *should*s, the most pressing of which was that I should have been with Mother. Although it was never stated, it was understood by the inmates of Clivedon Hall Gardens (with the exception of myself and possibly Grandmother) that my work was a matter of self-indulgence and I should be very grateful that I was allowed to do it. The fact that I worked because somebody must was too painful to voice. So Saturdays with Mother were my penance for indulging my whim the rest of the week. Sometimes we went to a gallery, sometimes I endured a tea party or an afternoon's gardening.

And if Mother happened not to need me, I should have been reading up the case law on the custody of children and preparing a bail argument for Leah Marchant. Above all I should not be spending yet more money, this time on a day out by the sea.

My perceptions of Meredith kept shifting. In the area of money, for instance, I had no idea about her true situation. She claimed to be poor but when Edmund said he couldn't find his bathing drawers, she told him airily that she would buy him a new pair in a shop by the seaside: "I can't believe there won't be mountains of bathing costumes in Eastbourne." And he was promised a bucket and spade and an ice cream. So many treats.

And then there was the question of her clothes, which were neither practical nor cheap. Perhaps the illicit rifling through Stella Wheeler's bedroom had sensitized me a little to the nuances of women's fashion. Stella's clothes, I suspected, with the exception of the nightgown, undergarments, and stockings, had been cheaply bought. The dyes had been saccharine, the fabrics creased. Most items in my own wardrobe could best be described as sturdy: skirts and jackets made to measure by Mother's quavery prewar dressmaker, Miss Pouncett, the rest off the rack at Debenham and Freebody. All Clivedon Hall Gardens clothes were expected to last season after season. Prudence was proud to claim that she still wore boots bought in 1906, resoled three times by a favored cobbler in Buckingham but otherwise good as new.

But Meredith's wardrobe was exquisite. The shades were subtle, the accessories carefully matched. Today she wore yet another low-waisted frock and little knitted jacket, a straw hat, yellow (of all colors) gloves, and matching bag. Prudence would never have recommended yellow. The principle by which we abided in Clivedon Hall Gardens was that each garment should match every other, so navy, beige, and especially black and gray were staples.

But the biggest mystery of all about Meredith was exactly what she was *after*, as Mother put it. How much money did she need to fulfill her plans? Where did she intend to live, long term? Had she tickets booked for a return voyage to Canada? I had been told to find answers to all these questions, but on the train journey, as we watched fields of cow parsley crushed by overnight rain, tossing hedgerows, a herd of cows each angled precisely in line with the others to face the railway line, farms tucked like models into their yards, towns and villages nestled into valleys exactly as described by a guidebook about the British countryside (according to Meredith), the sudden emergence of the sun between banks of cloud, and then the wide open plain and steeply rising down-land before the sea, we talked only of relatively neutral subjects.

"Tell me about Prudence," said Meredith. "What is her story?"

"There is no story. She is my father's only sister. My grandfather was a widower, so she was obliged to care for him and when he died and the family house was sold, she moved into the cottage which used to be the gardener's at the bottom of the garden. Prudence loved that cottage but when Father's money went, her allowance had to be reduced, so she eventually came to live with us."

"How did he lose his money?"

"Bad investments. After James died he grew reckless, although I think he was trying to secure our future."

"Poor Prudence for losing her home," said Meredith. "Poor you."

"Oh, we rub along quite well."

"But why do you put up with it? Why do you let her dominate those dreadful meals?"

"Does she dominate? I find her amusing, actually. I'm very fond of her. She's company for Mother, they're roughly the same age."

"It doesn't seem to me that they like each other much."

"They make the best of their circumstances."

"Oh, dear. What a way to go on." And she turned to the window, as if I was somehow culpable. "Everyone lives so meagerly in your house. Their lives seem so constrained."

I was silent. Meredith was surely not being deliberately obtuse but there she sat in her buttercup-colored lambskin gloves, eyes wide with concern, apparently oblivious to the irony that part of the cause for the Giffords' financial distress was sitting only inches away with his nose and fist pressed to the window, watching out for a first glimpse of the sea.

"What I have noticed about your house," she added, "is that everything in it is not only old but brown. Why is that, do you suppose? You live among sepia tones. I wonder, is that why everyone seems so low in spirits?"

After a pause, I murmured: "Everything was different before James died. We cannot seem to recover from that."

As I had somehow anticipated, the conversation was abruptly ended. Meredith put her arm around her son and said: "Look, darling, look at all these back gardens full of roses. This is Eastbourne, I feel sure. We must be nearly there."

Meanwhile, I reflected that perhaps she was right and Clivedon Hall Gardens really did have a pervasive brown hue. Only in odd little patches, other than in my imagination, did the house show a flash of color: a new pink soap in the bathroom (Mother's birthday present from a well-to-do bridge partner), lovely crimson in the kitchen where Rose was knitting a daring tea cozy in red and royal blue, Grandmother's collection of theatrical memorabilia, confined to her room to conceal the shameful fact that she'd once been an actress, a fistful of early sweet peas, grown by Prudence, hanging over the edge of their vase like the lilac, cream, and coral frocks of dancers.

⁂

In Eastbourne, I hovered in the doorway of a shop crammed with mainly pointless seaside items while Meredith bought her son blue-

and-green-striped swimming drawers, then a bucket and spade. Her method of spending money was a revelation. Out came a little purse (matching yellow leather) and from it a fistful of change, offered to the assistant to select and sort. "I still can't manage these farthings and thruppences and whatnot; take what you need." How careless it seemed not even to count what was given in change. Then at last we were safely away from the shops and high up on the promenade. "Of course there is water and to spare back home," said Meredith. "This, however, is proper seaside. This is what I was hoping for."

"It's pebbles," said Edmund, scanning the row of breakwaters. "No sand."

"When the tide goes out there might be sand," I said. He dashed ahead down the winding path to the sea and I felt a lightening of the heart as the breeze caught my hat and the air was suddenly full of salt and memories of more than a dozen childhood holidays in Cornwall. Not that those had been filled with unalloyed pleasure. There had been so many unconquerable tensions; Mother was always too cold or too hot and had to keep shifting her deck chair while Father grew impatient sitting on the beach with no function other than to bark injunctions at James and me, and disappeared on long, mysterious walks, thereby making Mother restless and leaving us all with a vague sense of failure that we had not proved interesting enough.

This day, on the other hand, promised a less precarious kind of pleasure. Meredith had the knack of simply accepting things as they came, whether it was that the sun was now shining so warmly and steadily that the few remaining clouds were visibly melting away or that the tide was timed to perfection, on the way out and revealing a bit of sand amid the pebbles, which allowed Edmund to build a shallow trench down to the water. Even the picnic was perfect, because Meredith had bought a few little extras from the baker and given a substantial tip to the servants for their trouble. "She will *ruin* those girls," said Prudence, "they are overpaid as it is."

After lunch, indifferent to the fact that she was revealing an eye-catching stretch of shapely lower leg, Meredith lay on the pebbles with her jacket behind her head. Edmund was befriended by a bossy girl a couple of years younger, whose frilled skirt was tucked firmly into her knickers and who insisted he help her create a gigantic face, complete with mustache and eyebrows, of pebbles and seaweed. So I too lay back, closed my eyes, and let the tumultuous week draw away from me in the waves falling and falling, the shocks and journeys and the new faces of demanding people: Leah Marchant, Meredith herself, poor Stephen Wheeler in his prison cell, and Nicholas Thorne, curse him, whose smile hovered in my inner eye like the Cheshire Cat's, even he was fading and mingling with the call of seagulls.

Except that a fly was tickling my throat and then the back of my hand—no, not a fly, Meredith, who fluttered a stalk of dried seaweed over my skin. "Tell me about the murder scene," she said. Her face overshadowed mine, but behind her the sky was now a vibrant blue. She had removed her hat so that her fine hair was blown up in wisps of reddish gold.

It was as if I was drugged; I couldn't at first think what she meant and my voice slurred with drowsiness. "Murder scene? I've never visited a murder scene."

"But you went to the dead woman's house."

"You know I did, to collect the defendant's clothes." Meredith was propped on her elbow so close I couldn't move. Her eyes, huge and inquisitive, trapped me.

"What was it like, to be in that poor woman's house?"

"Sad."

We stared at each other. I could see each individual lash, and yes, I'm sure hers were painted. "And what else?"

"Bleak. You know, hopeless."

"Why hopeless?"

"Well, obviously, the marriage had come to an awful end."

"But *things* are not usually hopeless. Things are just things. Anyway, did you find any clues?"

"We weren't looking for clues."

"Oh yes you were, I'll bet you were. I've read my detective novels, I know the score."

So there I was, literally breast to breast with Meredith, and there was the dead Stella Wheeler with her dank kitchen and seductive nightdress. And behind Mr. and Mrs. Wheeler were other, even more uncomfortable associations with their tragedy, not least the encounter outside Toynbee Hall, the fan swinging around and around in the little café, Nicholas Thorne adjusting the fabric in the knee of his trousers. "We shouldn't talk about the Wheeler case," I murmured. "For a start, I don't know much about it, and anyway, this is the weekend, I don't want to think about work."

"But it's in all the papers. I'm fascinated that the instant we arrive in London, Edmund's aunty gets caught up in a murder inquiry. Surely you can tell me what's going to happen next."

"I don't know. Nothing, according to the police. They seem to think it's cut-and-dried."

"Do *you* think it's cut-and-dried?"

"Mr. Breen is not satisfied. He says there is no motive. We are to pursue our own investigations alongside the police, who he doesn't think will do a thorough job, because they believe the evidence against Wheeler is overwhelming. So I'm to visit where Stella was a waitress, and Theo Wolfe, who also works for Mr. Breen, will talk to Stephen Wheeler's colleagues. Wheeler himself still hasn't said a word."

"That doesn't surprise me. Quite the reverse. In the war, in the hospitals, I saw quite a few men who couldn't or wouldn't speak because of what they'd seen or done. But you can't blame me for being interested.

What you deal with is so vital, don't you see? And it fascinates me how the intensely private, the circumstances of the dead girl's marriage, becomes a matter that is so public because of a crime. It was the same for me when I worked in hospitals. Although sickness is a very intimate state, it makes a person public property. I never could get used to the mix of the extremely personal and the fact that everything went on in full view of dozens of others. After all, it was in those circumstances that I came to know your brother James."

His name jolted me wide-awake. She was still hanging over me and there was a gleam in the back of her eye, perhaps in anticipation of my reaction. I was tempted to reach out my hand and push her aside, as if it was just her body that blocked my view of him. "Tell me," I whispered, "when you knew him, what was he like?"

"What was he like?" she repeated lightly, as if discussing the cut of a frock. "Why, he was like all the others, I suppose. Ill. Sick of the war."

"Describe him to me, please, as you knew him."

"Well, let's see now. I hardly knew him for long. You, on the other hand, were his sister all his life." She had clasped her hands between her breasts but still knelt with her face inches from mine. "So I'll trade you, Evelyn. First you tell me what he was like as a little boy." And she flung herself on her back, spread her arms wide, and closed her eyes.

In a flash of irritation—she was toying with me, surely, and must know how much this conversation meant to me—I sat up so suddenly that I was dizzy. Colors melded together in a bewildering soup of sparkle and glare until at last, by pulling the brim of my hat firmly across my brow, I could focus on Edmund, who was making a laborious journey up from the sea with his bucket.

"I want Edmund to have a father," said Meredith, tapping my forearm softly with her fist, "that's partly why I'm here. I want him to have a past as well as a future. So conjure up the young James."

"He was like Edmund to look at, though perhaps a little plumper in the face and taller for his age. Very determined, single-minded, affectionate."

"Yes, that's Edmund exactly. What else?"

"I was thinking when we first came down to the sea today that I remember James very clearly, Jamie, he was then, on our seaside holidays. He always was a perfectionist. We holidayed each year in Cornwall, near Padstow, and he loved to build sandcastles but woe betide us if the sea came in too suddenly or a dog sprang on his creation. He couldn't stand it."

"And when he couldn't stand something what did he do?"

She folded her hands behind her head so that her slight body was arched and I could see her ribs and the outline of her breast through the gauzy fabric of her frock. And again I was disturbed by the memory of Stella Wheeler's underwear drawer, the too-dainty knickers and the unseemly bust-flattener that had once defined the shape of her upper body. A pulse throbbed softly in Meredith's throat and her jaw and cheekbones were so fine and small that she appeared fragile. I chose my words with great care, as I had already learned to do with Meredith. "Got angry, I suppose, like most children. Shouted. It never took long to calm him down. Overall he was a sweet-tempered boy."

"On the other hand, I can't imagine that *you* ever made a fuss about anything, even when you were little."

But I would not be put off any longer. "And now, please, give me your impressions of James, those you don't mind sharing."

She didn't open her eyes. "Well, you'll be glad to hear that he bore his injury well. There had been talk at first of amputation, and when he heard his arm would heal he pretended to be relieved, but I saw in his eyes what I'd seen in others'—that even losing a limb would have been a small price to pay for being sent home for good. But he soon covered that up. And when he was better . . ."

I found that I had gripped her hand: "Yes . . ."

"He was quite noisy—loud with his fellow officers, but he was touching too in the way he'd sit by the beds of the men and read them letters or write for them, awkwardly, with his uninjured hand."

I saw him so clearly with his head bent, that beautiful inclination of the neck, and his bottom lip pushed forward. But I was not allowed to dwell on this image, because Meredith had leaped to her feet, picked up her hat, and said: "I'm off to explore this *authentic* seaside town. Keep your eye on Edmund, will you," and with a scrunch of pebbles, she was gone.

I couldn't fathom her. One moment we were exchanging confidences, the next she had deserted me so suddenly that I felt abused, as if she'd helped me up with one hand and knocked me down with the other. And, as was the case so often with her, I had the distinct impression that she had taken a good deal from me but given little in return.

So I was left on the beach with Edmund, who at that moment came running up to say that his new friend, Moira, was going to bathe and he would as well. Tearing off his shirt and sun hat, he raced away as fast as the pebbles would permit and was soon at the water's edge with Moira, who was bare-footed but otherwise fully clothed. I called after him to wait for me but he didn't or wouldn't hear. Moira's parents were snoozing in deck chairs, so I seized my bag, pushed my feet into my shoes, and ran after him, muttering to myself: "This is absurd, he shouldn't paddle so soon after lunch, disobedient child. Where is Meredith? She should be here to look after him." And then I decided with horror that I was turning into Prudence, in fact I must surely look like her in my city shoes and flapping dark skirt on that sun-struck Sussex beach.

Back I went to the picnic blanket and removed, with great difficulty, shoes and stockings, then my hat, hitched up my skirts, and staggered over the stones. My unaccustomed feet looked like beached-up water creatures and my progress was very slow, because my hair blew across my eyes and I stubbed my toes. The next moment, I had caught up with Edmund and Moira and was holding each by their cold, wet hands as we jumped the waves. Moira instantly pulled away and announced she was going back to her mother. Edmund, gratifyingly, stayed with me.

"I used to jump the waves with your daddy when we were children," I said. "We loved the sea."

"I don't have to hold your hand. Mommy lets me paddle without holding her hand."

"But I feel I must, Edmund, because I remember I lost your daddy once, when he was a little boy. I wouldn't want to lose you."

"How did you lose him?"

"He was angry with me and he walked away when I wasn't looking. We found him back at the guesthouse, on his bed, reading an annual. By then half the town was searching for him, even the police."

"Why was he angry with you?"

"He got bored, I think that was it."

"Well, I'm not bored." And he plunged forward and ducked his shoulders under the water then rose up, flapping his thin arms, stamping his feet, and shouting. "It's freezing. It's lovely. It's so cold."

Suddenly, like a new wave breaking, I was happy; my purest moment of happiness since James's death—no, long before, since war was declared and we knew he would have to go away. The only times that had come anywhere close were my graduation and the news that I was to be taken on by Breen, but both these events had been tempered by my family's ambivalence to them. It was the collision of water, sun, and memory, the blue horizon, the sudden bond with my newfound nephew, the touch of his wet hand, the way he had flashed me a delighted smile as he emerged from the water, his prancing figure. And beyond Edmund, the context of that day felt very promising, the fact that my work, awaiting me like a sleeping beast, in that moment seemed to me full of fascination and complexity. And at the back of all, an illicit tick on the very far edge of my consciousness, was Thorne. I had an absurd wish that he might see me like this, with my hair blown up in a cloud and my feet bare.

And perhaps I was happy to be in the present, because I'd remembered vividly the pain of the past as I took Edmund's hand: the lying on my stomach in the sand reading *Great Expectations*, and Mother's sleepy question: "Where's Jamie, Evie, can you see him?" Then the search, escalating to a frantic trawl of the beach, my father's return from his walk—"What do you mean he's lost? I thought you were keeping an eye on him." Father had stood in his cravat, panama, and blazer, one hand on the small of his back, the other shielding his eyes as he renewed the hunt. We had to begin from the beginning, because he couldn't believe we had looked properly in the first place.

In the end I was sent up to the guesthouse half a mile or so from the beach, just to check that he wasn't there, and I was so panicky that I could scarcely breathe. In the last few minutes before I discovered him, keeping a nervous lookout for me over the top of *The Boys' Own Annual*, I had a glimpse into a future without him and I saw that my family would be a husk and that I would spend the rest of my days as if forever running uphill in an attempt to find him.

But for the first time, today, with chill waves lapping my toes and this other little boy boldly doggy-paddling between breaking waves, I had a sense that even though James was gone, my life was full enough.

∽⟨⟩∾

Meredith's mood had been further altered by her walk. It was now I who bustled about collecting our things together while she looked on. She said we would take the omnibus to Beachy Head and look at the lighthouse, and when Edmund moaned first about getting dressed, then the sand in his stockings, she said, "That's enough, Edmund," so harshly that he was silent.

"What did you think of the town?" I asked.

"I didn't see much of it. I visited a church."

I tried not to show my surprise. Then she added: "Actually I got homesick. Isn't that absurd? Twenty-nine years old and missing my sisters and mother and a remote village by a lake."

"Why wouldn't you miss them?"

"Because I fought so hard to get away," she said so fiercely that I didn't probe further.

We walked on the upper promenade and Edmund hung over the railing to watch the band play a military march. All we could see around the edge of the little bandstand was the flash of brass and the conductor's epaulette. "Can we go in?" he asked.

"You'd be bored," said Meredith. "You'd have to sit on a deck chair and listen to the music without saying anything, like those other people who've paid for their tickets. We're best off here."

Edmund studied the occupants of the deck chairs, who sat in the concrete bowl of the arena: elderly couples, invalids, ladies with handbags gripped in their laps. One segment of the auditorium was devoted to wheelchairs in which sat youngish men missing one or both legs. During the war people used to say you could hear the guns thundering in France from promenades on the south coast, and at that moment I recoiled from the band's military cheer, the wounded soldiers, and the quiescent ladies with their handbags, because of what they represented.

Meredith wrenched Edmund away to catch the bus but it was not until we were safely on the top deck and riding out of town above a promenade punctuated by stumpy Martello towers that she spoke to me again. "Edmund and I may not be taking meals with your family in future."

"I don't understand."

"Prudence said yesterday that she thought Edmund should eat apart from the grown-ups. I won't have that."

"It's not for Prudence to decide. If you wish Edmund to sit up with us, then he shall."

"I do wish it. I'm not used to being separated unnecessarily from my son. And there are other things you should know. One of the reasons I came to Europe was that I want to learn to paint. I have been looking about and found a class on Tuesday evenings that might suit me. I'm hoping I can rely on Edmund being cared for. He will need bathing and putting to bed. He always has a story."

"Well, certain —"

"And there's the question of work. My father was very generous and I'd saved up to travel here but that money is fast running out. I'm hoping I can come to an arrangement with your family, that you will perhaps settle some money on me, but it won't be enough, I'm sure. So I shall look for work, but that will mean Edmund will have to be taken to and from school by someone else."

"What sort of work do you have in mind? Will you nurse?"

"Not necessarily. I have an appointment to see Doctor Marie Stopes tomorrow morning."

"*Marie Stopes.*"

She looked me directly in the eye. "Do you know her?"

"Not personally. But of course I know that she has a clinic in Holloway and I'm aware of the type of work she does." I spoke low, so that we would not be overheard by Edmund, but Meredith's voice was ringing.

"Don't tell me you disapprove of that too. I feel very strongly that women should be able to make choices about conception. If I can get work as a nurse in such a clinic I shall be very well pleased."

I did not rise to the bait and point out that she could have chosen nothing more likely to dismay the ladies of Clivedon Hall Gardens. Instead we rode in silence while I contemplated her latest demands. Was she being unfair? Certainly she was very direct, something to which we were not accustomed. Elaborate rituals ought to be gone through in the asking and granting of favors. And Marie Stopes. I was conscious that my reaction was tempered with something very close to chagrin. I was the rebel in Clivedon Hall Gardens. If boundaries were to be pushed, it should be by me.

"You'd like to make your home with us then," I said.

"I would never let Edmund stay somewhere he wasn't welcome."

"You are welcome, of course you are. But Meredith, you must see that if you intend to live with us we will have to make arrangements."

"What kind of arrangements? You talk so coldly. This is your nephew, your mother's grandchild. We are family. At least, I was hoping we might be regarded as such." She looked away, biting her lower lip.

I was ashamed. "We still haven't had time to work out where we stand."

"Is it so difficult?"

"Not difficult. Strange."

It was time to get off the omnibus. On the clifftop, the wind was strong and quite cool, a kite-flyer was winding the spool of a kite that was a mere diamond-shaped speck in the sky, and a skylark bounced higher and higher on the air currents. Near the edge of the cliff I hovered behind Edmund's shoulder, ready to grab him should he take a spring forward.

"Look, Edmund," cried his mother, pointing beyond the blade of white cliff, "look at the lighthouse, don't you think it's marvelous? I love lighthouses, I really do, because they are a sign of the good that men can do for each other. Imagine the danger of taking a boat out to the lighthouse amid those rocks in bad weather. And the lamp is never allowed to go out at night, whatever the circumstances."

That moment was forever to be associated with primary colors: the red-and-white-striped lighthouse, the blue sea, the yellow of Meredith's glove. Because, after a gust of wind had knocked us all a pace or so nearer the cliff edge, she suddenly turned to me and spoke vehemently but so quietly that her son could not possibly have heard: "You think I venerate your brother's memory, as you do. Well, you're quite wrong. I hate to think of him. The very last place I'd choose to be is with his family if it weren't for necessity. If I could tear him from my being, I would. But I cannot, because of Edmund. Come, Edmund," she added sharply, "it's time to go home," and dragging at the boy's hand she marched him away, shunted by the wind, toward the bus stop.

I stared at the lighthouse and tried to comprehend what she had just told me. I had imagined, until then, that she had been angling to become a rather ill-tuned member of our somber chorus of women in mourning for James. Instead, it was as if she had scrunched my image of him into a tight ball that was reopening slowly in the palm of her hand, creased, worn, different.

And perhaps it was true that she didn't really want to be with us, after all. Barely had I got used to the idea of Meredith and Edmund as plaintiffs than she had turned the tables and placed me, abruptly, in the position of need. I needed her and Edmund to stay.

Ten

I hadn't been long at *Breen & Balcombe* before I decided that Theo Wolfe was more decorative than useful. At first I couldn't fathom why Breen put up with him and thought perhaps it was because a family connection had given Wolfe an introduction to the firm. In fact I sensed that Breen, despite his well-aired leanings toward the Labour Party, was a little in awe of the Wolfe lineage and was content to nurture Theo, despite his extreme laziness, because he enjoyed looking at him, liked to hear scandalous anecdotes about his years at a prestigious private school, and had the lower-middle class's grudging awe of the upper. Furthermore, while Breen was in some areas a Spartan, in others his taste was expensive, even exotic. He loved good whiskey and one of his favorite possessions was a mahogany corner cabinet housing a pair of exquisite cut-glass tumblers and a decanter. Late on chill Friday afternoons he and Wolfe were to be found snugly seated before the fire, savoring the malt. Wolfe in Breen's eyes had the same function as the Liberty-print silk handkerchief that adorned his breast pocket on festive occasions. By anyone's standards a beautiful young man, he was roughly my own age, a little heavy about the stomach, with floppy hair, an irresistibly boyish smile, and a talent for avoiding strenuous work of any kind. A tendency to asthma had ensured a wartime of pen-pushing in the Ministry of Munitions, and on foggy days he never turned up in the office at all but allegedly lay at home gasping.

Had Breen employed a more useful junior partner, his own hefty workload would have been reduced and the firm's income correspondingly enhanced. On the other hand, Wolfe definitely had his moments. He was, for instance, excellent at hobnobbing with the opposition and was often given five shillings from the Breen & Balcombe petty-cash box to take a police prosecutor out to lunch. I had not witnessed him in operation but could imagine the affable passing of the wine bottle, the sharing of somewhat off-color legal anecdotes ("Did you hear that Judge Michael Fitch's wife has left him? Small wonder, given his well-known predilection for touring the back streets of Soho in search of a delectable . . ."), the skillful segue of the conversation from the subject of whose star was in the ascendant to whether the police prosecutor thought there might be any room for negotiation in a certain case dear to the heart of Breen & Balcombe.

It was by such means that we learned there was considerable irritation among all concerned with prosecuting the Marchant case, because the *Daily Mail* (courtesy of Wolfe, none other) had got hold of the story and was vilifying the pernicious authorities who, not satisfied with separating a mother from her innocent children, had locked her up despite the fact that her only crime was to show a maternal desire to hold her own baby.

The day before Leah Marchant's next court hearing, Wolfe lunched with his pal Wotherspoon, who worked directly for the divisional superintendent, and the result of their conversation was relayed to me by Breen on the courthouse steps.

"So," said he, whipping off his trilby and brushing its crown with his sleeve, "we're in luck. The police are willing to drop the charge, not a sniff of a committal, nothing."

"This is excellent news," I said, though I couldn't help feeling a little disappointed, armed as I was with a lengthy bail argument and Mrs. Sanders as character witness.

"My thoughts exactly. So when we meet with Mrs. Marchant, tell her to plead guilty."

"Guilty?"

He resettled his hat. "Ready, then?"

"Mr. Breen. She's not guilty. She's a mother. It was her own child."

"Legally, she was guilty."

"Perhaps legally. But all she did was hold her own baby."

"Miss Gifford, if Mrs. Marchant pleads guilty, the police, who as you know have endured a good deal of adverse publicity over this affair, have agreed to a conditional discharge. They will cite as reasons Marchant's previously good character and the fact she has already served a spell on remand in Holloway."

"If the police don't like the adverse publicity they should drop the charge."

"Can't do that. Can't be seen to be bowing to the pressure of the gutter press."

"But neither should we make our client plead guilty to something she didn't do. She'll have a criminal record."

"Will it make an iota of difference to anyone if your Leah Marchant has a criminal record?"

"It will to her. Surely it will make it harder for her to win her children back. And what about her prospects of employment?"

"She's a char, I believe, not a nanny. All her employers will care about is whether she's honest. We can get someone to write her a testimonial to that effect. In fact I'll write one myself."

"Well, I won't suggest that she plead guilty. It feels utterly wrong."

Now that I had crossed him, Breen's face seemed gaunt and severe, with heavily etched lines between nose and lip. "I wasn't aware that your feelings were at issue here, Miss Gifford."

"My feelings have nothing to do with it, obviously. But is it fair of us to ask Leah to plead guilty to holding her own child?"

"Fairness is hardly the question. Miss Gifford, you and I are paid to work within the constraints of the law, and in the eyes of the law Mrs. Marchant is guilty. If you're unable to accept this simple fact, tell me at once and I shall deal with the case myself."

He knew I was trapped. How could I back down from this, my first significant case? And I was far too junior to go out on a limb though his pragmatism dismayed me. We went down to the cells in time to hold a brief interview with Leah, whom a week in Holloway had subdued; she looked considerably tamer in a clean though overly tight frock (I suspect lent by the loyal Mrs. Sanders), with her hair scraped back in a bun. In fact, I could detect a glimmer, in her round forehead and full lips, of the girl who had caught the eye of Breen as she polished the grates of his elderly client and later attracted the attentions of that feckless seaman, Marchant.

As soon as she saw Breen, Leah actually seized his hand and kissed it. "I knoo you'd come. Now I shall be free."

Breen responded to her relief and delight like a cat caressed beneath its jaw. "My dear Mrs. Marchant. I am touched that you remember me after so many years."

"I wouldn't forget you, Mr. Breen. And now I've seen you I know for sure that me and the kids is safe."

Breen perched on the edge of the plank that passed for a bed and patted the space beside him as if he were offering Leah a velvet sofa. "Your case is being dealt with by Miss Gifford here, who has left no stone unturned to ensure that you will be freed. I want you to listen to her very carefully."

The jailer brought a chair for me and I sat facing the pair of them in that tiny cell, upright and lofty as a maiden aunt. Leah gave me a disdainful look and pushed her hand into Breen's. "I want you to represent me, Mr. Breen."

"Well, I shall, in a manner of speaking, because Miss Gifford and I work together, but once a lawyer has taken on a case it's most irregular to hand it to someone else. You are fortunate because you will have the benefit of Miss Gifford's advice as well as my own."

Throughout this conversation, the argument with Breen had been continuing in my head. Could I defy him? Must I do as he said? I wondered what James would have done in my place. Father would certainly have chosen the most expedient route, but James? I was frantic with the knowledge that James's life had stopped when he was barely twenty, before he'd had time to develop into a moral touchstone.

In the end, deference got the better of me. I owed Breen this much, surely. He had taken me on against all the odds.

"I have visited Caractacus Court, Mrs. Marchant," I said briskly. "Your friend Mrs. Sanders will appear in court this morning to offer a character reference and an undertaking that you can have your old room back, should such information be required. We're hopeful that proceedings can be completed today and you will be released."

"Eh? I was expecting a trial. How can that be?" Again she addressed Breen, who nodded toward me.

"We suggest that you plead guilty to the charge of child abduction. I will then give the mitigation—the reason why you did it—and afterward we expect the magistrate to accept your reasons and to agree to a conditional discharge, which means that you will be free."

"You mean, plead guilty to somethin' I didn't do?"

"Not exactly, as I . . ."

"Never."

"You see, you did take the child, Leah."

"What does she mean, *the child*?" she demanded of Breen, whose hand she still clasped. "Does she mean my own son, Charlie? 'Ow can that be abduction? I never heard such rubbish. No, I won't say such a wicked thing, that I was a criminal in taking my own child. Don't make me, Mr. Breen."

I plowed on. "If proceedings are concluded today we will be able to arrange for you to visit the children, or at least the girls. I have already written to the home."

"What does she mean, *visit them*? I don't want to visit my own children. I want them back. I'm not listening to 'er any longer, Mr. Breen, it seems to me she doesn't make no sense. All I want is my own kids back. Oh, Mr. Breen, I beg you, please set them free for me." Tears ran down her newly washed face and onto her hands and Breen's wrist.

I suspected that he was relishing every moment of this interview. Squeezing Leah's fingers, he removed a handkerchief (not the Liberty silk) from his pocket and handed it to her. Meanwhile, precious time was passing; we were due in court in ten minutes and we'd received no indication from Leah what she would plead.

"So may I repeat, Leah," I said, "that our considered advice is that you should plead guilty to this offense. If you do, we very much hope that you will be free within half an hour."

"Oh, yeah, and what if it doesn't turn out as you say? What if they say, 'Ho, guilty are you? Then 'ave six months inside.' I know what happens to people like me when they're in the 'ands of people like them."

"It's a risk," I began, but Breen stood, adjusted his necktie, and picked up his briefcase. "Miss Gifford has given you the benefit of our advice, Mrs. Marchant. If you don't choose to take it, that's up to you. We shall do our best for you, whatever the circumstances, but I make you no promises. We shall see you in court."

"Don't go, Mr. Breen. Oh, I beg you. And don't make me plead guilty to somethin' I ain't done."

"You've heard what Miss Gifford said: We are suggesting that you plead guilty to something you *have* done," and so saying he swept out of the cell, leaving Mrs. Marchant staring at me with burning resentment as if his unwelcome advice were all my fault.

Catching up with Breen on the cramped staircase, I whispered: "What will we do if she persists in pleading not guilty?"

"You will have to make a plea in open court for the case to be dropped. After all, we know it's what the prosecution wants. Failing that, you will have to get her bail. But let's hope she'll do as we told her. I suspect she might." It did not occur to Breen to hold the door for me, so I had to prop it open with my shoulder. In all my years as a student of law, nothing had prepared me for the state of inner turmoil with which I entered that courtroom. I hardly knew whether to hope that Leah would follow our instructions and plead guilty, or not.

ⵐ

This time, when Leah Marchant's case was called, the courtroom was relatively crowded. In addition to Mrs. Sanders, who was dressed head to toe in black, and a handful of other spectators, a couple of reporters lounged in the public benches, and beside me, in a supervisory role, sat Breen, though he pretended a complete lack of interest by filling in the *Times* crossword with one hand and leafing through the pages of a file with the other.

Also present was Meredith, who had insisted on being told the date and time of my next appearance in court. "If I don't see you in action, you'll never make me believe you actually are nearly a lawyer," she said. Her presence was a distraction; I neither trusted nor understood her, the words she had spoken above Beachy Head lighthouse were scorched into my consciousness and I feared what new surprises might be sprung on me. I had not been told the result of the interview with Doctor Stopes.

The same magistrate, Shillitoe, presided as before. When Leah was brought up to the dock, he made a show of shooting his cuffs and wiping his pen before peering first at her, then Breen, over the top of his spectacles. "Mr. Breen?"

"Huh," said Breen, as if awoken from sleep.

"I presume this is your case."

"This is Miss Gifford's case."

"Then why are you here, Mr. Breen?"

Breen's right eyebrow arched and he did not trouble to rise more than a few inches from his seat. "Forgive me, I presumed this was a public court of law."

The charge was read by the clerk, and the police prosecutor began: "Your Worship, as you know, the case is an unusual one, because it concerns Mrs. Marchant's attempt to kidnap her own baby. The 1891 Custody of Children Act gives the court the right to refuse Mrs. Marchant custody of her children if she be proved incapable, and her parental rights having been voluntarily relinquished by Mrs. Marchant when she gave the children in to the charge of the Good Samaritan's Home, Hammersmith, section 3 of the act gives the court a duty to decide whether it ought to restore said children . . ."

"I just took 'em into that blasted 'ome in the first place because I couldn't manage. Nobody told me I wouldn't get them back," yelled Leah from the dock. "Nobody told me what I was signin' my name to. If I 'adn't of tooken 'em in, if I'd kept them at 'ome I wouldn't be 'ere now. I curse myself for trying to care for my own . . ."

"Mrs. Marchant, kindly do not intervene in these proceedings unless you are invited so to do," said the magistrate.

"But they're my bloody kids."

"Excuse me, Your Worship," I said, "might I have a word with my client?" and I hurried to the dock, where I used its high oak sides to hoist myself up on tiptoe and whisper: "Leah. You must be quiet. Above all, don't swear or you will find yourself in contempt of court."

She glowered but said nothing more. As I swung around to face the bench, I caught a glimpse of Meredith, who was watching with such intense interest that it would have been no surprise if she had leaped to her feet and berated the magistrate.

"Are we now ready for pleas to be taken?" asked the clerk. "Leah Marchant. Do you plead guilty to the offense of child abduction?"

The dock was behind me, so I couldn't see Leah's face. Breen entered another answer on his crossword. At last, she murmured: "I might."

The magistrate's eyes widened. "*Might?* That's no reply. Guilty or not guilty?"

"They told me to plead guilty, even though I'm not."

"Mrs. Marchant . . ." began Shillitoe.

I remembered but chose to ignore Thorne's advice about not interrupting a judge: "Your Worship, we *advised* our client to plead guilty, we did not *tell* her to do so. I would ask that the charge be put again."

The magistrate raised his hand to quell me. "Sit down, Miss um . . . Mrs. Marchant, I want you to listen very carefully to what I have to say. You are charged with a very serious offense indeed. If you plead guilty, you may face many months of imprisonment, so you should think very hard before you give your answer. Under no circumstances should you obey blindly the dictates of your lawyer . . . legal adviser, if you don't agree with her."

I clasped my hands in my lap and gazed straight ahead to a point above the clerk's bald patch. Breen swiveled around and stared long and hard at Leah.

"Guilty, then," she said sulkily.

"I beg your pardon?"

"I plead guilty."

"Are you sure?"

"How many more times do I 'ave to . . . ?"

"Mrs. Marchant, please be aware that you are addressing a court of law. I don't like your tone."

The clerk said soothingly, "Now that we have a plea, perhaps the prosecution can give us the facts of the case."

The prosecutor, as if reading from a script prepared by Theo Wolfe and his lunch chum, outlined the facts and stated that although on the face of it there could be few offenses more serious than child abduction, in this particular instance the prosecution was well aware that there were many mitigating factors, as would doubtless shortly be outlined by the defense, which was why the case had, exceptionally, in view of its seriousness, not been sent to a higher court, and certainly if a lenient sentence, for instance a conditional discharge, were, on this occasion, to be passed, the prosecution would not object.

It was my turn. "Your Worship, I would support what the learned police prosecutor . . ."

"Then there's nothing more to be said, is there?" said the magistrate in a quiet and measured voice. "I have the full picture."

Breen threw down his pen, readjusted his weight, and folded his arms. I gathered my wits: "On the contrary, Your Worship, I of course want to be sure that you give due consideration to my client's circumstances before you sentence her, even though I am grateful for the police prosecutor's compassionate view of her offense. Her landlady, Mrs. Sanders, is here to vouch for her good character and devotion to her children. Would you like to hear her speak, Your Worship?"

"I would not."

The courtroom was so still that I could hear Leah's uneven breathing in the dock behind me. The magistrate had me on the end of a wire and I recognized that this was not a matter of professional dislike or suspicion, as I had previously assumed, but of mortal outrage. He saw me as an aberration, an enemy of the establishment, and I had no hope at all of reaching him.

"Are you minded then to go along with the police—?" I said shakily.

"I am minded to sentence this woman as I see fit, Miss Gifford. I won't be dictated to by you or anybody else." He smiled, showing small, white teeth.

Too late I heard Leah's sucking intake of breath. "I told you so. I told you what would 'appen when we was down in that fuckin' cell. Oh my Gawd, he's goin' to lock me up and I ain't never goin' to see my kids again."

"Silence, Mrs. Marchant."

Leah lurched at the door of the dock, but one jailer seized her wrist, the other whipped out handcuffs and held her while she writhed and yelled: "I ain't never goin' to listen to anyone again. You're all bastards. You don't care a damn for me an' my kids. I'm not waitin' any longer . . ."

The magistrate intoned: "Leah Marchant, for the offense of child abduction I commit you to three months imprisonment, that is penal servitude, with hard labor, plus another month, to run consecutively, for contempt of court. Four months in all. You may take her down."

The courtroom was suddenly abuzz and my own voice rang out: "Your Worship, you cannot commit a defendant to imprisonment of any but the first division for contempt of court."

"I'll do what I damn well like in my own courtroom. Take her down."

Breen uncrossed his legs, stood up, and lightly drummed on the desk while he waited for stillness to fall. His mouth was quirked into an incredulous smile and when he spoke his tone was jocular, as if he were conducting a conversation with a close but misguided friend: "Your Worship, this is quite unlawful. Imprisonment with hard labor cannot be imposed for contempt. We will appeal."

"Do so, Breen, by all means. Mr. Clerk, is the next case ready?"

I made a play of gathering and sorting my papers, then crushed them into my briefcase. Breen leaned across, screwed the lid onto my pen, and handed it to me, presumably to signal that he was firmly on my side. Meanwhile, Leah sobbed violently and shouted abuse as she was led down to the cells. A young lawyer, waiting for his own case to be heard, sniggered in the benches behind me. I sensed that Meredith's passionate gaze was on my face but I couldn't bring myself to look at her. The inside of my head was dark, apart from one thought, white and hard as a pebble, so that when Breen took me by the elbow, steered me across the foyer, ushered me to a cramped interview room, and closed the door, I could not prevent myself from saying in a choked voice: "You should not have intervened."

He had perhaps intended to utter a few bracing words of advice; at any rate, he was fired up to leap into action with his customary zeal and knock the British justice system into shape on behalf of the two victims of this disaster, Leah and myself. Therefore my words affected him like a blow to the cheek. I had never seen him so taken aback; he visibly stiffened and his eyes, usually full of fire, went cold. "I do beg your pardon."

"You made me look a fool, even more of a fool. It's bad enough that Leah is now facing months of prison. I was wrong on two counts. First, I allowed my ambition to stand up in court to take precedent over a client's best interests. As was clear to all, that magistrate had no intention of giving a woman advocate a fair hearing. Then, I went against my own judgment in persuading Leah to plead guilty. But at least I did it by myself, at least I was seen to be handling the case start to finish, however badly. But then you stepped in. It was on the tip of my tongue to ask for an appeal but you didn't give me the chance. Mr. Breen, have you considered how you would feel if I were to stand up in the middle of one of your cases and intervene with a point of law?"

He had a child's tendency to show that he was wounded by the jutting of his lower lip and the heaviness of his lids. Settling his hat firmly onto his unruly hair, he bowed slightly and said: "Forgive me, I shall try to be more circumspect in future."

My heart ached in the knowledge that I had spurned a loyal and influential colleague. "Mr. Breen, this afternoon, if you remember, I am visiting Stella Wheeler's workplace, Lyons. Will I see you afterward, in the office?" But he was gone and the door snapped shut.

Alone in that nasty little room, I stared at the frosted glass in the window and drew a long breath. Not here, not now, Evelyn, no self-recriminations yet. You must act first.

So I planned my next moves with the precision of a military operation: I would tidy my hair, adjust my hat, open the door, and cross the foyer to the usher's desk. There I would lodge our appeal. I would speak to Mrs. Sanders and explain what had happened. Then I would go down to the cells and face Leah. If Meredith was waiting for me, I would send her away. Under the circumstances, I did not think I could stand her pity or indignation.

What I would not allow myself to do for the time being was dwell on the disgraceful behavior of the magistrate, Shillitoe, or my impulsive criticism of Breen. And I would put off, until later, consideration of the awful truth that, largely because of me, Leah was further than ever from release.

But when at last I emerged from that evil-smelling interview room, there was no sign of Meredith. I filled in a lengthy form and delivered it in person to a senior clerk; still no Meredith. I went down to the cells and conducted a pitifully short interview with Leah Marchant, who turned her face to the wall. When I reemerged, by now longing for a little companionship, no Meredith. How typical of her to do the one thing guaranteed to disturb me most, in this case witness the fiasco of Leah Marchant's hearing, then disappear without a word.

Eleven

By two o'clock, I was *walking* down Regent Street in search of Stella Wheeler's Lyons tea shop. For once abandoning Prudence's dress code, I wore neither hat nor jacket, both of which were stuffed into the top of my briefcase. No wonder I drew curious glances. The day was dull and cool for the end of May, but I rolled up my sleeves and occasionally a fierce gust of wind ripped a strand of hair from its pins, so that when I glimpsed my reflection in a shop window it was a madwoman I saw, white-faced and Medusa-haired. Although the pavements were crowded with lunchtime shoppers, the crowds parted before me.

At the end of Leah Marchant's case, when I had gathered up my papers and clutched them so tightly that their edges scrunched in my hand, the goldfish bowl of the courthouse had seemed to shrink and enclose me and I thought I wouldn't be able to get out. And when the pebble words to Breen—*You should not have intervened*—burst from my mouth, I had glimpsed, again, that the end of endurance would mean an end to self-control. After all, I knew what it was to peer over the edge of reason into an abyss where images of the dead howled unobstructed along vacant passages of my consciousness. Last time I had ended up facedown on the hall floor, scarcely able to draw breath, my fists squeezed tight as they drummed the cold tiles.

I marched on amid office workers who dived in and out of shops or plunged across the road. London heaved and churned, billboards and summer frocks and omnibuses, but that afternoon I couldn't for the life of me see the point. Nor could I stand the churning faces, in and outside my head: the way Meredith, Leah, Thorne, Breen, Stella, and Stephen Wheeler spun round and round in the tumbrel of my mind.

"For heaven's sakes, have some consideration," said an elderly lady as I barged into her, and she grabbed my arm to hold herself steady as she adjusted her shoe. The encounter calmed me. I apologized profusely and waited patiently while she tied the lace. Being useful, after all, was safe territory; it had been my vocation since birth.

Here it was, Lyons tea shop. The door stood wide open and inside was the usual counter stacked with Eccles cakes, doughnuts, iced buns, and sausage rolls, upon one of which a bluebottle feasted. Beyond the counter was the restaurant with a green-and-brown-patterned linoleum floor covered with rows of tables and bentwood chairs. Swing doors at the back led to the kitchen and beside them a vast dresser was piled with crockery and napkins. Although it was not quite the end of the lunch period, business was slack and I might have chosen any one of a dozen empty tables. In the end I sat under the clock, facing the room. To my left, across the counter, I could see onto the street.

Because it was a cool day the ceiling fans were still, though when I looked up at their fly-blown wings I was reminded of the warm air that had wafted onto my face when I had tea with Nicholas Thorne. Thank God he at least had not been in court to witness my shame today.

The table needed a wipe, sugar was sprinkled across its top, and a fly landed again and again to feed. I didn't mind. I was alone, anonymous. I closed my eyes to the clink of crockery, the ebb and flow of other people's conversations, the roar of traffic on the street beyond.

A tea shop. How many thousand conversations about everything and nothing had been conducted here? How many love affairs begun and ended? I remembered Thorne's shapely hand moving among the tea things inches from my own, which had been primly clasped on the edge of the table (Prudence maintained that hands, particularly those belonging to children, should be constantly in view). The colors in my head stopped spinning. I smelled tea and sweet pastry, and faintly the disinfectant they used to swab the floor. Then I opened my eyes and the restaurant was spread before me, Stella Wheeler's premarriage world, where she'd worked nearly seven years: since leaving school until the eve of her wedding. It was as if the remnants of a pea-souper lingered in the room, a translucent pall of old cigarette smoke, bacon rinds, and coffee grounds. Despite the precision with which the tables and chairs had been arranged in rows, there was an impression of untidiness, something to do perhaps with the dingy floor and lassitude of the waiting staff. I was surprised that a girl with a taste for finery, like Stella, should have been content with such a humble workplace.

A waitress approached, languidly swaying her hips. She held a tiny notepad and raised her eyebrows uninterestedly to take my order. I picked up the tariff card, and out of habit asked for poached egg and a pot of tea, both considerably cheaper than at the Peter Jones department store. But in any case, I decided, for once I shall be like Theo Wolfe and make a claim on Breen & Balcombe's petty-cash box. If I were to be dismissed by Mr. Breen for insolence, at least I should not be out of pocket.

When the girl came back with my pot of tea (the egg would take longer, as it had to be put *fresh on*), she also brought a dishcloth with which to swipe the sugar granules onto the floor. "I was wondering," I said, "if I might speak to the manager. It's about someone who used to work here, Mrs. Stella Wheeler."

The girl had exquisite skin but irregular features, including a beaky, high-bridged nose and close-set eyes. Beneath the unwieldy cap her hair hung lank and dead straight. When she heard Stella's name, she clenched the dishcloth and pressed her pale lips together. "You did know Stella, then," I said.

"She was Stella Hobhouse when she was here."

"I realize that. But you did know her?"

"'Course I did."

"Do you think you might be able to help me? I have a few questions." The girl took a step back but hovered. Her eyelids were pink, as if from recent tears or sleepless nights. "I'm a lawyer, you see. This is a very difficult question to ask but I'm assuming you know what happened to Stella?"

"Of course. The police come in and asked us all questions."

"What did they tell you about her?"

"That she was dead. That she was shot."

"What did they want to know from you?"

She backed a little further and said, "I should fetch my manager," but continued to watch me with her light eyes, as if mesmerized.

"The thing is, we need to make sure that the police have collected all the information necessary," I told her.

"They said Stephen probably done it. They was asking if we knew how he treated her when they was together."

"I suppose that's partly what I want to know too. And I also would like to learn more about Stella."

"Why don't you ask the police?"

"We think they've made up their minds about Stephen and might miss something. We want to do our best for him so we thought we'd look into things ourselves."

"Did Stephen do it?"

"I don't know."

"Did he say he hadn't done it?"

"He hasn't said anything. He can't or won't speak."

She was now even paler and her large eyes were fixed, though not focused, on my face. "I knew him. I knew them both. I was at their wedding. Stell and me was mates."

"Can we talk then?"

"I should get my manager," she repeated, this time with even less conviction.

"Don't do or say anything that makes you uncomfortable. Take your time to decide whether or not you'd like to talk to me."

We exchanged names—hers was Carole Mangan—then she disappeared to fetch my egg (cooked to perfection and piping hot), and, when she'd unloaded her tray, darted away to serve a couple of ladies who came in laden with shopping and wearing hats that were surely far too heavy for the season. They dropped into their chairs, scattered bags about their feet, and exclaimed how *exhausted* they were and how they had spent far too much but never mind. Carole, in her well-trodden shoes, stood by patiently, waiting to take their order.

I wondered how proficient a waitress Stella Wheeler had been. Given her fastidious taste in underwear, I presumed she would have noticed the unsuitability of those hats, especially the one with dark brown velvet ribbons. And how had she endured the uniform, the calf-length sack of a dress and nurse's apron with its bib rising to chest height then split to cross the shoulders in wide bands? Had Stella worn her hair short or long? Short, I guessed; there had been no dish containing hairpins on her dressing table. And with a stab of excitement very far from my earlier despair I realized that Carole would know every one of these details. If they'd worked together for years, they must have had oceans of time to share intimacies.

I sensed that Carole was aware of me even as she took the latest order through to the kitchen and that though she was nervous, she was intensely interested in talking to me. When I'd finished my lunch, she came close again. "If you'll let me know the truth about what's going on, I'll talk to you in my tea break. Our manager doesn't tell us nothing. It's not fair."

"When is your tea break?"

"Half an hour."

I waited, at first fretfully, then more calmly. There were any number of uses to which I might have put that half-hour. Prudence's birthday, for instance, was imminent and I might have shopped for handkerchiefs or some equally unimaginative gift. Prudence was impossible to please, because she had so many negative opinions about things. There were bookshops nearby in which I could have looked up the latest legal publication or even found some little treat for Edmund. I could have taken a walk. But instead I remained at the table, sipping tepid, overbrewed tea and accustoming myself to Stella Wheeler's world. An older waitress stood listlessly in the doorway, arms folded, watching the street. Her cap was neater than Carole's, but her hair had been badly cut and sat unevenly on her collar. She adjusted her weight from one leg to the other, as if to relieve pain.

Time passed. An elderly woman came in with a couple of children a little younger than Edmund, who spent a painful length of time choosing between chocolate and banana milk shakes. Which would Edmund prefer? I wondered. Perhaps one day he would come with me to a tea shop. My heart ached at the thought of his sturdy legs swinging from the chair opposite. James had been for chocolate, every time. Carole reappeared with a trolley and began systematically clearing and wiping tables. I heard the hands on the clock above my head shift a notch and somebody drop a bit of china in the kitchen. A grubby boy arrived at the counter and asked if he could have something for a farthing. What an uncomplicated trade a waitress's must be, I thought, skimming the surface of other people's lives, their moments of celebration, exhaustion, or simple thirst a matter of complete indifference. In my own work I was expected to meddle, and look where that had got me.

Promptly at a quarter past three, Carole again emerged from the kitchen, this time without apron or cap and with the top button of her dress undone. She wore a pink cardigan and a straw hat, so that her ashen skin seemed rosier. When we were outside, I heard her inhale sharply and it was true that even the air in that street, reeking of manure and motor fumes, seemed fresh after the cigarette smoke and kitchen smells of the tea shop. She walked ploddingly with her handbag clasped in both hands and told me that she worked until six and caught the bus home to Balham. It was a long day—ten hours—and she missed Stella all the time and couldn't believe what had happened to her.

"We were mates," she said. "We used to get the giggles terribly, you know, about some of the customers. There's no one to have a laugh with now."

"Can you describe her for me?"

"She was quite moody. She liked her own way. But she was very pretty and always hugged you after she'd been mean, or bought a bit of chocolate, so you had to forgive her. And she was hardworking and would always cover for you if you was tired or sick. I think in all the years I knew her she was hardly ever off ill or late even."

"How long is it since you last saw her?"

"A couple of weeks. Like I said, I went to her wedding in April and then she came into town after work and we had a drink. I can't bear to think that was the last time I'll ever see her. I'll try and go to the funeral, although the manager says we can't all have time off. As far as he's concerned one person is more than enough and it'll probably be him." Her skin was so fine that I thought the tears might seep through rather than hang on the edge of her lids.

"Tell me about the wedding."

"Well, of course, because she was getting married she had to stop work, and she was excited about that, but then sad at the end, I think. We had a party on the Friday, and we'd had a collection, even head office chipped in, and so we gave her this tea service she wanted from

Lawleys—she and I were always walking past the windows and she had her eye on one set in particular—and on the Saturday we went to the wedding and she looked beautiful, but then she always did. It took her weeks to choose a frock, creamy-yellow, all floaty at the back. It suited her lovely because she was thin and it showed her ankles. But she said it wasn't to be so fancy she couldn't wear it afterward."

"Did you like Stephen Wheeler?"

It had dawned on me that I must not underestimate Carole—her responses were carefully weighed. "Does it matter if I liked him?"

"The thing is I don't know either of them. We are having to defend Stephen based on very little because as I said he's not talking to us yet, though we hope that might change."

"But his gun was there."

"It was. His gun and his gloves."

"He was nice," she said, taking the plunge suddenly. "*I* would have married him if he'd asked."

We smiled, though the expression in her eyes was raw and pitiful. "He was quite a bit older than she, wasn't he?" I asked gently.

"*Much* older—fourteen years or so. But he seemed so kind even though Stell said the war changed him, made him heavyhearted some-times. Whenever we met he'd shake my hand and give me ever such a lovely smile. And when he wasn't smiling he'd look sad again but I thought lucky old Stell, to have a man like that, who you could bring 'round easy enough, I thought, by taking care of him and treating him very softly. I used to be so jealous of her, the way he'd be there after work with his hat off, waiting for her. I thought she took him an awful lot for granted."

"And after she was married, do you think he was still kind to her? Were they happy?"

This drew a very sharp look indeed. "I don't know much about that," she said. She broke off suddenly. "Do you have a watch? I only have quarter of an hour for tea."

"Your time is almost up." We walked much faster back along Hanover Street while I decided which of a dozen questions was most important. "What did you talk about that evening in the pub after work?"

"Mostly about work, and the manager, and customers she remembered. She said she sometimes even wished she was still working, which we thought was mad because she'd been champing at the bit to get out."

"So she was a bit bored but otherwise all right. There was no suggestion that she was frightened or anything?"

"No. Definitely not. Just restless as usual, always looking around. There was a sort of spark in her eye that I'd not seen before. She said we should go out for tea in her house one Sunday afternoon when she'd got it all nice but she couldn't fix on a date for the time being."

But how long would it have taken Mrs. Wheeler, I wondered, to make her house presentable enough to hold a tea party?

We were on Regent Street again and the noise of cabs and carts was almost too intrusive for speech. "Miss Mangan, is there anything else you can think of that might help me? Any reason Stephen would suddenly turn on her? Nothing she might do to make him angry or jealous?"

"Jealous?"

"For instance, was she ever keen on anyone else?"

"The police asked me that."

"What was your reply?"

"We all have our admirers, even me. I gave them a list of men who used to ask especially for Stella."

"But there was no one special?"

"Not that I know of."

"Could I have a copy of that list?" We were at the doorway of the tea shop. "And Miss Mangan, might you have a photograph of Stella?"

"A wedding photo, yes."

"I'll call back then, shall I?" She nodded and gave me one of her shyly acute glances. Then she stepped across the threshold to the interior, which had grown much more crowded in the short time we'd been away.

Twelve

I dreaded *my return to the office,* where I would have to face Breen, but although I was back by four-thirty, a time when Wolfe was generally taking tea and Breen rattling off dictation, I found Arbery Street deserted save for Miss Drake, who was stabbing at the keys of her typewriter. I placed the Lyons receipt in her in-tray, bade her good afternoon, and descended to my basement office, where I made a note of my discussion with Carole Mangan and wrote up Leah Marchant's disastrous bail hearing.

Periodically, as I recalled the painful events of the morning, I glanced up at the corroded bars on the window, the lime-stained sink, and teetering stacks of files, thinking how ironic it was that after Leah's first hearing I had offered my resignation, whereas after her second I faced dismissal. At six o'clock I heard familiar movements overhead, presaging Miss Drake's departure; the whisk and clatter of a typewriter closed down for the night, the washing of cups in the new scullery, the upending of chairs so that the floor would be properly swept tomorrow morning. Next I heard her reluctant footfall on the basement stairs and a note was pushed under my door, typed on the inside of a thrice-used envelope.

Mr. Breen says you're to attend Wheeler's bail hearing with him in
Amersham. Ten-thirty sharp tomorrow. And afterward an appointment

has been made with Chesham Constabulary for a visit to the crime scene. Mr. Breen insists you wear sensible shoes.

Another slip of paper followed (my receipt from Lyons). On the back, Miss Drake had written in her famously regular copperplate: *Application refused. All expenditure pertaining to company business must be authorized before its incurrence.*

∽

The atmosphere in Clivedon Hall Gardens, when I arrived home, was even more frigid than at Breen & Balcombe, and with some cause: I was late for dinner, everyone was hungry, Meredith had gone out, and Edmund was misbehaving by sitting on the bottom stair and refusing point-blank to go to bed. His thumb was stuck in his mouth so deep that his lips lapped his wrist while he glowered at Prudence, to whom thumb-sucking was an anathema. Min was hovering exasperatedly at the top of the basement stairs. Had she been left in charge, like in the old days when James and I were children, she would have brooked no such nonsense.

"I've promised him a story," said Mother, trying to take hold of his free hand, which he snatched away and pushed under his thigh, "but he says no. He's being very naughty. He hardly touched his supper. We had no idea when you were coming so we insisted he ate his."

"But Meredith and I had agreed he would eat with the grown-ups." Faced with an intransigent boy, none of us knew what to do with him. Mother, it seemed, had forgotten all she ever knew about handling children, though if my memory was accurate it had always been her preferred duty to float downstairs in a mist of lace and rose water, ready to dine out or watch a play, rather than to stay in and put us to bed.

"It's no use his being hungry now," said Prudence, "he should have eaten when he had the chance."

The little boy pressed his knees together and pattered his fingers on the side of his nose.

"Oh, dear, are you hungry, Edmund?" asked Mother, and I knew she was terrified lest he was, because what could she do about it? She could scarcely defy Prudence.

Rather than reply, he lowered his eyelids so that his cheeks were shadowed by his long lashes. I admired his obstinacy. "Why don't you and Prudence keep Grandmother company?" I said to Mother. "I'll put Edmund to bed."

"But what if he won't go? We've all tried. Mother offered to take him up one of her collections."

My heart ached for Edmund, with his downcast eyes and wedged-in thumb; he must be very miserable. But I also knew that this had become a battle in which we were all joined. If I failed to get Edmund to bed, it would be a triumph for Prudence, who was bound now to be willing him to stay put.

Once Edmund and I were alone, I attempted to stroke his head but he flinched away. Had this been the six-year-old James, and such behavior of Edmund's was uncannily like his father's, I would have tickled, cajoled, and joked until I had persuaded him to race me up the stairs. But I was no longer nine and I had forgotten how to tease a small boy without hurting his pride, so instead I found myself addressing him like a court of law. "It seems to me you have three choices, Edmund. You can either stay there until your mother comes home, though I think you'll get very tired, or you can sit at table for us, which as you know is pretty dull, or you can come up with me and we'll have a story, and you can wait for your mother in your bed. The latter seems by far the most advisable course of action, but it's up to you."

Having waited a moment for the counterargument, which was not forthcoming, I offered my hand. When he made no move, I climbed the stairs anyway, very slowly. His will stretched against mine and I knew that he wanted to come to bed but was unable to rescue himself. In the end, I hung over the banister and whispered his name repeatedly until I saw the glimmer of a reluctant smile. This time, when I reached for him, he allowed himself to be lifted into my arms. I picked him up clumsily, surprised by his sudden, willing weight, and had to maneuver him until his legs were properly hooked around my waist. And it was like Eastbourne again, the waves breaking, the sun shining. His chest was pressed to mine, his arms clasped firmly about my neck so that his breath was in my hair as he twisted a loose strand absentmindedly around his finger. The smell of him, the green, lovely perfume of Edmund, James's child, sang in my blood.

When we reached the room he shared with Meredith, I set him down and helped him to undress, folding his still-warm clothes but resisting the temptation to press his shirt to my face, protecting his modesty by bustling across the landing to run water into the basin, holding the towel as he washed his hands. Then he nestled within the crook of my arm, as Jamie used to, while I read to him from the Brothers Grimm, the copy won by me at Sunday school in December 1902 and so well-thumbed that the back cover had nearly dropped away from the spine. In went the thumb again, Edmund's head fell back against my shoulder, and I read into the fluff of his hair. Once, toward the end, I kissed him, though he didn't appear to notice. It seemed to me that my lips had been starved of kisses all these years and that as I read I felt my lost self unfurling a little more, not just the sister but the mother I had never been, though my voice didn't falter: "And when the wolf came to the brook he stooped down to drink, and the heavy stones made him lose his balance, so that he fell, and sank beneath the water . . ."

I would have sat like that, though the awkward angle made my back ache, until Meredith's return—no, longer, until morning. Forever. But Edmund curled gratefully onto his side when the story was over, then rolled back and murmured: "We never said any prayers."

"Does your mother say prayers?"

"Oh, yes, we say prayers every night."

"What kind of prayers?"

"She has beads and we touch them. We always pray for my father. We ask Jesus to look after all the young men who died in the war."

So Meredith was a Roman Catholic like her parents, on top of everything else. In any event, I did not feel equal to praying with Edmund, since my worship these days was limited to occasional attendance at church when I raged at the banality of addressing a God who patently hadn't listened. "Shall we leave it for tonight, as it's so late?" I stooped to kiss his hairline, between brow and cheekbone.

"Mommy says we must never be too tired to pray because God is probably never too tired to listen to us."

I noted the *probably* and smiled. Trust Meredith to put in a caveat. However, I pressed my hands together, bowed my head, and dutifully recited the "Our Father," which seemed to satisfy him.

Then I kissed his forehead again, switched off the lamp, and went downstairs, my feet sprung with joy and triumph, only to find that a bowl of tepid celery soup awaited me in the dining room, where the others sat before their already empty bowls.

"We couldn't wait any longer," said Mother, glancing nervously at Prudence.

"I'm afraid I had to point out once again that it is unhealthy for a household to be dictated to by the whim of a spoiled child," said Prudence, adjusting her knife and fork on either side of her mat.

Min was already at the door, bearing a tray laden with the next course. Nobody spoke while she cleared the bowls and laid out the casserole dishes. Grandmother, as usual, seemed largely oblivious to the poisoned atmosphere, though she occasionally raised her head as if to catch the currents in the air. I helped myself to potatoes and waited for the next salvo.

"She goes out without a word of explanation," hissed Mother the instant Min was gone. "No wonder the child is upset when his mother would give no indication of what time she'd be back. And she's asked me for money. She says she has nothing to live on and must have an allowance." I ate a few mouthfuls, hungry despite the significance of the occasion: money being discussed at mealtimes. "Prudence and I agree that she is quite impossible. It's as if she's come with the deliberate intention of living on us. Well, there's no more money—no matter how deserving she is—and that's that."

Mother, when roused to anger, tended toward petulance rather than effectiveness. She was better suited to acquiescence. In her heyday, she had charmed most comers, especially male, through her upward glances and winsome smiles. She could meet a dozen of Father's colleagues in an evening and remember every one of their names; inquire, as if she knew them intimately, after their wives and daughters; suggest birthday gifts; make witty critiques of concerts and plays; and leave not a heart untouched by her tenderness. Mother, after all, was the daughter of a successful and rather daring actress: Ibsen was often mentioned in the same breath as Clara Fielding—Grandmother's stage name. This somewhat risqué fact was overlooked, even perhaps envied by Father's colleagues, because Mother was beautiful and had a white, pillowy bosom.

But now the men weren't here and there was no one to save her except that poor substitute for husband and son: me. "Prudence says this has all gone on long enough. Meredith seems to be running rings around us," she added. "I know she was James's . . . and we must . . . But her expectations are entirely disproportionate."

Prudence cut a cube of braised steak into quarters and raised a segment to her lips without bending her spine a notch to meet it. "In my view, her sudden coming is very irregular. I suspect she has something to hide."

"But don't you love Edmund," I cried, "don't you want to keep him here with us? I would pay any amount to make that possible." Grandmother's neck shot forward as she craned to hear what had roused me. "Grandmother," I enunciated, "don't you love Edmund being here?"

"Oh, I do. He's a dear little boy. So intelligent and polite."

"No," said Mother suddenly. "I won't put up with that woman just because she's Edmund's mother, whatever anyone says. It would be different if it was just the boy, I accept we have a duty to him. But I cannot manage with her in the house."

It was on the tip of my tongue to ask *Manage what?* but Prudence said: "I fear for your mother's health, I really do. In my view this is putting intolerable strain upon us all."

"Will you speak to her, Evelyn? Tell her we have no money."

I ate a meager bowl of semolina pudding and jam while pondering my next move. The situation was complicated by the memories of Saturday's conversation with Meredith on Beachy Head, and Edmund's arms about my neck as we climbed the stairs.

When Meredith came home, I was already preparing for bed, but with a brisk knock she burst into my room, decked out in strings of red beads and a long coat embroidered with multicolored flowers. She reeked of smoke and alcohol, her eyes were shining, and she dropped a bulging carpetbag in the doorway. Her slender little ankles were exposed and her shoes were pointed, with wide straps. I, on the other hand, was wearing an ancient nightgown, so well-washed that it was gray rather than white, and my large feet were bare.

"Look at you," cried Meredith, "straight out of a painting by Millais or Rossetti. You ought to be floating in water with your hands pressed together on your breast. If that judge could see you now, a voluptuous nymph rather than a bluestocking in a gray jacket, how surprised he'd be. But, incidentally, I have come to tell you what a sensation you were in court this morning. Everyone was talking about you in the foyer afterward. Were your ears burning? I was so proud to know you."

"I was horrified by what happened, actually," I said.

"Horrified? But why? You were lancing a boil. Don't you see, that beast of a man was exposed for the senseless bigot he really is." She kicked off her shoes, jumped onto my bed, tucked her feet under the sheet, and fell back on the pillows as if fully intending to stay awhile.

"That poor woman, Leah Marchant, is in prison tonight because of me," I said, dragging my hairbrush through tangles with such force that the hair crackled.

"Oh, yes, but I don't suppose it matters that much. I was talking to a friend of hers called Mrs. Sanders and she said at least being locked up would keep Mrs. Marchant away from the bottle another night— since she lost her children she's been drinking heavily apparently. Your ears must have been burning, we both said how much we admired you and how brave you were. Do you know, as I was watching you I really thought to myself: This is a historic occasion, I am witnessing practically the very first time that a woman in England has stood as an advocate in court. But listen, you are not alone in making history. This evening I attended my very first art class."

She sprang up and unpacked various items from her bag. "I went along to the art school in Chelsea and they had no vacancies, at least not for beginners, but they did have a notice board filled with cards written by teachers offering classes and I found one in Bloomsbury. The teacher, who's called Hadley Waters, was gassed so he's very thin and wheezy but he studied at the Slade and has his own studio where the classes take place, and he happened to be holding one this evening so he invited me to join it as a tryout. He didn't even charge me and his class turns out to be just what I'm looking for. There are five other pupils with very mixed experience, including another beginner like me. We experimented with perspective and the human form. I'm so happy."

A clutter of paints, brushes, and boxes piled up on the floorboards until finally a sketch pad emerged, which Meredith held to her chest with both hands. Thus displayed was the drawing of a female nude seated on an upright chair with her back to the artist but her head turned so that it was as if her name had been suddenly called. Thankfully, all but the side of her breast and the cleft of her buttocks were hidden from view.

Though I knew virtually nothing about art, I could tell that Meredith had flair. With minimal strokes of charcoal, she had depicted living curves, not to mention a distinctly hoydenish glint in the model's eye. "It's because he worked at the Slade that Hadley Waters has the confidence to allow a mixed class to tackle nudes. I'm so relieved. The last thing I needed was to spend months drawing flowers or some such. I particularly wanted bodies, whole, healthy bodies, having been a nurse, you know."

She perched on the side of the bed and held the drawing at arm's length, then darted across the room, propped it against the wall, and gave it further scrutiny. Her ability to confound me was quite extraordinary. Somehow the fact that she had made such a proficient drawing of a strange woman wearing no clothes made it impossible for me to raise the subject of funds. And then she cried: "I forgot the most important thing of all. We have been invited to a party. You and me. In Kew, wherever that is. Actually on the river, Hadley says. Can you imagine, I go to one art class and I come home with a party invitation? Hadley says we must go because he thinks everyone will be there, including Augustus John and that the house where the party is to be held is itself a work of art."

"A party? We can't go to a party given by strangers. We won't know a soul."

"We'll know each other. You can be quite sure that I only agreed to go if you were invited too. It's a fortnight on Thursday."

"Oh, dear, I'm sorry but I think there's a concert at the church that night which Mother would like me to attend."

"That's all right, we'll go on to the party afterward. It probably won't start until terribly late. I can't tell you how thrilled I am—it was my dream back in Canada to find a world of culture in London and now I have, and so easily. Hmmm, would you smell the inside of my bag? Don't you just love it, oils and linseed? I feel like an artist already. I'm sorry that I had to rush off this morning, by the way, before I had a chance to tell you how brilliantly you performed, but I had so much shopping to do."

"Meredith. Forgive me asking, but how are you able to afford all this?"

She sat back on her heels, let her hands drop between her knees, and gazed up at me. "I still have a little of the money my father gave me. He was as generous as he could be."

"Mother says you spoke to her today and asked for an allowance."

"Oh, yes. I did. Perhaps I should have waited until you were home but I'm eaten up with anxiety about how Edmund and I are to manage and I thought the best way would be to bring it all out in the open. Unfortunately the job I went for yesterday was not quite right so I shall have to try elsewhere. I found Doctor Stopes surprisingly conservative on some matters, notably the question of marriage. She and I didn't exactly see eye to eye. So you see, until I do get work, I must have some money to live on."

"The thing is, as I told you before, we can barely make ends meet here. We are quite ready to house you and Edmund for as long as you like, but none of us has a specific allowance. Prudence has some savings, I believe, but very little. We're all having to scrimp and make do."

Her eyes had hardened. "Well, I'm afraid I am not prepared to go on like that. I have been making do since Edmund was born, and I cannot stand it any longer." She piled things back into her bag, and I felt sorry that her pleasure in them had been tainted by our conversation. But I was also aware that her movements were a little clumsy and wondered if alcohol was behind her shrillness.

"Shall we speak again tomorrow," I asked, "when we're not both tired?"

"Tomorrow you'll be out again, into your wonderful world where you are significant, Evelyn, and I shall be cooped up here in these terrible rooms. I must have some money. I'm not asking for much. Twenty pounds a month is what your father used to send me, but I don't expect anything like that. Half would do."

"That is still a huge amount, almost as much as I pay the girls."

"Then I have come to a new prison. Worse than being at home. Have you any idea how it feels to be so confined? Perhaps I should find other lodgings, in fact it's possible that there may be a room in Hadley Waters's house."

"I should be very sorry if you were to take Edmund away. That's not what I want."

"Evelyn, it's not for me to tell you how to run your affairs, but I've been thinking, couldn't you raise money on this house?" She had changed tack again and now spoke more softly. "Perhaps you could borrow money against its value or let a room." (Her voice did not falter, although we both knew the only empty room was James's.) "And it's beyond me why your mother pays for two women to cook and clean when she and Prudence sit around all day and complain about the cost of everything."

"It's what they were brought up to do. They don't know any other way. It would be cruel to expect them, or indeed Min and Rose, to change now."

She was very still, watching me, and my heart beat faster, because I knew she was weighing something up in her mind. Sure enough, she next said, "I have something to show you," and she opened the door, crossed the landing, and disappeared into her own room while I picked up the nude, who had an overbite and a weak chin, and wondered what new blow was about to fall.

When Meredith came back, she stood so close that I could pick out the individual strands of embroidery silk on her coat. From a little leather wallet she withdrew a scrap of paper, stained and soft, which she handled with her fingertips and cradled in her palm lest it break apart at the creases. When she passed it to me, gentle as if it were a fragile living thing, a wounded butterfly, I began to weep.

"He wrote it while he was dying," she said. "They found it in his hand when they recovered his body and they brought it to me."

On the paper was one word, very faint, scrawled with a blunt pencil and smeared with dirt. I knew the writing, I would have known it in any circumstances. The word was, in fact, a name: *Meredith*.

Thirteen

The next morning, I obediently took the train to Amersham in good time for Stephen Wheeler's hearing. Much to my relief, I was an hour ahead of Prudence, who would later travel the same line on an annual birthday visit to her old home.

It was a haunted journey. From a smeary window identical to this, Stella Wheeler had gazed at the lanes and hayfields of Middlesex with, I suspected, no great interest in the bucolic pleasures they offered. Everything I had learned of her so far suggested a girl who had preferred the city to the country; her family home had been in the suburb of Acton, and she had chosen to work in central London. I guessed (though I'd seen no details) that the costume she'd worn for the fateful picnic had been planned rather in accordance with a fashion-book fantasy of what ladies might wear in the country than with a mind for practicality. And I imagined that Stella would have sat opposite her husband instead of beside him, with the picnic basket on the floor between them. Perhaps Carole's wistful *I would have married him* and her comment that Stella had taken her suitor somewhat for granted had convinced me that the affection between the Wheelers had been rather greater on his side than hers.

And as for Wheeler, what had been in his mind as he journeyed to the farthest reaches of the Metropolitan Line? What murderous thoughts? Perhaps none at all. Perhaps, despite all the evidence to the contrary, he'd simply anticipated a picnic with his new bride, a pint or two in a country pub, and a return in the late afternoon, refreshed and sunburned, for a night of marital harmony—I shunned the word *passion* as being too Ethel M. Dell—at home in Harrow and Wealdstone.

Unlike other ladies on the train, I had to uphold the pretense that I was an articled clerk with a future before her, so I somewhat self-consciously opened my briefcase (inherited from Father) and removed my notes from the day before. Perhaps I could use the fact that I had won Carole Mangan's trust to buy more time in Breen's employ. I had no idea how deeply Breen was hurt but I imagined that he was the sort never to forget a slight. And because I felt unable to apologize, I was in a double bind: I wanted to work for him but at what cost? Must it be always on his terms, regardless of a conflict with my conscience or the damage he might choose to inflict to my dignity as a lawyer?

The Lyons tea-shop notes occupied me for a while but my mind would stray to the previous night. It was almost as if Meredith had stage-managed the sequence of events: the child on the bottom stair, his head on my shoulder, her renewed request for money, and the subsequent suggestion that she should leave. I couldn't possibly let Edmund go now he'd allowed me to put him to bed. And surely to do so would be a betrayal of James. My brother's tortuous death was a raw wound in my consciousness, the pain made more acute by the addition of one small detail, the scrap of paper unspeakably stained. What had it cost him, with his one good arm, to extract the paper and pencil from his pocket and scrawl her name? Only hers.

Later, as I reached the courthouse door, I expected the usual chilly reception from staff and fellow lawyers but instead an usher actually bowed. "Miss Gifford, I presume? I have a message for you, ma'am. Mr. Breen says if you would be so kind, could you join him downstairs in the cells?" At least he was courteous as he led the way, although unable to resist a conspiratorial twinkle as if he were playing a parlor game.

Downstairs in the interview room, I discovered that the firm of Breen & Balcombe had turned out in force while a police officer stood in one corner, hands folded, staring straight ahead like a parody of himself. Breen was seated at one side of a small, square table, left arm hooked over the back of his chair as he gazed piercingly at Wheeler, whose head was dropped in his hands. He was wearing the jacket in which he'd been arrested and a clean shirt, presumably one collected by Breen during our trip to the house in Byron Street. Wolfe was note-taker. I had never seen him sit full-square on a chair, he always contrived to balance on one buttock with the other leg thrown across his thigh or extended before him, a posture which gave the message that while everyone else might be taking these proceedings seriously, he really could not. I imagined that he had been lolling thus on the fringe of events since he was at school.

When I was introduced by the usher, Wheeler made no move but Breen snapped to his feet and pulled the fourth chair from the table while even Wolfe half rose and made a gesture, as if toasting me, with his pen.

"Miss Gifford," said Breen, handing me into the chair with disturbing ceremony. "Stephen, this is the third member of our firm, Miss Gifford. She will be working on this case alongside me. Miss Gifford, you should know that Mr. Wheeler's recollection is now clear and that he denies the charge of murder."

My heart pounded with relief. I was not to be dismissed or cold-shouldered then; in fact, I was now formally included in the most exacting proceedings handled by Breen & Balcombe in living history. It was as if yesterday had been a triumph for me rather than a fiasco.

"So, Stephen, I'll ask you again, was there anyone else you can think of in Stella's life who could have had a motive for killing her?" Breen said.

Wheeler shook his close-cropped head upon which the hair grew dense as fur.

"As far as you were concerned, on the morning of her murder everything was as usual between you?"

"Yes."

"And I know you've told the police already but when was the last time you'd seen the gun and the gloves?"

"They was in my shed. To be honest, I'd forgotten they was there. I moved into the house in January, to get it ready for Stell, and I didn't really know what to do with that military stuff." Wheeler's voice was as dismal as his bearing and I doubted whether, even when times were good, he had spoken vigorously.

"Did Stella know about them?"

"Of course. I showed them to her when I took her 'round the house after I moved in. That was the last time I seen them."

"Stephen, I know this is a very personal question, would you have said you and Stella were happy together?"

Breen spoke the word *happy* tentatively, as if it were in slightly poor taste, and by way of reply Wheeler huffed air through his nostrils and nodded three times, slowly. I thought I understood him well enough: since the start of war, the notion of happiness had seemed a distant thing, like a flash of sunlight in a dark wood. But I could not help thinking that, even setting aside the ten days of imprisonment accused of murder, Wheeler hardly cut a romantic figure, or one who was cut out to be a promising husband for a wayward girl bride. His body was bulky and round-shouldered, his neck short, and his face, though regular-featured, too fleshy to be striking. Hair grew thickly on his wrists and throat, and his left hand was badly disfigured, having lost all but the thumb and index finger.

"Miss Gifford, do you have any questions for Mr. Wheeler?" asked Breen.

"I have one question." My female voice must have struck a chord with Wheeler, because he looked me full in the face for the first time, revealing eyes of a touchingly liquid gray. I drew a sharp breath, because I was reminded suddenly of other eyes, as desolate as Wheeler's. James, toward the end of his last leave, had become increasingly detached, aquiver, like an unshelled mollusk, with the anticipation of going back. "Mr. Wheeler, what did Stella do all day while you were at work?" I asked softly.

"Looked after the house. Did the shopping and washing and things like that. What else would she do?" It was clear that he hadn't liked the question, though he stared at me defiantly.

"Mr. Wolfe?" said Breen. "Anything else?"

Wolfe, in between doodling in the margin, had been dashing down notes in handwriting that would later have Miss Drake tut-tutting as she attempted to type them up. "The hat," he said, in his asthmatic drawl, "I think your wife was wearing a hat on the picnic?"

"Of course."

"Did she wear a hat most of the time or was she inclined to take it off when she could?"

"She didn't like the sun on her face, if that's what you mean."

"I believe her hat was found with the picnic basket. We've seen it in the box of exhibits."

"I don't know what you're talking about."

"I mean, when you left her to go off for a drink, do you recall whether or not she was wearing her hat?"

"She was lying in the shade. She had her hands on her chest and she was holding the hat between them." His mouth contorted at the memory and he bowed his head.

The hearing was due to begin in ten minutes, so we shook Wheeler's too-soft hand and went upstairs to courtroom 1, which was crowded with press and spectators among whom our arrival caused quite a stir. I found myself sandwiched between Breen and Wolfe and realized that a conversation must have taken place between them to ensure my inclusion and protection. Though I did not look directly to my left, I glimpsed a number of women's hats and realized that Wheeler's family was probably present, perhaps Stella's too. And then any further consideration of the Wheelers was pushed out of my head altogether, because I had caught sight of the black-clad figure folded into a lawyer's bench behind me, Nicholas Thorne.

Before I could recover, Breen turned, gave him a nod, then whispered to me: "I understand you've met Thorne already. We've arranged a meeting after this hearing. Incidentally, Wheeler's boss, Thorne's prospective father-in-law, is also in court—over there to the left. Sir David Hardynge. It will do the case no harm if Imperial Insurance is prepared to supply Wheeler with a character reference and there's even talk of them paying his costs."

After a decent interval, I glanced across at the gentleman in the frock coat and pinstripes, very dapper, with thick silvery hair and a glossy mustache meticulously combed, his fingers folded lightly over the handle of a cane. His bright, curious gaze was partially concealed by the thick lenses of his spectacles, but as he glanced at the dock in anticipation of Wheeler's appearance, he caught my eye and gave me the brisk, appraising stare of a powerful man.

The court was ordered to rise and the bench of three magistrates entered, self-important with the prospect of dealing with a murder rather than just the watering-down of milk by a local farmer, next case on the list. Wheeler, handcuffed between two policemen, was led into the dock and there was a frisson among the observers, a scratching of pencils on paper as the press sprang into action, and I heard a sob. When I glanced around again, Wheeler's eyes were wet because he'd seen his family and Sir David Hardynge, who smiled with great kindness. I turned back hastily to face front—any movement of my head meant that I risked meeting Thorne's eye.

The entire proceedings were thrown into sharp relief by my disproportionate and ungovernable reaction to Thorne. I was actually trembling, and the side of my body nearest him, which he might have reached out and touched, ached. And though Wheeler should have had my full attention, my mind instead was processing several impressions, each of extraordinary clarity. I felt, more than at any time of my life, significant, though I wore, as ever, a gray suit and misshapen hat. I felt, acutely, the proximity of Breen and Wolfe, and, behind me, Thorne. And this heightened consciousness played on my comprehension of what was taking place: I regarded the tragedy of Stella Wheeler and her workaday husband in the light of what was happening to me as I stood in front of Thorne, a man whom I had met only twice but who had the power to change the color of air.

Meanwhile the hearing proceeded. The defendant was identified as Stephen Anthony Wheeler, date of birth September 14, 1888, aged thirty-six. The indictment was read out: That on May 17, 1924, at approximately three o'clock in the afternoon, the defendant Stephen Anthony Wheeler had, with malice aforethought, murdered his wife, Stella Jane Wheeler, formerly Hobhouse, by shooting her once in the breast with a single bullet, at close range, with his revolver.

Dead silence in the courtroom.

"Are we ready to take a plea, Mr. Breen?"

"We are, Mr. Clerk."

"Stephen Anthony Wheeler, to the offense of murder with malice aforethought, do you plead guilty or not guilty?"

"Not guilty." Another ripple of excitement as the legal machine rolled on. An early date was set for committal proceedings to the Aylesbury Assizes, bail was refused. A woman sobbed in the public gallery. "No, no, no," she moaned, "it can't be true." In less than ten minutes the prisoner was removed to the cells—he did not look again to the public gallery—and the hearing was over. At once there was a bustle in the courtroom as the spectators and press filed out; Thorne crossed to Hardynge's side, held open the door for him, and they left the courtroom together.

"Very well," said Breen. "Divide and rule. Wolfe, you and Miss Gifford are to speak to the Hobhouse clan, I'll deal with the Wheelers. And at eleven-thirty we're to meet with Thorne in the King's Arms."

So Wolfe and I drew Stella's parents aside and interviewed them in a little room kept for the use of victims. The mother, pale and tremulous, was slender, barely forty, with hair neatly cropped under a heavy hat. Her elegant mourning clothes showed considerable attention to detail; the gloves fastened from wrist to thumb with a dozen tiny buttons, a handkerchief edged with black in her fist and her slim shoes immaculately polished. The father was much less fine-featured, slight of build, a chauffeur by profession. He turned his hat around and around and said that he might lose his job over all this, he'd already had three days off work, today was the fourth, and there was the funeral still to come.

Also present was a married daughter, Julie Leamington, three years older than Stella, and for the first time I glimpsed what the dead girl might have looked like. Julie was a dressmaker and, like her mother, impeccably turned out though she had inherited the father's prominent nose, small mouth, and wide-set pondering eyes, so that her appearance, in the uncertain light of the witness room, was Madonna-like. She was very slender, with a long, delicate neck and fine hands. Unlike her parents, who were so engrossed by their tragedy that they seemed not to have noticed that I was a woman, Julie regarded me with considerable curiosity and suspicion.

Wolfe, who proceeded to surprise and impress me with his handling of the interview, did not act so much with tact as with the easygoing indifference of the wellborn. When he was offering his condolences, his detachment contrived to be professional rather than offensive—I suspect he bestowed the same degree of sympathy on these parents bereft of a daughter as he might on a friend who'd lost a bet. The effect was to quell any potentially emotional outbursts, at least at first. His frame was comfortingly large, his smile amiable, though at the same time managing to convey that he was communicating with the Hobhouse family across a considerable social divide. "I expect the police have been asking you all sorts," he said.

They nodded.

"You must feel utterly bemused by it all, as are we, we must admit. But we need to get to the bottom of this so we can account for the dreadful thing that happened to your daughter. So if you don't mind, we'll try and put a few pieces of the jigsaw in place. Could you bear it? Very well, can we just clarify first of all one or two things. I think Mr. Wheeler rolled up at your place on the Saturday night? How did he seem to you?"

Mrs. Hobhouse pressed her handkerchief to her mouth and spoke through the cloth. "We welcomed him. I can't bear to think of it. We could tell he was out of sorts. Panting, you know, flushed after his bicycle ride. We wondered afterward if he was the worse for drink. Turns out he'd come to us fresh from murdering our child."

My pitying respect for Mrs. Hobhouse was growing by the minute. I saw her as a woman jolted out of a quiet existence by this violent event, but determined to play her part well. Her bearing suggested a self-conscious desire to be dignified in her grief, as if she was an actress thrust before an audience despite being somewhat unsure of her lines.

"Mr. Wheeler denies that he killed her, Mrs. Hobhouse," said Wolfe. "We mustn't lose sight of that. I was wondering, is there anything more you could tell us about Stella, the type of girl she was?"

Hobhouse, who I decided was the weaker partner, spoke emphatically, "She were a lovely girl. Quiet. Worked hard at that restaurant of hers. Loved to dance. Couldn't wait to be married."

"She was a child, I believe, when she first knew Stephen."

"He used to come over and play with her when she was no more than a babe," said Mrs. Hobhouse, "take her for rides in a go-cart, which was a thing she loved. Our families were bound up together by church connections. Stephen adored our Stell. He wrote to her all through the war. I didn't think it was appropriate, her being so young, but it was wartime after all, so I hadn't the heart to stop her sending letters back. And she stayed loyal to him afterward, which is to her credit though I always thought she could have done better. She had several admirers, not all of them fit for marriage, it's true, but she didn't need to marry *him*. She was by no means desperate."

"Any admirer in particular?"

"None special, as I told the police."

"Do you think Stella was happy?"

"Happy in what?"

"Her choice, you know, her marriage."

"Oh, she was happy enough. Our Stell was the type of girl who had to be wed. She was restless at home. But I wanted her to be sure in her own mind. I asked her a few times, the last was on the night before her wedding. I said, 'Are you sure, Stell?' and she was cross with me, she said what did I think she was putting us to all that trouble and expense for, if she wasn't sure? She was very fierce as she always was when she'd fixed her mind on something."

"Mrs. Hobhouse, the way you're talking makes me think you had your doubts about the wisdom of your daughter's marriage?"

"I thought she was very young and he was quite old by comparison, but she had set her heart on it and that was that."

"She was lucky to have him," the sister said suddenly, an odd remark—

though the waitress Carole Mangan had said much the same—given that Stella was now dead, apparently by her husband's hand. "At least he was alive, with only three fingers missing. Had the luck of the devil in that war, he did. I lost first one fiancé, then another."

"You're happy enough with Michael, aren't you, Julie?" asked her mother.

"He wasn't my first choice." I noticed that Julie was resting her palm on her stomach and wondered if she was expecting a child.

"Yes, but Michael isn't moody like Stephen was," said Mrs. Hobhouse. "Stephen did have awfully bad moods."

There was a pause. "That's frightfully interesting, Mrs. Hobhouse," said Wolfe, examining his nib. "Mr. Wheeler was moody, you say?"

"Only since the war and very rarely then. He was the sweetest-natured boy before that. Far too soft for our Stell, I sometimes thought. She was a girl who needed keeping in line. But I do blame the war for the fact he did get very low from time to time, Stell said. I believe he could have opted for home duties, you know, after he was gassed, but no, he would go back. I used to think they should pass a law that took a man out of the trenches once he'd survived for, say, two years."

"What form did his moods take?"

"Oh, you mustn't make so much of a small thing," cried the mother. "The fact is, he killed our Stell. And that's not what you do when you get low, is it? Just because he went quiet sometimes doesn't give him an excuse to kill her."

"What about finances? Do you think the couple had any money worries?"

"I doubt it. They were short, of course, but Stephen was very careful with money. It's one of the reasons it took him so long to marry her, he was saving up."

"Mrs. Hobhouse," I said, "could you tell us when you last saw Stella?"

Tears spilled over her lids. "She came for tea and to fetch the picnic basket in the week before she died. She was excited about the picnic, poor soul. I offered to go over to her and help her get the house nice, but she didn't seem to want that. She said she liked to come home and go upstairs to her own room and look at her old things and I thought why not, after all she's still a child."

"What kind of things did she keep in her room?"

"Oh, you know. Dolls. Old clothes. We never got 'round to clearing it after she was married. We didn't have time."

"Would you mind, I wonder, so that I could get to know better what Stella was like, if I came and had a look at her bedroom sometime?" The mother nodded. "I went to see where Stella worked, you know, at Lyons. Apparently she had a wonderful record, never ill, never late. You must have been proud of her."

"She was a very good girl. But we brought up both the girls to be conscientious."

"Good job," said Julie sullenly. "Looks like I'll be slaving away till the end of my days. *He'll* never get off his backside and find work."

"Julie," said her mother sharply.

"I talked to Stella's friend at work and she told me Stella had hardly been late once in all the years she'd worked there," I said. "That's an outstanding record."

"Oh, I should think that's an exaggeration," said Mr. Hobhouse. "The buses and trams aren't that reliable. You was always shouting at her to get up in the morning," he reminded his wife.

"She was a very good girl," insisted the mother. "I always knew where I was with Stell."

"Come off it, Mum," said Julie. "She was no saint. What about the night when she never came back at all because she missed the last train? Dancing down the Trocadero with her friends from work she was. You were worried sick."

"When was that, I wonder?" asked Wolfe, adding tiny leaves to a line drawing of a weeping willow.

"Lord, I can't remember. Some time in April, a couple of weeks before she were married."

"Was Stephen with her?"

"Not that I know of. She was out dancing, is all, having a last fling. He knew she loved dancing. He liked to watch her when they were someplace together, being flat-footed himself."

"Stell said not to tell him when she used to go down the Trocadero," said Julie. "She knew he'd get into one of his states. He didn't like her going down there."

Now that the Hobhouses' hitherto united front was fractured, the atmosphere in the room had soured. Nevertheless, their acquiescence thus far had surprised me. I tried to imagine how we would have reacted, a few days after the news of James's death, had we been confronted by a barrage of questions from those trying to exonerate the German who had fired the shell. But the Hobhouse family had responded meekly to our probing, I guessed, because they had been schooled all their lives to do as they were told by professional people.

∾

Half an hour later, the firm of Breen & Balcombe met Nicholas Thorne over morning coffee in an upstairs private room at the King's Arms, where Thorne achieved the difficult balancing act of showing deference to Breen's reputation and experience while not in any way diminishing his own status. Nor did he reveal that he and I had parted on a very strained note the previous week, and I was conscious that a bond was created between us by the very fact that we chose not to share details of our meeting with the others. He sat in an easy chair, legs stretched before him, a diminutive coffee cup and saucer in his hand, indulging with Wolfe in the kind of male joshing that never failed to annoy me. In a rapid exchange, they established a network of common experience and acquaintance: Radley, was it? Ah no, Rugby man myself. Then Christ Church. Did you know Saint, Rentoul, Marshall Hall? Either Wolfe or Thorne had dined with the first, scouted for another, knew a friend of a friend whose sister had married a second cousin of Hall's. Then their talk drifted on again: Poor old Jeffries . . . Colossal promise, brilliant career ahead of him . . . last days of the war . . . The brother survived. Not half so sharp . . .

Breen was between them, spaniel-like, smiling his grammar-school-boy smile as famous legal names were tossed about easily as bonbons. I, on the other hand, sipped my tepid coffee and tried to assume an expression of tolerant disdain. My heart had told me Thorne was perfect, my head already knew that he was not. What a shame to find him guilty of being so tediously true to type.

Even so, he moved me so that the air around him seemed to oscillate with color like a shattered rainbow. Surely I was not so shallow as to be stirred by spotless cuffs, knife-sharp creases, or fineness of cloth? So what was it? Perhaps he reminded me a little of the dead boys I had known, my brother and his friends, Peter Shaw who had kissed me under the canal bridge. Like them, Thorne bore himself eagerly, as one anticipating an ever more interesting future. Like them, he had a boyish laugh and the ability to switch mood from jovial to solemn in a flash. He was undoubtedly the most beautiful man I had seen in years, not so much for the regularity of his features and the cleanness of his limbs as for the openness of his gaze, his slow but momentous smile, the particular inclination of his head when he was listening. And I loved to hear his voice, which was clipped, bright, and full of easy laughter. I wondered what kind of war he'd had, that it could have left him so apparently unscathed.

"To business," he said at last, drawing himself upright and unaccountably managing to wrong-foot us, as if only we had been indulging in idle chat while Wheeler suffered. "Sir Hardynge has decided that Imperial Insurance will fund Wheeler's defense. He's very cut up over this case, thinks the least we can do is make sure we get the very best barrister for the job. Wheeler has been with the company since he was sixteen—his position was kept open during the war, of course. Had it not been for the slight conflict of interest I might have worked on the case myself." His smile was self-deprecating, but we were left in little doubt that his days of working on briefs in a junior capacity were all but over. "We are somewhat embarrassed over the police assumption that the motive was an insurance claim and find it hard to believe Wheeler would be so misguided as to think he could get away with it. After all, he, more than any man on earth, will have been very clear about the terms and conditions under which life insurance is bought—he will have explained them himself to numerous clients. But one way or another, in the circumstances, I can only help and advise, and perhaps suggest whom we might instruct. Marshall Hall would have been ideal but he's taking on far less work these days. There's Burton Wainwright."

"Could we afford him?"

"Money is not at issue here. We want to do the right thing by Wheeler."

"Then Wainwright would certainly have my confidence," said Breen. "You'll be aware that the evidence against Wheeler is very strong except for the matter of a plausible motive. I would like to believe he's innocent but at present there is not a single scrap of evidence to suggest another culprit. We are therefore pursuing a parallel line of defense, at least for the time being; that Wheeler is not in his right mind, whether or not he committed the murder. Had he maintained his silence I would have gone for a fitness to plead hearing but he now speaks very coherently indeed. The fact remains that Wheeler served nearly four years in the trenches, the crime is insanely unsubtle, and his response when arrested was that of a broken-spirited and bewildered man. Burton Wainwright has, I believe, dealt with other such cases and would therefore be an excellent choice."

"Stella's family told us that Wheeler has been moody since the war, something Miss Gifford's waitress at Lyons mentioned too," said Wolfe. "Breen, you spoke to the Wheeler clan. What had they to say on the subject?"

"That he was often withdrawn, not himself."

"Any money worries?"

"They thought not. But he had a terrible war. Refused to rest, even when offered the chance. Saw countless slaughtered. Finally got sent home with half a hand missing just weeks before the ceasefire. Who would not be damaged by such experiences?"

"Who indeed?" said Thorne. "But I'm afraid the counterargument to shell shock as mitigation is very powerful. The prosecutor will ask, Where would we be if every ex-soldier whose nerves had been shot to pieces took to killing his wife?"

"And the murder was hardly unpremeditated," I said, and found myself abruptly the center of attention.

"That doesn't mean a thing," said Breen. "The mad have their own logic."

"It seems to me," I added, "that his plan was both ridiculously ill-conceived and meticulously well worked out. If Wheeler really killed his wife and hoped to get away with it, why did he hide the gun and gloves next to her body? And why didn't he take the opportunity to bury her properly, given that he had most of the weekend? Besides . . ."

"Besides?" Breen prompted.

"Besides, Wheeler says he didn't kill his wife and I believe him."

"What makes him different from every other murderer who pleads not guilty in our courts?"

"He was trusted. I met a friend of Stella's who knew him quite well, and today her sister. They both trusted Wheeler."

Thorne smiled. "I'm afraid most murderers are trusted by those who know them well."

I could scarcely add: And I would defend Wheeler with the last atom of my being because he reminds me of James, not for his appearance or demeanor, of course; Wheeler was nothing like my slender, straight-backed brother. It was the way that war had swallowed these hopeful young men and spat them out as strangers. I remembered the soiled scrap of paper upon which James had scrawled Meredith's name. He had marched to war one person, died another, just as Stephen Wheeler had returned moody and sorrowful and was now engulfed by this new tragedy. In my book, he should be cherished and protected if for no other reason than that he had been treated with such abject lack of humanity in the past. "If he'd done it," I said weakly, "I think Wheeler would not lie about it."

Breen said with surprising warmth: "Well, Miss Gifford, you have the makings of an excellent defense lawyer. You speak of our client's innocence with conviction, exactly what we need."

All this time I'd barely looked at Thorne, but as we prepared to leave that small upper room where the smell of spilled beer and old cigar smoke lingered in the dust, Breen said: "I was wondering, Miss Gifford, if we might instruct Thorne on the Leah Marchant appeal. It's up to you, of course, I wouldn't dream of interfering but it seems to me a good opportunity to ask him. I have to watch my step with Miss Gifford," he added to Thorne. "She can be very fierce."

"I'm well aware." Thorne shook my hand and looked directly into my eyes. In the street below two dogs were rivaling each other in barks. A window was open behind him and a shaft of sunlight fell, a parallelogram, onto the intricate pattern of the rug. It seemed to me I could smell that sunbeam, a hint of bonfire.

"Drop me a note at my chambers," he said, "if you so wish." Then he released my hand and handed me his card.

I picked up my father's briefcase, passed through the low doorway ahead of him, and went down the crooked stairs to the public bar. "I saw Thorndike's *St. Joan*," he said as we emerged onto the street. "Did you, by any chance?"

I nodded. He smiled. "I thought you would have done."

"We're off to visit the crime scene, Thorne," called Wolfe. "Care to join us? We could just about squeeze you in."

He laughed. "Thanks. I'll have to give it a miss. Con. at two." And I tried to dislike him again for being so busy, for using the slang of his chambers to such crushingly exclusive effect. Why not say conference? But with what terrifying speed he was becoming enmeshed in my life and at what risk to my equilibrium? I did not watch his departing form as he strode off toward the station; instead I turned resolutely away and threw back my head, pretending to crave the sun.

Fourteen

Wolfe's *blue Austin tourer lurched* and spluttered jauntily along the Chesham Road. Breen sat in the front with his hat off and his hair like a dandelion clock around his bald patch while I twisted sideways to accommodate my legs in the backseat and prayed that the journey would not last long enough to make me sick. My eyes were alternately blinded and dazzled as we flashed in and out of dense shade; first deep woodland, then head-high hedgerows. Due to the engine noise, I couldn't participate in conversation, so I was mercifully free to pursue my own thoughts.

I was lecturing myself: you have seen Nicholas Thorne three times, Evelyn. You know him to be arrogant, ambitious, engaged to an heiress. Do not behave like a lovesick girl. Put him out of your head at once. So he was in my mind all the way to Chesham as I relived the walk on sun-baked cobbles from Toynbee Hall to the tearoom, the way he had swung my father's briefcase back and forth, the competence of his hands among the teacups, his voice today in the upstairs room, gentle, cultured, full of laughter.

He was still with me as the car jolted to a halt under a wall near the church, where a policeman was waiting in the shade of the lych-gate, detailed to accompany us to the crime scene. When we followed the track through the churchyard and on up the hill, Thorne was ghostly at my shoulder. Breen, in his element, took off his jacket and walked in his shirtsleeves with his waistcoat undone and his striped braces exposed. Wolfe, far less fit, panted behind us, complaining of the seed-heads, pollen, wild flowers, the *smell*, all sure to lay him low. And ahead of us ambled the policeman, heavy-hipped in his sweltering uniform.

It was a near-perfect day; a light breeze, a few puffs of cloud, the track shaded. Only the company was wrong. A skylark soared, like at Beachy Head, and the air was filled with birdsong and the whirr of insects. Cow parsley and ragwort clustered in the hedgerows, cattle lowed in a field nearby. We came to a stile by a copse and beyond it a gap in the hedge and on the other side an uncut hay meadow dense with color. Prudence could have named every flower but I was able to identify only campion with some misgivings, poppies with certainty.

Under the hedge, out of sight of the path, a squarish patch of meadow had been trampled down. "This is where the picnic was held," said the policeman, "according to our man Wheeler, although by the time we comes up here on the Sunday morning, he's removed all the evidence and taken it home so we have only his word for it. It's true the grass was crushed and my colleague found a bit of gristle that might have been corned beef, but that's all we got."

It was a dreamy, isolated spot, a twenty minutes' walk from the town yet absolutely cut off from it. The Wheelers could have got up to anything there but I imagined a languid Stella lying back on her elbows and telling her husband to keep off, anyone might come along. "The poor young girl was wearing pink," said the constable, who had been present at the finding of the body.

What had she been feeling? Restless, bored, sleepy? And Stephen, according to his own version of events, would have been aching for a pint while trying to entertain his flighty young bride with his plodding conversation. Or was his heart pounding and his hands shaking because of what he had in mind?

"Of course she weren't shot here," said the policeman, "that much we do know even though he denies until he's blue in the face knowing of the place where she was buried or how to get there from here. We think they must have walked half a mile or so to them woods across the valley."

"Only one witness has come forward who saw them on the way up the hill from Chesham at twelve," said Breen. "Isn't that extraordinary? We're within a stone's throw of the town."

"You could be hours out here and never see a soul, especially weekends. I can take you to where she was shot and buried if you like. Shouldn't be more than half an hour or so, there and back."

Wolfe said he would wait for us in his automobile on account of his asthma, then the constable went ahead as before, followed by Breen and finally me. The path sloped quite steeply down to a dry valley and up the other side so that the view was constantly changing. Meredith would have dubbed the countryside *quintessentially* English—that is, well-managed, its wildness confined to patches. We walked in silence for a while, as if out of respect for Stella, who had been a few minutes from death as she swished through these grasses. But with Breen ahead of me and not a word said about our disagreement after the Leah Marchant hearing, I could not be quiet for long. "Mr. Breen, yesterday I was hasty. I . . ."

He gave a bark of laughter and put up his hand to silence me. "I knew that would be on your mind, Miss Gifford. Never undermine a good argument by backtracking. You were right and you know it, at least on the question of my intervention over the appeal. Learn to stand your ground without self-recrimination."

On we went, along the side of the hill with a cluster of farm buildings ahead and a soft breeze funneled through the valley. Nothing else was said but I smiled at the back of Breen's head and loved him.

"We think this is the way they must have come," said the policeman as we approached a coppice. "It's the most direct, though again we've found no evidence. But there's a number of routes Wheeler could have taken, once he'd killed her, to cut back to the picnic spot and then on down to the town. We think he must have done it before he had his drink—there's no sign of a revolver in the pub and why would any girl hang about for an hour or more on a hillside waiting for her husband to drag her farther away from town and shoot her? Which means he was sitting in the Queen's Head, sipping his pint in full view of other customers even though he'd just killed his wife. See, there's a matter of nearly three hours between when they were sighted walking up to the picnic spot and when Wheeler had his pint. Definitely time for all kinds of murders to be committed. And of course Wheeler knew this area well, on account of his being a bit of a fisherman and coming out here to fish in the Chess since he were a young boy. It goes without saying, by the way, that neither the Wheelers nor the woman who found the body, come to that, should have been in these woods, strictly speaking. They're private."

Stella had been discovered deep inside a pheasant covert with a picket fence all around to contain the birds. The gate had been padlocked by the police. Inside, the woods were cool and dim, the tracks thick with leaf-mold and quiet except for the pheasants, who occasionally clattered shockingly among the trees. We came to a clearing pungent with the smell of cut bracken, where there were more signs of much heavy-booted trampling.

The policeman spoke lower and lower as we drew closer to where Stella had been found: "We think it's likely he prepared the ground in advance. Shallow as it was, two feet, if that, the grave was a neat affair, probably all ready and waiting for her."

What had induced Stella to enter these woods? I felt a soft lurch, as if a bird had taken flight within me, because I thought it could only have been sex. There will be shadows, she must have been told, and a bed among the bracken. No one will see us, only the pheasants. Perhaps she had lain down willingly on her green mattress, all unknowing of the fact that a few feet away a trench had been dug to receive her body. And perhaps, after the shot had been fired, she had time to stare up through a blood-red haze to the glittering leaf canopy and to hear, after the affront of gunfire, the hush of the breeze through young birch leaves. Perhaps she had thought of the old days in the tea shop with its tariff cards and tin trays and hideous caps as her memories unwound from their spool until she was a child again in Acton. Perhaps, if I stared hard enough, I might see a trace of her, a wisp of Stella Wheeler. But no, there was nothing.

⚬✖⚬

My father and I visited my brother's grave in 1921, on Valentine's Day. As we approached the graveyard near Arras, the sun came out so that the landscape which had hitherto been shades of gray, like in all the photographs, was tinged with pale green and yellow. New buds simmered under the surface of bare twigs. At first we saw farmland and villages clustered around unbroken churches, but gradually the landscape sickened; no hedges or trees, the ground pitted and deeply furrowed though furred with early spring growth. Rusty heaps of metal and wire littered the edge of the road. Houses were under construction amid heaps of rubble.

We were members of a group of mourners invited by the regiment, who deemed the graveyard just fit to be visited, though only temporary wooden markers had been placed at the heads of the graves and the entire field, as far as the eye could see, was crisscrossed by duckboards. Once there, Father and I walked in single file. Throughout the journey, I had avoided touching him, because I knew that instead of comforting me he would expose me to his grief, obscenely raw so that his face was a mask of suffering and his eyes refused to recognize me. He repeated "My son, my son, my son" as if he were in a movie and the titles had to be kept simple.

As I studied the impossible field of graves, I could not fathom that each represented a man or that a place so orderly had been the scene of thousands of violent deaths. The symmetry of it made me recoil, as if the air were still poisoned. How dare you take more care of the dead, I thought, than of the living? I despised the live soldiers who accompanied us and even the men who lay dead under earth. It is men, I thought, with their unassailable conviction that half the population is more stupid than they, who have done this.

Stretching out my gloved hands to the sunshine, I tried to reach my brother, who was lying under the soil of this plot 386 and who had died, we were assured, yards from here. Of course I wanted to know details. Where exactly had he climbed from the trench? What about the boy stranded on no-man's-land, where would that have been? The officer, embarrassed, answered vaguely and edged away. So the only true image I had was the mud. The duckboards lay over acres of mud. One of our party lost his footing, floundered, and only by grasping another man's arm was able to drag his foot free. I realized then that we had sent my brother to live and die in mud, like an animal.

Still I thought I must surely be able to pass through time to him, that it was only time, that wretchedly impenetrable fourth dimension, that held me back, because here I was, on the very spot where he had last been alive. But he seemed farther from me than ever in that French place, on French farmland, a few feet under the new-sown lawn of the cemetery. I had no sense of him at all as I looked at his name on the plaque, LIEUTENANT JAMES CARTWRIGHT GIFFORD, 13642, 15TH LONDON REGIMENT, or the date relating to his curtailed life, NOVEMBER 20, 1917, AGED 20. These digits had nothing to do with him.

But later we passed out of the temporary gate, walked down a lane

edged on either side with broken ditches, and came to the remnants of
a stone barn with walls three foot thick, which must have stood for
centuries before it was mown down in an hour by shell and rocket fire.
Only a corner was left, but the resourceful farmer was once more using
the building for straw and had erected a tarpaulin to protect it from the
rain. I felt a little consoled, to see the building thus reclaimed for its
proper use.

And I knew, as I laid my hand on the stone and closed my eyes to
the glare of the low sun, that my brother had sheltered here. I felt it as
a shock to the arm. Meanwhile, Father walked on, all unknowing, absorbed with the dead, and without regard for me, his living girl.

Fifteen

That evening I was again greeted by music on my return to Clivedon Hall Gardens and the entrance hall was an altogether unfamiliar place. Sunlight had got in through the open door of the drawing room, and I saw our commonplace red tiles as color traps, their little yellow scrolls like tender signatures. The smell of cake-baking wafted from the kitchen so that it was as if the house had been sprayed with an essence called Home. Meredith was throwing a birthday party for Prudence.

"My goodness," she had cried, "don't tell me you never even celebrate birthdays properly in this house. We can't have that, can we, Edmund? Edmund and I are very fond of birthdays. In fact we are *experts* at birthdays. You shall have a party, Prudence, whether you like it or not."

Normally, birthdays in Clivedon Hall Gardens were marked by an opening of cards at breakfast and presents after dinner. Before the meal, we drank a small glass of sherry. We called our gifts *tokens*; I had bought a posy of anemones for Prudence from a florist near the station and a pincushion with felt petals, like a rose, from a shop in Amersham. Neither of these offerings seemed sufficiently openhanded in the light of Meredith's celebration.

In the first place, Rose had been induced to bake a special cake, which was now being served in the drawing room even though it was six o'clock and barely an hour before supper, thereby putting everyone's (but especially Edmund's) appetite at risk. Then every surface was bedecked by shop-bought flowers, roses and freesia spilling out of vases and nodding in the breeze from the open French window. There was—surely not—*champagne*—and there were candles on the cake. "Just five, Prudence, I'm guessing one per decade?" Prudence, flattered despite herself, put her hand to her breast and tried to look fifty.

Meanwhile, Marcia Freer and Henry Burr crooned, "What'll I do, when you are far away, and I am blue . . ." from the gramophone. Prudence's cheeks were very pink but then she'd spent the day in Buckinghamshire and had caught the sun while in the garden of her friend Miss Lord, who had provided a generous lunch consisting of chicken in some kind of jelly and shaped into a loaf ("It sounds very unusual but I can assure you was delicious, Miss Lord's girl is a very imaginative cook") and strawberries. All four of Prudence's intimate circle had been present and emphasized, as always, that their lives just weren't the same without her.

So perhaps she was mellower than usual, because she'd had a dose of church gossip—the organist was the chief concern, being too arthritic to hit all the right notes reliably, particularly distressing at funerals. Furthermore, Prudence had taken the opportunity to visit her old cottage, though here a slight shadow had been cast. The current tenants were keen to keep the cottage on but had traveled to Scotland for the summer, which meant that the rooms were vulnerable to *damp*. "Miss Lord says she will go in to air it regularly but I feel it's a great imposition."

Or perhaps Prudence was rosy-cheeked because even she could not resist the pleasures of a party, despite the fact that Rose had been exceptionally heavy-handed with the cochineal in icing the cake, which was the color of beetroot stain. Prudence took a delicate sip of wine before turning to the small pile of presents, which included one from Miss Lord, *The Essays of Elia*, bound in calfskin and rewrapped in its tissue paper so that Prudence could have the pleasure of opening it again in front of us.

Mother was wearing her second-best blouse and attempting to participate wholeheartedly in the festivities, although I could tell from her frequent glances at the flowers that she was wondering how on earth all this had been paid for. She took angry little sips of champagne, as if by drinking it faster she would make it cost less. Fortunately, I provided an outlet for her irritation. "What's that dirt on the hem of your skirt, Evelyn? Could you not make some small effort?"

So I fled to my room, threw off my work clothes, and stood for a moment in a slip as the draft from the open window fluffed my skin. *What'll I do, when you are far away* . . . Then I dressed in my one summer frock, bought a year ago, in unexceptional cotton voile with what Mother called a *hideous* line; it had a broad sash tied at the hip and a pleated skirt. Glancing in the mirror, I thought of Nicholas Thorne as he stood on the pavement and asked me about Saint Joan. Of course now I scrutinized my reflection for signs that I was like her, or her theatrical representation, because surely that had been his message. I too had caught the sun, even though I'd worn a hat, and my eyes were unusually bright. But perhaps Thorne, noticing what James used to call my *furious* jaw, saw me as a fanatical trailblazer rather than a passionate, utterly compelling girl-saint.

I smiled at myself and there I was, simply a no-longer-young-enough woman in a pale frock and with a touch of wistful excitement in the eyes, God help me.

"At last," said Meredith when I reappeared downstairs. "Now the party can begin."

We sang "Happy Birthday" lustily, especially Grandmother, who was tone-deaf, and Edmund, who had an enthusiastic treble. Then Prudence blew out all five candles in one breath.

"Did you wish?" cried Meredith.

"Of course." What would Prudence have wished for? A return to her cottage, money, a man (even this might be possible to a devotee of Ethel M.), a resolution to the Meredith problem?

Then the presents were opened. Mother had bought a novel by Dorothy L. Sayers, titled *Whose Body?*, which Prudence set hastily aside, because she was not used to murder stories and was probably unsure whether they should be cast in the forbidden category of *light* fiction. My pincushion was received with restrained enthusiasm. Grandmother had crocheted a set of mats for Prudence's dressing table (I seemed to remember a similar gift being offered the previous year), and Edmund's present was also homemade, a representation of Aunt Prudence herself with stuck-on buttons for eyes and nose (one of which fell off as Prudence presented the picture to us for inspection). Fortunately, Prudence's good manners never failed and she thanked him gravely.

"And now mine," said Meredith, "also artistic, I'm afraid. Like mother, like son," and she presented a scroll tied with a blue ribbon. Having unfurled it, Prudence rotated it a couple of times then held it at arm's length and squinted before turning it outward so that we could all see. It was a piece of stiffened fabric with unbound edges, linen perhaps, painted with an abstract design in strong shades of red, orange, and brown, spots, zigzags, and stripes, which contrived to form some kind of unified whole that could, by a stretch of the imagination, be a face framed by symmetrical locks of hair, or perhaps it was something else entirely, a crest of some kind, or nothing at all.

"I found it in a market," said Meredith. "Don't you think it's stunning? I believe it's from Guiana. Whatever, it's a completely original design. I thought it would be perfect in your room."

Prudence's bedroom in Clivedon Hall Gardens was as near a reproduction as she could manage of her old room at the cottage: sprigged wallpaper and white work cloths. The picture-rails were hung with a cross-stitch design behind glass, depicting a cottage garden, a couple of faded photographs of our stiffly Victorian Gifford forebears, and a reproduction of Constable's *Hay Wain*. This new work of art (if such it was) would be glaringly out of place.

"Let me see," said Grandmother, removing her spectacles and holding the fabric half an inch from her eyeballs. "Oh, the beautiful colors. And what a clear pattern."

Prudence and Mother were in agreement on the subject of modern art. In order to qualify, a *great* painting had to be representational and worked with invisible brushstrokes. Ideally, a moral should be drawn from it, which made Holman Hunt's *Light of the World* probably the most perfect picture in existence. *Modern* art was therefore summarily dismissed as lacking in skill and *crude*, the latter being a heinous crime only surpassed by lateness and blasphemy. However, this was her birthday, Meredith had given her a present (I think Prudence shared my suspicion that the gift had been chosen to perplex rather than to please), and she must be thanked.

"And will you put it up in your room?" demanded Meredith with the eagerness of a child. "Do you have a frame?"

"Perhaps I shall find one among some of my stored items in the attic," said Prudence, setting the fabric aside. But she could not quite leave it alone and I saw her glance at it again and even stroke it while we waited for the dinner gong. Her head tilted and her lips pursed as she tried to decide whether or not she was being duped. When we filed into the dining room—Mother firmly gripping the half-full bottle in case the girls got hold of it—Prudence left the painting behind on the arm of her chair, but then, as we crossed the hall, went back to fetch it, saying that if we didn't mind, she would hang it over the edge of the sideboard so that she could look at it during the meal.

"When is the next birthday?" asked Edmund, who was excused soup these days. "Mine's on July 31."

"And after that will be Evelyn's, on August 14," said Mother, who had recklessly poured another glass for herself and Prudence but just a thimbleful for Grandmother, Meredith, and me, as if we were all three underage.

"And how old will she be?"

"Goodness," said Prudence, "we never ask a lady her age."

"I shall be thirty-one," I said.

There was a painful silence. "That means you're older than Mommy," said Edmund.

"But only by two years," said Meredith. "And the thing about Evelyn is that she has crammed so much into her life already."

Mother, at the end of the table, laid down her spoon and Min came forward to remove the bowls. We were on dangerous territory, and I waded in to change the subject. "You'll never guess where I've been today."

"Oh, good Lord, I forgot, you have been to the murder scene. How *fascinating*," cried Meredith.

"We won't want to hear about it at table, I think," said Mother, wiping her mouth.

Grandmother spoke into the silence. "By the time I was thirty I had finished with the stage and was expecting you," she told Mother.

"That's it," said Meredith, "this room is filled with exceptional women. I am in awe of you all." Nobody else seemed to notice the irony of this remark made by a woman who had crossed the Atlantic to nurse behind the front lines and conceive a child out of wedlock.

"I've always missed it," said Grandmother. "There's nothing quite like the fear of that curtain going up and having to encounter the dark space on the other side. Now that's what I call being alive, a lit stage and an audience in darkness. Oh, one is so aware of oneself quivering in the footlights and nothing else matters except that first word which will decide the fate of actor and audience. I was someone who always had to be in the light."

"Which was your favorite part, did you say?"

"That would be Nora in *A Doll's House*, which I played in Manchester."

"And you wore such stunning costumes. Edmund loves the picture of you as Titania . . ."

"It was a very long time ago," said Mother. "Why bring up the past? You have not acted for *years*, Mother." Tears were brimming, and she laid down her knife and fork, put her hand to her head, and pushed back the chair. "I'm so sorry, Prudence, on your birthday . . . my head. It's the heat. Forgive me, forgive me." Then she was gone from the room and we heard the rush of her feet on the stairs.

Edmund was wide-eyed for a moment, but soon tucked into his mashed potato. Meanwhile, Meredith said: "Prudence and I are off to the Tate Gallery tomorrow. While you were upstairs getting changed, Evelyn, I made her promise to come. It's such a pity you're not free too."

"I've never been to the Tate," said Prudence, "one ought to make the most of being in London."

"Of course, it's work for me," said Meredith. "I have to prepare for my next class with Hadley Waters and at the moment there's no plumbing the depth of my ignorance."

"I don't expect I shall like everything in it," said Prudence, "but one has to keep an open mind." Suddenly, across the table, I met Meredith's eyes and I was eleven again, at the back of class with my best friend Margaret Bagshott, struck by an agonizing fit of giggles. Meredith and I tried to suppress the laughter, we put our hands to our mouths and dabbed away our tears while Prudence looked from one to the other of us, smiling uncertainly: "What did I say that was so funny?"

 oxo

Mother was not laughing when I went upstairs half an hour later; she was at the dressing table, still wiping tears from her eyes. Despite the season, the windows were tight shut, the curtains drawn, the lamps lit, and there was a leather-bound album open on her lap, containing photographs of James and myself as children, solemn figures in intricate clothes, posed in the garden or a studio, the arm of the lanky girl invariably flung around the neck of her sturdy little brother. In one, James sat on my knee, his own legs so short that they stuck out dead straight, a coil of my hair falling onto his fist. He stared as if mesmerized into the camera; I was watching his face.

Keeping my distance, I perched on the edge of the bed and said briskly: "It was so good of Meredith to arrange a party."

"You know I can't stand birthdays. I cannot bear to count the passing years. Evelyn, it's for your sake I feel so unhappy tonight."

"Oh, Mother." I took her cold hand and squeezed it. "Don't be unhappy on my account."

"You have missed out on so much. I wish you'd marry."

She could have no idea how that night especially her lament touched a raw nerve. Springing to my feet, I said coldly: "On the other hand I have had a fascinating day, one such as few women, I think, have ever experienced. If I had a husband to care for and a clutch of babies I doubt if such a day would have been possible."

She put the album aside and turned on me with equal force, very pale but with a gleam in her eye that may have been due to the unaccustomed champagne. "I don't want to hear any more about your grubby life. You are willful and cruel because you insist on talking about work all the time, even though you know I can't bear it. You have abandoned me. My life is in ruins and you will not help me."

"What could I do to help, Mother?"

"You could be *here*. You could try to behave like a proper daughter. You could save me from having to deal with that terrible woman, day in, day out."

"I shall soon be earning money at least."

"I would sacrifice the money tomorrow if it meant I wouldn't be so alone."

"You have Prudence. You have Grandmother and the girls, and your bridge parties. Now you even have a grandchild, Edmund. You are better off than most when it comes to company."

"I didn't choose any of this. My life is nothing to what it used to be before the war. Can't you see? All this has been thrust upon me against my wishes. And all that I loved, all that I strived for has been torn from me. Oh, if only James had lived. Instead he ruined everything."

"What do you mean, he ruined everything? Mother, he was killed, he could hardly help that."

She shot me a strange look, half angry, half frightened, then seemed to recover a little. "Of course. What I mean is, I can't help it, Evelyn. I sometimes think you have taken his place—you have used his death to get what you want."

She had never voiced her resentment so explicitly before and I think we were both shocked. "Or perhaps I'm keeping something of him alive," I said shakily.

By way of an apology perhaps, she put out her hand and I pressed it reluctantly. Her lace sleeve came to a point on her knuckle and had tiny buttons along the cuff. When I was a child, it was considered one of my privileges to be called down to her bedroom to help with fastenings before she went out, but I was always sulky, because the task brought me up close to the side of her that was forever pulling away. Now she had allowed her hair to fall from its pins so that it was half tumbled down her back. From this angle, in this light, she might have been younger than me. For a moment, we watched each other, neither of us moving, neither of us able to break the silence. I felt dreary to my soul that this conversation, like so many others, had ended with us locked into positions of mutual disappointment, each incapable of being what the other wanted.

Sixteen

Leah Marchant's appeal was scheduled for a ten-thirty hearing on Friday morning, before Recorder Martin Hestlethwaite. I arrived early to find no sign of Thorne or indeed the defendant, Leah Marchant, who was of course to be brought by prison van. The wait was torture for me, because I would not listen to the voice of reason within my head: You sent Thorne the papers. He has the facts of the case and they're all he wants from you. Apart from that, you are nothing to him.

At ten precisely, Thorne strode in, immaculately turned out, ineffably calm, though perhaps a little warm after a brisk walk. Removing his hat, he ruffled his hair in a gesture I had come to anticipate. "How was the trip to the crime scene, Miss Gifford? I was so sorry not to see for myself. Perhaps I'll wander up there next week. Could you spare the time to show me, do you think?"

Was he seriously proposing so intimate an expedition as a walk in the Chesham fields? I said: "It's late. We should go down and see Leah Marchant at once. She should be here by now."

"Lead the way."

He followed so close that I distinctly felt his knee brush my skirt as we went downstairs. Fortunately, when we reached the cells, I had only to stand by and watch as the machine clicked into action for Leah Marchant's benefit. And there on display were all the tricks he'd used on me: the frank smile, the eyes suffused with sympathy, the hearty handshake, the inclination of the head as he commiserated with her on the appalling treatment she had received thus far at the hands of the judiciary. "I promise that I shall do my level best, Mrs. Marchant, to ensure that you will walk free this very morning."

Neither Leah nor I was required to speak. She, of course, was be-dazzled by the gloss of the man. To her, the authoritative voice, the tailored clothes, the scent of him must have been unutterably alien, and she behaved as though starstruck, whispering monosyllabic responses and never taking her eyes from his face. Thorne showed a detailed knowledge of the case, including the names and ages of her children, although he'd probably not read my notes until minutes previously. The interview ended in yet another prolonged handshake, and five minutes later I was seated behind him in court, mesmerized by the way the ties of his wig nestled at the back of his neck.

It was immediately obvious that Thorne and the recorder, Hestleth-waite, were more than nodding acquaintances. When introduced by the clerk, they acknowledged each other formally but an underlying famil-iarity was indicated by a flicker of the judge's eyelid. In the presence of Thorne and Hestlethwaite, the police prosecutor was apologetic. The events of the last hearing, he inferred, had been an aberration. Even though the police had felt there was considerable mitigation, events in court had persuaded the magistrate, in his wisdom, that only a custodial penalty would do.

Mrs. Marchant, who was again supported by her friend Mrs. Sand-ers, never took her adoring eyes from Thorne. A tear trickled down her left cheek. When allusion was made to her unfortunate attitude in court during the last hearing, Thorne glanced at her incredulously, as if strug-gling to understand how any judge could possibly have taken offense at such a sweet-natured woman.

He rose to his feet and it seemed to me that others in the courtroom held their breath at the unfolding of his great height. His delivery was restrained, that of a rational man barely having to exercise his wits in order to steady a minor wobble in the British justice system. "At any point, Your Honor, do stop me if you think I've gone far enough. I'm sure you will be as dismayed as I am that this case has come thus far and that the woman before you has now served weeks in prison. Your Honor, in the third decade of the twentieth century, I for one am appalled to find myself representing a mother cut off from her own children not for loving them too little but for loving them too much."

We emerged from the courtroom ten minutes later, with Leah's sentence remitted to six months' conditional discharge and a letter from Hestlethwaite instructing the matron of the Good Samaritan's Children's Home in Hammersmith to allow Mrs. Marchant an interview with her two oldest children at the earliest opportunity. In another five minutes, we all met in a private room, together with a *Daily Mail* reporter who made enthusiastic notes as Leah gabbled her gratitude to Thorne.

"Mrs. Marchant," I interrupted, and received a resentful glare. "I shall write to the home and accompany you there. The *Daily Mail* has very kindly agreed to fund your case until your children have been released to you."

"Can't Mr. Breen come with me or Mr. Thorne?"

"I am your legal representative."

"How does it feel, Mrs. Marchant, to be represented by one of our first lady lawyers?" asked the reporter wolfishly.

Leah chose not to answer but instead vowed that she would henceforth be working twenty hours a day in order to provide a decent home for her children.

"Don't make promises you can't keep," said Mrs. Sanders, who'd been talking to Thorne about landmarks near Toynbee Hall familiar to both. "I've only got the promise of ten hours' work a week for you so far."

Thorne sat on the table edge, arms folded, apparently enjoying the aftermath of the case. Was it fair of me to question his motives? Surely his interest in Mrs. Sanders was genuine rather than to make a point of displaying the egalitarian leanings acquired at Toynbee. When the two women were ready to go, he rose and bade farewell as if this had been a social event rather than an appeal.

Afterward, the empty room seemed strikingly intimate though the door stood ajar. While I packed my papers, he loosened his bands and ran his fingers across his scalp to release hair flattened by his wig. At last, I said stiffly, "Thank you, Mr. Thorne. You made that seem very easy."

"It's always easy when there has been an insane judgment such as the one passed on your Mrs. Marchant. I do have some faith that justice, or in this case plain common sense, will assert itself where necessary. You were treated unfairly at the last hearing. Miss Gifford, I have given you much thought since we met and believe me, I do understand the great mountain you have to climb. It's hard enough to get a toehold in this profession when one is male and has friends."

"The trouble is I must cut my teeth on real clients. It is they who suffer."

"Beginnings are always tricky and I cannot think of an institution more entrenched in its own traditions than the law, excepting of course the Roman Catholic Church. After all, both depend on tradition for validity, to some extent. I suspect that what you must come up against all the time is our collective resistance to change. I confess I'm guilty of that sin too, as you did not hesitate to point out when we last met."

"Why would anyone who loves justice resist change if it is necessary?"

"Ah, but you see my brothers-in-the-law don't see that change *is* necessary. They believe that we perform perfectly adequately without women. And of course you're a threat."

"But they should be interested in justice." The strain of exchanging ideas with a man whose image had haunted me night and day made me speak more harshly than I should. "Why do they want things to remain the same? Was the past so perfect? Was it fair?"

"Steady on, Miss Gifford. I wasn't trying to defend the past, merely explain the present."

"Isn't it convenient that you are able to dismiss the past instead of admitting that it perhaps doesn't bear scrutiny?" I said.

"To which particular aspect of the past are you alluding, Miss Gifford? I do feel it's always safer to deal in specifics."

"I'm surprised you have to ask. Is there an adult alive who could look back over the last decade with any degree of gratification?"

Too late I saw the conversation hurtle away from me and only afterward did I have time to analyze the real cause of my anger. While the argument was actually taking place, I blamed my loss of bearings on Thorne's insufferable self-satisfaction. Later, I realized that his reference to our tea together, his acknowledgment of a connection that I had tried to convince myself meant nothing to him, had thrown me entirely off balance.

He was no longer smiling. "It seems to me, Miss Gifford, that you are perfectly right in holding my unfortunate sex largely responsible for the war and all that followed. But surely you weaken your case by seeing us as a collective. By herding us together you remove responsibility from each one of us. I like to consider my sex and yours as comprising individuals, each of whom has free will."

"Generally, I think you'll agree, women have not been seen by lawmakers or society as individuals. We women are always banded together as the weaker sex, if we are allowed to have a characteristic at all."

"So you're a suffragist, Miss Gifford?"

"Don't categorize me. I don't want to be put into a box any more than you do. I too want to be seen as a human being."

We stood, one on either side of the table, as if the air had developed a viscosity that trapped us. I would not be the one to look away. It seemed to me that his eyes had a different light in them today, a spread light, like a candle behind glass. I think, for a moment, my body actually inclined toward his before I came to my senses. "If you will excuse me, I have a luncheon appointment."

"Perhaps we are walking the same way."

"I shall be taking an omnibus."

"You are still angry with me. I have done nothing to convince you that I am on your side."

"It ought not to be a question of sides. It ought to be a matter of justice. Good day, Mr. Thorne."

Then he did something very odd: reached out as if to push the door open wider for me but instead raised his hand to cover his eyes. As I passed him, he said: "Miss Gifford, I wish you well, I really do. But forgive me for saying that I also wish with all my heart I had never clapped eyes on you."

☙

How I caught the right omnibus bound for Holborn or found the correct change I have no idea. When the conductor moved away, I sat with closed eyes, all other senses stifled by the stench of diesel while the earth recovered its equilibrium and I my wits. His last words repeated in my mind, over and over.

I met other women lawyers every couple of months or so, at the Law Society, where we ordered lunch, made a point of lingering over coffee, and entered the date of our next rendezvous in our diaries before leaving. There were many cheaper and nicer places to go, but one of our unspoken motives was to assert our right to use the building now that we were members and had forced the issue of *facilities*, so that a ladies' cloakroom had been installed for us, at vast expense (they said), in what had formerly been a coalhole in the basement. We considered it our duty to make our presence felt where we could (we were not admitted to the reading room), in case anyone forgot us or thought we would fade away.

Usually I anticipated these meetings with a passionate sense of pride that here we were, the groundbreakers, still going strong four years after we first gained access to the society, still full of verve and hope. As I climbed the steps between grandiose white pillars, I thought I knew how Grandmother must have felt when she made her entrance on stage, into the limelight.

When I met with Carrie and the rest, we were so relieved that now, after weeks of maintaining an air of unassailable determination in our daily work amid male colleagues, we could let down our guard and vent our feelings, there was always a little verbal jostling as to who should go first. But on the whole, we listened attentively, rejoiced in each other's triumphs, and offered advice and commiseration over setbacks. Rivalries that had surfaced in the battle to find work were now suppressed by our joint resolve to overcome the iniquities of the professional world. United, we presented a much more formidable front against the pin-striped brigade, who rustled their newspapers and lowered their voices when we were near.

But that Friday, as I nodded to the porter, I felt apprehensive at the prospect of meeting my friends. There they were, assembled under a portrait of Edward Leigh-Pemberton, president in the mid–nineteenth century and therefore spared the horrors of dealing with women law-yers, four ladies in dark colors and last summer's hats, their voices light and fluid in that austere setting, full of news and opinions. Last time we had discussed whether our newly formed association of women solici-tors had played into the hands of the male establishment by setting us apart, and the debate was scheduled to continue today, but I had such little appetite for the discussion that I almost turned tail. I couldn't imagine that any of them would understand how I felt and I expected no sympathy, because I thought I had betrayed them by falling in love.

Carrie greeted me with her customary appraising stare, then, before I had time to shake hands or draw up a chair, cried: "Evelyn, I saw you. I *saw* you last week at Toynbee Hall. You came late for the concert and at the end I tried to fight my way over to you but you'd gone."

To hide the sudden heat in my face, I ducked my head and began unbuttoning my jacket. "I shouldn't have been at Toynbee in the first place. I was due back in the office, but I was passing that way and couldn't resist the music. Afterward, I had to dash."

"It was a wonderful concert, one of the best we've put on, I think. But surely you must have known I'd be there. Why didn't you look out for me?"

"I was so hot. I . . ."

"Well, not to worry. We've been talking about Toynbee, actually. They're giving me more work. I intend to specialize in family law. I don't mind what comes my way really but it seems a good field to choose because so little is being done to improve the rights of married women. It's not fashionable or lucrative but it matters."

I settled deeper into my armchair, pretended to follow the conversation, and even managed to order a bowl of soup. In this company, it was quite acceptable to acknowledge that one was short of money. And then Carrie suddenly embarked on a subject that was entirely pertinent to me and therefore set my nerves jangling again: she too was in love, though, Carrie being Carrie, her love was straightforward. She was engaged to a solicitor, who, according to her, was as radical and ambitious as she. Of course she loved him unequivocally and of course her love was reciprocated. Such was her confidence, none of us dared suggest that marriage may prove detrimental to her career or that engagement to a successful lawyer might be seen as compromising our ideal of achieving success and recognition by our own merits. Her good fortune in finding not only a healthy man but one in sympathy with her ambitions was so extraordinary that we felt awe rather than jealousy.

Which made my own pathetic state all the more absurd. There was no question of my confiding in these women. So you've fallen in love too, they'd say incredulously. It must be catching all of a sudden. Who is he?

And some of them, on hearing the name Nicholas Thorne, would be even more disbelieving. But he's already engaged to be married. He's bound to be a silk one day. What are you thinking of?

In any case, their conversation had moved from the subject of love to the more pressing one of money. Our current rates of pay, those of us who received any fees at all, were untenable. Why should we be paid so much less than our male colleagues for doing the same work, usually in half the time? Maud, the most committed suffragist among us, was so vexed by the question that she had canvassed her MP and brought it up at a political rally. "It's the only way. We have to make our presence felt with every element in society but especially those in public office. We have to keep challenging the norm or they'll think they can get away with it. They pay us pin money in the expectation that we'll be grateful for anything, as indeed I'm afraid we are."

"There isn't time to fight battles on too many fronts," said Carrie. "My own feeling is that we should concentrate on the law. We have to prove ourselves as lawyers and we don't want our cause to be tainted by association with shrill women who are simply looking for a cause, any cause."

I was thinking: What if Carrie had reached me that day in Toynbee after the concert and insisted I took tea with her? What if there'd been no rush along the hot pavement, no Thorne carrying my briefcase, no argument in the tea shop? What if I'd not seen him between the day of Leah's first court appearance, when he touched my arm and gave unwanted advice, and Stephen Wheeler's bail hearing in Chesham this week? Perhaps his impact would have faded in the intervening days, leaving the faintest scorch mark instead of an indelible scar. As it was, the image of him flared in my mind and every word and glance we'd exchanged made him more ineradicable. It was too late.

Carrie said: "Once we have an expertise in a certain field of the law we are uncrushable, because we are needed. If we're too generalist, we are dispensable. I said to Ambrose . . ."

Nonsense, I told myself, you're not in love. How would you know what being in love is? It's so long since you felt anything for any man that you think the faintest spark of interest, a raising of the pulse, is being in love. You don't even know Thorne.

So I set the thought of him aside and heard myself talk quite calmly about the Wheeler case (which they'd read of in the newspapers), the fact that we had our own line of inquiry, and that I was to visit Stella's house on Monday. Then we discussed Leah Marchant's predicament, and Carrie had much to say concerning the iniquities of a law that would probably ensure that Leah never recovered her children. "You do realize how much money she'll need before they are released. Each day they're in the home will cost her more, because in order to get them back she'll have to recompense the charity for their board and lodging. And then she'll have to show that she can provide for their moral and financial needs. I mean, the authorities might conclude that the children are indeed better off in an institution, have you thought of that?"

"I've never seen Leah Marchant with her children or visited the Good Samaritan's Home so cannot make a judgment. But given she surrendered them voluntarily in the first place, this all seems very unjust."

"She will have been told the rules when she placed them in the home but been so desperate to get away that she won't have listened. How could a woman, forced to surrender her children, think rationally? Did she sign a document? Can she read? But you should visit the home. It's possible you might be pleasantly surprised. Is it one which sends children to the colonies?"

"What do you mean?"

"One thing you'll need to check is where the home stands on child migration. I don't expect you want the children mixed up in that."

"I don't understand."

"Surely you know that this country ships masses of children to the colonies every year, particularly Canada and Australia. It's government policy, has been for years, to support charities in sending unwanted children overseas to underpopulated outposts of the empire. After all, there are hundreds of perfectly good homes for them out there, people crying out to adopt a child."

Maud said: "For some, that must surely be an excellent solution. I heard of a boy who was given his own land in Canada and is now a prosperous farmer."

"Yes, but I also know critics of the scheme. Some of the children they send abroad are very young. And I don't know what checks are made, once they're out there."

"But what has this to do with the Marchant children?" I asked. "You are surely talking about a scheme for orphans. The Marchant children have one if not two parents."

"I'm just warning you to be vigilant. At Toynbee all kinds of things come to light. I've dealt with the case of a woman who recently married a good man, prepared to take in the child she'd been forced to give up because it was conceived when she was sixteen and turned out by her family. But when they made inquiries they were told the child had been adopted and was enjoying a comfortable life with a well-to-do family in the West Country. I've written numerous letters but the only response from the charity is that they feel it's important for the child not to be contacted by its natural parents at this late stage. That mother is adamant she never agreed to the child being adopted and the charity is refusing to show me the papers they say she signed. If it's all aboveboard, why the secrecy, is what I want to know? The only way forward might be to take the home to court, bring it all out in the open, let them prove they went through a due process and that your client's children are indeed still in this country."

"Where else could they be?"

"Where indeed? It seems to me that charities are overzealous in having children 'adopted' and coy about admitting what form these adoptions take. If these Marchant children are healthy and personable, they would be considered ideal candidates for Canada. It's such a cheap, neat option."

Before I left, I arranged to call on Carrie in her offices to look at papers she had collected on the welfare of children taken into care. But I was cursing myself for not consulting her earlier. If only I hadn't been distracted by Thorne that day at Toynbee I would have acted with greater urgency. Carrie had pulled me so firmly back into line that the turmoil of the morning now seemed an aberration. My vocation was clear: to rescue the Marchant children from the abyss into which they appeared to have fallen.

Seventeen

On Monday, I visited *Stella Wheeler's childhood home*, 83 Manchester Street, in a grid of mid-Victorian terraces off Horn Lane in Acton. The house was substantial compared to Stella's and set back a few feet from the street, behind a low front wall shielding a diminutive garden with a rose bush in the center and borders crammed with lobelia.

The front step was swept, the door had recently been washed, and the hall smelled of baking. Mrs. Hobhouse greeted me with the words "I've been cooking for the funeral. They say the body will be released early next week. Of course for now I can only do things that will keep. Dundee cake." She showed me into the front parlor, which was stuffy with underuse and into which had been crammed a collection of oversized furniture presumably passed down from previous generations. Mrs. Hobhouse's housekeeping, unlike her daughter's, was decidedly up to scratch. Even the fire irons, I noted, had been dusted, and the antimacassars were newly starched.

"I'll fetch the tea," she said. "Will you be all right in here for a moment?"

The parlor spoke volumes for Mrs. Hobhouse's respect for good-quality old things, coupled with a love of what was new and fashionable. The sideboard, for instance, was Victorian oak, but on it was arranged a modern tea service with a stylishly inconvenient pot—probably a bad pourer—patterned in orange and green. In the middle of the mantel was a black-and-white vase with Egyptian figures and at either end were framed wedding photographs, one for each of the Hobhouse girls.

Julie's was on the left. Her unfortunate groom, Michael, had an awkward posture, and even in that formal pose his bride, in an ethereal lace frock, looked impatient as she held herself rigid while supporting him on her arm.

In the other, identically framed photograph, I at last met the younger daughter, Stella, as she stood beside her new husband, Stephen Wheeler, in a church doorway. One glance confirmed my belief that the Wheeler marriage had been a mismatch. Stephen's feet were planted too far apart, his shoulders rounded, teeth showing through his beard, a trilby clutched to his soft belly with one hand, the other on his new wife's slender hip. She had a girlish form and was evidently well aware of her own beauty; her posture and restrained smile suggested that she was holding herself carefully, as if she were modeling her clothes rather than participating in a wedding. She wore her hair in a dainty bob, and her headdress had two small earpieces with artificial flowers clasping the veil on either side of her forehead. Her face had the regular beauty of a line illustration in a women's magazine, though her nose was perhaps just a little too broad. Her eyes, like her sister's, were wide-set, but she had a prettier mouth and was altogether much finer-featured than Julie. Though her frock had a demurely square neckline, there was a heaviness in her eyelids that was somehow affiliated to Wheeler's hand on her hip, bunching the fabric of her skirt. A little bouquet of lilies was clasped to her breast.

"I can hardly bear to look at that," said Mrs. Hobhouse, who had brought a tray of tea.

"When was the date of the wedding?"

"April 26. They'd not been wed three weeks when she . . ." Tea was poured and I was provided with napkin, plate, knife, and rock bun, but it was clear, despite this hospitality, that Mrs. Hobhouse was not comfortable with my visit. She treated me with reserve and once or twice gave me a slightly hostile glance. The house, save for the ticking of a clock, was silent and I thought of the hours she must spend alone in it now that her daughters were gone.

"You must be wondering why I'm here, exactly," I said. "Forgive me if it seems intrusive but I wanted to see Stella's room, just in case there was anything the police had missed, anything that might give us a clue as to why she died."

"Do you think I haven't been through that a thousand times? There's nothing in her room, I can tell you. I can't help thinking, Miss Gifford, that it's *his* things you should be looking at, not hers. He's the one who did it."

"I understand how you must be feeling and I'm sorry. I won't stay, if you'd rather I didn't. It's just that the police are so sure of Stephen's guilt that they are going to set an early trial date. Just supposing Stephen isn't the right man, supposing it was someone else."

"But it was his gun."

"Mrs. Hobhouse, there's no motive. And it's just possible someone could have used Stephen's gun. Anyone could have got into the back-yard. The shed wasn't locked."

She was momentarily startled by this idea, then slumped back in a gesture of total exhaustion. With her mouth slack and her eyes closed, her face aged twenty years. "I've thought this through. In my view there's no doubt Stephen did it. He wasn't right in the head, I can see that now, and I reproach myself for not taking more notice before. Our Stell was scared about staying too long when she came here that last time lest she wasn't home when he got back."

"What was she afraid of, exactly? Did he lose his temper with her, do you think?"

"She never gave me details. I think he could be unpleasant, you know, go silent. I don't think he hurt her, if that's what you're getting at.

But even when they were engaged the fact he kept such a close eye on her caused friction between them. His jealousy would have provoked her into being difficult."

"Can you explain what you mean by difficult?"

"Sulky. She was always a bit of a sulker. And I expect if he asked her questions she didn't like, she wouldn't give him straight answers on principle."

"But do you think, aside from that, she ever gave him cause to be jealous?"

"You're talking about the dancing that Julie was going on about. He didn't really mind that. But you see this terrible thing has happened and what's on my mind is that Stella may have played up deliberately, not realizing that he was far more dangerous in one of his moods than any of us realized, and what he might do to her in the end."

She led me upstairs to Stella's bedroom in the back of the house, overlooking a symmetrical garden with vegetables and berry bushes. The room smelled of clean bed linen and the fruitcake baking below. There was a narrow bed against one wall, a space where a dressing table had once stood—the rug was dented with castor marks and there was a pale oval patch on the wallpaper—a wardrobe and a chest of drawers. The only incongruous item was a dressmaker's dummy with a half-made black skirt pinned to its waist. The surfaces were painfully bare.

"I miss her terribly," said Mrs. Hobhouse. "The last time my Stell slept here, it was the night before her wedding."

"Do you mind me opening the drawers?"

"Do what you like. The police have been through anyway. I don't feel anything's private anymore. But you won't find anything."

I recognized the room's appalling sense of abandonment. Everything in it, so familiar to Stella, was disconnected and cheapened without her. I opened a few drawers but the contents were so sorrowful that I closed them hastily; clothes too unloved to be moved to the bride's new home, a child's prayer book, a doll with a celluloid face and a wonky eye, and a waitress's uniform cap and apron, presumably left over from Lyons.

"In the top of the wardrobe are some wooden bricks and such I was keeping for grandchildren," said Mrs. Hobhouse.

I held an irrational belief that whatever I was looking for would never be found while Stella's mother was present. In the end, I asked if she could perhaps find me paper and pencil, since I had foolishly forgotten my own. This did the trick; she backed away and left me. Very softly, so as not to offend Mrs. Hobhouse, I closed the door and something swung against me, a cotton robe with frilled edging and a faded design of roses. With some reluctance, I brought the cuff to my face. The fabric smelled of the room and very faintly of a sweet perfume I remembered from Stella's wardrobe in her new house. The pockets were empty.

Other than that, the room at first yielded no secrets. The rails at either end of the bed could have done with a fresh coat of paint, and I imagined Stella's damp stockings hung there to dry overnight. In the narrow wardrobe was a child's woolen coat with a velvet collar and on the shelf above a sun hat and the collection of toys in battered cardboard boxes.

I shut the wardrobe door and looked into the mirror. On the eve of her wedding, Stella would surely have tried on her dress one last time and paraded here, turned sideways to examine her profile, contorted herself to get a glimpse of the back view. She must have sat on the bed, crossing and recrossing her legs to inspect her ankles in the glass that now reflected only my pale face, framed by the dark rim of my hat. I hoped Stella had enjoyed her dancing days while she had the chance.

የ

I used to be invited to parties even before Meredith arrived to shake us all up, though generally I didn't go; experience had taught me that church socials and gatherings organized by former school friends, now married, would unfailingly disappoint. But I remembered a time, before the war, when I had sat thus before a mirror and lifted the hair from my neck because I was nearly an adult and had acquired a slender throat and a rather intriguing set of curves between chin, breast, waist, and hip. I remembered, on the evening of a party, believing that I was on the verge of everything and that life was a precipice over which I longed to fling myself.

And today, gripping the edge of Stella Wheeler's mattress, I felt the same as during the concert at Toynbee Hall. Love, love was what I wanted. I saw reflected a thirty-year-old virgin with creases on her brow and a frown between the eyes, and recalled the hopeful girl who had attended lots of parties until at last she got herself kissed under the canal bridge. The ghost of the murdered Stella Wheeler clung to the robe hanging on the back of the door and whispered: You could have had more. You had the chance to find out more and you didn't take it. Well, more fool you.

The man in question was of such a high rank that I had to fall back against the wall when he passed me in the corridor. We women were mostly employed in the bone-cold rooms of the censorship office crammed so close that our elbows collided. Our days were spent dipping our pens in black ink and scrubbing out dates, times, and places from the back of a hundred thousand postcards. After my brother's death, I worked like an automaton, because it seemed to me that every postcard must in any case be from a dead boy, the last product of his pen a spattering of unoriginal words many of which I ruthlessly crossed out. Sometimes I was tempted to stuff a sackful under my blouse and burn them, to spare the families the hope, on seeing his handwriting, that a beloved boy was alive.

We all assumed that any other woman in the building not engaged in the censorship office must be doing something much more interesting. There were some locked rooms we didn't go near, because the work that was done inside was of such high security that only the cleverest women who could also type or knew languages were admitted there. So finally I persuaded my father to bring a typewriter home from his office and in the small hours taught myself to touch-type (amid complaints from the girls, who slept in the rooms above mine, that the hammering was keeping them awake) and successfully applied for a transfer to a much snugger office, where I typed up decoded messages about the movements of German troops. Nobody ever discussed the information we passed on, but among us there was a warm and unspoken camaraderie, founded on pride.

One officer, a colonel, noticed me and I sensed that when he entered the room he sought me out and took pleasure in seeing me there. He was quietly spoken, reserved, and had been injured in the left arm. The spring and summer following my brother's death felt cold and I was cocooned in layers of wool and grief, so the world held few connections for me except the keys of my typewriter. This unassuming man, though, occasionally caught my eye and smiled.

A few weeks before the armistice, there was a party after work to celebrate a birthday. As I was leaving, the officer approached me with a stunningly straightforward invitation. "It's Miss Gifford, isn't it? Would you have dinner with me tonight?"

It must have cost him dear to ask. I knew that he was married, with a family in Dorset, and I suspected he was not a habitual philanderer and that this was a rare and uncharacteristic venture for him. So I agreed at once, touched by his interest, flattered, and too numbed by grief to know what my true feelings were anymore.

The streets were wet and a light drizzle was falling. He was gentlemanly, shielding me from the traffic and adjusting his pace to mine. Dinner was in a discreet restaurant, subterranean, with tables pushed into little alcoves so that we were more or less alone, and it occurred to me, when I realized the intimacy of the place, that he was perhaps more accustomed to clandestine suppers with ladies than I had imagined. I made a safe choice from the menu and thought that Rose could have managed a much better leek-and-potato soup than this. He drank several glasses of wine to my one as he talked about the first year of the war, when he'd seen active service at Aisne and Ypres where his arm had been wounded. He considered himself much better suited to intelligence work than combat. "I'm indecisive, a poor quality for a military officer but in many ways an excellent one for someone working in intelligence. I can be relied on not to do anything rash. It has taken me three months to get around to inviting you to dinner even though you are the most attractive woman I have seen for a long time. Ah, you look surprised, which I suspect is typical of you. You seem to me quite unaware of your own power."

Smiling, he lowered his eyelids as if pursuing a private thought, and I knew that he would want to make love to me, and that I would let him. I was curious, after all, and found him intriguing, even though he seemed not to find any incongruity in talking about his wife, who bred dogs, or his three sons, two of whom, thank God, were too young to serve, one out in France. I was required to disclose nothing about myself.

He had a quiet apartment near the restaurant, full of beautiful pieces of porcelain and glass. "I'm a collector," he told me. "Even in France I found time to seek out bits and pieces. I can't resist them"—and he gave me a globe of hollowed-out glass that filled my hand with crimson.

I never could stand the truth of color. At that moment, I wished he had been less kind, less tentative, because now that I liked him more I wanted him to make love to me less. I couldn't imagine how it would come to pass that we would remove our clothes and lie on his bed.

He took the bowl from me and put it down. "You have beautiful hands," he said, "it was the first thing I noticed about you. But I have some advice. After the war, never let on you can type unless you have no other choice. I think you are much too clever a woman to spend your life typing up other people's letters."

I smiled cautiously. He was holding my elbow as he looked down at my hand and I made out the shape of his skull under his thinning hair. His thumb moved from my arm and instead stroked my breast. The trouble was, in the end, that I was quite incapable of losing myself in his touch and therefore could not stand the thought of the mechanical act ahead. He was too polite, I too indifferent.

I took a step back and withdrew my arm. "I'll go now," I said.

His face closed up and the corner of his lip, under the mustache, tightened. In the neat spaces of his apartment, my own movements were calm as I collected my gloves and bag from the hall and let myself out. But during the long walk home, I cursed myself, not for accepting his invitation to dinner but for failing to take the opportunity that had been offered.

⁂

I glanced again into Stella's mirror and it was then that I saw her, almost concealed from view behind books on a shelf above the bed, with just a foot extended past a copy of *Little Women*. Pushing aside the book, I discovered a statuette, so small that it would almost have been covered by my fist, of a naked girl connected to a plinth by one tiny foot, running, hair flying back, hands raised above her head, small-breasted, every detail distinct, even the fuzz of pubic hair and her little toes. I knew practically nothing of art, less about sculpture. All I knew was that this little bronze, suggestive but exquisite, was entirely out of place in a bedroom where no other item had cost more than a guinea.

When Mrs. Hobhouse returned, we made an inventory, beginning with the dressmaker's dummy (modeling her half-made dress for Stella's funeral), the robe behind the door, and the bed, and continuing with the contents of the wardrobe and drawers. We even took out the box of toys, noted the farm animals, and counted the bricks. In a further battered box was a collection of dollhouse furniture, roughly made but with working doors and drawers. "My husband used to make it for her. She loved small things when she was a child," said Mrs. Hobhouse, beginning to weep.

I opened each miniature drawer. Inside were trinkets, a windmill from a charm bracelet, a tiny shell, and an odd assortment of dried-up things such as one might find on a nature table in school: an acorn in its cup, a sycamore key, and a conker case.

"Funny girl," said Mrs. Hobhouse, "she will have kept those for her dolls." I didn't contradict her, but the chestnut case, though discolored, was quite soft and its smell too distinctive to be anything but last season's.

Last of all, I went to the bookcase and took down the bronze dancer. "Oh, that," said Mrs. Hobhouse. "I didn't know she kept that here."

"Where did it come from?"

"She bought it herself. I hate the thing."

"Mrs. Hobhouse, might I borrow it, if I take great care of it?"

"Whatever for?"

"I want to show it to Mr. Breen. It seems rather unusual to me."

Her eyes were fixed on the statue and I realized that it was asking a great deal, to take away something of Stella's. "I'll write you out a receipt," I said. "I won't keep it long."

Afterward, she followed me downstairs. "Well, that was a waste of your time. I'm sorry."

"Not wasted," I said, "I wanted to know more about Stella and now I do."

"Such as what? What do you know?"

"Why, that she was much loved, Mrs. Hobhouse."

Perhaps it was this last remark that made her trust me finally, because as I left, she put her hand on my arm. "I'm worried that there won't be hardly anyone at the funeral. Will you be there?"

Eighteen

O*n the night of the art party,* I had agreed to attend the first half
of the concert at St. Mark's, though such an arrangement was in
direct defiance of Prudence's maxim that a task done halfheartedly is
best not done at all. Next day, I was to visit the Good Samaritan's Children's Home with Leah Marchant, so I worked late in preparation and
went straight to the church. The approach to the hall was through an
overcrowded graveyard and into a dim little lobby, where Mrs. Gillespie
sat at a trestle table upon which were displayed a small pile of handwritten programs and a wooden bowl of change. A brown envelope had
been left for me, inscribed with the information that Miss Prudence
Gifford had reserved a ticket for Miss Evelyn Gifford but that the ticket
was so far not paid for. Admission to the concert cost one and sixpence
(program and refreshments included), all proceeds to the Church Bell
Restoration Fund.

It required extraordinary willpower to cross the threshold from the
golden light of a mellow June evening and enter the gloomy hall with
its smell of bare feet (an expressive-dance class was held on Thursday
afternoons) and floor polish. There I was confronted by a dozen or so
ladies in second-best hats, and a handful of gentlemen, spread out across
five rows, the choir assembled at the front in their frilled white blouses,
and Mother twisting around on the lookout for me.

As I edged my way into the vacant seat beside her, she murmured in a low voice reserved for the interior of ecclesiastical buildings: "You're not still intending to go to this wretched party, are you? *She's* turned the house upside down. She intends to wear *trousers*, did you know? I doubt if we shall ever get the boy to sleep while you're both out."

Mother's breath smelled of tea and huffed the veil she had worn since James's death, its black spots a dreadful plague on her skin. As the choir launched into "An English Country Garden," I found myself longing to be at home with Meredith. At this moment, Edmund would be perched on her bed, offering advice while she dressed. The art party had turned out (horror of horrors) to be fancy dress, on the theme of the sea, and Edmund had revealed a disturbing (Prudence's word) aptitude for rifling through Grandmother's chests of old clothes and producing just the right garment. "However," Prudence had added, "I think you should be more graceful about the party, Evelyn. After all, you might meet some proper artists there." Now that she had been to the Tate and was in possession of a scrap of painted linen from Guiana, she considered that she had a toe in the modern-art world and was therefore licensed to criticize those of us reluctant to engage with it.

Perhaps it was the experience of having been recently in Stella's bedroom or even the witchery of the bronze dancer, but I wanted urgently to be with Meredith and Edmund, decked out in my summer frock and the sheath of blue satin that was to transform me into a sea nymph. I wanted to pick Edmund up in my arms and bury my face in his neck while I tickled him, a new ritual we had.

The choir had now, with more courage than competence, launched into a Gabrieli madrigal. Midsong, I whispered to Mother: "I'm sorry, I have to go . . . I don't want to be late . . ." and then, surprising even myself, I clambered past three pairs of unyielding knees. The doors had been left open and beyond the porch was the tiled path leading to the gate, the grasses and yew tree bathed in slanting sunlight, and the head of an angel with long stone tresses hanging over the grave of a child.

࿐

Before we left for the party, I showed Meredith the bronze dancer, fearful that, out of the context of Stella's bedroom, the statue might seem less exceptional, but she stood on my palm as exquisite as before, light pooling in the hollow of her throat.

"My, my," said Meredith. "Where did you find this?" She took the dancer to the windowsill, where its soft curves and strong legs darkly glowed against the muslin curtains.

"Do you think she's valuable? She belonged to the dead girl, Stella Wheeler."

"Did she now?" Meredith put her hand to her mouth. "So Stella held her too. Doesn't that just bring us so close to a murder victim?"

"What do you think?"

"I think she's lovely and probably worth a small fortune. She's quite modern, I'd say, I swear I saw something like her in a gallery in Toronto."

I persuaded Meredith that we should travel to Kew by bus, since we had hired a cab for the return journey, which was likely to be very costly. We attracted considerable attention from other passengers, given that she was indeed wearing green trousers under a diaphanous tunic, a costume adapted from Titania's, found by Edmund in one of Grandmother's boxes. He had suggested that to look more nymphlike, I should tie my hair loosely with a blue ribbon; I thanked God that Mother and Prudence were safely interred in the church hall and had not witnessed me leaving the house.

Our hostess, Lady Jane Carr (no mention was made of a husband), owned a low, redbrick villa backing onto the river, and as we approached,

we heard jazz, perhaps being played in the back garden. The front door
was opened by a bored-looking woman holding a cocktail glass and wearing a clicking necklace made of wooden fishes. She neither took our
names nor introduced herself to us. Instead she drifted upward, weaving
her way between a mermaid and an octopus who drank beer directly from
the bottle.

The first-floor drawing room ran the width of the house with a door
at each end and a row of windows reaching floor to ceiling and overlooking the garden, where people were dancing wildly to the jazz band.
Meanwhile, in the drawing room, which was decked out with balloons
and streamers, a man and a woman sat in one corner, he playing the
guitar, she the banjo, both severely dressed and intently watching each
other's fingers, so that to see the jazz dancers below in their flashing
colors and to hear the passionately rhythmic music in this room was to
be in a dreamlike state of dissonance.

Guests had arranged themselves about the furniture, and a group of
devotees hung over the musicians with rapt expressions. Some were in
extravagant costumes, others simply wore a symbolic badge or sash, but
there were too many colors, the blues and greens confused me, what
with the dizzying music and the women's painted faces. Too often lately
I had found myself in situations where I didn't know myself, and now
here I was in the midst of the bohemian set, my companion the unreliable Meredith, who was utterly transfixed by the party and stood beside
me wide-eyed and speechless. Then, seizing a couple of cocktail glasses
from a tray held by a waiter dressed as a sailor, she thrust one into my
hand. "Hadley said there'd be absinthe. Maybe later."

Apparently, nobody here knew the Clivedon Hall Gardens rules of
behavior. They dressed differently, talked differently, touched each other
differently. I couldn't categorize them socially or work out how much
money they had. I even grew sentimental about my mother, who in her
heyday had been an expert hostess, and on seeing strangers would surge

up to them with a string of pleasantries designed to make them feel they were *very* special to her, and a proposal to introduce them to people they would *absolutely* adore.

There was no sign of Meredith's teacher Hadley Waters or of the promised Augustus John (surely one would recognize him), and as far as I could tell from snippets of conversation, not a single person was talking about art. However, after another few sips of whatever was in the glass, my perceptions changed and I liked the room and the people in it a little better. The house was indeed a work of art, so that the walls themselves had been treated as canvases and were covered by primitive, two-dimensional paintings of furniture and even a painted window with a painted woman's face, thick-nosed and heavy-browed, like the banjo player's, peering in. Along the door frames were drooping tendrils of painted ivy.

Meredith cried: "How marvelous. Do you think your mother would mind if I decorated my bedroom like this? Only joking, really. Hadley hasn't taught us how to draw flowers yet. But let's go outside and find him and the others. There's *no one* in here."

We went down, stepping over the loungers on the stairs. A passage led through the house to a glass door opening onto the garden. There was no sunlight left, and cool air was blowing from the river so that some women had picked up blankets from the grass and draped them around their shoulders. "Look," said Meredith, "over there, I think *he's* famous." She pointed to a man who could certainly be someone. "Epstein or Kramer, I can't decide which."

The band, which had been resting, was tuning up in its arbor, and there were shrieks of laughter as a girl in a fringed skirt tried to blow into a trumpet. A sad-looking, long-faced woman with hair cut at right angles, dressed in masses of blue drapery and smoking a black cigarette in a jet holder, moved apart from a nearby group and introduced herself as Jane Carr, our hostess, and were we having a lovely party? Did we know Carrington and dear Ralph, who had promised to call if they happened to be in town . . . ? Almost at the same moment Meredith was greeted by a thin man in a pirate's outfit complete with red head scarf, gold earring, cardboard dagger, and eye patch. Hadley Waters.

"But Hadley," exclaimed Lady Carr, "you will never convince me that you are *dangerous*."

Hadley, who was willowy-framed and long-haired, had two women in tow. The first I recognized as the model in Meredith's picture of a nude; there was no mistaking those harelike eyes and protruding teeth or even the droop of her unbound breasts under the fabric of a clinging jersey dressing gown, which she wore over a knitted bathing costume. "You'll know Margot," Hadley said, and she and Meredith kissed extravagantly, "and this is another regular at my Tuesday class, Sylvia Hardynge."

The other woman held out a cool white hand first to Meredith, then me. I managed to meet her eyes, which were remarkable, dark gray and with an alluring internal sparkle, and I even smiled, but it was as if sound and movement had been sucked violently from the party and there was just this other woman and me, and somewhere else, waiting inevitably to reveal himself, Nicholas Thorne.

Sylvia's beauty was such that it was hard to look away. Her abundant black hair fell in tendrils and she was draped in some kind of white Grecian robe, which she said was an attempt at Artargatis, sea goddess. She wore her clothes carelessly, but the gown revealed the pearly skin of her shoulders and breast and the perfect lines of her long body. Even as something in me died at meeting this lovely creature, I registered that her laughter at her own incompetence with the paintbrush was infectious and her voice had a pleasing, slightly sardonic confidence. Then I saw that she wore a sapphire ring on the third finger of her left hand.

"I believe I know your fiancé," I said.

"Oh?" Her lovely eyes widened.

"I work for a firm of solicitors. I met him, Mr. Thorne, in connection with a murder inquiry."

She was enthralled. "He mentioned you. Said he'd been upbraided by a woman lawyer for being too old-fashioned and stick-in-the-mud. Good for you. I'm delighted to meet you. Anyone who pulls my Nicholas down a peg or two . . ."

"What about you?" I asked. "Have you an interest in the law?"

She didn't quite like the question. "I have no intention of studying the law, if that's what you mean. Daddy's not keen on women having careers as such. But I am getting myself embroiled in politics. Daddy's standing for Parliament at the next election. I have a feeling that might turn out to be my thing too."

"Do you go to political meetings?" cried Meredith. "Could I join you? I keep meaning to go but haven't yet."

"But would you be in my party?" And there, again, was that throaty laugh. "I'm with Tom Mosley. I follow him slavishly, from right to left. Daddy's appalled, but there it is."

"How could I know which party to be in, until I tried them all?"

"'Somebody Stole my Gal,'" said Hadley, cocking his ear to the band. "Shall we dance? Do let's," and he led his harem of three aspiring artists onto the dance floor, which was a platform of wooden boards set up on the grass. I hung back and, as soon as they'd forgotten me, went on and on, retreating until I was among trees.

Lanterns had been strung across the dance floor so that light reflected in the sequins and rhinestones on dresses and headbands. Some of the frantically dancing couples leaped onto the grass and kicked off their shoes. The band played faster and faster and Sylvia Hardynge threw back her head so that her long white throat gleamed. She was laughing down at little Meredith.

He would come. There was no escaping the pain. I wanted Nicholas and Sylvia to meet so that I might watch them together from this safe distance and lay to rest the ghost of my own nonexistent love affair. And there, sure enough, was Nicholas, a latecomer in boater and blazer, kissing Lady Carr on both cheeks then standing with folded arms beside her and surveying the garden in the uneven light from the lanterns and an extraordinary crescent moon, which had, in the last few minutes, risen above the river, with the old moon burdening its lap like a fat, round cushion.

I merged myself deeper with the trees. The pain was such that I rubbed the old wound in my cheek against a trunk in an effort to divert sensation elsewhere than my heart. And at that moment, I saw Sylvia detach herself from Hadley Waters's flailing embrace and spring off the dance floor toward Nicholas. Seizing his arm, she raised herself on tiptoe and kissed his cheek and lips, then reached up and gave his boater a teasing nudge so that it tilted over his forehead. Perhaps she complained she was chilly, because the next moment they set off toward the house, she clinging to his arm, the trailing hem of her robe a pool of ivory, her hair a swathe of black silk, and disappeared.

By midnight, the garden was so cold I was numb, and the absinthe had almost run dry. My soul had shriveled and my thoughts were bitter morsels of complaint. I wanted to be at home, in my bed. Unlike every other woman at the party, I had to get up for work next morning. I wanted to sleep and never wake. I was very hungry. I was a fool. I was pitiable. I should have known better.

Hadley Waters, on the other hand, had grown damp-eyed and sentimental. "We should take a boat out on the river," he said. "Might I have the pleasure of rowing you ladies?"

By now the band was improvising somewhat melancholy themes,

which wafted across the water to where people floated in cushioned rowing boats with lanterns swinging from hooks on the prows, like illustrations from *The Twelve Dancing Princesses.* Hadley claimed to be an expert oarsman and Margot and Meredith were both keen to go on the river. I couldn't imagine anything less inviting than the Thames at this hour but thought when it was over it might be one-thirty, time for the cab, and if I let Meredith disappear in the boat without me, there was no telling how long I'd be left on the bank waiting for her.

Margot sat in the prow facing Hadley, who had the oars, and Meredith and I were side by side in the stern. Drink had loosened Meredith's tongue—she talked in a high, fast voice, her accent much stronger than usual: "How wide the river is here, but do you know, it makes me homesick for Canada where the rivers run so fast and clear. Your aunt Prudence was very impressed by the Turners in the Tate, by the way, our trip was a roaring success. Water, she said, is difficult to paint but *he* managed wonderfully. Why is it that even when Prudence pays a compliment, it sounds like a decree? You Maida Vale ladies have everything sewn up, don't you? You don't have room for doubt."

I recognized wearily that she wanted to pick a fight, so I trailed my hand in the water and changed the subject. "I was talking about Canada the other day, incidentally. I'm told that our country sends hundreds of orphans out there each year. Did you know anything about that?"

"Of course. Not that we want all of them. You're only supposed to send us perfect children and instead you fob off defective ones on us. If a child is already half-witted, it's not nearly such fun for a farmer out on the plains to knock the living daylights out of him."

"Meredith, what are you saying? I was given to understand that our children go to good homes."

"Oh, I'm sure some do, Evelyn, if that's what you'd like to believe."

"It's not a matter of belief. I'd rather get at the truth."

"Truthfully, then, I have worked in hospitals where your migrant

English children, your rejects or home children as we call them, have turned up riddled with sexual disease or mentally defective."

"I didn't know I . . ."

"Did the news not reach you here of little Charles Bulpitt who hung himself in a barn, he was so abused by his master? Oh, it's a common sight, when you visit a Canadian farmstead, to see a ragged home child leading in the cattle or some such. Mother's cousin had one as a housemaid. That worked out all right, I think; she was a good worker."

"How could I not have known about this?"

"On the other hand I'm sure your aunt Prudence would applaud the scheme on the grounds of its justness. If a child is to be destitute due to the improvidence of its parents, at least let it be useful."

It grew colder despite the cushions and even a rug thoughtfully provided by Lady Carr. The river, poisoned by my conversation with Meredith, was horribly dense between little puddles of light cast by the lanterns. Behind us, Lady Carr's garden was like a painted film set. Then Meredith's mood changed entirely as she tucked herself up closer to me, crying: "Isn't it cold?" Reaching both her arms around my waist, she rested her head on my shoulder and kissed me under the chin. "Glad you changed your mind? Happy to be here?"

That night she wore an exotic fragrance, very musky, and the heat of her tense little body transferred itself to mine so that despite the shock of intimacy, I welcomed her closeness. A bottle was passed among us and I took a reckless swig, mesmerized by the sight of Hadley Waters's blade dipping in and out of the river, the fall of a few drops of water as it flew along then sliced the surface tension with a deliciously tiny plop.

He and Margot were planning an exhibition. "But I don't think we should restrict it just to paintings," he said. "I think we should go foraging in the flea markets for anything we consider to be art, jugs, radiators even, all welcome so long as they have lovely shapes."

"I like the idea of an exhibition of *things*," said Meredith. "Evelyn's aunt Prudence and I are going to the British Empire Exhibition next week to see what *things* there might be to look at from those far-flung places. Prudence says that primitive art is fine so long as it is done by primitive peoples. But you know, I love all beautiful things. I don't care if they're useful or not so long as they're good to look at. That's why I've acquired Evelyn as my very best friend. She's a bit useful, I suppose, but more than that she's very beautiful, though she doesn't know it."

"Surely you are too begrudging," cried Hadley, "in saying that she's only a *bit* useful."

"Oh, in a court of law she's no doubt invaluable. But in the house-keeping department, not at all. To this day she has no idea how to make a bed or boil an egg."

"Who wants to know how to make a bed?"

"Actually, I do, I'm an expert bed-maker, being a nurse. My corners are knife-sharp, I can tell you."

"Of course, I forgot that's what you did in the war," said Hadley. "What a handy person to have in the art class. Next time I drive a nail through my palm, I'll call on you."

"How very Christ-like," said Margot, leaning forward to stroke him. "Did you really do that once?"

The bottle was passed again and the conversation now drifted into a litany of gruesome accidents as Hadley dipped his oars ever more slowly. His knees were touching Margot's and eventually slotted between them. There was a lot of jiggling of the boat as they began a series of long, closed-eyed kisses that made my heart beat hard and uneven until at last I forced myself to look away.

Meredith, who had been drinking steadily, snuggled deeper beside me under the rug and buried her face in my lap. "I love you," she said. "I love you and I hate you, did you know that? I love you because you're Evelyn and one minute you're stiff and starchy as Prudence, and the next you're this bold, amazing woman, braver than almost anyone I know. And I hate you because you're the sister of James and your eyes are tight shut." She paused, her head pressed to my breast as she clung to me.

I saw the coming revelation rather as I might have watched a demolition ball hurtling toward me; there was no possibility of ducking or interrupting its momentum. Alcohol and cold had disempowered me so that it was easier to lie still beneath the blanket and wait than to offer any resistance or attempt to change the subject. Besides, wasn't I always greedy for information about James, anything that would return him a little more solidly to me? Meanwhile Margot had shifted and she and Hadley, now side by side, drew in the oars and ran their hands over each other instead.

Meredith stroked my neck. "I've wondered for years whether I would ever tell your family the truth about what happened. Part of me wants to keep it a secret, to protect you, I suppose. Part of me wants to tell you, so that you have the full picture. Which is the path I should follow? Tell me, do. I'll leave it to you to decide for me."

I looked up at the stars. "You know I want to know more about James."

She adjusted her weight so that her head lay on my shoulder and her breath, full of spirits, fell on my neck. With her finger she traced my features; nose, jaw, breastbone. "I'm too drunk to know what I'm saying, almost. I only know that it's now or never, here on the river, where the boundaries are all gone. If I leave it any longer it will be too late and you'll be striding out of my life again, as you do each morning, leaving me to boil with frustration in the house."

I lay like a sacrificial victim, arms by my side. It was as if Meredith, and the obsidian river, and that bright bowl of a moon had enchanted me. She took a strand of my hair and wound it around and around her finger, held it up as if to examine it in the light, cast it aside and picked up another. "You see, we were a religious order, nursing in a general hospital quite a way behind the lines. By the time the men got to us they'd been patched up to some extent or their wounds were sufficiently minor that they'd been brought straight back to us, by minor I mean frostbite, gas, suchlike. The lucky ones, and there weren't so many of them, were sick enough to be sent home but not so ill that they wouldn't recover in the end. The unluckier ones would be maimed for life. The unluckiest of all, we nurses used to say among ourselves, made speedy recoveries and were sent back posthaste. Your brother fell into the latter category."

She had brought me up close to a window and James was on the other side. My nose was pressed to the glass; yes, if I looked deeper, if I strained my eyes, I would see him. I caught hold of her fondling hand and held tight. "We have no idea about his last days. We hadn't seen him for months before he died. He wrote from the hospital, said he was injured. We knew that. Tell me, please, what did he look like? How was he, in himself?"

Her eyes were huge and reflective in the dim light. "To me he was just an ordinary boy."

Ordinary? James? No: beautiful, ambitious, funny, quick-tempered, impetuous, but ordinary? No. No.

"He was very young," Meredith was saying, "his skin was young, like so many of those boys, and he was exhausted when he arrived and his wound was in a bad state, quite a slash to the upper arm, severe loss of blood, though it mended quickly. His voice was unusual, with a throaty quality to it and similar intonations to yours. Were you aware that you and he both slice off each sentence at the end, as if you are in too much of a hurry to linger on the final word? And then, as he got better, he grew mischievous and childlike, reckless, as many of them did. It was the release of being away from the lines for a while. We had to put up with all kinds of pranks, I can tell you. Your brother was a ringleader, a practical joker, not that there was much scope in the hospital. But they got access to a typewriter and sent 'round a directive to bed-bound patients that only those reduced to one limb out of four were henceforth to be sent home, the rest would be considered fit for duty, trenches widened to accommodate wheelchairs and ramps provided alongside fire-steps. Most took the letter in good part. Some men wept."

"It seems a cruel thing to do. James wasn't cruel."

"You don't think so? Or perhaps it was just that like so many of them he had gone beyond knowing what was reasonable."

"His values would not have deserted him, even in those conditions."

"Oh, is that what you'd like to think, my dear Evelyn? How saintly you are with your strong bones and your pioneering spirit. You think the world operates in black and white, don't you, Evelyn, and if there are gray areas then hey, the law will sort them out. I think it remarkable that you have reached the ripe old age of thirty and still believe that there is clarity about what is right and what isn't."

I didn't know what I had done to rile her. "We ought not to talk anymore," I said, "in case we say something we regret. We have both drunk too much. Please."

She lay watching me, with one dainty arm crooked behind her head. "I've weighed up what to say. I know that if I do tell you, something will be broken forever. Bizarrely there's a part of me that wants to preserve your memories of him. You are all so frail, creeping about in your old museum of a house. Why, I can see the imprint of your father's head in a cushion on a drawing room chair. I swear that James's boater hangs at a certain angle in the hall because that's how he left it. I've done an experiment, pushed it another way but half an hour later it's always back in its old position. It's as if you all took a deep breath when you heard that he got killed and you've never let it out again. Now what if I break this spell, I think, and tell the truth about their precious boy? What then?"

"Nothing could make me love or miss him less."

"Oh, that's never been my intention. No, no, we all need to love

as much as we can. Perhaps, you know, a whiff of human frailty might
make you love him more. Well, the truth is this. James fell in love with
me, like so many of them did. We were ministering angels, after all, in
our white veils and aprons. Those men emerged from the pain and the
horror to find that we had created order and had quiet voices and gentle hands. We were women. But unlike the others your brother was
greedy. It wasn't enough to look—he had to touch, too. He grew hungrier and hungrier, pursued me, wouldn't leave me alone, refused to take
no for an answer, found out my routine until, on the evening before he
was due to go back, he came looking for me with just one idea in his
head."

I watched the candle within the lantern flicker as it swung back and
forth. Dimly I was aware that the lovers had settled into the bottom of
the boat, murmuring and nuzzling.

"Say something," she said.

I was silent.

"Do you understand what I'm telling you?"

"Of course I understand. There's Edmund."

Her voice came in stabs. "Ah no, no, you don't understand. I'm telling you that he forced himself on me."

I said not a word.

"Well?" she said.

"Please, no, don't."

"Ah, I was ready for denial. I know you'll say it wasn't rape. I couldn't
understand your brother until I met your father, and now that I've met
you too I have an even clearer picture of why he did it. Oh, James was
brought up decently, had a sense of decency, but there was a kind of
stranglehold on his emotions, a point where he simply went blind and
gave in to desire because he didn't recognize desire for what it was. He
thought that desire had to be satiated, like hunger or thirst. There was
no stopping him, he would not listen to me or, I suspect, to the voices

of all you others in his head." She looped her arm around my neck and pulled herself up so that her mouth was actually on my ear. "Let me tell you one more thing," she whispered. "Then you'll believe me, perhaps. You see, I wasn't just any nurse. Like I say, I was with a Roman Catholic order. I was training to be a nun. I had taken vows. You didn't ask where it was I went at night, to be alone, where he found me. Can't you guess?"

I thrust her away with such force that my elbow flew back and cracked against the side of the boat. "I don't believe you. Why do you want to hurt me like this?"

"I don't want to hurt you. It's the truth. I'm telling you the truth because I want my life back. I did not choose Edmund. I love him, in the end, though I thought I never would, he had done such damage to what I was. But when he was born I felt this tug at my heart and I could not help but embrace him. But why should that one moment define my life? I didn't sin, yet I find myself with no vocation, no future, and hardly any money, forced to love the child conceived in a moment of struggle and fear. And because of Edmund, I have to relive that moment again and again, the fact that though my mouth opened no sound would come, that I felt so little and powerless, in such pain and shock, not just my body but my soul, my own self, all I wanted to be, violated. In the end I couldn't live with the imbalance of that, of knowing you were all here, oblivious to the damage he'd done."

It was impossible to follow what she'd said. Instead I was scrabbling to recover my old images of James: James in uniform, the hardness of his warm cheek when I kissed him, James mortally wounded and so innocent. "Did you make this allegation about James to my father?"

"No. I did not."

"Why not, if it's true?"

"I took pity on him."

The pair in front had emerged from their embrace and in a clumsy, giggling effort to regain their seat, tipped the boat so furiously that one of the oars fell into the river. Margot gave a little scream, stood up, clutched hold of the side, and tried to reach it. Too late I saw what was happening, cried out, and shifted my weight, but the next moment Margot had tumbled in after the oar with a wild cry and a great splash. I suspect that the fall into the water was partly self-willed, because she surfaced, shrieking with laughter, hair plastered to her face.

"Never mind the oar," shouted Hadley, a little more sober. "It's floated too far away. And no, don't try and pull on the boat there, you'll have us over, work your way round to the front and hold on to the prow . . ."

Meredith and I sat side by side, not touching. My face was set in a travesty of a grin, as if I thought that was the correct response to losing an oar and a passenger, and I discovered that I was wet through. The bottom of the boat was inches deep in river water and Margot had splashed us all. Meanwhile, the commotion had attracted the attention of other boats, a few of which came pitching or gliding down the river, depending on the oarsman's skill or degree of inebriation. "Are you all right?" "Is everyone safe?" came voices across the water.

"We've lost an oar," called Hadley, hauling Margot back into the boat, where she slithered in her trailing robe like an ungainly fish. "Hard to find it in the dark," someone said after a few minutes. "I tell you what, grab hold of our painter and we'll tow you in."

By now we had drifted a long way downstream but at last, after more shouting, squealing, and rocking, our boat made ungainly progress back to Lady Carr's jetty. Margot was shaking violently under the sodden blanket. I thought perhaps Nurse Meredith would spring into action but she said nothing and I couldn't bring myself to look at her. As we neared the jetty, we saw that quite a crowd had formed, including Lady Carr, whose jet beads glinted in the moonlight. And, with the inevitability of all the events of that fateful night, I saw Sylvia Hardynge, shrouded in a shawl and hopping from foot to foot, and beside her Thorne. I looked away to the far bank, which was mercifully dark, and then closed my eyes as the boat sailed with surprising grace and speed to its mooring.

Everyone was shrieking instructions to Margot, who had to be helped out of the boat, swathed in a dry blanket, and rushed up to the house. Arms reached down to Meredith and me. I allowed my hand to rest briefly in some warm, male clasp, then stood shakily upright, though I could scarcely feel my hands and feet. My dress clung to me, the blue satin sheath drooped from my shoulder, my hair was matted on my cheek. I walked through the crowd, still with that polite smile stuck to my lips, and looking to neither right nor left. Meredith was ahead. And now I was on the lawn, feet squelching in wet shoes, the strip of blue satin knotting around my thighs, and I was past the empty dance floor and the arbor where the band had been, I had almost reached the gate at the side of the house, I would walk straight home, I thought, anything to get away, but it was too late, I heard his voice behind me full of incredulous laughter: "Miss Gifford, Sylvia said you were here but I thought she must be mistaken. What an extraordinary coincidence."

I stood stock-still in my drooping clothes, aware that my frock clung to me, was even perhaps translucent, and that my hair was in rattails. Half turning my head, I murmured: "Forgive me for not stopping, Mr. Thorne. I am very wet. If you'll excuse me."

But he came closer and put the back of his finger to my arm. "You are freezing cold. Can I offer you my jacket? No? How are you traveling home? Sylvia and I could take you in . . ."

"Thank you. We have a cab." I moved on. From the corner of my eye I had seen the group who'd thronged the jetty hurrying up toward us, led by Sylvia and Lady Carr. Then at last I was at the side of the house and out on the street, where miraculously a cab was waiting with Meredith already crammed tight into the far corner of the backseat. For a moment I wondered whether I could bring myself to get in with her.

Then I thought of Edmund, of work in the morning, and of Thorne, who was staring after me.

We did not speak on the journey home, though from time to time one or other of us shivered violently. At Clivedon Hall Gardens, I paid the cab driver and unlocked the front door while she waited wordlessly on the step. Once inside, she slipped away and ran upstairs.

Rather than follow I waited until there was no further movement overhead, then went into the dining room, where I drew back the curtain. Moonlight fell on the table set for breakfast, on the looming furniture.

I sat in my customary chair, from whence I could see the portraits of Father and James. My brother's eyes were shadowed in the inadequate light but the lines of his cap and shoulder were clear-cut as ever. I went up close and drew my fingertips over the glass. Never, I think, had I wanted him back so badly.

But my father. Even now I could smell the whiskey on him, a sickening whiff of hair pomade and spirits. At night sometimes, after the war, I had woken in the small hours and known that he was still up. When I crept downstairs, I found him at the table, his tumbler pushed among the breakfast things, the decanter unstoppered, his head sunk low. Sometimes, if I could bear it, I sat with him.

Once he did speak, weeping unrestrainedly so that tears and saliva dribbled onto his plate. "I killed him," he said, "my son," and he glanced at me with cowed eyes to see if I would offer any comfort. "I could have kept him back. I could have pulled strings and got him a safe posting. Instead I forced him to sign up early. I envied him. I thought the war would be glorious and swift and that it would be better for the firm if he volunteered. I told him he was a coward when he admitted to being afraid."

I could not even bring myself to reach out and touch his wet hand. I did not trust those whiskey-fed tears or know how to forgive him.

But now I had words alright. "Why, on top of everything else, did you not tell me about Meredith and Edmund, Father? It's too much for me to bear." I knew why. Father had preferred to wallow in the death of an innocent boy. To have acknowledged that James had darker urges, had loved a woman, would have sullied the process of grieving, complicated the guilt. And so he had kept James's memory simple, like a martyr's.

I did not believe Meredith. I loathed her. But she had altered my image of James forever. Desire hung about the polished surfaces of that room. I felt it twitch and mutter even within the tightly folded and rolled napkins.

Nineteen

W hen I arrived at Caractacus Court at ten o'clock the next morning, or rather the same morning, in yet another cab, courtesy
this time of the *Daily Mail* fund, I was greeted by Mrs. Sanders, who
invited me to go up and view the transformation to the Marchant living
accommodation. She told me that Leah had been scrubbing floors both
in her own house and other people's since her release, and had already
saved five shillings. Leah stood at the entrance to her room, arms folded,
as if to say, I told you so, wearing a jaunty hat and well-brushed jacket
and skirt. Thanks again to the newspaper, her debts to Mrs. Sanders had
been paid and her old room refurnished with a couple of beds and four
dining chairs. There was even a rug to go before the fire and a cradle for
the baby when she got him back, though I doubted that an eighteen-
month child would fit into so small a bed. Less promisingly, I distinctly
smelled alcohol on her breath.

Once in the cab, neither of us spoke. Leah was pent up, clutching a
canvas bag containing gifts for the children, as stipulated in a letter from
the home: grapes and colored chalks. Apparently, she still regarded me
as enemy number one, because she turned her face to the window and
refused to engage with me. And I, reeling from the events of the previous night, was in no mood to speak to her. My eyelids stung and my
pulse raced—I had slept for perhaps an hour and a half. Poor Leah,

engaged in the mission to save her children, could have no idea how remote she seemed to me or how unfit I was at that moment to be her legal representative. But then, as rain slashed against the window, she suddenly said: "You tell them to let them kids come home with me and I'll give them such a treat of fish-and-chips. Mrs. Sanders will mind them evenin's when I go cleanin' them banks. Mr. Breen give me a reference so I shall have no trouble gettin' as much work as I like."

"Mrs. Marchant, please don't raise your hopes. There is no question of the children coming home with us today. This is a visit simply, in which we must begin the process of convincing the authorities that you are a fit parent. So of course we shall tell them the good news about your work and you will be allowed a brief interview with your children, fifteen minutes, they said, but that is all."

"Do you think I can bear to see my children and then leave them again? I thought they was comin' 'ome."

"It was explained to you very clearly after court that the judge had ordered that you have a visit. Nothing was said about the children coming home. There is a long legal process to be gone through first." I spoke sharply and she said nothing more but stared sullenly out of the window.

The home was set behind a pair of gates bearing the sign in wrought iron: GOOD SAMARITAN HOME FOR DESTITUTE CHILDREN. There was a yard with hopscotch marked out before a gray-brick building with high windows and double front doors set in a Gothic-style frame and painted green. "That's why I chose it," said Leah, "because I seen the hopscotch."

We sat in the entrance hall, where a flight of stairs rose dead-center, divided on a little landing, and then continued to left and right. The unplastered walls were painted dark green to shoulder height, cream above, and there was a hospital smell of antiseptic covering up something less palatable. Although the building was quiet, there was a definite atmosphere of lives held in abeyance.

The matron kept us waiting for several minutes, which I thought ill-advised. Leah could not sit still but crept again and again to the foot of the stairs, peering up as if expecting her daughters to come running down from the landing. The quiet was punctuated by the occasional distant closing of a door or the echo of a woman's voice, and by Leah's loud sighs and rummaging in her bag. Sometimes she fiddled with her hair and twitched at her skirts or glared accusingly into my face. Thanks to my father, I was all too familiar with the symptoms of one overfond of alcohol but deprived of the bottle. By the time we were summoned into the office, Leah was wild and my heart was in my boots.

The matron, Miss Buckley, was dressed in a formidable costume of pale gray linen with a silver badge on the lapel: an engraving of the home complete with its cathedral-like doors and the Latin motto *Ut prosim* above it. Her hair, cut in a chin-length bob, was brushed into a shiny gray helmet. Considerable effort had therefore gone into her appearance and yet she had achieved what most women would strive to avoid: an air of utter restraint that betokened a kind of negative vanity. I sensed that she would be rigid.

When she opened her mouth, I knew we were doomed. Her voice was too high and girlish for a woman well into her forties, and though she smiled a good deal, her eyes were hard. Her desk was completely empty except for one closed file, and she indicated that we should sit on two hard chairs opposite. I thought with surprising nostalgia of my basement office stuffed with files and papers, which at least showed that for decades Breen & Balcombe had been grappling with human transactions. Surely this room ought to have some sign that its business was children? But no, the only obvious reference was a pious painting of a child at prayer beneath a crucifix, on which a lurid figure of Christ hung with blood dripping from brow, hands, and feet. For a moment, I was distracted by the memory of Meredith's drunken disclosures about her vocation and had an absurd urge to laugh—today she and Prudence were off to the British Empire Exhibition. Did Prudence really not know that Meredith was a Roman Catholic, and therefore a viper? And once again I was flooded with dread of Meredith. She sickened me utterly, the way she had insinuated herself, used her son to win our trust, and then attempted to destroy my brother's memory.

"I think it's wonderful, Mrs. Marchant, that you should have come to visit your little ones. You'll find them in very good spirits," said Miss Buckley.

Leah nodded eagerly, setting a pair of ornamental cherries wagging on her new hat. For the time being, she was very composed in her dark clothes, her hands folded tightly on the bag as if it contained her pent-up excitement.

"There are just one or two things I need to say," added Miss Buckley in her oversoft, overmodulated voice, "before I bring the girls in."

"I'll see them alone. By the way, we'll be private, won't we?" said Leah.

Miss Buckley acknowledged the interruption with a slight lift of an eyebrow. "Ah, no, not this time. As I was about to say, we have very strict rules about visits from our parents. It can be upsetting for our little ones to see their mothers, and your two, Mrs. Marchant, have only just started to settle. In some ways they're coming on beautifully—you'll see that Ellen has completed her first sampler and dear little Cathy is learning her alphabet. We think she's very clever."

"She is clever," said Leah. "They both are. I want them home."

"Shall we talk about that afterward?" said Miss Buckley quietly.

"I think it would help Mrs. Marchant to accept the current situation if there was some hope." My voice, abused by last night's unaccustomed alcohol and lack of sleep, sounded rusty. "Perhaps you can explain the process to her."

"She will need to show that she can provide a good home for the children, of course. Where is the husband?"

"We are attempting to contact him. He is at sea." So far we had sent three letters to shipping companies, inquiring after Sam Marchant, all of which had been sent back stamped NOT KNOWN. "But even if he is unavailable, I think we will be able to prove that Mrs. Marchant has provided the children with a comfortable home and we are checking to see that there are places for the girls in a local school."

"Well, that all helps. We have to be sure that we are returning our children to safe homes, where they will be cared for as well, if not better than here. But for the time being, I want you to listen to me very carefully, Mrs. Marchant. You shall have fifteen minutes precisely with the children. We are very strict about a first visit. Miss Gifford and I will be with you at all times. It's appropriate to give them a little present, if you have one, and ask them about their studies. When they come in you may shake hands and later you may kiss them good-bye, but otherwise we discourage physical contact because the children find it too disturbing. And I must warn you that if you fail to keep to any of these very easy rules, we shall be forced to end the interview early and the board will be notified. As I said, we have learned from painful experience, the shorter the better at first."

Leah said nothing more but sat with her head back and her bottom lip clenched in her teeth. I felt nauseous. Miss Buckley rang the bell, there was a few minutes' silence, and then the door opened and two little girls were ushered in by a mistress dressed head to toe in beige.

They were aged perhaps seven and five and wore identical gray frocks and white pinafores. The younger had brown hair pulled into a tight tail at the back, the elder's fine, near-white hair was parted at the center and worn in two thin braids. In her right hand was a scrap of canvas. Both had huge, greenish eyes. At sight of their mother, they stood stock-still, hand in hand.

"Oh, my Gawd. Oh, my precious girls," breathed Leah.

The girls didn't move but the younger turned her solemn eyes toward the matron, who nodded. "I've been telling your mother that you know your ABCs, Cathy. She's very pleased."

The child stood, watching.

"Give Mother your ABCs."

Both little girls stood as if frozen to the spot, hands tightly clasped, watching their mother.

"Cathy," said Miss Buckley in her soft, sweet voice, "do as I say."

Nobody moved. Finally, the matron said: "You may shake hands with your mother then, if you can't remember your ABCs, and with Miss Gifford."

The older girl's gaze flickered to me, and my lips managed a frail smile. The child was an inch or so shorter than Edmund, but whereas his eyes were trusting and inquisitive, this little girl was expressionless as she came up to me, sister in tow. One after another, I felt their small hands in mine; both were cold and neither returned the pressure of my fingers, then they were quickly withdrawn.

"I believe your mother has brought you a present," said Miss Buckley.

Leah produced the bag of grapes, squashed so that the juice had bled into the brown paper, and the chalks in a little cardboard box. Both packages lay in her lap.

"The girls will be allowed to share with their friends after tea," said Miss Buckley. "And now I think, as nobody has anything to say, our time is almost up so . . ."

One of the children gasped, as if she had been holding her breath all this time, and at the same moment Leah's spine seemed to collapse and she held out her arms. The spell broken, the children hurled themselves at her and all three were knotted together, their heads pressed close.

"Very well," said Miss Buckley. "It's time to part now."

They were sobbing, covering each other with kisses, arms wound tightly together.

"Come, Ellen," ordered Miss Buckley. "Bring your sister away."

The group tightened, the sobs grew louder. I pushed aside my chair and backed to the wall. Had Leah not been between me and the door, I believe that I would have walked out of the home into the cab rather than face that scene. The matron marched up and tried to pull one of the girls away but she stuck fast. "Help me," Miss Buckley commanded and when I didn't move, opened the door and called sharply: "Miss Hands."

"Oh, good God," I cried, "this is inhuman. Could she not have five minutes alone with her children?"

"It's because I am human that I won't allow this. The judge promised in his letter that the mother would behave herself. Have you any idea how long it will be now until these girls settle again? Night after night the older one soils her sheets."

The other woman came in and there followed a nightmarish attempt to wrench the children from their mother. Their fingers were unpeeled one at a time from their grip on her clothes and hair, their eyes were wild as they felt themselves torn away, struggling, howling, writhing, but at the last moment Cathy, the youngest, got a hold of her mother's skirt again and the pair once more clung to each other.

At long last and much too belatedly, something in me broke. "No," I shouted. "No. This cannot be right. Miss Buckley, if you leave them alone, I undertake to return these children to your care in five minutes."

Her immaculate hair had come adrift, her collar was askew. She stared at me venomously and returned to her task.

"I shall report you to the board for cruelty to these children," I said, very quiet now. "You are perhaps unaware that we have powerful friends."

"We have rules."

"Yes. You have rules, but in extreme cases I believe rules have to be bent. Even I, a lawyer, believe that."

Miss Hands, the minion, had given up the struggle and was looking at her fingernails as if to detach herself from the proceedings. Leah now had both girls on her lap, tightly clasped, the grapes a sodden, purple mass on the floor beside her foot.

And then the matron abruptly gave up and left the room, followed by Miss Hands. I closed the door. "Leah. You have five minutes. Five minutes. If you don't let the children go after that, I can guarantee that you will never get them back. Do you understand me?" She was whispering into their hair, showering them with kisses. Their crying quietened.

I went to the window overlooking the yard and the treacherous hopscotch. Again I remembered the conversation in the boat with Meredith and I recognized the danger; because of what had happened at the art party, I was a different woman this morning and there was no telling what I might do next.

As if in proof, I now began to look around the room. In one corner sat Leah. The youngest child was telling her about Sunday tea, at which they had jam and sponge cake. And in the morning was church. According to Cathy, the service was three hours long at least. My hand rested on Miss Buckley's empty desk with its inkstand and ledger complete with fresh blotting paper and behind it a filing cabinet. On one wall was the crucifix, on another a very bad painting in oils, presumably of the Good Samaritan at work. And to the left of the window was a notice board with a dozen or so typed or handwritten lists and memoranda pinned to it.

Three minutes had gone by. Somewhere upstairs a handbell was rung and then carried some distance along a passage, still jangling relentlessly. The girls were attentive as rabbits to a dog's bark. "Playtime," said Cathy. "We go out to play now."

"Hopscotch?" asked Leah.

"Skipping. We skip."

When I have read every notice on this board, I thought, I will tell

Leah that it is time to go. There were details of the local doctor and hospital in case of emergency, a list of board members, weekday and weekend timetables (two visits to church on Sunday, morning and evening), and the dates when a nurse would come to inspect the children for nits. And pinned to the bottom right corner was a handwritten page:

The *Metagama*
Date of sailing, September 22, 1924.
150 children. Aged 8 and above.
Placements, various, domestic, agricultural
Fee £13.00 per child.
Submissions by August 11, 1924.
Agency Barnardo's, in association with
the Church of England Advisory Council on Empire Settlement.

I looked from the notice to Leah and her children and remembered Carrie Morrison's warning and, in the boat last night, Meredith's scathing judgment of the government's emigration policy. Was this to be the fate of these children? What if Leah could not resist the bottle and her drunken husband was never found?

The filing cabinet was unlocked, and when I peered inside, I found that the partitions were neatly labeled: ACCOUNTS, MEDICAL, BOARD MEETINGS, CHILDREN ADMITTED 1920, 1921. And in the third drawer I found what I was looking for—MIGRATION—and in a folder:

Canadian Outfits for Girls

1. Warm overcoat
2. Hat
3. Sets, warm underwear . . .

4. Comb

5. Prayer book . . .

I crushed the page into my pocket. My time was almost up. Frantic, I again scanned the notice board and found the somewhat yellowed sheet:

Board of Trustees

January 1923

Bishop Ogilvie

Reverend Hawkins

Thurrock

Curren

Smythe-Engleby

Carlyle . . .

Ten names in all. I unpinned the notice, folded it up small, and put it in my pocket. Then I told Leah: "It will look much better if you surrender the children now rather than be forced."

A gush of endearments followed. The children, I noticed, were more stoical than the mother; the younger, Cathy, clutching the chalks, the older again holding tight to her sister's hand. They were now keen for the moment of parting to be over, while Leah was too wrapped up in the drama of the moment to help make it happen. When I opened the door, Miss Hands was in the passage, looking frightened. The children were hugged violently, then surrendered. I was relieved to see that Miss Hands smiled down at them kindly, that they took her hands fearlessly and then were whisked away with merciful speed.

"We should wait for the matron to come back," I said. "We should apologize for the earlier scene."

"She's the one who should be sorry."

"Leah, she holds all the cards. Don't you understand? She could report you to the board and they could forbid further visits."

But after a quarter of an hour or so, it became clear that Miss Buckley would not return to her office. Her absence was the last word, and I realized that she was even more formidable than I had thought.

Twenty

fter depositing Leah at Caractacus Court, I made my way by omnibus to Arbery Street, where I intended to tell Mr. Breen about the disastrous episode at the children's home. He was not about, however, so I sat in the basement and wrote a verbatim account. At one point I went upstairs to make tea, offering Miss Drake a cup as usual, today more than ever for the sake of companionship.

"Thank you, no. I shall have my tea at a quarter past four."

"I can wait."

"I wouldn't dream of putting you to the trouble."

I tried to catch her eye; I so longed for a little warmth, but she went on hammering at the keys.

❦

By the time I let myself into Clivedon Hall Gardens, the family was at supper and Meredith's voice rang clearly through the half-open dining room door. "There were wonderful artifacts from Africa, Prudence was very taken with them, weren't you, Prudence?"

"Certainly. I have a great fondness for color. The exhibition gave one a sense of one's place at the center of an empire teeming with opportunity and inspiration. My criticism is that there was too much to see in a day. Far too much. I shall have to go back. The silks from India . . ."

"And of course I could not keep away from the Canada Hall even though I knew it would make me a touch homesick," said Meredith. "They insisted that our chief claim to fame is that we make good butter. Can you imagine? When we have so much richness . . ."

I was determined not to sit at the same table as Meredith and had actually reached the foot of the stairs when Min appeared from the basement with a tray of liver and onions. "Are you going straight in to dinner then, Miss Gifford? I imagine you won't be wanting soup."

So I sat next to Prudence, managed a few mouthfuls, and after a while began to register a disturbing change, which in the circumstance had a macabre irony, as if the fates were laughing at me. Surely I must be imagining it but no, absurd though it seemed, Prudence too was perhaps in danger of falling a little in love. There was Meredith with her huge eyes and darkened lashes, cutting Edmund's liver into slivers, some of which she slipped onto her own plate so he wouldn't have to eat it all. And there was Prudence, alert to every move, no longer huffy with disapproval but gruesomely teasing, posting remarks across the table as if daring to see how they might be received.

"No, Meredith, I did not like that Aboriginal shield. On the contrary, I found it horrific. You always seem to prefer items connected with blood, I notice, whereas I liked the more domestic artifacts, the . . ."

"Blood and death," said Meredith, with her mouth full. "Even you cannot deny their existence, Prudence. My art teacher, Mr. Waters, instructs that they are the themes of so much of art. Oh, and love, of course." Here she looked Prudence full in the eye and I felt the poor woman quiver beside me. "You show me a great painting, Prudence, and I'll show you . . ."

"In Hunt, for example, *The Light* . . ."

"Hunt is not a great painter. It's time you came to terms with that. He's great with his brush. He's great at telling a story, but he's not a great painter. He does not push back the boundaries of our understanding, he is insipid."

"How can you say that . . . ?"

The rest of us were excluded. Mother interrupted from time to time with an admonition to Edmund to keep his elbows off the table or eat up his nice liver, but she'd been defeated at bridge in the afternoon and consequently had a headache. Grandmother, who was fond of liver, ate with her usual dedication to the task and for once did not bother to pick up snippets of conversation. Only I, it seemed, spotted the danger to Prudence's peace of mind.

The subject of the art party came up over the blancmange. "Meredith tells me you had a lovely time," said Mother, a little resentfully, "but that you nearly drowned in the river."

"Hardly."

I would not meet Meredith's eye, though she exclaimed: "Oh, it was so good to see Evelyn having fun for a change. You should have seen her knocking back the absinthe."

There was an awful silence. "Absinthe," said Mother faintly.

"Not in front of Edmund," said Prudence.

"Why not? What is absinthe?" he asked.

"A poisonous drink. So poisonous that it's against the law in most countries."

"And Mommy drank it?"

Meredith hugged him. "And so did Aunty Evelyn and look, we're both still alive. It's not poison, Edmund, unless taken in great quantities."

"All alcohol is a form of poison," said Mother. "It's a poison to children, Edmund, and to some adults who don't know when enough is enough. But absinthe. I'm surprised at you, Evelyn. Your father always used to say that if, as a lawyer, he was ever found dabbling in anything approaching an illegal substance, he would expect to be struck off."

Meredith laughed. "Absinthe, like all drink, is delicious, Edmund, and don't let anyone 'round this table tell you otherwise. Your father, as I recall, was especially fond of spirits." I flinched from this reference to James, which was accompanied by a sideways glance at me as if to say: Remember what I told you. "What your grandmother means is that like so many grown-up things, drink has to be treated with respect. Why, I bet you've drunk plenty of absinthe in your time, haven't you?" she asked Grandmother, who was sucking blancmange through her remaining five teeth.

"We got hold of some once for a first-night party, the play was a Sheridan, I believe. I have never been so sick. But afterward I dreamed that I was a ballerina. I've never forgotten that dream. So vivid. So lovely to float through the air and then leap clean off the edge of the stage."

Meredith helped herself to more blancmange; she had a very sweet tooth and was undaunted even by Rose's lumpy milk puddings. I broke in hurriedly with an offer to take Edmund upstairs for a bedtime story, and to my relief, he came willingly, holding my hand as if we were old friends. I had visions, as I got up from the table, of his performing the same trick as the Marchant girls and clinging to his mother's skirts. He chose the story of Briar Rose, the abused girl whose fate was decided by the whim of a couple of wise women and whose only other claim to distinction was that she slept for a hundred years.

Afterward, he lay against me, full of questions. "But she'd be a hundred and fifteen when she woke up. How would she be able to stand?"

I thought of those little Marchant girls trapped in a place they hadn't chosen and my anger grew, like the wise woman's in the story, until when Meredith came up to help Edmund with his prayers I was in a furious state. Wicked, wicked woman for slandering my brother. And now she'd compounded the wrong by seeking to corrupt his son with talk of absinthe.

After Meredith had kissed Edmund on the forehead, he at once curled on his side, ready to sleep. I took her pointy little elbow, pushed her into my own bedroom, and shut the door behind us. "I can't bear it, what you said about my brother. Admit you were lying."

"Evelyn, aren't you tired after our late night? I am." She did look exhausted, sunken-eyed, the bones prominent in her forehead.

But the counterarguments had been building in my head all day. I would take her story apart until there was nothing left but the lurid shreds of her twisted imagination. "You know what bothers me most of all, that you said you were training to be a nun, that you would lie even about that. You love clothes, beautiful things, art, pleasure. Forgive me but I see nothing of the nun in you."

"Oh," she said wearily, her hands loose on her lap and her head bent, "and what is your image of a nun, I wonder? I wanted to be a nun because I loved God, it was that straightforward. I was a fool, I guess. I had such a clear sense of what I would do it was bound to go wrong. I would devote myself to God and I would nurse. And then in the war, in those hospitals, my faith—I guess that's what you'd call it though it doesn't fully explain what I felt—at first grew even stronger. I could do what was required of me, I knew. I could love those men, those pitiable men, I could love our enemy who sometimes came to us in a pulpy mess as prisoners, even the profiteers and the politicians and generals who had sent men to their deaths in such monstrous numbers. I didn't get angry or rebellious or resigned, because I had sacrificed my will to another's. What I *thought* was irrelevant after that, what I *did* and believed was all that mattered. Yes, I had surrendered, and it was a good feeling. I let go. I did my work. And then your brother came along." She glanced at me and her eyes were sober, as if she were struggling to be entirely truthful but I didn't trust her, I thought her a consummate actress and that this gravity was just another ploy. "He saw me as a challenge, something to break through to. He wanted me, all of me, body and soul, my full attention. He couldn't stomach the fact that I might actually have something else, *someone* else on my mind."

"My brother did not rape you. He was incapable of hurting anyone. He was kind and respectful. He wouldn't do that to any woman, because he loved *me*. He would think of it happening to me."

She lay back on my pillow, curled on her side, and drew her knees up to her chest, watching me. "It's not my intention to make you think too harshly of him. I understood him and perhaps in some ways I wanted him. I had wanted so many others. I wanted to be held and kissed and made love to. I wanted oblivion. Of course I did. But don't you see? I had wanted it but given it up. I had turned my back on that kind of comfort and he violated the choice I had made. That was the worse thing he did, almost worse than forcibly entering my body."

"But if you wanted him, you must have given him a signal."

"What signal, exactly? That I found him handsome and amusing? That I felt sympathy for him? That I rejoiced in his recovery and was so sad because he had to go back? Yes, I felt all those things. Is that what you meant, Evelyn?"

"I think he must have believed . . ."

"You were about to say, he must have believed that when I resisted him I was just playacting. Then you think as your brother chose to. You are no better than he. I might have known. God, you British middle classes, you cannot be in the wrong, can you, especially not if you want something that you can't have? He regarded my resistance as an obstacle, simply, to overcome." She unrolled from the bed and stood so close that we almost touched and I saw every detail of her small throat and her moist mouth and her hair falling in feathery wisps on her forehead.

"He raped me, Evelyn. Believe it. Accept it, please, so that we might put it behind us. So that we might be on the same side."

Her breath was on my chin and her eyes were pleading and ardent, turned up to me like a saint's at the foot of the cross in a bad painting. Perhaps it was fatigue, the lingering nightmare of the art party or the visit to the Good Samaritan Home, perhaps it was the unwanted intimacy of that moment or that she seemed so false, so determined to act out her part, but I couldn't stop myself, my hand came up and I struck her on the right cheek, not hard but enough to shunt that piteous look from her eye. "I don't believe it. I used to think I would help you, that we should accommodate you for the sake of Edmund. If you want us to care for him, we will. He shall be ours. But I want nothing to do with you and your lies and your wickedness. I want you out of my life."

She was still for a moment, not reacting even by putting her hand to her reddening cheek. Then she closed her eyes briefly, drew a deep breath, and left the room.

Twenty-One

It rained sporadically all the way through Stella's funeral. We had to prop our umbrellas in the porch, where they were so numerous that I wondered if I would ever recognize mine again. Trickles ran across the flagstones and collected in a puddle by the step. Inside, the church smelled of wet fabric and lilies and I was confronted by rows of black-clad backs and heavy hats. Stella's mother, Mrs. Hobhouse, had feared that there would be a lack of mourners but instead there were rather too many and I saw her glance around in bewilderment at the crowd of strangers: reporters, voyeurs, and police officers. The coffin, in lonely splendor on plush-covered trestles, was decorated with a single wreath of roses, placed above Stella's smashed heart.

In between hymns, we heard the wind bluster on the windows and a sudden spatter of hail. It was fitting somehow that a girl who had died violently in sunshine should be laid to rest in rain. Since the war, all churchgoing had seemed to me inexorably connected to death rather than resurrection. My brother's memorial service, held in the church we'd attended all our lives, had left me untouched, even faintly bored, and I was outraged when later I saw his name inscribed on the plaque in the side chapel among the other war dead. How dare they confirm something I didn't believe to be true? My father's death, on the other hand, had been marked by the same kind of bombast that featured in most aspects of his latter years. He was buried with considerable ceremony, mourned by a congregation of senior legal colleagues in their tailored coats and top hats. The address from the pulpit was by an archdeacon, because our vicar didn't consider himself to be quite grand enough, and the wake had been in the gloomy parlor of a hotel near Baker Street. What I remembered most was the smell, at midday, of last night's whiskey and cigarettes.

They were a sorry parade in my mind, Brother, Father, Stella, and behind them a million others. Waste, waste. I stared at the coffin and willed that girl to rise up and tell me the truth. What happened, Stella? Why did someone believe you needed to die?

A couple of pews ahead of me, an older man and a young woman stood a little apart from each other. I recognized Carole Mangan, the waitress at Lyons, by her bony shoulders clothed in a too-large black coat and the wisps of her fine blond hair sticking out from under her hat. Stella's family was clustered together, except for the husband of the disdainful sister, Julie. He had been consigned to the pew behind and remained seated throughout. The hymns were so conventional that they could only have been chosen by people who rarely went to church, and the vicar gave a brief, embarrassed address about a young girl's life cut off in its prime by a wicked act, presumably a deranged mind . . . so much killing and death already this century, you'd think we'd had enough bloodshed. . . . In the end his voice trailed away as if he was worn out by the futility of his own words.

And then we all trooped out, jostled in the porch to retrieve our umbrellas and straggled down a path under a yew tree oozing rain to a square of land that had been newly annexed to form an extension to the cemetery. Poor Stella had again been shortchanged. If it were me, I would much rather lie among the snugly lichened or half-fallen gravestones in the old churchyard than in a bit of virgin earth that had hitherto been wasteland.

I stood well back from the other mourners, feeling more than ever an intruder, and wondered if any of them knew secrets about Stella, notably where she had found the bronze dancer that was even now weighing down my briefcase. If Meredith was right about its value, no one here was moneyed enough to have given the statue as a present—worn shoes, uneven hems, ill-fitting coats, and greasy hat-brims all betokened shortage of funds—except perhaps the elderly gent who had accompanied Carole Mangan, a senior figure from Lyons who wasted no opportunity to point out to the press the showy wreath sent by the company as a mark of respect, and then shook Mr. Hobhouse heartily by the hand and drove off in a waiting taxi, far too important to linger.

After he'd gone, Miss Mangan, who had been standing at the edge of the grave, glanced over her shoulder and shifted surreptitiously toward me, as if afraid of drawing attention to herself. Rain had reddened the end of her nose and her skin was made sallow by her black costume. She had brought me a wedding photograph, different from the one on Mrs. Hobhouse's mantel, because this was of the bride and groom and all the guests, including Carole herself wearing a pale, drooping dress and a hat with a turned-up brim. Stella's smile, as in the other photograph, was like a model's in a fashion plate.

"Do you know who everyone is?" I asked.

"Stella went through it with me but I don't remember them all, no. Most were family friends. There were three of us from work. You can borrow it if you like."

"Can you spare a moment to talk to me?"

"I have to be back in the restaurant by one."

"May I travel with you some of the way perhaps? Are you going by bus?"

We said good-bye to Mrs. Hobhouse, who wore a dazed smile and scarcely seemed to know who we were, then set off through the now half-hearted fall of rain toward the omnibus stop. "I have the list you asked for as well," Carole said as soon as we were alone, and withdrew a handwritten sheet from her bag. "We did our best, me and the other girls. We argued over some. Number three, for instance, we was never quite sure if he came to look at Stell or Jeannie—Jeannie left about the same time as Stell. And seven is so poor he hardly seemed worth mentioning. She'd never have bothered with him."

"Do any of these men still come to the tea shop?"

"A few. The wheelchair boy sometimes. Before she left, or at least before they found out she was getting married, they was all regulars."

"Did the police ask about any of these men?"

"Obviously. I gave them the same list, just told them, didn't write them down. But they didn't seem that interested after I said Stella had never gone out with any of them."

"How did you know? How could you be sure?"

"Stephen met her most days after work. I don't see how she could have kept another man hidden from him or me, for that matter."

"There must have been some occasions when Stephen wasn't able to meet her. What about her lunch breaks or days off?"

She shrugged. "We had few enough days off and I presume she spent most of them with Stephen. At lunchtime we often get less than half an hour. Of course I don't know what she did with every minute. I only know what she told me and it was pretty ordinary stuff and, for the past few months, errands to do with the wedding. Sometimes I would go with her at the last minute—she never minded, so I doubt she was having secret assignations."

"The thing is, Carole, there are one or two things I've found that don't quite fit into the picture I have of Stella. For instance, when I was in her house I couldn't help noticing she had beautiful clothes, especially underwear."

Carole blushed. "She loved clothes. She'd have starved to save for a pair of silk stockings."

The omnibus came and we sat side by side on the top deck, I with the umbrella propped between my knees. It took several minutes for the conductor to reach us but I waited until we'd paid for our tickets before I showed Carole the scrap of paper I'd found in Stella's sponge bag. "Do you know where this ticket is from?"

"No idea. It's nothing to do with Lyons, I can tell you that."

"And here's something else I want you to see." I opened my case and showed her the dancer lying in its nest of tissue. "I found it in Stella's old bedroom, in Acton. I think it might be worth quite a lot of money."

She peered into the case. "Never seen it in my life."

"You don't think the manager, for instance, that man who was here, might have given it as a wedding present."

"Are you joking? We had a whip-'round for the tea set, like I said, but the manager didn't chip in. We had to plead with him to let us have a bob or two for her leaving party."

"What about someone from your list?"

She shook her head. Then she gave me a sidelong glance and said, "There is something that I should mention while I have the chance, though it's nothing much. Do you remember I told you that Stella was nearly always on time? It's preyed on my mind ever since, because one day in April, a couple of weeks before her wedding, she come in at about ten o'clock, two hours late, with mud on her shoes and her dress all crumpled, and it was obvious she hadn't been home all night."

"Her sister thought she'd once stayed out dancing at the Trocadero and missed the last bus home."

"She hadn't been dancing that night. She wasn't wearing dancing shoes. When I asked her why she was late she just said she'd overslept and missed the bus. But I knew she was lying."

"She had mud on her shoes?"

"That's it. She wore outdoor shoes and changed when she got to work. But I saw them in the cloakroom, caked with mud and little bits of grass, you know, when you've walked across a muddy lawn that's just mown. And her coat had a stain on it too, like a brown smear. And I knew she'd done something she was ashamed of, because of the way she behaved the rest of the day. It was always the same, when she'd been unkind or gone too far mimicking a customer or some such, she always went quiet and tearful and would hug me again and again as if she wanted to be sure and make someone love her. She was like that all morning, couldn't do enough for the customers but kept looking at the door, as if she were expecting someone, or coming up to me in the kitchen and kissing me."

"So where do you think she had been?"

"I have no idea, that's the thing. Somewhere not that nice. The coat had an odd smell, you know, like it had been left in a damp bathroom. Oh yes, it made me think of hospital wards or an old bloke we have in sometimes who doesn't wash himself." She glanced at me anxiously. "And to be fair, I'd forgotten all about it. If it hadn't been for the fact that she's dead and you keep asking questions, I wouldn't have brought it to mind again."

We got off the bus on Holland Park Avenue. The rain had almost stopped and I sensed that Carole wanted rid of me; there was something shameful about discussing the dead girl's secrets only minutes after she was buried. I said I would take the train back to Euston Square, but I was sorry that we had to part; her honesty, her desire to do the right thing were endearing and I thought she would be a good friend, if only I could win her trust.

At the last moment, I asked her to have another look at the dancer. She seemed afraid to touch it but in the end held it in her bony fingers. "Isn't it heavy? Did it cost a great deal? I shouldn't fancy it in my home. My mum would have a fit."

"I don't know what it's worth. I'm going to try and find out."

"What use is it?"

"It looks nice, I suppose, that's all."

"Stella loved to dance, it's true. But not like this, obviously . . ." Her pale eyes, as they met mine, were a little fearful. Then she thrust the statue back in my hand, her bus came, and she rode away.

Carole's list:

Gentlemen Admirers. Stella Wheeler

1. Married man. Wore a ring. Bowler. Dark overcoat. Big nose, mustache, specktacles for reading. Seemed tired. Lunch times only. Never ate. Just coffee. Read *The Times*. Watched her ankles.
2. Boy. Eighteen-ish. Clerk of some sort. Sore neck from his collar. Pimples. Sunken cheeks. Worshipped Stella. Would spend his last penny on a bit of toast, just so he could hang around at a table.
3. Gentleman. Old. White hair, mustache. Spectacles. Brief case. Always polite. Never seemed to mind who served him but we thought he looked out for Stella or Jeannie. Took the same table each time. Back to the wall. Under the clock. Watched, and sometimes got out papers and worked. Would visit odd times. Always in week, never on Saturdays. Sometimes away for weeks at a time, we'd almost forget him, then he'd be back.
4. Another gentleman. Mr. Griffiths. A bit younger than the one above. Bald on top, longish straight hair round ears. Fifty? Pin stripes. Big tips. Liked all the girls and we liked him. Asked about our love lives. Wanted to know what we did weekends. Sometimes came a few days together, then a long break. Still comes in from time to time.

5. Young man in wheelchair. Late twenties. No legs. Mother used to bring him. Proposed to Stell every month or so. Loved her to flirt with him.

6. Fat man. Banker, he told us. Bowler hat. Smelled of cologne. Ate cakes, loved cakes, sweet tooth. Natty shoes. Used to grab Stell's hand sometimes when she passed and ask if she'd go on a date. She used to say the touch of him made her shudder. When she told him about Stephen he said he'd got far more to offer than an insurance clerk.

7. Another cripple. Harry. Missing one arm, one foot. No job. Loved Stell. Must have drunk gallons of tea for her sake. Heartbroken on afternoon she left. Said he'd never come back and never did.

8. Prince Charming, as we called him, too good to be true. Very tall, very well turned out. Posh voice. Not more than thirty. Always an umbrella. Made no secret of his feelings either, though overdid it rather, we sometimes thought. Used to tease her. Brought her a posy once. Enough to make her quite hopeful—we girls used to build it up into a romance and plan a silk wedding gown for her, and a trousseau. But then, a month or so before her wedding, he stopped coming.

Twenty-two

I arrived at the office of Breen & Balcombe very wet and hungry, my fingers itching to take up a pen and do routine work, to keep myself steady after the turmoil of the art party and its consequences. But the minute I let myself into the hall, Breen's voice rang from his study: "Gifford."

"Mr. Breen."

His office, that strangely metamorphic place, had transformed itself into a no-nonsense hub of business and he was in the kind of mood when an interview with him could go either way; he would spark fire one minute, be reasonable the next. A vast document on heavy parchment was spread before him and a pencil tucked behind his ear as he played to the hilt the part of overworked lawyer. There was no sign of tea, whiskey, or any of the other Friday treats.

"Door," he yelled. I shut the door. "Now where have you been?" he said on a long sigh, as if I could have been to the Antipodes, for all he knew.

"To Stella Wheeler's funeral, as I . . ."

"And what was the value of that? Remind me."

"Her mother asked me to be there. I didn't think . . ."

"It seems to me you've done a lot of not thinking recently, Miss Gifford. I have a letter here from Miss Buckley, matron of the Good Samaritan Home, copied to the chairman of the board of trustees, Bishop Ogilvie. Here it is, two close-written pages on the subject of your unprofessional and provocative conduct."

"I had no choice, sir."

"Hah."

"I think if you'd been there, if you'd seen the children with their mother . . ."

"You see, this is it. When I told them I might take you on my colleagues said to me, steer clear of the woman, any woman. You're mad, Breen, to consider it even. Women cannot see the wood for the trees, they said. Or to put it in the words of a particularly eloquent journalist: 'Women see through a stone wall what is not on the other side.' *Personally* you might well have felt pity for the children, Miss Gifford, *professionally* you had no right to do anything other than your duty as a legal representative. As it is you've probably set the cause back irretrievably. Miss Buckley writes that you used threats against her."

"I merely pointed out . . ."

"The entire affair shows a lamentable lack of judgment."

"Mr. Breen, I could not bear to see those children suffer. We must rescue them—they are in danger of being sent to Canada or Australia if we don't. I saw a notice of sailing on the notice board. My friend Miss Morrison says it's common practice to ship foundlings abroad."

"What are you talking about? *Canada*. Don't be so ridiculous. How old did you say the Marchant girls were?"

"Seven and five, which I admit seems young to be migrated, but apparently some are. And they'll be sent there one day, possibly, if we don't get them back."

"Well, you've just raised the stakes on that. Miss Buckley also states that you removed something from her office. I'm assuming that is simply not true."

I didn't know whether to laugh or cry as I took the documents bear-

ing the names of board members and the list titled CANADIAN OUT-
FITS FOR GIRLS from my briefcase. As I unfolded them, Breen sank his
head in his hands, recovered, picked up the papers, studied them, and
tossed them down again. "You are in serious trouble, Miss Gifford. You
could be struck off for this. It constitutes a complete breach of trust,
professional misconduct, the lot. What were you thinking of? You could
have copied them out."

"There wasn't time."

"I suspect our only option will be to grovel. I hate that. Tell me again
what you meant . . . *Canada*."

"Miss Morrison says that some children are migrated overseas and
adopted. But it may be worse. I've heard that some children are forced
to work as domestic servants or farmhands. Others are mistreated."

"I'll get Wolfe to look into it. You stay clear. Don't even breathe until
I give you permission. Off you go now, for God's sake. It's likely the
police will be here any moment to arrest you for theft so before they
arrive you might as well draw up a couple of affidavits for me."

Instead I sat in the chair by his desk and lifted my sodden briefcase
onto my lap. "There's something I've been meaning to show you, sir. I
brought it from Stella Wheeler's bedroom."

He gaped. "You didn't steal it."

"No, no, I gave Mrs. Hobhouse a receipt."

I took the statue from the briefcase and stood it on his desk. Then,
for good measure, I unfolded the ticket I'd found in Stella's sponge bag.
Breen threw himself back in his chair, twiddled his thumbs, and looked
at the dancer from under his lids. In the meantime, the room had
changed, as if the statue had drawn all the feeble light from a drizzly
afternoon to itself and Breen's office was merely a backdrop. He leaned
forward and advanced his chin close. "Now that, I'll admit, is fascinating."

I breathed more freely as I watched him adopt a new pose, that of
fine-art connoisseur. He didn't touch the statue at first but got up and

walked slowly around the desk so that he could view her from every angle. Then he sat down again and picked her up delicately by the plinth to study her, head to toe. "You are right, she is beautiful. Utterly. Modern. It shouldn't be too difficult to find out where she was bought. A limited edition I shouldn't wonder, French, you have to admire the French, not a Bourdelle but possibly a copy. Probably worth fifty pounds or so, quite outside our little waitress's league."

"And then there's this. If you remember, I found it in Stella Wheeler's sponge bag when we went to the house."

"As I said at the time, possibly significant, possibly not. When all's said and done it's a cloakroom ticket."

"The thing is, sir, I think it probably is significant because I've found out that Stella was a collector. She'd carefully tucked away a conker case and acorn cup and other little bits and pieces in such a remote part of her wardrobe at home that there was a good chance they would never be found. Her mother thought they were remnants of her childhood but they weren't, they were freshly fallen. And now Carole, a waitress who worked with Stella, has told me that in April Stella stayed out a whole night and wouldn't say where she'd been. She came into work next day with a stained coat and dirty shoes."

"Well?"

"Well, don't you think, Mr. Breen, that this all points to a love affair of some kind?"

"A love affair? She'd only been married a fortnight." Despite his bluster—the words *love affair* were spoken incredulously, as if to say no one in their right mind would embark on such a thing—he didn't appear to be much shocked but nodded as if this was what he'd been thinking all along.

"I've been pondering it for some time. And now Carole has given me a list of men who admired Stella, although she's pretty sure none met her outside work."

Breen's face was a mask of incredulity. "Miss Gifford, a man's life is hanging by a thread. A trial date has been fixed. And you have *been pondering* a theory that could change everything. If Wheeler had cause to be jealous he has a motive for murder, don't you think?"

"I do. But what if Stella had become a nuisance to a rich admirer? Blackmail . . ."

He flung himself back in his chair and yelled: *"Wolfe."*

Miss Drake appeared. "Mr. Wolfe, as you may recall, has an interview with a colleague from the war office."

"Curse the boy. Then we'll meet first thing Monday, eight o'clock sharp. See he gets the message."

When Miss Drake had gone, I said: "Don't you think we should tell the police?"

Few things delighted Breen more than throwing obstructions in the way of the police, though he made a show of prevaricating by chewing his lip and looking at the ceiling. "In time. Not now. I don't want them asking clod-hopping questions of our poor Mr. Wheeler. Things are not straightforward. We've had a report from Wheeler's medical officer and we think there's just a chance we may be able to run an argument of unfit to plead, after all, though it's a very high threshold to cross. The defense has to convince a judge and jury that the defendant is incapable of understanding what is going on. There are many pitfalls. If we lose the argument and Wheeler, after trial, is found guilty, our chances of mitigating on the grounds of diminished responsibility are damaged because a jury has already decided he *is* of sound mind. At this stage, until we've clarified our line of defense and had a conference with Wainwright, I want to play all our cards close to our chest. And by the way, I had a call from Thorne. Says he'd like to take a look at the crime scene for the sake of completeness or some such nonsense. Damned nuisance he couldn't have come with us the other day. I said you'd go with him on Monday afternoon, keep you out of mischief." He stared at me blandly.

"No, I can't," I said.

"I beg your pardon?"

"No. I have too much work. I am at least a week behind with . . ."

"Wolfe can't take him on account of his asthma, and I've far too much on so you're all we've got, I'm afraid." He threw a sheaf of documents across the table. "You should read this report from Wheeler's medical officer. Despite the little matter of Miss Buckley of the Good Samaritans I'm minded to set you up for a cozy tête-à-tête with Stephen Wheeler, woman to man, see if you can get anything else out of him, especially now you suspect there was a third party in the marriage."

ฺ

Wheeler's medical report shed quite a different light on a man I had come to regard, hitherto, entirely as a victim of circumstance.

When recruited in August 1914, Wheeler was deemed of "inferior" health due to a slight weakness of the lungs (asthma, like Wolfe) and the fact that he was somewhat overweight and pigeon-toed (the examining MO noted that Wheeler had been confined to a desk ten hours a day since leaving school more than a dozen years previously), but was nonetheless considered fit enough to join up. Army life seemed to have been good for his health, because there were no other entries until an account of chlorine gas poisoning in 1915, which affected his already damaged lungs and resulted in severe bouts of coughing. A healthier man would have suffered less, wrote the MO, who added that Wheeler received the news that he was to be returned to England *without comment*.

This lack of responsiveness became a feature of the report. When he was again examined, prior to being sent back to France, it was noted that he showed no sign of emotion, either pleasure or distress, at the thought of being returned to the front line. Later, when treated for a

slight wound to the foot sustained through a display of extreme careless-
ness by a private with an entrenching tool, the doctor noted that
Wheeler made light of the pain, hoped the other chap wouldn't be
disciplined for it, and asked if he could be patched up by nightfall when
he was due to go on patrol, a duty he seemed to relish despite its dan-
gers. *Wheeler is one of the type of personalities who are much depended on by
their fellows,* noted Doctor Reardon. *His behavior is utterly consistent, will
never show an excess of emotion, notably fear, and even under heavy shelling
remains calm.*

When he was finally invalided out, due to the loss of three fingers
on his left hand caused by handling a malfunctioning grenade, Wheeler
had displayed some irritation that he would not see the war through to
the end.

In a handwritten postscript to the typewritten report, Reardon had
scrawled: *Wheeler was in many ways the ideal soldier, unflagging, always
ready to volunteer for difficult tasks, utterly dependable, able to sleep and
maintain normal functions in the most challenging conditions. When I was
asked (along with other officers) to select men to perform the most taxing of
duties, his was often the first name that came to mind. One of our regiment
was convicted of desertion and firing on a military policeman while already
on suspended sentence for a like offense. When Wheeler's name was drawn for
the firing party, I was relieved. I knew he could be relied on and that he would
not flinch.*

*I have noted that there are types of personality that survive better in war
than in peacetime—a man like Wheeler thrives on the routine of war and the
absolute necessity to obey orders. The shocks of trench life register less with this
type than with others. At times of greatest trial to the emotions, such as after
a battle, in burying the dead, he worked tirelessly. I have never known him
to break down. You will note the commendations, in my view much deserved.*

*And yet despite, or perhaps because of, the above, I would strongly recom-
mend that Wheeler be examined for his psychological fitness to plead. What is*

acceptable, even convenient in times of war, does not allow a man to survive in more normal circumstances. His fellows thought Wheeler "odd" despite his trustworthiness and bravery under fire, and I wonder now, on reflection, whether he wasn't of a particular type of personality that experiences difficulties in engaging in normal human relationships, and whereas in the face of constant danger most men do at some stage show signs of fear and shock, such a man as Wheeler cannot make a genuine display of such emotions at any time. In the circumstances, I wonder if Wheeler is capable of comprehending the complexities of the British legal system or, more to the point, if the British legal system could possibly comprehend Wheeler.

∞

I spent the afternoon in my musty basement, plowing through a heap of paperwork, much of which would have to be taken home to do at the weekend. Each envelope had been slit open by Miss Drake, the contents examined, refolded, and put back. She did not prioritize my papers in order of urgency, as she did for Wolfe and Breen, or take it upon herself to respond to more obvious, nonlegal queries, so I had to wade through an indiscriminate heap of licensing applications, maintenance orders, letters from an affronted husband and a self-righteous wife, a property search, a couple of requests for appointments for the signing of wills, a query over an eviction order.

Then there was the letter from Miss Buckley of the Good Samaritan Home, which made very unpleasant reading indeed, since it was full of exclamation marks and rhetorical questions about my qualifications and fitness for my job, and the fact that she felt duty-bound to write a full report to the board, given that her authority had been so severely undermined. My poor father, I reflected, must be spinning in his grave. Had he not, against his better judgment, paid more than five hundred pounds for my university education, articles, and professional fees, yet here I was, once more in peril of losing my position and altogether hopelessly out of my depth?

And in Clivedon Hall Gardens, disaster had struck. My fault again. The smell of smoked haddock, it being Friday, was pungent as I unlocked the front door. At dinner there was no sign of Meredith or Edmund and the atmosphere was funereal. Nobody replied when I commented on the rain and asked how they had all passed the day. Finally, I said: "Where are our visitors?"

"They are flat-hunting," said Prudence, making the sensational gesture of flinging down her fish-knife and fork and pushing aside a near-untouched plate. "Meredith says that you have told them to leave."

I picked a bone from between my front teeth and took a sip of water. How typical of Meredith to avenge herself with this precipitate gesture.

"Your mother and I think it unforgivable that you should have acted without consulting the rest of us," added Prudence.

"You surprise me, Aunt Prudence. I thought that you and Mother disliked Meredith being in the house. I thought you would have thanked me."

"There is such a thing as Christian charity. We would have given the girl a chance, time, to find somewhere suitable. We would have made her welcome until then. Why were you so cruel to her? Why?"

How could I announce over fish pie that Meredith had accused James of rape? "I'll discuss it with Mother later," I said.

Mother, with the dazed expression of one who has been given her heart's desire only to find it was not at all what she wanted, had finished eating and was dabbing her mouth with her napkin. At eight o'clock, while we were eating tapioca, the front door opened and then we heard feet on the basement stairs. Meredith had doubtless arranged to have supper put back in the kitchen by Min and Rose, who adored her.

Meanwhile, I planned the forthcoming conversation with Mother. How would she respond if I told her about the alleged rape, given that her entire world was built around the spotless shades of her dead son and husband? In the end, I took the coward's way. When she and I were alone together, I said that she had been right all along, we simply couldn't afford to accommodate Meredith and so I'd told her to go. I had, however, offered to take care of Edmund.

"It seems so sudden," said Mother, glancing nervously at the door. "I wish you'd consulted me."

"I'm sorry. We'd had an argument, she and I, to do with the art party, her drinking. I believe that she is a very difficult woman, full of bitterness. I should like to help her but I don't think our way of life is compatible with the one she longs for. Above all, however, we must continue to support and protect Edmund."

Mother's mood was odd, as if her mind was on something else. She stood up, drummed her fingers on the dressing table, swept across the room to the writing box containing James's letters, glanced at me, began to speak, changed her mind, and started again. "Oh, of course. I've wondered if what she really wanted was for us to adopt him. Then she'd be free. Certainly we must do the right thing by Edmund. Well, perhaps it will be a blessing that you have spoken out . . . But I can't help thinking, Evelyn, that with all your expensive education, you might have handled it better."

⟨∞⟩

It was a miserable weekend. Edmund was to be found in odd corners, big-eyed, pretending to read a book and full of questions none of us chose to answer, about what was happening and where was Mommy, until at last Grandmother invited him into her room to play board games and look through an album of opening-night good-wishes cards.

Prudence put on her hat and a martyred expression and went out on mysterious expeditions while Mother paid calls and held a bridge afternoon. I was ostracized by all but tried not to mind, telling myself that I was glad Meredith was leaving and that I had far too much work preparing for a morning in the magistrates' court on Monday—routine for an experienced lawyer, an ordeal for me—to be bothered with domestic matters. The proposed excursion with Thorne haunted me.

Meanwhile, it went on raining. Meredith spent long hours walking the streets looking for somewhere decent and affordable (as I heard her tell Min on the stairs), and returned wan and soaked to the skin. The girls fussed over her, ran her a hot bath, and made a dainty supper because she'd missed tea. On Saturday evening, I decided I ought at the very least to apologize for striking her and say there was really no hurry, she could stay until she'd found alternative accommodation, but when I knocked on her door, she appeared briefly, fragile as a flower in her delicate robe, and actually flinched away as if terrified I would slap her again. Later I heard Prudence knock and gain admittance. Their conversation went on and on.

On Sunday, Meredith took Edmund to church, having first established that I had decided not to go that day. How could I pray for strength in exercising the Christian virtues of restraint, continence, and humility, when in truth I wanted none of them?

By the time the five of them came back to lunch, it was perfectly clear to me that I now was the outsider, and that the others, even my mother, had united to protect the wronged little Meredith and her fatherless son.

Twenty-three

On *Monday morning, even Wolfe turned up* for an eight-o'clock meeting, somewhat rumpled and with one cuff link in his pocket because he'd not had time to fix it before leaving. The bronze dancer stood in pride of place on Breen's desk, concealed under a duster.

"Wheeler's trial date has been fixed for July 14 at Aylesbury Assizes," said Breen. "We have a not-guilty plea and nothing whatever to support it except a couple of character witnesses."

"And no plausible motive," said Wolfe.

"Miss Gifford has come up with a motive." Breen paused for dramatic effect, then swept the cloth from the dancer. Miss Drake, notetaker, took one look and gave me a reproachful stare, as if to say she might have known I would sully the place with obscene statues. Wolfe sat up a little as Breen continued: "Jealousy. This statue is evidence that there may have been another man in Stella's life. The dancer, which she could never have afforded to buy for herself, is presumably a gift but we don't know from whom. Not her husband, I would suggest, given that it would have cost half a year's income. And I don't see Wheeler purchasing such an item. There is also a night, a fortnight or so before her wedding, when Stella went missing with no consistent explanation to her friend or sister. All we know is that she appeared at work with stained clothes, which smelled bad, and mud on her shoes. And then there's this cloakroom ticket which Stella hid away in her sponge bag and a list of customers at Lyons who took a fancy to our Stella when she was a waitress." He laid out on the desk the scrap of paper, Carole's list, and Stella's wedding photograph.

Wolfe picked up the dancer and turned her in his meaty fingers, a glint of appreciation in his eye. "It should be possible to find out who sold her, even who bought her. But the kinds of establishment I have in mind are very exclusive. They will want to protect the identity of their customers. What about the police, what do they think?"

"The police searched Stella's room but overlooked the dancer or thought it unimportant. It's up to you to do their work for them, Wolfe; I'm sure you have ways of encouraging even the most discreet tradesman to divulge a little information, in the interests of justice. Miss Drake, unlock the cash box if you would, and provide Mr. Wolfe with five pounds' worth of half-crowns. And now the ticket in Stella's sponge bag. Does it mean anything to you, Wolfe?"

"It could be anything. A raffle ticket? A cloakroom ticket? Number 437. No, it's slightly larger than a raffle ticket, wouldn't you say? I've seen this type a good deal, Breen, haven't you, among our clients, as issued by the police when they confiscate clothing or such. But our Stella didn't have a criminal record, did she? And what about the stains on her clothes? What were they? Mud, blood? Do you suppose she had an accident or was lost, or was perhaps induced or forced to lie down in her clothes—is that what you're thinking, Miss Gifford?"

For a moment we were silent as we pondered those murky eighteen hours between Stella leaving work and turning up late next day. Then Miss Drake spoke for the first time. "Of course," she drawled, putting the tip of her pencil daintily to the middle of her bottom lip and pausing, to emphasize that she was doing us a favor by uttering a word, "she might have had a medical emergency, but of a very specific nature."

"You mean she sought an abortion," said Wolfe.

"Child murder," said Miss Drake firmly.

Breen sighed. "It had crossed my mind, though one might have expected something to show up in the postmortem. And if it was the case that Stella was in some kind of desperate situation, would she not have told her friend at work? I thought you women talked about anything and everything." But having looked from Miss Drake to me, he didn't press the point—apparently he didn't find that we were representative of our sex.

"Stella's friend at Lyons did mention that the clothes smelled of hospitals," I said.

"I could find out . . ." said Wolfe.

"I daresay you could," said Breen, "but in the meantime, on the basis that it's possible our poor victim had a medical emergency, I think Miss Gifford should visit our hospitals to see if she spent a night there. Miss Drake will find the name of her family doctor and speak to him. I may make a few inquiries among our female clients who might have a better idea than us where a girl might go. And Wolfe, get someone to check police records for the night Stella was missing, in case she ended up in custody. And now," he added, nodding dismissively at Miss Drake and me, "I'd like to speak to Mr. Wolfe."

☙❧

An hour later, I was in Shoreditch Magistrates' Court, making licensing applications, this time before a bench of four lay magistrates, one of them a lady in a startling white hat. For once I found myself greeted smilingly by the bench, I suspect because the novelty of a female advocate broke the tedium of granting the Railway Arms an extension until eleven o'clock for a coming-of-age party; another, a week on Saturday, for an engagement. The magistrates pushed back their chairs and discussed each case sotto voce as if they were deciding guilt in a capital offense, and when granting the application did so with an air of sighing magnanimity.

Later, this time with Wolfe yawning on my left hand, supposedly to lend his support, I defended a landlord prosecuted under the Intoxicating Liquor Act. "A woman was responsible for the legislation in the first place, it's surely fitting that you should take on the extra work it brings," Breen had said, though he'd once told me he approved of the bill, describing it as one of the very few recently introduced onto our statute books that might enhance the quality of our lives.

The landlord's defense, disclosed to me when he turned up five minutes before the hearing, was that it was ridiculous to expect him to ask every young customer his age before serving a pint, and that bloody ("Excuse me, miss") woman MP hadn't thought through the consequences. "Other landlords manage it," I told him. "I shall simply suggest to the court that it was an uncharacteristic lapse and that you have a clean record for this type of offense." I did not add that with Lady Astor's bill only months old it was to be hoped no landlord had accrued a record.

"By the way," murmured Wolfe as we sat together under the dock while the magistrates retired to consider their verdict, "the Marchant case. Breen told me to look into it. Devilish hard to get the children out by legal means, I'd say. The Good Samaritan Home is notoriously evangelical. Takes a hard line on the sort of background those children come from. The chair of the board, Bishop Ogilvie, is teetotal. Can't stand drink, can't stand the fact that some children don't have a father or attend church."

"So what must we do?"

"We'll need to pull strings, Miss Gifford. I doubt your Mrs. Marchant, from what I've heard, will be able to prove to the courts that she's a fit mother. Homes like the Good Samaritan will argue that children should be severed from the vicious influence of home."

"We have money. She will work."

"Money isn't enough. If the home's taken against her, they will spy on her and inspect her to see if she has the moral rectitude to bring up the children."

"And if she hasn't, according to them?"

He shrugged. "Then the home will dispose of them as it sees fit."

We sprang to our feet as the magistrates came back and fined my landlord ten shillings.

Afterward, still brooding on my conversation with Wolfe, I waited an hour and a half for the case of a young boy (one of Breen's habitual clients) in the children's court pleading guilty to stealing a pineapple. I so wanted to see Miss Buckley and the Good Samaritan Home subjected to the due process of law. It wasn't just that Buckley and I had been locked in positions of violent antipathy for those few minutes in her office, it was that Leah had all the cards stacked against her: the home had money, influence, tradition, righteousness, religion on its side. Poor Leah had only love (and the home would even regard her type of love as dubious), Mrs. Sanders, and me.

Meanwhile, Wolfe, with characteristic ennui, represented a wife beater who was pleading innocence on the grounds of severe provocation (adjourned for trial), and defended successfully in the brief trial of the son of a fellow solicitor accused of dangerous conduct on a bicycle.

After the pineapple case (adjourned for the child's mother to attend), I was at last free to go.

Twenty-four

By the afternoon, the weather had cleared, and I took the Metropolitan Line train to Chesham under a blue sky studded with puffy white clouds. Though I would not have admitted it to myself, I had made a concession to the fact that I was meeting Thorne by wearing a much lighter blouse than usual, with mother-of-pearl buttons and a slightly scooped neck, though, in view of the recent unsettled weather, my shoes were suitable for all seasons.

As the train rattled out of Wembley Park, I was conscious of a clearing of the mind that had nothing whatever to do with the sunshine. It was as if the tangle of home and work fell away and instead I was untrammeled as an arrow shot cleanly from its bow.

I had not experienced the world in such vivid colors since the July before James was killed, when he was on leave and we picnicked on Primrose Hill, lying on our backs afterward, elbow to elbow, hip to hip. When I turned my head, about to say, "We'll buy an ice cream, shall we, on the way home?" I saw that a tear had trickled from the corner of his closed eye, down his cheek, and into his ear. I didn't say a word. We got up a few minutes later and walked home. I never mentioned the ice cream.

It was as if all the years since then I had been semiconscious but now was abruptly wide-awake, with everything so present to me that I blinked in the sudden burst of color, sound, touch. Beyond the train window, tranquil farmland gushed past, greens and creams and browns, and within the compartment the smallest detail came into sharp focus, so that instead of filtering out the inconsequential I saw it all: a crumpled ticket, the ridges in the floor where cigarette butts, mud, and fluff were caught, a mole the size of a farthing on the cheek of a child opposite, the way his mother's wedding ring cut into her swollen finger. A sane voice in my head repeated: You are a legal clerk accompanying a barrister on a tour of a murder scene. That is all. You are absurd to attach any other significance to the meeting. But that voice was drowned out by a roar of expectation.

In a terse telephone conversation with Thorne's clerk, I had arranged to meet him behind the church. I had a map and a penciled plan of the terrain, together with a list of instructions from Wolfe: *Check timings; consider hat; how did Wheeler conceal weapon?* It was barely a ten-minute walk from the station, across the High Street, through a cluster of little cottages, and up the lane leading out of the town, where Thorne was waiting for me beside a natty Ford. He leaned on the churchyard wall and wore a summer-weight suit and beautiful shoes, highly polished, with stitching across the toe and narrow, neat laces. His trilby was perched on the wall beside him and his hair had flopped onto his brow. When he saw me, he gave a start, as if of surprise, and raised an eyebrow. I walked up briskly and put out my gloved hand, registering that both his pose and his reaction to my arrival had been staged and that he was possibly nearly as nervous as I.

"Very good of you, Miss Gifford, to give up so much of your valuable time."

It was on the tip of my tongue to remind him that I had no choice in the matter but I was determined not to quarrel. In fact, my plan, upon which I had dwelled at length during the small hours of three successive nights, was that he should find my company so dull that he would want nothing more to do with me. If I didn't see him again, I reasoned, my wounded heart would begin to heal. So we set off in silence along the path running under the churchyard wall and through the gate into the field.

At first, my strategy worked. I told myself that he was just a man, after all, product of a good private school, the type I had known at Cambridge only perhaps more able and ambitious than most. Well, I had nothing to fear. What was all the fuss about? In fact, when I glanced at him, I told myself: he is too tall to be truly desirable and you know him to be as ambitious and as guilty of chauvinism as the rest—I wonder you ever found him attractive. Sylvia, the socialite, is welcome to him.

"No ill effects from the art party, Miss Gifford?" he said at last.

"None. You?"

"Oh good Lord, no. But then I didn't take a dousing in the river. And Sylvia keeps a weather eye on my drinking, if that's what you meant. I'm never allowed to knock back so much that I can't drive her home."

"I thought your fiancée very beautiful."

"She is. Sometimes I forget how beautiful, so that when I see her after an absence I'm quite taken aback."

I nearly laughed aloud. Until that moment, my treacherous heart had allowed the hope to flicker that Thorne had engineered this trip because, despite his engagement, he was as interested in me as I in him. The flame was extinguished by his devotion to Sylvia—expressed abstractedly, as if he was actually immersed, for that moment, in her loveliness—and it served me right. Well, I knew how to encourage men to talk about their heart's desire; I had learned the trick at my mother's knee. "Have you been engaged long?"

"Rather too long. I've known her for years, since she was a bouncy little girl. I was at school with her brother, Donald. He and I were best friends. I used to spend weeks of my holidays in and out of the Hardynge house in Belsize Park." I pictured those favored children, several rungs above my own family on the social ladder, flitting from one pleasure to the next, tennis, cricket, cycling, theater, dancing. "My own home was much humbler," he added, "my father is a solicitor in Reading but the Hardynges welcomed me nonetheless. And when I got back from the war I found that Sylvia had become this astonishing young woman. How could I not ask her to marry me?"

I congratulated myself on dealing with the subject of his fiancée with generosity and detachment, although I could not help dwelling on the strangeness of his last question. Nonetheless, the exchange, in which Thorne had disclosed so much and I so little, had given me the upper hand. "According to the police," I said, consulting my notes, "this is the path taken by the Wheelers, no question. A witness has come forward, a farmer's daughter who passed them here, on the brow of the hill, about midday. She gave a very detailed description of Stella's pink dress and hat."

Thorne paused and looked about. Near his left hand, a pair of blue butterflies touched midair and flitted away, and from trees to the left I heard the faint knocking of a woodpecker. "The reason I wanted to come here," he said, "was that I thought it essential to understand the lie of the land. You will gather that I'm frustrated at not being involved in the case myself but Hardynge takes a great interest and so do I. Maybe I'll notice something that I can pass on to Wainwright."

"In the end details of the crime may prove irrelevant. Mr. Breen is still considering a fitness-to-plead argument."

"Is he indeed? Fiendishly difficult. Especially given Wheeler's coherence both at the police station on the day after the murder and subsequently in jail. I'm surprised at Breen. He hasn't a chance. Wainwright won't entertain the idea."

"Perhaps Mr. Wainwright should have met us here today," I said curtly, stung by the criticism of Breen.

"I confess it never occurred to me to ask him, Miss Gifford. Probably I was being selfish . . ."

Altogether he was far less at ease than on other occasions; his irritation at Breen seemed uncharacteristic and even his movements lacked the wonderful fluidity that had so drawn my attention before. He opened a gate, held it for me, and closed it after us. I didn't look up at his face as I passed but mumbled my thanks. Afterward, I remembered how the hinges groaned, the snick of the latch, and under my hand the warmth of weathered wood polished by decades of passing cattle.

"Did you have a good weekend, Miss Gifford?"

I quickened my pace. The breeze was light and fragrant but my heart ached. At that moment, as my shoulder had so nearly brushed his arm at the gate, as I turned away my head though I knew he was smiling down at me, I had so yearned for him to touch me that to keep up this façade of indifference seemed unendurable. "Much as usual, thank you."

"We played tennis, would you believe. Whenever it stopped raining we dashed onto the court, never mind the risk of slipping. I spend more time than I can afford playing tennis, always on a Saturday, sometimes Sundays too. The Hardynges have a grass court and Sylvia and I are quite addicted, though neither of us is half as good as Donald, who was an ace. Do you play, Miss Gifford?"

"Not anymore. I used to."

"So how *did* you spend your weekend?"

"Mostly working."

"I might have guessed. I'll bet you drive yourself atrociously hard. Do you ever let yourself have a holiday, I wonder?"

"I try to. Last week was exceptionally busy so there was catching up to do. Unusually for me, I was out of the office a good deal."

"Why was that?"

"This Wheeler case, among other things. And then the Leah Marchant affair is dragging on. If you remember, her children are being looked after in a home from which we're now trying to extract them."

"Of course. Any progress?"

"We are afraid it will be difficult to have the children released. Their home life is far from ideal. Mr. Wolfe suggests we may need to pull strings."

"You have only to say the word and I'll see what I can do to assist."

I was silent, caught by the twist of anger that habitually followed one of his assumptions of superiority, whether imagined by me or otherwise. Then I said: "Thank you. I'll consult first with Mr. Breen."

After a few moments, Thorne tried another tack. "So, when the Wheelers came up here, he was carrying a picnic basket and she presumably a little handbag of some kind. Has anyone mentioned a handbag?"

"It was scarcely more than a purse, I believe, the same color as her dress, containing comb and compact—it was buried with her."

"Has anyone made a suggestion yet about where Wheeler hid the revolver on the way to the picnic?"

"We presume it would have been in his jacket or the picnic basket."

"A revolver is quite bulky and heavy. And there's another question I have. It's odd that Wheeler should have been in possession of such a weapon during the war, let alone after it. They tended to be the preserve of officers."

"I believe Wheeler was promoted to corporal during the war."

"Nonetheless. Noncommissioned officers didn't usually carry revolvers, as I mentioned to Breen the other day." We were walking briskly, despite the heat. Though I didn't look directly at Thorne, I couldn't avoid his shadow, which sometimes tangled with my feet. "If you like, I could carry your jacket, Miss Gifford."

"Thank you. No. I prefer to keep it on." This last remark was so churlish (and untrue) that I had to make up for it by saying the first thing that came into my head: "Actually, it's possible that you could help me with the Leah Marchant case. I'm afraid to say that when she and I visited the children's home things went very badly. My fault as much as hers. I had an argument with the matron."

He laughed, youthful, delighted, and for a fatal moment I caught his blue, brilliant eye. "Now, why doesn't that surprise me?"

"I was most unprofessional, I admit, but the sight of two little girls clinging to their mother's skirts unhinged me. So now I have to find a way of extracting the children, knowing that I have lost any hope of the matron's sympathy. And I have found that they are vulnerable in another way. Did you know that this country apparently ships hundreds of foundling children to colonies overseas?"

"I had heard, at Toynbee. And I believe there is to be a government commission to look into the practice this autumn. Surely the Marchant children are too young."

"I'm not so sure. And if they're too young now, they won't be in years to come."

"What you need is contacts, Miss Gifford. If you could find out who is on the board . . . Why are you laughing at me?"

"I was ahead of you, Mr. Thorne, I took a list of board members from the matron's office. I intend to write to each in turn but maybe I should save myself the trouble and hand the list over to you. You're bound to know someone, there are a few titles, I'm sure a word in the right ear from you would save me six weeks' work."

"Do I detect a note of bitterness there, Miss Gifford?"

"Really, you can't blame me for having a chip on my shoulder." It was happening again, the fatal allure of pitting my wits against his. "I've heard all kinds of arguments against women entering the legal professions, the stuff about special spheres and women having no understanding of relevance or analogy or evidence, but there is one that nobody quite brings themselves to mention: that unless their fathers happen to be high up, women will lack the connections that make all the difference between success and failure in the law."

"It's the same for men. Connections help men to get on too."

"Connections they have formed over generations, at ancient schools and universities, through family and friends."

"Miss Gifford, I do sympathize with you, I really do. In fact you'd be astonished to hear how much my views have changed since I met you. But in one thing I cannot sympathize, this constant wailing that life is tough for women in the professions. Instead of griping about your disadvantages, why don't you make use of them, turn them on their heads? After all, it's a device we use all the time in demolishing an opponent's argument. You, as a woman, have the advantage of surprise and novelty. You are a pioneer, which in your place I would find extraordinarily exciting rather than a bind, as you seem to. I do believe that women have different qualities from men, you can't persuade me otherwise, but you should play on them. Even your enemies can't deny that women are often intuitive, eloquent speakers. Since you and I last met I've listened to another of your female colleagues performing in court—a Miss Cobb—very impressive."

"Yes, but the reverse is used against us too. Our critics translate intuition and eloquence into an overreliance on instinct, too much talk. Now here, I believe, the infamous picnic took place."

Since my last visit with Breen and Wolfe, summer had deepened in that unremarkable field. Rain had fallen, so that the meadow grass was taller and the hedgerow busier still with insects. A cloud swept across the sun and at some distance a tractor engine wheezed into life. "Are you looking for anything in particular?" I asked. "Mr. Wolfe, for instance, is very intrigued by the fact that poor Stella became separated from her hat, which suggests that Wheeler . . . the murderer, I should say, whoever he was, perhaps took the trouble to carry the hat back to this picnic spot though he'd buried her handbag and shoes. Wolfe thinks that a girl as fashionable as Stella would not have left it here herself unless she was in a great hurry."

"I gather she was shot more than half a mile away, is that right?"

"It is, and although I've never met Stella, I just can't understand why she agreed to walk so far. I've seen the type of shoes she wore. It's one of the things that troubled me, why she should stray such a distance from the picnic spot. There must have been very powerful persuasion."

"You don't think she was forced at gunpoint?" Thorne stood with his hands in his pockets, hat crushed under his arm, absorbed apparently in studying the ground. I slid my jacket off at last, very conscious of my bare wrists and the thin layer of cotton voile on my upper arms. He glanced at my throat and away.

"My own belief is," I said, "that Stella may have had a love affair."

In the silence that followed there came again a thickening of the air, the muffling of other sounds, birds, a distant tractor. "I see," he said. "Based on what evidence?"

"Various clues, little things she'd kept tucked away out of Stephen's sight. The trouble is, if I'm right and he was consumed by jealousy, it would make him more likely to have killed his wife rather than less."

He nodded and walked on, so that I wondered if he too had found the words *love affair* unendurably resonant. Our pace, under the hot afternoon sun, was much slower. The joy of being with Thorne, of finding him companionable and sympathetic, overcame my determination to keep him at arm's length, and I talked freely about how I came to study law and my experience of postwar Cambridge. He had a most engaging way (probably honed through years of escorting Sylvia) of adapting his stride to mine and inclining his head when listening. For the first time in my life, I gave voice to the guilt I felt at having benefited from James's death. "I doubt if Father would have had the money or inclination to let me study and apply for articles if James hadn't died."

"Yes, but you know, we are all victims of chance. I'm not so very different from you. Hardynge has proved an extraordinarily kind and influential patron but it's partly because his own boy, Donald, will never be a barrister now. In that sense I too am a replacement son. I didn't have too bad a war, fortunate postings, my luck was in, I suppose you could say. Like so many others, I feel a great surge of guilt sometimes that I am in one piece, that I even have one or two fine memories, of *fun*, would you believe? But Don didn't survive—he did, physically, I mean he's alive, but his nerve broke and he's confined to a hospital—not far from here, in fact. I don't think he'll ever be right."

"What happened to him?"

He swiped the hedgerow with his jacket. "He was in Wheeler's regiment—Second London Rifles—most of the men from Imperial Insurance joined at the same time. Donald fought bravely but then there was an incident . . . forgive me, the details are private to the family . . . and he collapsed, mentally I mean. Since then he has been moved from one institution to another, seeking a cure. At present he's in a place not that far from here beyond Princes Risborough." Long silence. "Suffice to say the Hardynges are utterly stricken, still. I think in fact they'd all have been better off if he were killed outright—I'm sure they know that too, which makes things all the worse for them. Sir David visits weekly, the mother seldom, Sylvia when she can. She's a trooper. I used to go quite often but my visits distressed him—they think I'm too much a re-minder of the war."

"Is it just a matter of luck, do you suppose, that enables one man to pull through the war in relatively sound mind, another not?"

"You're thinking of Wheeler and the fitness-to-plead argument. All I can say is that if you and I, Miss Gifford, were to see a bull charging us from the other side of this field, we would each react differently. Of course if we were trained to run, we might run, or trained to face it with a bayonet, we might do that, but if terror got the better of us, who knows what we might do? Why, you, I suspect, would argue with it and I would attempt to pull rank and then if we both had any sense, we'd run like the clappers. And afterward you might recover in a minute, while I would shake for hours." Inevitably, I loved to hear his laughter, deep-throated, soft.

"But Wheeler had a good war—I've seen the medical report."

"A good war? War is so extreme. At times it was such lunacy I could have thrown up my hands and walked away, never mind the conse-quences. We were hungry, tired, bereaved, and often shaking with fright. Death was a second away. On the mornings of an offensive we woke up knowing that half of us would be dead by evening. When I ordered my men to attack, I was ordering them to be shot. And even when we thought we were safely at rest behind the lines, mishaps occurred. I saw a man who was tapping out his pipe against a tree one minute lose his head to a bit of flying shrapnel the next. Nothing would surprise me about what a person would do, or become, under those condi-tions. He might stand up in full view of the enemy and stroll out on no-man's-land to pick up a dead friend"—here he glanced at me and I thought, he *knows*, can it be possible that he knows about my brother—"or on the other hand, I've seen a brave man cry because a tin of cocoa dropped from a shelf onto a duckboard. But we're lawyers, Miss Gif-ford, we know all this. We often represent people who have behaved impeccably all their lives and then go and commit some extraordinary crime."

"But have you ever known a good man do something really wicked, not just weak or cowardly but downright wrong? Could war make a man do that?"

"Wicked? I don't think so. I've seen a man lie his way out of the front line. I've seen petty thieving. I've seen men blow a week's pay on a game of cards or ten minutes in a brothel. These things aren't wicked, are they? Ill-judged, desperate, reckless. But wicked?"

We crossed Drydell Lane and entered the bridle path, a green tunnel leading up the side of the little valley, today more sun-baked and somnolent than ever. As the quiet countryside rolled away from us, Thorne and I were well beyond sight or sound of other human beings and it dawned on me, in the hush of midafternoon, why Stella had been brought so far from the picnic spot. And I also knew that I no longer had any intention of holding back from Thorne; that instead, given that this was probably the only hour of my entire existence that I would spend alone with him—or indeed any man I found so desirable—I would take from it what I could.

Nevertheless, what I chose to say frightened me so much that I shivered, even in that airless track. "A woman called Meredith turned up on our doorstep, it was through her that I came to be at the art party because she shares a teacher with Sylvia. She claims—she is, I mean there's no doubt about it—the mother of my brother's son, conceived while she was a nurse in the war. My father had met her once but I didn't know of her existence even. Or the child's. And then last week at the party she told me that my brother had forced himself on her. You see, I cannot even bring myself to say . . . *raped her*. I adored my brother, I know he wasn't capable of such a thing. Later she and I had such a dreadful argument that I struck her."

The sun was very hot despite dense leaf cover, yet in places the mud underfoot was not baked dry and I had to step aside or follow a higher bit of ground. A bee, languorous with the weight of pollen, thudded against my hand. In the long silence that followed, I wondered if Thorne knew that he had just been presented with my heart.

"There, up to the left," I said, thinking, I'll change the subject and give him the chance to escape my confidences, "is the copse where Stella was killed."

But Thorne said: "Are you afraid that this woman, Meredith, may be telling the truth about your brother?"

"I don't trust her. I think her capable of manipulating anything. But one thing, I believe, is authentic. She showed me a note in my brother's handwriting. Just her name. Nothing else. She claimed that he wrote it while he was dying. I do believe in that note and I puzzle over it, why he would have written her name, just hers, out of love or guilt or perhaps as the beginning of a message. And I suppose I am jealous that it was her name, not mine. He didn't write to me before he died."

"You haven't answered my question."

"I don't think I believe her, no. But she's sown the seeds of doubt. I thought I knew my brother inside and out. It was bad enough to realize he'd had an affair. I was a fool, naïve. I didn't believe he'd ever loved any young woman except me."

"Does it make any difference whether she's telling the truth?"

"Surely it makes all the difference in the world. Above all to the memory of my brother. I loved him. I thought I knew him."

He sighed, took my jacket, combined it with his own, slung both on his shoulder, and looked down into my face. "Miss Gifford, your brother is dead. What you have left is a mother and her son. And the memory of a boy who before the war was, I suspect, as gloriously clear-headed and ardent as you. Ever since I met you I've been meaning to say that I'd heard of a Gifford, a Captain James Gifford who died after nearly twenty-four hours in a shell-hole, one shoulder and one eye missing. His bravery was something of a legend. I'd heard it was a heroic death and that he'd crawled out of the trench to rescue one of his men. How old was he, nineteen, twenty? Poor boy, he had little enough time to learn how to love a woman other than you. He's dead and surely in anybody's book that's punishment enough. Ah, don't cry. This bloody, bloody war. It goes on and on, doesn't it?"

As we faced each other across the little lane, I realized that this was the most intimate conversation I'd ever had with another soul. And I also half understood that we were laying our cards on the table one by one and that we were edging closer while maintaining a show of keeping ourselves apart.

"To look at it from another angle," Thorne said, "why would this woman lie to you?"

"Because she can. To increase our sense of obligation?"

I walked ahead, wiping my eyes first on my sleeve then, belatedly, a handkerchief. Oh, I should not allow myself to cry; he would think me so weak and girlish. So I gathered pace and was almost running by the time I reached the little thicket where the pheasants were confined behind their wire fence and Stella had been buried under bracken. At the gate, I fumbled with the chain looped around and around the post. Thorne didn't help but stood with folded arms, peering into the trees.

"I remember a wood in the war," he said, "blasted clear of most of its branches, the few remaining hung with bits of bodies, gas caught in the fallen leaves so that men were stumbling about groping for their masks, blind and screaming. If that day you had told me that I would survive, and that I might stand once again at the top of an English valley, before a pheasant covert, with a woman such as you beside me and a quiet sky above, I would not have believed you."

"And yet there's Stella Wheeler," I said harshly. "We're here because she was murdered. English woods are not as peaceful as you had hoped."

I got the gate open at last. The woods were hushed—perhaps the pheasants felt the heat and were huddled into shade and there was no wind to ruffle the leaves—and the bracken had grown higher since last time. Now the leaf cover was so thick that hardly any sunlight got through and the green was deeper, dustier. It was as though we entered an emerald cave with needles of light flickering here and there. I floated across the soft floor of the wood in a nugget of time other than my own. I had stopped crying, my heartbeat had slowed, my mind was quiet, and it seemed to me that I was half Stella—the girl whose cotton robe still drifted perfume from a hook on the back of a bedroom door—half Evelyn, and I knew, as I had known the first time, exactly what must have drawn Stella here.

"Nobody would hear the shot, that's why he brought her so far. And I think she came willingly with whoever brought her, believing that they would make love."

If I reached out, I could take him. He stood so close that I felt his heat and sensed the tremor of his nerve endings. My hand was still, lying against the side of my thigh, a mirror of his a few inches away. I knew without any doubt that he had engineered this trip because he couldn't help himself. He was as absorbed by me as Peter Shaw had been, and the officer with the crimson glass bowl.

I pointed out trampled bracken and a bit of rope tied from tree to tree, marking the place where Stella had fallen. But even the shallow pit in which she'd been buried was already half covered with new undergrowth. There were signs, a beer bottle, a chocolate wrapper, that others had been here, locals and sightseers probably, taking a look at the crime scene. Thorne studied it all carefully and we consulted the map. "If he'd left the coppice this way, he'd have had to pass the manor house but eventually would have come to the Missenden Road, which would have brought him quite quickly into Chesham. Or he might have run back to Drydell Lane and gone into town that way. If, on the other hand, we pursue the theory that it wasn't Wheeler who shot her but someone else, he might have left a car in a lane nearby and escaped in any number of directions, toward Great Missenden or Wendover or across to Hertfordshire."

"What do you think? Could it have been anyone but Wheeler?"

"I don't know. It was a well-planned killing. Quite neat. Wheeler lacks a plausible motive unless as you say he was jealous, so let's suppose it was someone else who wanted Stella dead. Is it really possible that he could have known about the picnic, ensured that Wheeler went down for a couple of beers, and in the meantime lured Stella to her death, shooting her with a revolver known to be Wheeler's? And why would anyone do that? She was just a little waitress, hardly a threat. Though

Wolfe's right that the question of the hat is intriguing. Wheeler said he found it with the picnic things, but a lady would never normally be separated from her hat. Look at you, I've never seen you without one. But if all we've got is a slight problem with a hat, it looks very bad for Wheeler: a premeditated crime like this, a shooting in cold blood for what the prosecution will say was purely financial gain, and a refusal to admit guilt."

We decided to leave the coppice by the western gate, a route that someone other than Wheeler, intent on escaping, might have taken. "You've seen Wheeler," I said. "Do you honestly think that Stella would have been persuaded to march all this way to these woods, presumably on the promise of a little lovemaking with him? If I were her I would have protested that there were plenty of other places much nearer to the picnic spot where we might have been private. And I would have complained about the damage that a frolic in woodland might do my pink dress. I would have been totally bemused, in fact. No, I don't think Wheeler could have lured her all this way."

It would have to be you, Nicholas, I thought. If it had been you who found me lying on a picnic blanket when Wheeler left me, if you had stood over me, held out your hand, and said: Come, I know a place . . .

We left the woods and followed the farm track up the little valley to the lane. And yes, there was a fringe of trees where an automobile might have been concealed, even a tire track in the dried mud at the edge of the road. Quarter of an hour after shooting Stella, a man might be in Great Missenden or Amersham, less than half an hour would bring him to Princes Risborough. "It is possible," was Thorne's verdict, "but not probable. There's no evidence at all. In my experience the simplest explanation is usually true."

I had stopped thinking about Stella. Nicholas walked a little ahead and I noted the immaculate crease in his trousers, the dust on his shoes. We were between trees again, in sudden shade. In a few minutes, I took my jacket from him. Soon we reached the farm and beyond it the long, sloping track leading down to the town. "It's so hot," he said. "I should have thought to bring a flask or such. Could we not sit for a moment?"

"Of course, if you want to." There was nowhere obvious except a dusty verge, so I stood with my arms folded while he made a show of looking around. Then he sighed, as if with exasperation, and the next moment had taken a hold of my upper arm and was looking into my eyes. "Miss Gifford. You must forgive me. What I'm about to say is something I've been rehearsing for days. And I still think I'm mad to say it. But I find I must. I cannot live the rest of my life knowing I missed the chance. You must know, Miss Gifford, that I find you devastatingly attractive."

I stood with my arm at a somewhat awkward angle, and the sleeve of my blouse rucked up under his long fingers. The fabric of his shirt was of an open weave and the collar was soft, attached, the kind Edmund might have worn. After one startled glance at his face, the look of desperate appeal, I stared instead at my scuffed shoes.

Remember this, I told myself. Never forget a single detail. There was a freckle above the knuckle of his thumb and I was amazed that I should have been given the chance to study so intricate a part of him.

At last he let go of my arm and said, very clipped: "Forgive me. Forgive me. I have behaved unpardonably," and started to walk away. I watched the distance grow between us.

Well, Evelyn?

"I have thought, until now"—my voice was tentative, a slender thread— "that the strongest feeling I would ever have for a man was grief." He was still. "But now there's you."

He was a few paces away, shaking his head, and when he looked at me at last his eyes were soft with doubt. "What are you telling me?"

"I think of you constantly, until I infuriate myself. I try to brush you from my mind, because of Sylvia."

He bowed his head, nodded. His hat was off and the angle of the back of his head, nape to crown, reminded me of Edmund. "Very well, Miss Gifford. Evelyn Gifford. I understand you. I have behaved very badly. Let us forget I spoke."

Voices clamored in my head: the voices of Prudence, Mother, my own. You can't have him. You shouldn't, you mustn't. Be strong. Bear the hurt of parting now to avoid much worse pain later. I cried: "Do you think I will ever forget what you said? How could you be so cruel? Could you not have exercised a little more self-control?"

"It appears not."

"Haven't you thought about Sylvia?"

"I have tried to consider Sylvia but I can't. I can only think of you."

"This is just because I dare to argue. You think it's exciting to meet someone who answers back, especially a woman. Can't you see that? You should put me out of your . . ."

"Yes, that's so true." He laughed suddenly. "All true. Each time, I can't wait to see you because I don't know what you'll say next, what fresh remark of mine will be demolished. You must have noticed how I've cropped up time and again these past few weeks. Why do you think that is? Except for the art party; to see you there was the most extraordinary shock to me—when we ran down to the jetty and you of all people stepped out of the boat in that mad dress and with your hair so wild. I think you are astonishing."

"I'm not astonishing. It's just that I'm educated and ambitious and you're not used to women like me."

He laughed again. "Miss Gifford, what gave you this abominably low opinion of yourself? Look at you. I admit, I dreamed of women during the war and they certainly weren't like you. I wanted softness, I wanted to slide away into someone quiet and gentle and accepting. But then I met you and felt a spark in me, and I did, yes, find you exciting but beautiful too."

The empty track rolled away on either side. His skin was damp and his smell was of soap and male sweat, so like my brother's. I had time to imagine the heat of his mouth before he kissed me, but not its softness.

"I thought you wanted to put me in my place, I thought . . ."

His second kiss was the merest brush of the lips, feather-light. He whispered, "I am falling in love with you. Will you believe that? Would you please not argue this one point?"

"How can we . . . ?"

I felt the unknown bulk of his body against mine, the texture, the shape of his tie and shirt buttons as he kissed me again. He seemed to me an expert but then who had I to compare him with, apart from the boy under the canal bridge and my would-be lover at the War Office? Their ghosts were present, in the shade, and Stella's, and even my brother James's, but then the astonishing intimacy of his kiss blotted them all out and I was just Evelyn Gifford kissing Nicholas Thorne among trees in a lane between wheat fields, with his arms drawing me closer and my hand on his upper back, and my hat pushed off as he caressed my hair and neck.

After a few minutes, he pulled me deeper into the hedge so that we were a little hidden from the lane. This time our hats and jackets were flung down and I was drawn up under him, my back arching over his arm, his hand on my chin and his kisses dark and beautiful. I felt them as a tearing inside me, as if a strip of membrane had been ripped from throat to thigh and I clung to his warm, strong neck for fear of dissolving altogether.

I drew back at last, but he whispered: "Don't say anything. We won't say a thing. I don't know what this means. I can't think. This has happened and can't be undone."

He kissed me again and smiled into my stunned eyes, and solemnly, in between kisses, tucked strands of hair behind my ears. Then I put on my hat and we walked sedately away, although my hand was tightly clasped in his. As we neared the town, we separated and by the time a hay cart lumbered past, followed by an impatient motorist, I wore my jacket and he was decorously ahead of me. Gradually we entered the bustle of the little town and found that the rest of the world was still as it had always been, that cabbages and plums were displayed outside a greengrocer's and that the baker's window, this late in the day, was almost empty, except for a cottage loaf and three tea cakes. At the Queen's Head, where Stephen had his two or three pints after leaving Stella on the hillside, dead or alive, we stared, standing so close that Nicholas's elbow touched my upper arm, at the redbrick, large-windowed pub, shuttered against the heat of the afternoon. And then we turned up the lane leading to the church, where he had left his car, passing the wide-open doors of ancient cottages and the shrouded windows and shut doors of much grander houses.

I wouldn't let him take me home. Instead, he agreed to leave me at Ruislip Station, where I would catch a Metropolitan Line train. The engine started easily and he drove, as he performed everything else, with casual competence. "Tell me what you are thinking," he said as we left the enclosed lanes of the town.

"I'm trying not to think anything."

He kissed my palm. The car was very hot but he didn't unfasten the roof. I sat, butter-soft, helpless, my hands folded on my lap, turning from time to time to convince myself he was there, the side of his mouth quirked up as he drove, a little hunched forward by the low roof of the car. The smell of the Ford, leather and oil and polished wood, seeped indelibly into my memory of that afternoon.

At the station, he sat beside me on a bench at the far end of the platform, waiting for the train. "You're so quiet," he said.

"Be grateful."

"But I'm not grateful. I like your words. All of them."

I laughed. Our hands lay on the bench. He drew the tip of his index finger along the inner side of my wrist as the boy Peter had once done.

The lines sang, the train was coming. "I'll speak to Sylvia." He squeezed my hand, then kissed my cheek. "I'll write to you."

I stepped into the train and took a window seat. There he stood on the platform. Nicholas. I put my hand on the window, one last gesture before he disappeared. His eyes were full of shock and tenderness and longing, as mine must have been. The train drew out of the station; I fell back against the hard seat and closed my eyes. I had no substance, was simply a parcel of light.

Twenty-five

On Wednesday, *Mother invited me* to help her deadhead in the garden, where she took the unprecedented step of asking me to meet her for lunch next day. I was so taken aback that I thought she must have got wind of the fact that I'd been kissing someone else's fiancé and wanted to put a stop to it. Then she added: "Let's meet in the Lyons you keep talking about, where your murder victim worked. I'd like to see for myself."

"I thought you hated that sort of thing."

She wouldn't meet my eye but made savage snips at a dogwood. "Life would be so much easier if you didn't argue all the time, Evelyn." And then she hissed: "I want to talk to you about Meredith somewhere away from the house."

ex☉

Next morning, Breen and I drove to Wormwood Scrubs to interview Wheeler. Breen's shoulders were hunched as if he carried a great burden. "The man is as good as hung unless we can save him from having to plead in the first place. Or unless you can work a feminine magic, Miss Gifford, and get something more out of him today. Wolfe has left no stone unturned to find the origins of that wretched statue but it's proved to be trickier than we'd hoped. She is one of a limited edition of fifty, French, imported last November and bought by a number of so-called exclusive dealers and stores—you're perhaps not aware, in Maida Vale, that these sorts of pseudo-classical figures are terribly in vogue at the moment. The damnable thing is that Harrods, for instance, had three, and a few were sent out of London to Edinburgh, York, and Birmingham. So it will be impossible to track down her purchaser with any degree of certainty unless we have some idea of his age or what he looks like. I've set Wolfe to making matches with Carole Mangan's list but it's a thankless task to expect a shop assistant to remember a purchaser who might at some date have bought a bronze, and to pick him out of the motley crew she describes. Always assuming, and it's quite a leap, that it's someone on the list who gave Stella the dancer."

"And the missing night, the cloakroom ticket?"

"We have no proof that any of these things are connected, or are significant. I'm afraid I lean toward Miss Drake's view of the type of thing Stella might have been up to. But in any case all this is pointing toward a motive for Wheeler, not an alternative culprit."

We were silent as the cab stuttered along the Harrow Road, but then, having encouraged me to think the worst, Breen, exactly as if manipulating a bench of magistrates, turned the tables. "Don't look quite so despondent, Miss Gifford, I happen to think it's worth persevering, if only we have enough time. In my experience, the truth has a habit of bubbling to the surface like gas in a swamp. Truth has its own imperative, I find. Thanks to you we know something very significant: that Stella did indeed have a benefactor who could afford to spend more than fifty pounds on a statue."

"And whoever it was, it was a thoughtless present," I said. "Of all the things he might have bought, like clothes or jewelry—Stella would have loved jewelry—he chose something useless, the kind of present suitable for someone who already has everything, unlike Stella, who had

virtually nothing. And a naked dancer? How was she supposed to explain that away to her husband?"

"Miss Gifford"—he leaned forward—"it was a clever present, don't
you think? Exclusive enough to turn a poor girl's head but not so rare
that the purchaser could easily be traced. And suggestive . . . Do you
know what I think? That it's the sort of gift a man might buy if he
wanted to put ideas into a girl's head."

"Ideas?"

"If Miss Drake is right—or at least is thinking along the right
lines—ideas were indeed put into the girl's head. With disastrous consequences."

The cab was warm, though the windows were pulled down. We were
static behind a tram and the air was fumy. All in all, the conversation
was far too personal for my liking. Surely Breen must see my bubble of
joy; surely he must know that I had been reconstituted by love. That
morning, a letter had been delivered to Clivedon Hall Gardens, addressed in a hand that made me tremble. I had snatched it from the
breakfast table and put it in my pocket to open on the way to work,
leaving the crowded bus five stops early so that I might read it without
someone looking over my shoulder.

Dear Evelyn,

I write this because I think you might be as disbelieving as I am of
what happened. I have lost count of the times I have relived our walk.
My fear is that I shall simply wear the memory out . . .

The letter was in my pocket; I felt the corner of the envelope against
my thigh. So yes, I knew all about the ideas that a beloved man might
put in a girl's head. I knew that in some circumstances body and soul
were pitched toward one goal. Surely Breen could tell that I was molten
with expectation?

"To give a girl a present like that suggests a relationship that has already become intimate," he said, "or perhaps one in which intimacy is being denied. We know that Stella liked dancing. In that light, the bronze is both flattering and quite shocking."

I suspect, as I said, I may be falling in love with you. Trained as I am to analyze and dissect, I try to work out why this very inconvenient thing has happened. Inconvenient. I suspect you'll smile at that word (I should like to watch that dawning smile). But I was so solidly fixed on a particular course, and now this.

I can't write more until I have spoken to Sylvia. You will understand that I am trying to remain as true to her as possible. There is a crisis with Donald—I cannot speak to her at present.

"Don't you think, Mr. Breen," I said, "that such a man, knowing Stella has been murdered, must be wondering whether there is some danger of the police finding the bronze dancer and asking awkward questions? He must be very worried."

"My thoughts exactly. But I have concluded, on the contrary, that he probably feels quite easy. He couldn't have known that Wheeler would have the good fortune to be represented by the excellent firm of Breen and Balcombe. The police missed the dancer after all and we're only pursuing that particular trail because you were observant enough to notice her."

But might you and I meet again in the meantime? Tea? Some noisy, public place where I won't be tempted. Fortnum's. Thursday next, five o'clock. I'm bound to be through at court by then. You can reply to me at my chambers. Mark the letter *Personal*.

Nicholas.

Mr. Breen, meanwhile, had changed tack completely and was addressing the Marchant case. "We have received a letter, Miss Gifford, from your friends Mrs. Sanders and Mrs. Marchant, requesting an interview. They have drawn up a petition, it seems, to have the children returned."

"Should we meet with them?"

"*You* should, of course. They need to know it's going to be a long and tortuous process. And you should draft a letter of apology to Miss Buckley, at the same time requesting a meeting with appropriate members of the board to discuss the future of the children. Meanwhile, I'll get Wolfe to follow up a few leads, make some connections, see if he can find someone who has a lever on a board member. If he's right and the home is intransigent, we will need to apply pressure on many fronts."

☙❧

By now I had some experience of prison routine, the unlocking of numberless doors and gradual immersion into a stifling interior ever more remote from the street outside. Wheeler was waiting for us in an interview room that had the sole luxury of a high, barred window, open a fraction. In the moment before he rose to greet us, he was even more depressed-looking than before, as if his jowls and shoulders had been dragged down by weights. He might have been boneless, slumped into his soft, heavy body. I could not see him as a fighter, sinuous and brave; I could not imagine him rushing forward to battle. A prison officer stood in one corner, arms folded in a posture of utter indifference.

But when Wheeler saw us, he got to his feet, more animated than I'd ever known him before. "Well?"

Breen shook his hand. "Nothing much to report as yet. But I've brought my colleague Miss Gifford to see you. She's done a great deal of work on your behalf and has lots of questions." Wheeler showed no sign that he remembered me but sank down in his chair, as if he'd used his last ounce of energy. "I'm just Miss Gifford's escort," added Breen. "It didn't seem right to send a lady on her own to a prison, so I'll get on with some work while she's talking to you. Forget I'm here." And he settled himself as if he were snugly in his office, extracted a heap of papers from his briefcase, and unscrewed the lid of his fountain pen.

I was wearing the same blouse as on my trip to Chesham with Thorne—I could scarcely bear to dress in anything else. But these days I understood the effect of a woman's uncovered wrists and throat, and when I took off my jacket and hat, I was aware that the gaze of all three men, even Wheeler, flickered over my exposed flesh.

"Mr. Wheeler, I'm here because I believe you didn't kill Stella. However, at the moment we can't find another suspect so we have to prove to the jury that it was impossible for you to have done it because you had no motive. In fact, quite the opposite. Do you understand? So I'd like to talk to you, if I may, about you and Stella. I thought I'd start by asking about before the war. When you left, Stella was just a little girl, really. Twelve."

He said nothing.

"You fought bravely. We've read the reports. You joined a regiment recommended by your employer. So you were among your friends."

Not a word.

"And Stella wrote to you all that time. It must have been a comfort to receive her letters. But she was still very young and you didn't expect her to marry you when you got back. All these years since the war, you never seem to have put pressure on her. Her sister, Julie, says Stella might have married any number of men but she chose you."

Wheeler sat with one arm flat on the table, head low, mouth so slack that a line of saliva trickled onto his sleeve. The prison beyond the interview room muttered and boomed and clanged, and I was reminded of the Good Samaritan Home and those other pent-up lives.

"Mr. Wheeler, I went to visit your mother-in-law in Acton where I saw your wedding photographs and talked at length to Mrs. Hobhouse. Meanwhile, Mr. Breen has spent time with your own family who told him you'd kept all the letters Stella wrote you during the war. We'd like to use them as evidence during the trial, if we may, to show how devoted you were to each other." Still he said nothing and my voice rose and quickened. "You see, the prosecution is going to find it very hard to prove that you shot your wife in cold blood simply for the insurance money, especially given the length of your courtship and your faithfulness to each other. We think that's a wholly implausible argument." Wheeler suddenly looked up, and the glance from his gray, moist eyes was startling, as if he knew and felt more than he could ever say. "So the prosecution will also try to show other reasons why you might have killed her. And one of them might be that you were jealous about her. Your mother-in-law says you were jealous sometimes, is that true?"

A further sinking of the shoulders.

"Stella loved dancing, didn't she?"

Suddenly he smiled; a sad smile but full of fond memories. For the first time I noticed that he had unusually good, very white teeth.

"And I'm told that you, on the other hand, never danced."

He shook his head.

"That must have been hard for you."

Another piercing glance. "I loved to watch her dance," he said in his low, sorrowful voice and I felt a thrill of triumph that he'd spoken to me at all. "I loved to see her happy."

Breen, who had been scribbling notes in the margin of a letter, paused to take his pen apart and inspect the ink holder.

"I'm sure you wanted her to be happy, Mr. Wheeler," I said softly. "Tell me about Stella's dancing."

He leaned forward and studied his damaged hand. "I would go down to the Palais with her and watch. I'd buy her a drink or two, she preferred lemonade when she was dancing. She used to wear little frocks, showed a lot of leg, and soft shoes, and after she had her hair cut she wore a slide to stop it falling over her eyes, but it always did in the end. Because she went wild. Her arms and legs would fly up so fast I could scarcely see them. She was such a wonderful dancer others used to stand still and watch. She knew all the latest, Charleston, the lot. She used the word *syncopation* all the time. She'd practice on the pavement and at home, singing to herself, 'At the Jazz Band Ball' and such; 'It Had to Be You.'"

"Did she have any special partners?"

"She'd dance with anyone, the girls from work, her sister Julie. Sometimes a young man would ask her but after one or two dances she'd point me out and swap partners so they didn't get ideas."

"Was there ever a man she danced with more often? One she seemed fond of?" He gave me such a baleful, dismayed look that I quickly added: "I believe sometimes she went dancing when you weren't with her."

"I didn't mind her going dancing with the girls as long as it wasn't down the Trocadero. I didn't like that place."

"I was talking to one of Stella's workmates, Carole. She said one morning in April Stella came to work having been out all night. Do you know anything about that?"

"What do you mean, all night?"

"Carole said she was late to work and her clothes were unchanged from the day before, and her sister Julie says the same, there was one night that Stella didn't go home."

"Well maybe she did stay out. It's not a crime. It doesn't have to mean anything."

But he was so rattled that I suspected he had known nothing about that missing night and was in danger of clamming up while he pondered its implications. "And after you were married?" I asked gently.

"After we was married it was a bit different. Mainly because of money. She didn't have her own money anymore, except the housekeeping. The rent and the wedding, the honeymoon and all took most of what I had and we was saving to buy our own house."

"So how did the two of you spend your evenings, after you were married?"

"Talk. She would sew bits and pieces to her dresses. I was always very tired after work with all those figures and the traveling. She wanted a gramophone or radio, we was hoping for one as a wedding present but it didn't happen. Too pricey, I suspect. And anyway, we needed practical things, saucepans, cutlery. We was intending to go out more, once we'd saved a bit more money. Stell loved the pictures. Anything. Charlie Chaplin."

"Did she seem happy?" That word again, but now I felt I could use it with authority.

There was a ponderous silence. "Stella was never happy," he said at last. "I knew her most of her life, since she was a very young girl, and I never knew her happy. I tried to make her happy. She said I made her happy but I didn't. In the end I thought, well, maybe if I marry her, she'll be happy."

The prison officer shifted his weight. Breen's pen hovered over a document.

"Why wasn't she happy?" I asked.

"Who knows? Sometimes she said she was bored. She wanted more than she could ever have. She was always saying, 'If only this,' 'if only that.' And she would set her heart on a new pair of shoes or a hat, as if they would make her happy. Sometimes I was doubtful about marrying her because she was so restless and discontented but then I thought, she says she wants to be wed, maybe if we have children, they'll make her happy."

He leaned toward me as if desperate to confide. I remembered Nicholas, the kiss in the hedgerow, thistles, briar rose, and I touched Wheeler's hand, near where there were scars instead of fingers. "Stephen. When you were married, was it all you hoped for, at night? You had waited for her such a long time."

He gave me a burning, wounded look. "It was all I'd hoped for."

I now dipped into my briefcase and took out the scrap of paper I'd found in Stella's sponge bag. "We found this. Do you recognize it?"

He knit his brow and drew the paper toward him across the table. "Where d'you find it? I don't know what it's about." He touched it again, puzzled over it, and shook his head. Next, with fast-beating heart, I took out the bronze dancer and placed her on the table, where she was utterly incongruous, the only perfect, lovely thing in the room. Wheeler stared dully. "What d'you bring that old thing here for?"

"You've seen it before?"

"'Course I seen it. Couldn't stand the thing. Wouldn't have it in the house. I didn't know she'd kept it."

"Where did she get it from?"

"Heck knows. She got hold of it shortly before the wedding. Said she'd bought it as a little present to herself. Waste of money, I told her."

"We've had it valued. We think it's worth more than fifty pounds."

He was all gray at that moment, a swamp of misery, and it was clear that he had known the dancer was valuable and that there was no innocent explanation.

"Mr. Wheeler, I must ask you this. Do you think the dancer might be a present from a man who . . . ?"

He got up, sallow, furious. "She would never. My Stell. Never. Never. She wouldn't dare. She wouldn't hurt me. She told me, she swore to me."

I let his words settle before I persisted: "So you did discuss the possibility that she might have been . . ."

"You seen a picture of my Stell. She was lovely. The loveliest-looking girl I ever seen in my life. Don't you think I would worry that she might fall for someone else? Look at me. Look at the state of me. A cripple. Old. Can't dance, can't earn enough to buy her treats. She was all I ever wanted. I dreamed of her all my life—the thought of her kept me going through the war. She knew that. She knew. She would never be so cruel. She didn't have to marry me but when she did, I thought that would be the end of her wanting all kinds of other things."

"And wasn't it?"

Silence.

"When you say *other things*, do you mean other men?"

Another agonized look. "I don't know. I didn't believe it possible there wouldn't be, you see. I called at the café often. I knew there was men watching her. I thought it would end, once we was married and she was out of that place."

"And yet you still suspected her."

"I thought a baby would stop all that sort of trouble, that I'd never have to worry about her again."

"But of course, it was far too soon after your marriage for Stella to have conceived."

The little room was very hot and airless with just the slit of an open window. Breen's voice cut in, matter-of-fact. "Stephen, whose idea was the picnic, yours or Stella's?"

"Idea? Well, hers, I think. I can't remember."

"And tell me again, what happened while you were up on the hill. Did you suggest you went down to the pub or did she?"

"I don't know. Me, I suppose. She wasn't bothered."

"What happened then?"

"I've told you a million times, nothing happened. I left her. I went to have a beer. I come back and she was gone." He buried his face in his arm and wept.

Then, out of the blue, Breen said: "In the war there was an incident when you were picked to form part of a firing squad, do you remember?"

Silence.

"Describe to me what took place that morning."

But Wheeler was weeping too hard to reply.

⊗⊙

On the way back in the cab, Breen asked: "How is it looking to you, Miss Gifford?"

"It looks to me like he was eaten up with jealousy, sir."

"In which case we're done for. The man is so coherent there's no way we can attempt to prove he is mentally unfit. Thorne was right." His bright eye fixed on me. "Thorne telephoned, by the way. Said he'd talked over the fitness-to-plead question with Hardynge and Wainwright. Wheeler was far too competent an employee, they suggest, right up to the Monday after the murder. And his behavior in prison has been impeccable. If he'd maintained his silence it would have been another matter but you've heard how lucid he is. There's no chance of us winning on that. So it's back to motive. We won't tell the police about the dancer until we've found out its provenance and what happened on that missing night. When we're in possession of all the facts, we will decide what to do with them. But I tell you one thing, Wheeler is making very deliberate choices about what he discloses. He's a dark horse, in my opinion, brighter than I used to give him credit for."

"And you still think he's innocent."

"I still have no opinion, Miss Gifford. As I've said, I believe, for the time being, what my client wants me to believe."

"Why did you ask him about the incident in the war?"

"Because there's a danger the prosecution will pick up on the fact he was part of a firing squad and therefore, they'll say, practiced at killing in cold blood."

Twenty-six

I arrived at Lyons well before Mother, because I wanted to speak to Carole Mangan privately. I spotted her at once, near the kitchen, indistinct in the smoky restaurant, one foot resting against the wall, a lock of pale hair hanging over her brow. Though white with fatigue, she ushered another waitress out of the way. "Is there news?"

"We are making progress. You have been an immense help, more than I can say. But it's possible we may call on you again if we need to, if any of the men on your list prove to be important and we need to have them identified." She nodded. "And I was wondering, could you tell me any more about the day Stella came in late, when she hadn't been home?"

"Not really. She was tired and grubby. Secretive. That's all."

"Did you have an idea where she'd been? You must have wondered."

She rubbed fruitlessly at a tea stain on her apron. "I suppose I did. She was so tired. And frightened and upset. I thought she must have had a bad time with someone—not with Wheeler, he'd never treat her bad—but if so, why wouldn't she say?"

"And yet you didn't suspect her of having an affair?"

"There were no signs, no. And why would she, if she was engaged to Stephen? Why not just break it off with him?"

At that moment, Mother arrived, a somewhat incongruous apparition from Clivedon Hall Gardens, dressed in her usual hat with the spotted veil and a black double-breasted coat, both far too heavy for so warm a day. She removed one glove, and looked about nervously as if she'd never been anywhere so lowly before, though I suspected that before her marriage, in the days when she was merely the daughter of a former actress and struggling schoolteacher, she would have been grateful for meals in establishments far humbler.

"This is my mother, Miss Mangan."

Mother smiled at Carole in the queenly fashion she reserved for lower classes not directly in her employment and said nothing. Because we so rarely had lunch together and this, I insisted, was my treat, we ordered expansively, croquettes with potato salad, and tea. Mother agreed that the meal sounded tasty but took little interest and instead scanned the room as if seeking out spies at other tables. She seemed determined to make an effort to establish good relations, however. "So tell me what you've been doing this morning."

"Mr. Breen and I visited Stephen Wheeler in Wormwood Scrubs."

She adjusted the front of her veil. "And how is that case progressing?"

I could not think of the Wheeler case, even in her presence, without being flooded by memories of Thorne's kisses in the hot lane. "Badly. But I'm sure this place is significant. My theory is that Stella, the victim, who was a waitress here, had a rich admirer. And the obvious place for her to have met such a person is while she was on duty."

"*Rich*, you say, how rich?"

"Rich enough to have spent fifty pounds on a present."

"Surely nobody that rich would come here. Why on earth would they, when there are so many restaurants and clubs around Piccadilly, just down the road? Your father was scarcely what I'd describe as rich, but I never knew him to set foot in somewhere like this. Can you imagine?"

She had a point. Father's haunts had been his club, the hushed dining rooms of expensive hotels (if a client were treating him), or the smoky restaurants around Chancery Lane. He and his colleagues feasted on roast beef, not poached eggs. "Perhaps Stella's gentleman came in on the spur of the moment," I said, "in need of a cup of tea, and Stella happened to catch his eye. She was very pretty, by all accounts."

We watched Carole clear a table and give the surface a perfunctory wipe. "Depend upon it, there is another explanation." Mother had assumed her role of glamorous hostess, expert at making connections. "He will have met her elsewhere then found out where she worked. And she, the little minx, will have ensnared him and given him just enough promise of future favors that afterward he came back time after time."

"Mother, it almost sounds as if you talk from experience." I caught my breath. There she was, my veiled, inadequate mother, who had spent her adult life lavishing love on husband and son, caressing, praising, nurturing. But really, was that the only side of the story? What had Father been up to on the nights he was late home? She seemed oblivious as she dipped into her handbag, removed a handkerchief, and dabbed at her nose. Or was there just a hint of self-consciousness, a tremor in her hand? "What about that other nasty case," she asked, "the woman who injured your face?"

"We are still trying to get her children back."

"I can't understand why the home wouldn't be glad to get rid of them and return them to the mother."

"It's not that simple, we have to prove that she is able to care for them."

"And is she? She didn't treat you very well."

"Not by herself perhaps, no, but I believe she has a good friend who will help and, in the long run, the children would be better off among people they know than shipped abroad to heaven knows where."

"Goodness me, Evelyn, it seems to me that you are taking a great deal on yourself—all this responsibility for other people's children."

Our conversation was suspended as Carole set out our lunch. Instead we talked of Grandmother's deteriorating sight and of Prudence's cottage, which she planned to visit to ensure that mice or burglars had not got in while the *wretched* tenants were in Scotland.

"But actually," said Mother, shifting forward and speaking in a low voice as if about to divulge a state secret, "did you know that Prudence has offered the cottage to Meredith, once the lease has expired at Christmas?"

"That's very generous of her."

"I shall never understand Prudence. One minute she is calling the girl an impostor, the next she is taking her side."

"What does Meredith say to the offer?"

"I'm afraid she laughed. She said she and Edmund would die of boredom if they had to live in the country."

"Nonetheless, it's generous of Prudence."

"Oh, it is—I don't deny it. And so unlike her." Mother approached her face even closer to mine, so that her veil brushed my cheek. "You know that Prudence has also offered Meredith money. All she has. Her next suggestion was that she, Meredith, and Edmund set up house together in town on the proceeds from the sale of the cottage."

"But that is extraordinary," I exclaimed obediently, though in truth I had seen this coming.

"She says Edmund is heir to the Gifford name and that someone must ensure he is supported. She has changed sides *completely*."

"And what does Meredith say to this?"

"She too seems to have changed her tune. Evelyn, I'm not sure that Meredith knows what she wants; I think all this talk of expensive apartments is bravado but I'm equally sure the last thing on her mind is a ménage à trois with Prudence and Edmund." She poured the tea, her fingers delicately crooked over the clumsy pot. "The fact is, Evelyn, since your precipitate action, telling Meredith to leave, I have been thinking. It is my belief that we have a duty to her and the boy and we cannot simply send them away. Oh, I don't blame you entirely. It is partly my fault, I admit, that we pitched ourselves against her in the first place. I was so shocked when she arrived that perhaps I was not as welcoming as I might have been and my response affected you. It was up to me, after all, to set the tone. Well, I've considered all the possibilities and we simply can't afford to rent her a flat in London. So what I've thought is this: perhaps we could create Meredith a little apartment within our house. It wouldn't cost us much to make her a sitting room, even a little kitchen, but we would at least be offering her a home. I was thinking of the second floor, where she could have the spare room—and James's room."

I was stunned. That she should offer James's room, his shrine, was extraordinary. "It would mean sacrifice on your part, I'm afraid," she added, taking up a fork and pushing her croquette aside. "If we were to give them a sitting room, and Edmund his own room which of course he must have in time, you might have to move to the top floor."

"I don't understand you," I cried, "this is the complete opposite of what you . . ."

"Hush, Evelyn." Again she looked nervously about. "Don't make this more difficult than it is. Can't you see, we owe Meredith a home?"

The food was too peppery for my liking but I ate several mouthfuls while I decided whether now was the time to disclose the terrible allegation Meredith had made about James. The trouble was that since my conversation with Nicholas I was less sure; the edges of my outrage had been blurred. Meanwhile, Mother snapped open and shut the clasp of her handbag. "The truth is, Evelyn, I have not been quite honest with you. Your father did tell me about Meredith and the child though I must admit that over the years, because I'd heard no more about them, I pushed the fact that they existed to the back of my mind. I knew of course that your father had met her in London, and that she was expecting . . . I was too upset at the time, so soon after James's . . . And we decided we must keep it all quiet, what good would it do for everyone to know that he'd . . . ? The woman was going back to Canada after all. We thought we'd never see her again."

Mother's eyes and mouth were wet as she gave me a nervous look then again opened her bag. "We did something else which you may find hard to forgive. I think you will be very angry but I'm prepared to risk that. James wrote to us after he'd left the hospital, a day before he was killed. The letters arrived a fortnight or so following the news of his death while you were at work. He told us about Meredith, that he had treated a woman badly is how he put it, and that he wanted us to care for her, should she come to us for help. He said he loved her and would have married her if she'd returned his love but that unfortunately she did not. I made your father burn the letter. I was very angry, actually beside myself, given this news came so soon after his death, to think of this woman toying with my son. And it was so unexpected to receive that sort of letter instead of his usual affectionate . . . It was so unlike all his other lovely brave letters."

Her hand was in the bag, hidden from view. "Until Meredith turned up again, I never regretted not telling you. I was jealous of you, as a matter of fact, because you had such a fine, unsullied image of your brother, whereas I had to imagine . . . But one thing I have always regretted, and that is the need to hide from you the fact that he had also written to you, and we didn't give you the letter because we thought it would contain a confession about what had happened with this woman. I've never opened it, my conscience is clear on that front, but nonetheless. I could not bring myself to destroy it—it was yours—and now I have decided to give it to you because I know you are very angry with Meredith, and I'm hoping that whatever James wrote will convince you to be kinder to her."

She brushed the surface of the table with the side of her hand and placed on it a small, poor-quality envelope. When I didn't move or speak, she gripped my arm and I saw that a tear was caught in the webbing of her veil. "Evelyn, don't be too hard on me. We wanted you to think well of your brother and we thought this would upset you too much."

Carole was hovering to clear the table. Mother's meal was uneaten. I picked up the letter and put it in my lap. "I'll pay for the lunch," I said. "You go."

"You're not too angry with me?"

I forced myself to speak calmly; anything to be rid of her. "You go now, Mother. Why don't you do some shopping while you're in town? Buy a new hat. Something summery and small with a turned-up brim. No veil."

My voice was a stranger's, low and toneless. Nevertheless, she was so relieved I had not made a scene that she responded laughingly: "I have never known you to care about what I or anybody else wears. What has come over you?"

She kissed me through the veil, then hung her bag over her arm and walked uncertainly away. At the door, she turned and waved. As she went past the window, her back straightened and I knew she would go to Selfridges and look for a hat both to please me and as a reward to herself for being so brave.

The restaurant had quietened a little. Carole approached, glanced at James's envelope, and offered to bring me a fresh pot of tea. Nothing changed in that constantly changing place, the ebb and flow of diners, the straggling queue at the cake counter, the flies, the waitresses in their black dresses. I imagined Stella's arriving late one morning, her eye sockets bruised from a sleepless night. She must have glanced at the clock to see how late she was and then, as she hurried to the cloakroom, felt calmer, because here she was again, safe. Carole said Stella had looked often at the door that day, as if expecting repercussions from whatever she'd been up to. A fortnight after the missing night she was married, and in another few weeks murdered. I had no truck at all with the idea that these things in Stella's life were unconnected. One thing led to another.

NOVEMBER 19, 1917

Dearest Evie,

It has become my habit to write you a last letter and when I come back safely to tear it up. So here's another. I usually write the same noble words. How much I love you and hope you won't grieve for long, and that I've had a good innings and no regrets. I ask you to care for Ma and Pa but be sure not to let them talk you out of a brilliant career.

If you get this it will be because I've taken another hit and this time James Gifford is no more, poor lad. Well, my dear sister, my dear touchstone, here's a thing I have newly learned, that death is by no means what I fear most. Or to put it more eloquently, I would rather die than continue living in the shadow of my own lost innocence.

When I was hit that time a month or so ago I tried out death. I lost so much blood I had to be carried on a stretcher. My head rolled from side to side and I thought any minute some sparking thing would fall from the sky and do for me. Further from the front it was quieter, I was shunted into an ambulance and in the dark I felt life wash away. I grew colder until the pain went and I slept sometimes. And then I lay in the hospital in and out of dark hazes, aware of upright figures among the prone ones. I would snap suddenly into consciousness and realize that there'd been a change, an end of activity because another boy had died. Once, I followed.

Do you know, it really wasn't so bad? We trod a soft floor and our hands groped forward in the dark until we found ourselves in a crimson room, velvety, hushed. You would have loved the color of that room, Evie, the color of apples and roses and the rubies in that shop where you bought my ring. A color to keep you warm. Any minute, I knew, another door would open to another dark corridor and endless silence would begin. But then there was a tug on my wounded arm and I came back and was looking into the eyes of a woman who wouldn't hear of me dying. I was patched up and tucked up and made to drink vile stuff and when I woke again my head was firm on the pillow.

You were always better at everything than me, Evie. I don't blame anyone for the way I turned out but I came here and found I wasn't equipped to kill or be killed. I hadn't been tested. I was rightly afraid of what James Gifford might do, in those circumstances. The one bit of advice I dare to give you, if you do practice the law, is don't look at just the act, look at the cause; don't depend solely on the law, depend on justice. Even if I live I could never now come home. I could not enter that house, climb those stairs, lie peacefully down on my bed. I have fallen in love with a woman here, the one who wrenched me back to life—she actually used the words "I don't want you to die, Captain Gifford," and so I lived. Evie, if she should visit you by any chance, for God's sake be kind to her, and love her, and try to convince her I was a good man but not the best. And that when I was lost I found her, and held too tight.

There's a hellish racket overhead. Imagine Rose in a temper, clashing her pans. Doesn't come anywhere near.

Good-bye, my very legal sister.
James

Twenty-seven

When I arrived home after ten o'clock that night, Mother was still waiting up for me. "Where have you been, Evelyn?"

"Working late."

She hovered about me, took my hat, and hung it up next to James's. "I told Rose to keep back a plate of cottage pie because I didn't know when you'd be in. I was afraid . . . Oh, Evelyn, I've been so worried you wouldn't come home at all. What must you think of me?"

"Really, does it matter what I think?"

"Of course it does, Evelyn, please, don't be cold."

"I must speak to Meredith. Is she in?"

"She's with her art group. She didn't say when she'd be back. When I told her my idea that she might have an apartment in this house she laughed at me. She said she had to be free and she couldn't think of anything lonelier than being within the household but not of it."

"She has a point." There was a hat box on the hall stand. I took off the lid and inside was a purple velvet hat with a padded brim and matching rosettes. Not summery, not dainty, but at least not black.

"It was in the sale," said Mother.

I nodded, took the hat, and put it on her head, adjusting it low on her brow. She peeked out at me, fearful, and I saw how her prettiness had disintegrated through the strain of these fruitless little stabs she made at controlling her life.

"Please talk to me, Evelyn. Say you've forgiven me."

"I can't yet."

"I knew this would happen. I knew you would be angry."

"Give me time, Mother. Good night now." I walked relentlessly upstairs, away from the thin figure in her lilac cardigan, who must always be appeased.

Edmund's door was open. He was fast asleep, and the landing light fell on his bed, where he lay on his back, one arm flung out so that his half-clenched fist hung in space.

ॐ

Next morning, I waylaid Meredith as she and Edmund were running down the stairs on their way to his elementary school in Lisson Grove, and asked if I might keep them company.

Even Meredith would not give me the cold shoulder in front of her son, so the three of us set off, she very chic in her Eastbourne yellow summer frock and hat, Edmund sturdy in shorts and long socks, myself giraffe-like in a dark skirt. Edmund, never slow to seize an opportunity, insisted on walking between us so that we might swing him over the cracks in the pavement, but as soon as he'd left us, crossing the school yard with heartrending confidence, a pall of silence fell and Meredith started to walk away, even when I called after her: "Would you mind, could you spare a few minutes? I want to talk to you. We could perhaps go to the park, if you had time."

"Oh, I have all the time in the world. But you, surely not."

"I want to apologize for what happened, if you'll let me." The last thing I expected was to see tears start to her eloquent eyes and hang on the lashes. "Meredith, however shocked I was I should not have struck you. It probably doesn't help at all that I've never done such a thing in my life before. I offer you my unreserved apology and beg you to forgive me, if you can."

She stood with bowed head until a nursemaid asked her to step aside so she could get by with her push chair. This prosaic street of villas and box hedges hardly seemed the right setting for a highly charged scene, whether of reconciliation or rejection. James's letter was lying in the briefcase with my love letter from Nicholas. How could Father's bag, the street, or the city contain such words?

"I would like us to start again, right from the beginning," I pleaded. "Meredith, you have received very poor treatment from my family for so long. I want to make amends."

I was walking toward Regents Park, and to my relief she did follow, though lagging slightly behind. We crossed the Outer Circle and entered the park proper near the boating lake, made unattractive by a frisky little breeze and an overcast sky. Meredith, in her light frock, clutched her goose-pimpled arms. She wouldn't meet my eye and I felt a pang of nostalgia for the much chirpier Meredith, who had taken me on a trip to Eastbourne: unpredictable, infuriating, even dangerous, yes—but vivacious, intriguing, tricky.

Once we were in the park, out of sight of others, she began to cry in earnest. She did this tidily and well, so that tears ran neatly down her cheeks to be caught in a diminutive handkerchief. "I have been so afraid that Edmund and I would be destitute. I was cursing myself for the way I told you what happened, when I was drunk and not able to consider properly what I was saying."

I glanced down at her, struggling to see her through James's eyes, to understand what he had loved. Was it just that hers was the first face he saw when he regained consciousness? Or was it her difference from us, the Gifford women, that drew him, the fact that she was small and ardent and driven by an inner light very different from ours?

"You have to understand that what you told me about James seemed entirely out of character to me at the time. What I have come to realize is that I probably didn't know him well enough to judge how he would be when he was away from me. I was just his sister. I didn't know what war was like."

"That's it," she cried. "We all behaved out of character. But you see, if we hadn't been changed by what we saw and did, why then, we'd have been made of stone. Evelyn, I want you to know this. I didn't tell you what happened between me and James to shock or blackmail you or kill your love for your brother. I told you because that's what happened." The bizarre thing was I wished I had believed her before I read James's letter. It seemed to me so clear now, that she was telling a version of the truth. "But I should have said more. I shouldn't have left you to imagine the very worst. He wasn't actually violent to me. I scarcely realized what was happening because I wanted so much to cling to him—by then I was lost too, Evelyn, the war had done for me finally and to hold a young man in my arms when he needed me seemed the only reasonable thing left to do—and then, too late I realized that he was expecting far more than me, was blind and deaf to my protests."

After a long pause, I said, "I understand Mother put a plan to you and you turned it down."

"Certainly I did." Meredith was actually grinning. "Can you imagine if I were to live in the midst of you but conveniently tucked away; Prudence and your mother on the first floor and me and my friends crashing up and down the stairs in the small hours. It would never work. And besides, I've changed my mind about what I want. I was at Sylvia Hardynge's house last night. She has a studio in the attic."

Despite the chill air, I stood still. "Sylvia?"

"Surely you remember her from the art party; fiancée to that barrister acquaintance of yours. She invited us back for cocktails after class to see her work. Hadley is very taken with her. We all are, except Margot, who's jealous. Sylvia's family lives in this mansion with a semicircular drive, columns to the porch, servants skimming about, mother and father out at the opera. Sylvia says they're all running around looking for distraction because her brother, who's in some kind of asylum, is very sick and they're at their wits' end. For some reason he could be thrown out of the place he's in at present. But apart from the mad brother, Sylvia, it seems to me, has everything, including a studio, so I can't be too sorry for her. It's a wonderful room, part of the roof has been glassed so that it's full of light in the day and stars at night. I should like something similar."

She was teasing me with this extravagant request and I tried to laugh. Nicholas would undoubtedly have been up to that studio in starlight. I imagined how he and Sylvia must have stood together, like at the art party, his arms around her, their kiss, and all about them Sylvia's blank canvases.

Meredith's face was peaky with cold, and her fingertips purple. We took a path that led to the north of the boating lake. The wind had blown debris from beneath the trees, and scraps of dried leaves, the very last of last year's, whisked across my foot. The ghost of a memory stirred but flickered away.

"We'll talk another time," I said. "You are too cold here and I have to go to work. But do we understand each other a little better? I do so want to find a solution."

At the junction with Grove End Road, where I was to catch the omnibus, we parted. I should have liked to embrace her, to set a seal on my apology, but could not yet. "I was wondering," I said, "if you can spare the time, would you come with me on a trek around London's hospitals? I'm not acquainted with how hospitals work, you are. Could you, would you help? It's to do with Stella Wheeler, the girl who was shot."

I half expected a rebuff, but instead the old light came to her eye.

"Why, I'd love to. This is your *murder* case, you mean . . . Oh yes, please."
Then, as the bus came, she asked wistfully: "Where are you going now?"

"To the office first."

As I stepped aboard, I felt a pang for her, dressed to the nines in her yellow frock, and for the first time I fully comprehended what it was my brother had taken.

Twenty-eight

Though *I would not have admitted it* even to myself, I arranged
the meeting with Leah Marchant and Mrs. Sanders quite deliberately to take place on the afternoon of my tea with Nicholas. I was
planting an obstacle in the way—assuring myself that it was not too late
to change my mind about embarking on a love affair.

So, punctually at three, Mesdames Marchant and Sanders duly arrived in Arbery Street, both smartly turned out in clean frocks and best
hats, impressed by the awful significance of being in a lawyer's office.
Miss Drake, who always behaved impeccably with clients, greeted them
with quelling courtesy and ushered them upstairs to our bare little meeting room with its empty bookcase and round table covered by a felt
cloth. Having offered to bring us tea, she left the door ajar. Wolfe was
present in the building in case of trouble but had been told not to show
his face otherwise.

The meeting began quite well. Leah Marchant, who'd recently had
such a severe haircut that her dead-straight bangs drew a sharp line
under her hat, was quiet, ominously so. She sat much too still and stared
at me fixedly. Mrs. Sanders produced from her bag several sheets of
paper on which were written names, addresses, and signatures (or
crosses) of friends and neighbors who had signed a petition stating that
Mrs. Marchant was a responsible parent and ought to have her children

returned. "Leah says she was treated shameful by that woman in the 'ome. Quarter of an hour, less, is all the time she 'ad with them kids," said Mrs. Sanders. "We've 'eard nothin' since. She's sick of messin' about. She wants the kids back. So we've tooken matters into our own 'ands and this is what we come up with."

"That's very helpful, thank you. I shall ensure that this is sent to the chairman of the board."

"And in the meantime, we was wantin' to know what you've been doin' to get the children back."

"Well, in the first place we have been taking advice. I was as dismayed as Leah by the matron's attitude. However, we don't want to upset the home any further. We must tread carefully since it's a delicate area."

"*Delicate* for who?"

"The difficulty is that now the home has the right to keep the children unless we can prove that they will be materially better off with their mother. I'm afraid that the next step will be an inspection of the children's living conditions, should they be returned. We would recommend that if you are not a regular churchgoer, Mrs. Marchant, you become one, so that we can get a priest to vouch for you. And it would be very helpful if there were relatives—your own or your husband's, who could show an interest in the children."

Leah's face had reddened. Mrs. Sanders said: "Maud Grant over the way 'as a different man in every night and four kids under five crawlin' in the gutter and nobody inspects 'er."

"We will next write to the board, perhaps at the same time as we send your petition," I continued, "requesting an interview with the chairman, Bishop Ogilvie, and for a timetable to be set when these investigations can begin. And in the meantime we may instruct an independent person, a health visitor or similar, to support you over the coming weeks."

Mrs. Sanders put a restraining hand on Leah's. "It's all takin' so long," she said, "we can't understand it."

When Leah wept, her whole face was awash. "I want them back. I don't understand. I want them back. They never will come. I know now. I might as well give up."

"Now, now," said Mrs. Sanders.

"It's you," wailed Leah, shaking a wet finger at me. "If it wasn't for you I'd 'ave them. You are what's keepin' them away. I seen the way they treats you. You don't 'ave the power."

"It's not a matter of power, Mrs. Marchant, it's a matter of . . ."

"You set yourself up as somethin' you're not. I need a man to do this for me. They'll listen to men. I don't understand Mr. Breen not 'elping me."

The situation at that moment seemed to me hopeless, given that there was no trust on either side. How would this volatile woman ever clear the obstacles the system had set her? And was she a fit parent?

"We'll go now," said Mrs. Sanders hastily, then murmured to me: "I told her not to say these things. The fact is, Miss Gifford, I believe that you will succeed because you want it as much as we does. That's what I tell 'er. It's not just another case to you."

I shook their hands and watched them go down the narrow stairs. Leah, I noticed, left a faint, sweaty after-smell.

It was only a quarter to four. Even if I made a laborious note of the discussion, there was still plenty of time to reach Piccadilly by five. I had not managed to escape, after all.

My parents had escorted me to tea at Fortnum & Mason more than a dozen years ago, as part of my eighteenth-birthday celebrations. They still cherished the hope that I might become a young lady—not a debutante, we weren't in that league—but Mother dreamed that her bookish, wild-haired girl could yet be transformed, butterfly style, into a vision of lacy garments and soft white skin, capable of breaking a string of hearts. Excursions such as tea at Fortnum's were designed to tantalize and refine. Instead I was bored. It was the summer holidays and James was staying with a school friend in Devon. For me, education was over forever. I had nothing to talk about, nothing to look forward to as I slouched over a plate of cakes for which I had no appetite. Father glanced at his watch and consumed a coconut tart in one mouthful. Mother said that the pale blue spotted taffeta gown she'd bought me was very becoming, "If only you'd sit up, Evelyn." In truth, it was more of an effort to slouch in those tight corsets.

Today, anticipation of seeing Nicholas again was such that my legs hardly seemed attached to my body as I trod the deep-piled carpet in the wake of the very superior headwaiter, to whom I said that I was meeting a gentleman, Mr. Thorne. All the tables seemed to be occupied by aloof ladies in exquisite hats—there was no sign of Nicholas. I was shown to a table facing the door, where I tried not to mind that my clothes were shabby or that I felt displaced there among the starched cloths and waiters whose feet made not a sound on the carpeted floor as they whisked about with trays held high or pushing trolleys of cakes, their waistcoats and intensely white aprons so unlike those of their poor relations at Lyons.

My sense of dissonance grew until my head was spinning with other settings to recent unease—the boating lake at Regents Park, the prison interview room, Lyons, and James's letter dropped into my lap—and I wondered what on earth I was doing amid these splashes of gilt and scarlet and cream, the muffled clinks, the murmur of conversation that signified wealthy people at leisure. In any case, Nicholas would surely not turn up, if for no other reason than that my note in response to his had been so cold—*I shall be pleased to meet you at five on Thursday* . . . *Sincerely yours*—because I had dreaded it falling into the hands of Miss Drake's equivalent at his chambers.

At the next table was a grandmother wearing floor-length bomba-zine. Her granddaughter swung a stockinged calf under a frill of apricot voile.

My head knew that the most likely reason for Nicholas's lateness was business in court, but my heart argued: If he felt for me as deeply as I for him, nothing would keep him away. Then I thought of another, far more invidious cause of absence: he's realized his mistake, he's told Syl-via of our little fling, and she's brought him back into line. How could she fail, with those long lashes, the brilliance of her eyes, and the undu-lation of her hips in the white satin gown? And as the minutes passed, as a waiter pausing by the table asked me pityingly (it seemed to me) would I care to order tea while I was waiting (of course not, I had less than one and sixpence in my purse), I thought frantically that the whole affair had been a terrible joke, Nicholas had suggested Fortnum's to humiliate me, to impress upon me that this was his world and I could never be part of it.

I had only to look at the other ladies, cut in the Sylvia mold but not as lovely, silk stockings, hats adorned with pleats and feathers, hair art-fully arranged so that one little curl fell crisply on the forehead or in front of the ear, gowns draped at the neck and hips, embroidered sashes in jewel colors—sapphire, ruby, emerald—kid gloves, hand-painted scarves in fabrics Stella Wheeler would have sold her soul for, to know that I could never compete.

Still Nicholas did not come. I'll give him just a few more minutes, I thought. It was gone twenty past five. Surely they would not be serving tea much longer. Because I'd handed in my briefcase at the cloakroom, I had nothing to read but the menu: *Anchovy toast . . . Smoked salmon . . . Cucumber . . . Selection of freshly baked . . .* My bones had gone liquid with misery as I anticipated leaving the store and plodding back to Clivedon Hall Gardens, the fumy pavements, the overcrowded omnibus, the un-locking of the front door, dinner at seven, as usual. My world was splintering into shards of gray and black; it was the death of James all over again, I couldn't bear it, I must leave before I broke down in a shameful flood of uncontrollable tears.

"Evelyn."

He was standing over the table, shockingly formal in black jacket and waistcoat, pinstriped trousers, hard collar; Nicholas, his eyes full of loving concern, his hand when he took mine very warm. One glance at his face, that unique and perfect ensemble of features, made my blood sing.

"I have been in agonies," he said, hooking his foot around the leg of a chair and drawing it to the corner of the table so that he could be a little closer to me. Immediately, that alien place, the indifferent waiters, the lavish red drapes, the chandeliers, the chattering ladies, became insignificant. "The slowest judge in the world—fraud case. And then to top it all he was taken ill at three, something he'd eaten at luncheon. We waited half an hour and I was sure we'd get away early, adjourn till tomorrow, but just as we were packing our papers, back he comes, says we'll plow on to the bitter end. I should never have risked making this arrangement with you, I might have known we'd run late, but I had to see you. Oh God, you look done in, you're so pale and you've had no tea."

The relief was a painful rush of heat to numbed senses. I couldn't let go of the nightmare all at once. "I wondered if it was wise coming here," I said stiffly. "I feel sure somebody will recognize you."

"*Wise?* I'm not able to be wise at the moment. I didn't think about it at all, I'm afraid, this was the first place that came to mind. And it's not so bad. If someone does spot us, I'll pretend we're in a meeting. But God, you're right. This is the very last place we should be. I want to be alone with you."

Undone by the look in his eyes, I wanted to laugh or cry or seize his hand and cover it with kisses. As it was, the superior waiter brought tea on a trolley and there was endless fuss with a silver teapot, slop bowl, strainer, jug, wafer-thin cups with wide-brimmed, fluted edges (Prudence would not have approved—the tea could not retain its heat in such cups). Nicholas was not as deft as in the café near Toynbee, I noticed, his hand was shaking as he passed my cup. In that highly charged moment, as tea spilled, as our fingertips met on the edge of the saucer, I could almost have wished for the old Evelyn, who, sensing the danger, had stood up abruptly and walked away.

But it was too late. I sat so helpless before him that he laughed, buttered a scone, spread it lavishly with raspberry jam, and put it on my plate. "Eat. You must. I insist." Then he added, in a low voice and with more tenderness than I had ever known: "How are you?"

I could only shake my head.

"Are you aware that I have thought of you every single waking moment?"

"And I you."

We were pinned to our seats by the clink of china and the sudden trill of a piano improvising a sleepy bit of jazz. A couple of ladies drifted past, jasmine perfume, the flutter of lace. And beyond this cocoon, beyond the swathed windows, was the clamorous city, which would soon draw us apart again.

"Tell me you have been all right."

"I have not been all right, Nicholas, I have been very shaken."

"Good, good. I want you to be shaken, at least a little. You deserve to be, since you have utterly shattered my peace of mind."

"I have tried to concentrate on work. The trial is so soon. We think Stella really did have a lover. But on the other hand, if Stephen knew, and I think he did, then he had cause to be jealous . . . he has a motive . . . it's looking even bleaker for him. There is a statue, a bronze dancer, someone must have bought it . . ."

I, who had been praised at Oxford for my ability to carve an argument from a ragged collection of ideas and facts, now was incoherent.

My mouth formed words but the rest of my being was yearning to be closer to him; I was mesmerized by the slightest movement of his hand or eyebrow or lip. A crease the size of a thumbnail came and went in his left cheek near his mouth when he smiled. Fleetingly, I caught his eye. After that, I couldn't speak at all.

He said: "I was praying that you would not think, when you read my letter, that I was making an excuse for not talking to Sylvia. My mind is made up, I've not wavered for a moment."

"Please, yes, you must tell her. I cannot stand secrets."

"But it's a matter of timing, do you see? If you'll let me, I'll tell you a little more about Donald. I have hesitated, as I said, because of loyalty to his family, but it seems to me that the decision not to betray is far from clear-cut. You are what counts. For you to be unhappy, to be filled with doubt, seems a higher form of betrayal."

I dared to touch his hand with my fingertips. "Don't tell me anything that feels wrong. I trust you."

I did trust him. Even I could not disbelieve the evidence of my eyes. He was muzzy with desire, as I was, and a tremor ran through his hand at the brush of my fingers.

He shook his head, leaned his chin on his palm. "Evelyn Gifford. What have you done to me? I want to kiss you. I want to hold you and show you how very, very beautiful you are but we have to be civilized, so I will tell you a little about Don, if I may, because I don't want you to doubt me. He's not at all well. Physically, he seems in the pink of health; if I took you to visit him you would see an immaculately dressed young man, with hair and mustache perfectly trim. On a summer's afternoon like this one he'd be on a veranda drinking tea. But when we came closer, the illusion would become a little frayed though he would stand up very formally and shake us each by the hand. After that he'd say nothing at all. He can't, because his thoughts are shot to pieces. The war. Drugs. Recently they changed his medication and he became violent and nearly throttled a nurse. It is pure luck that he was discovered before he murdered her."

"What happened to make him like this?"

"The war. He was always oversensitive, perhaps overmothered, constitutionally unfit for the shocks we had to endure. His father, Sir David Hardynge, as head of Imperial Insurance was proud of the firm's contribution—money and men, including his own son. He regarded the war as an opportunity to extend his influence and would not entertain doubts, so Don was one of the first to sign up. He hated every moment, went into that war a brave, brilliant boy and came out like this."

The tearoom was emptying while the piano played languidly on. At five, time had stretched endlessly away, second by second. Now nearly an hour was gone.

"Can the family bear any more unhappiness?" I said. "How can you hurt Sylvia at a time like this?"

"Sylvia deserves better than a man who is thinking all the time about someone else. And she is tough, I think, not to mention proud. She would never be satisfied with less than everything. She is ardent and wholehearted about all she does. However, I will wait, if you'll allow me, until the family has got over this current crisis."

"You know, Meredith was invited home by Sylvia after the art class. I was shocked when she told me she'd been in Sylvia's house. It all felt so terribly close, as if Sylvia and I are brushing up against each other in the dark. Or rather, she is in the dark . . ."

"I know. I know, it must end soon. But there's another thing that makes a difference. I'm away next week. Manchester. Fraud case. It seems callous to tell her and then bolt. We need time."

"You'll miss the excitement of Wheeler's trial," I said, trying not to show my disappointment that he was going to be away.

He paid the bill while I was brought my jacket and briefcase. I had intended to tell him about James's letter and my attempt at reconciliation with Meredith but there had been no time. And again I felt regret for the time before Nicholas and I had kissed, when our talk had been edgy with expectation. Now we were so sad, so strained, and I knew I would spend the next week missing him, and regretting the things I hadn't said.

As we walked from the restaurant, he held my elbow. "Next Friday evening when I come back. We'll meet then. That will be our beginning. I'll fetch you in the car. But for God's sake let's be alone somewhere. I can't go through a charade like this again." He urged me past the lift to the glass doors leading onto the empty stairwell. The stairs marched down, down in gracious symmetry to the basement. I walked ahead of him, slowly, my hand on the banister, conscious that step by step the ground floor was approaching, the street door, parting. I felt the life flow out of me. He was leaving, it was so cold, so clinical, with another meeting arranged in a week's time. The prospect of this tea had sustained me through the past days, and the world beyond Nicholas seemed a chill and very complicated place.

As we came to the last landing, he got ahead of me, spoke my name, and kissed me with such violence that I lost all sense of anything but the taste of him and the cool wall at my back. The sudden contact with another body, the heat and hardness and incredible demands he made of my mouth, the sense of being taken over and broken down into little fragments of Evelyn opened me up to him so freely that for a moment I stood with my back and palms and calves pressed to that wall, unresisting as his hand covered my breast and his knee nudged my thigh. The inside of my head was dark with sensation and my untouched body hot and yearning. I broke away at last, half blind, gasping with desire, fumbled to take hold of his hand, and we ran on down, emerged onto the pavement, and headed toward the bus stop.

There, at last, within earshot of a couple of elderly ladies, each with a formidable handbag, one with darting eyes under an antiquated center parting, I recovered a little, straightened my hat, and managed something of my usual crispness. "By the way, Mr. Thorne, I have relented, since seeing you last. I need your help, if you can give it. This is a copy of the names on the board of trustees responsible for Leah's children."

"Good God," he said, scanning the document, still with a sheen on his lips from our kiss, "I know both these ladies, Manningtree and Curren. Cannon Mullins. No, not heard of him. And I don't know the chairman. But there's certainly plenty here for me to go on."

"I might have known you'd be friendly with the ladies."

"Miss Gifford, we have already established that I am an impossible snob and move only in the most select circles."

"How will you approach them? What will you say?"

"I'll do as I'm instructed by a solicitor. How would she like me to proceed?"

"Two things. I want the children released. And I want to know the policy of the trustees in relation to sending children to the colonies."

"The latter should be easy, the former more difficult. Perhaps we should talk again, Miss Gifford. Next Friday evening, then? In the meantime, I'll write."

For the benefit of spectators, we shook hands. The omnibus arrived and we were caught up in a throng of passengers waiting to board. His hand slid away from mine. I was swept forward. When I looked back, he was standing in the shade of a green-and-white awning, hatless, smiling.

Twenty-nine

M eredith *proved a stalwart* and indefatigable companion—if any-thing, a little too ready to enter into the spirit of our search: she was happy to discuss the possible reasons for Stella's disappearance that April night, with embarrassing frankness. "On the one hand, Evelyn, you are saying that it's possible she may have sought to end a pregnancy. On the other you think her unknown admirer made her a present of the bronze dancer to encourage intimacy. Does that add up?"

"Nothing adds up."

"So we are looking for signs of a girl who may have met with a medical mishap or been forced to visit a hospital when an amateurish attempt to intervene in a pregnancy went wrong . . ."

"Do you think it's hopeless, in your experience? Would you remember such a case, three months on?"

"You have the wedding photograph. Your Stella has quite a distinctive face. So no, I don't think it's hopeless."

We began with St. Mary's in Paddington, closest to Stella's home, Meredith sporting a new hat in powder blue with an outsized brim that winsomely framed her little face. At first I thought her dress inappropriate—she looked rather a lady member of the board of visitors than an ex-nurse on a somewhat sordid hunt for traces of a murdered girl—but by the end of the morning, a combination of the hat, an engaging smile, and a confiding glance from Meredith's enormous eyes had gained us at least a glimpse of record books.

From the moment she stepped onto the polished boards of a hospital corridor and heard the distant sound of trolley wheels, metal clashing on metal, the sluicing of water, smelled disinfectant and sick bodies, Meredith acquired stature and briskness at odds with her usual, nervier demeanor. I remembered James's description of her expert hands, this neat little woman with unquenchable energy, and again I saw her difference from us. It wasn't just that we were six inches taller and our limbs long and ungainly, but that our natures were so fixed, our ideas so earnestly focused on our own small horizons. The Meredith I now glimpsed was wide open, accepting of all she saw. Nothing disturbed her; noise, endless waiting, encounters with authorities determined to give nothing away or nurses too busy to speak to us. Again and again she stood her ground until the right questions had been asked, the right member of staff summoned, Stella's photograph scrutinized, records checked.

At St. Mary's, where we presented our letter of introduction typed by Miss Drake on "Breen & Balcombe"–headed notepaper, we drew our first blank. "Even if she were here that night we wouldn't necessarily have a record. We simply don't have time to write down all the ones who aren't treated or admitted. All sorts drop in late at night and most we turf out, you know, the sweepings from the park, vagrants, girls too tired to keep going. Sometimes the police bring them through for a quick checkup. They don't all get recorded."

I produced the cloakroom ticket. "Do you ever issue patients with tickets like this, you know, if they have to wait, or undress and hand in their clothes?"

"If only we were that organized."

We began the day traveling from one hospital to another by omnibus, ended it in cabs, too exhausted to consider the dwindling contents of Breen & Balcombe's petty-cash box. I think we knew, by the time we'd visited Westminster, St. Thomas's, and Guy's, that our quest was hopeless. There was no record of Stella. And yet, despite the apparent futility of our pilgrimage, I had a sense that we were creeping ever closer to the truth. Perhaps it was simply that we were taking some action, any action, or perhaps it was because we covered so much ground that we must surely be crossing and recrossing the dead girl's tracks. Or perhaps it was that by eliminating this one possible explanation for her disappearance that night we were leaving the way open for another to emerge.

Most of the time, during those tiresome journeys from hospital to hospital, Meredith and I were silent. It was as if we were circling each other like fencers afraid of a sudden jab, the opening of an old wound. She relented toward me a little as she teased me for loitering at the entrance to emergency departments, for the *Prudence* mouth, as she called it, I put on when there was a bad smell or unpleasant sight.

Once, I saw another side to Meredith altogether. At Guy's we were kept waiting nearly half an hour on a wooden bench. Around us was the usual motley collection of sick and walking wounded, and a mother in a stained skirt and shapeless hat, holding a young baby who screamed relentlessly for ten minutes on and on, back arched, gummy mouth wide, limbs thrashing. Twice the mother approached a nurse and twice the baby was briefly examined and the mother told to wait: "Just a moment longer, we'll be with you soon."

Meredith, I noticed, had started to tap her little foot as if irritated by the wailing like the rest of us. But when the baby stopped crying at last and seemed to relax in its mother's exhausted arms, she sprang up, asked, in a commanding voice, permission to hold the infant, put her finger to the side of its throat, her cheek to its lips, and said in a low, insistent voice: "Follow me. We will find a doctor." The next moment, both women had disappeared.

Meredith came back alone quarter of an hour later and sat beside me, feet neatly pressed together, hands folded on her bag. "I should have intervened sooner," she said. "I could tell the baby was very sick. The staff tell me there is an epidemic of measles at the moment. There aren't enough nurses."

"Will the child live?"

"I hope so."

An administrator came at last and perhaps because of the recent drama, Meredith was given the attention due one professional by another. For once the Breen & Balcombe letter was not needed. There was no record of a Stella Hobhouse or indeed any other girl roughly her age attending the hospital on a Tuesday or Wednesday night in mid-April.

As we left, I noticed that the bounce had gone from Meredith's step and she murmured, perhaps to herself: "Yes, yes, I know. I hear it so plainly."

"What is it?" I asked.

She laughed. "Nothing. Hospitals. It feels as if I was being drawn back. And I don't want to be, I hoped I'd left them behind."

"But if it's your vocation." In the circumstances, I wondered if my choice of word was a little tactless. "Meredith?"

"It wasn't just your brother. I was sick to my stomach. It was obscene, what we did, patch men up so they could go back and get killed. It was the opposite of medicine. I was sick of it."

☙❧

Theo Wolfe had little more luck than we, though what with his pocketful of half-crowns, well-bred drawl, and the suggestion in his bearing that he had all the time in the world and just saw no reason for going away unless he was given the answers he required, he had found that most of the very exclusive art dealers on his list were prepared to cooperate: the trouble was, they didn't come up with an answer. By showing copies of Carole Mangan's descriptions (immaculately typed by Miss Drake) and the bronze dancer, he discovered half a dozen or so possible candidates for her purchaser—in fact one, the white-haired gentleman with the mustache, had apparently bought the dancer no less than three times from three different places, if the salesmen were to be believed. Wolfe even acquired names and addresses for four of the buyers who fitted Carole's descriptions of Stella's admirers.

He then took a taxi to Lyons, lay in wait for Miss Carole Mangan to leave work, gave her, by way of a reference, my name and a card from Breen & Balcombe, and swept her away to stake out the gentleman purchasers one by one, to see if she might recognize a regular visitor at the café. None was.

The next day, Friday, Wolfe returned to Smedley's of Piccadilly, where the salesman had assured him he'd consult his records after work, and come up with the identity of the gentleman who'd bought a bronze dancer and who matched the third description on Carole's list. As Wolfe told us later, he entered the emporium with a spring in his step, convinced this was the one, skirted a somewhat obscene picture of a laughing Egyptian girl and, by way of shocking contrast, a vast oil painting of the Vorticist School, and approached the desk. Today a woman was seated there, browsing a catalog. Dressed in a cream linen frock with a brown collar, she treated Wolfe with indifference once she realized he had no intention of buying. When he asked for the salesman of the previous day, she said the man in question had not turned up for work. Wolfe then confided that he needed to speak to him on urgent business and could he have a forwarding address, but the cream-linen woman said she had no knowledge of his whereabouts, could not be expected to dig out bits of information for all and sundry, but would leave a note for the manager, currently on a buying expedition in Paris, if required.

At last, by means of flattery coupled with a ten-shilling note and the

hint of a threat to do with obstructing police business, she was persuaded to rifle through a filing cabinet, produce a log book, and come
up with the address of the former employee, in Isleworth.

Here Wolfe found a tall, run-down house owned by a desperately
thin landlady who said that the man in question, a Mr. Rintoul, had
gone.

"Gone where?" asked Wolfe.

She presumed, on his holidays. He'd not said much but then he
never did. Left with his suitcase that morning.

"Surely you must have some idea where he went."

No idea. But he liked the sea, as she recalled. There was a cousin
somewhere in the West Country.

Would anyone else know his whereabouts, did he have any relatives
locally, might Wolfe have a quick look in his room to see if he'd left a
forwarding address?

Certainly not. Who did Wolfe think he was?

"The salesman has disappeared," said Breen during a gloomy late-
afternoon conference, "and coincidence always makes me uneasy. But
on the other hand, it's hard to see that he would take us much further,
even if we found him. The police don't know we are looking for the
purchaser of a bronze dancer, let alone a mythical lover, so it's a very
long leap to suggest that this shady figure might in some way be connected with the murder other than to provide Wheeler with his motive."

In other areas, too, the collective endeavors of Breen & Balcombe
had drawn a blank. Miss Drake had persuaded the wife of Stella's doctor to disclose that Miss Hobhouse's health had been good and that
there were no gynecological issues, and Wolfe had got a crony in the
police to trawl through the records of stations in Central London for
the Tuesday or Wednesday in mid-April identified by Carole, but found
no trace of Stella.

"I'm convinced now that Wheeler will be found guilty next week," said Breen, "so much so that I'm beginning to regret my decision to let you sit in on the trial, Miss Gifford. You won't learn as much about advocacy as I'd hoped. How, in the circumstances, could a jury come to a verdict of innocence?"

Thirty

W When the firm of *Breen & Balcombe* arrived at the Aylesbury Assizes, we had to force our way through a swarm of excited ladies in second-best hats, waiting to be admitted to the public gallery of the courthouse in the old town hall. I glimpsed Mrs. Hobhouse in her funeral garments, and daughter Julie gripping the handles of the wheelchair to which her husband now seemed to be permanently confined. There was no sign yet of the Wheelers.

Burton Wainwright, whom I met for the first time in a lawyer's conference room, deigned to take my hand and say what a novelty, no, a positive honor it was to come face-to-face at last with one of these legal women he'd heard so much about. I thought him an unpromising figure, massively built and so fat in the face that his jowls and chins hung well below the wings of his high collar. The bottom three buttons on his waistcoat failed to meet, and his trousers were old and rumpled. Yet he exuded an air of confident bonhomie, as if he had just enjoyed a very large, alcohol-laced lunch, and he shuffled his way so casually through a bundle of notes that I could only hope his confidence was not based on a fatalistic belief that the outcome of this trial was inevitable.

Because I was to be merely a spectator to proceedings, I did not accompany Wainwright and Breen to the cells; instead, Wolfe and I sat in the lawyers' benches and waited. He bit at a hangnail, then opened a copy of the *Times* while I thought about Nicholas. The week stretched unendurably far ahead; surely there could be no possibility of a letter tonight, was he thinking of me or was he so absorbed by his fraud case that I had been pushed to the back of his mind? And at such a distance, would he remember only the worst of me—the arguments, my worn-down heels, the unruliness of my hair?

The prosecutor, Michael Warren, was a short, genial-faced man with slow delivery and an apparently playful twinkle in the eye, but the judge, Mr. Justice Weir ("Not good news," said Breen, "Weir enjoys a reputation for hardheadedness.") had cold eyes and unnaturally pale skin, drained of all color by the vibrant red of his robes. Wheeler was brought up to the dock, where he stood in what I guessed was his wedding suit, utterly dejected as his mother wept in the public gallery, the quill in her hat jolting with each sniff. Her husband was motionless, hat on knee, gazing into the middle distance.

The jury was sworn (there was one woman, dressed top to toe in brown, including a hideous hat like a pith helmet), and proceedings opened with exactly the same lack of drama that marked the start of any trial, from theft of an apple to treason.

"Stephen Wheeler," said Warren, "is more than fourteen years older than was his young wife. Their families were friends through church, and the young boy, Wheeler, lacking siblings of his own, had always shown affection for the two little Hobhouse girls, Julie, the older sister, and Stella. This affection was demonstrated in delightfully innocent ways—his mother tells how he built the little girls a go-cart and bought treats at Christmas. Stella was twelve in 1914 when Wheeler went away to fight but she maintained a regular correspondence with him—letters which will form part of the defense case—no doubt motivated by the patriotic desire of a young girl to lift a soldier's spirits. At the end of the war she was sixteen years old but Wheeler by all accounts made no attempt to court her at first, doubtless all too aware of the significant difference in age and experience. He had sustained an injury to his left hand and he might have considered that this disfiguration, albeit comparatively minor, had damaged still further his chances of winning a lovely young bride.

"But over the years affection apparently turned to romantic love. The couple were married this year, on April 26, when Wheeler was thirty-six, Stella twenty-two.

"Less than a month later, on Saturday, May 17, 1924, Stephen Wheeler, the defendant, and his new wife, Stella Jane Wheeler, traveled by a Metropolitan train from Harrow and Wealdstone in Middlesex to the town of Chesham in Buckinghamshire, in order to enjoy a picnic. After an early lunch, Wheeler left his wife alone while he went for a drink at a local hostelry. When he returned to the picnic spot some two or three hours later—we have only Wheeler's recollection as to how much time actually elapsed—she was gone. The following day, when she had still not returned home, Mr. Wheeler at last raised the alarm. On the Monday morning, her body was found in the woods and nearby, in a separate shallow pit, were discovered Wheeler's own military gloves and his Webley service revolver.

"Wheeler had a distinguished war record, and the prosecution does not seek to diminish that in any way. I cannot be alone in acknowledging the sadness of an event that has brought a man who served his country with such distinction to a court of law, charged with murder. However, Mr. Wheeler, or Corporal Wheeler as he then was, was responsible for one important lapse in discipline during his years of service, and one that he has freely admitted both to the police and to the senior army officer brought down to interview him. Unusually for a noncommissioned officer, Wheeler had been issued with a revolver because he volunteered for night patrols and raiding parties. At the end of the war, however, he omitted to surrender this weapon. The jury would be right in thinking that such an irregularity was not unusual in the huge demobilization that took place between 1918 and 1922 involving nearly two million young men, but the question they might well ask themselves is, What kind of person would wish to keep a revolver as a souvenir of the war? Papers, mess tins, medals, gloves, yes. A revolver?

"At any rate, the revolver found a home behind a rafter in the roof of Wheeler's shed, tucked away, he says, in a tin box containing odds and ends. By Mr. Wheeler's own admission, only he and his wife knew that the box was there. That box, when seized by police, was found to contain medals and documents but was empty of more significant contents—the revolver and the gloves—both of which were found buried close to Wheeler's murdered wife.

"Another key element of the prosecution case is an insurance document, which will be produced for your perusal later. Wheeler purchased life insurance a month prior to his wedding, at a favorable rate, since he was a long-term employee at Imperial Insurance. On the death of a spouse, the survivor, under the terms of the policy, was entitled to the princely sum of ten thousand pounds.

"The jury will also hear evidence from the family, particularly the dead girl's sister, that Wheeler was a jealous man who kept a close guard on his fiancée. Young Mrs. Wheeler was an attractive girl who worked in a Lyons restaurant. It is the prosecution case that Wheeler was driven by the twin urges of jealousy and greed to end his young wife's life. Of course the defense will say that nobody in their right mind would hope to get away with such a crime. The prosecution will argue that Wheeler was not an educated man, but performed every act of his life ponderously and systematically. Perhaps the rashest thing he ever did was marry a girl so much younger than himself, and it took him six years to make up his mind even to that. The prosecution will reason that it's quite in keeping with such a character to plan a crime meticulously, but possibly not to have a fully developed sense of its consequences."

Warren's first witnesses, fellow passengers on the Metropolitan Line to Chesham and a couple who had been in Chesham at about eleven-thirty on the Saturday morning, gave brief evidence that Stella and Stephen Wheeler had indeed set forth on a picnic. Only one girl, a farmer's daughter, Elizabeth Shearman, who walked into Chesham regularly on a Saturday morning and returned by omnibus, and had met the Wheelers on the hill above the church, was subjected to cross-questioning by both Warren and Wainwright, who seemed fascinated by the details of what Stella was wearing.

Miss Shearman was a self-important girl with thick ankles and a heavy chest crushed under an overelaborate blouse. A blue cloche covered her shingled hair and she leaned on the witness box as if settling in for a cozy chat. "Pink, she was wearing pink. A pink frock. White gloves. Can't remember what color shoes. Something light."

"And was she carrying anything?"

"*He* was. He had a picnic basket which knocked against his legs, I noticed. He looked awkward, a bit self-conscious. She might have had a little handbag on one arm. I can't be sure."

"And what did she wear on her head?"

"Why, a hat of course. A little straw hat. Very pretty, but I remember thinking it wouldn't be much use on such a hot day because it hardly had any brim."

"Here are three hats, Miss Shearman. One of them is Stella Wheeler's. Can you pick out her hat?"

"Why yes, it's the one with the little straw rosette on the side. I thought it was a pretty hat. I might even have asked her where she bought it, if I'd had time to chat, except . . ."

"Except . . . ?"

"They seemed in a bit of a hurry. She was walking behind. They weren't talking. They didn't look happy. She'd picked a few flowers, I think."

The prosecutor asked permission to reexamine. "She wasn't happy, you say."

"I'd say . . ."

Wainwright, surprisingly nimble, rose to his feet and said incredulously: "My learned friend is expecting the witness to indulge in speculation about the state of mind of someone she passed on a hillside."

"The point came out under defense questioning," said Warren. "Surely I'm at liberty to pursue it? Miss Shearman, could I confirm that you stated in open court that the couple didn't look happy, that Wheeler was leading the way, and that he seemed in a hurry?"

"That's right."

"Hardly what you'd expect from a couple embarking on a romantic picnic."

"With respect, Your Honor, we can't ask our poor witness to play guessing games . . ."

The next group of witnesses were the publican of the Queen's Head and two of his customers, all of whom gave evidence that Wheeler had entered the pub by the street door about half an hour before closing time and had drunk three pints, slowly and deliberately, without speaking to anyone but the landlord. He had seemed low-spirited and he couldn't be drawn into conversation. When closing time was called, he'd departed.

"In what direction?"

"Couldn't say for sure."

Wainwright was eager to cross-question the publican about Wheeler's so-called depressed bearing. "You must see many drinkers in your pub, Mr. Pool."

"I do. That's what we're there for." (Broad grin at the jury, a few of whom responded.)

"Some must come to drink, others to pass the time of day in conge- nial surroundings, some but not all for both."

"That's right."

"So Mr. Wheeler was not unusual in preferring to keep himself private."

"Not unusual, no. He did seem low, though."

"Your Honor," said Warren, "I would like you to rule on vague terms such as *seem low*."

"By all means," said the judge. "Perhaps Mr. Pool would be so kind as to describe Mr. Wheeler's appearance that afternoon so that the jury can make up its own mind as to whether he was low or not."

The publican, whose mouth was overcrammed with yellow teeth, was delighted to oblige. "He was dressed in a checked shirt, some kind of dark trousers, heavy boots. He looked hot and threw down his hat beside him on the bench. He sat over his beers like this, with his arms resting on the table. And he didn't look 'round or up, just stared down at his pint."

"One further question," said Wainwright. "Was Mr. Wheeler carry- ing a lady's hat?"

The publican gaped.

"Please answer the question, Mr. Pool."

"No. Just his own hat."

ୣ୬

During the lunch recess, I asked Wolfe to elaborate on the significance of the hat and he flashed me the kind of grin he usually reserved for asking a favor of Miss Drake. "Ladies and hats, Miss Gifford, in my not-inconsiderable experience, are inseparable. So either Stella was in such a hurry or so frightened that she left it behind when she went off with whomever it was killed her, or her murderer removed it from her head after he'd shot her and took it back to the picnic site. Wheeler certainly didn't have it in the Queen's Head, so the former explanation seems more plausible. But was she really so afraid of him that she would allow herself to be escorted, hatless, to a copse, so that he could kill her?"

"If she was at gunpoint?"

"It was a long walk. Nothing I've heard about Stella suggests an easy or compliant character. It's the one thing about the day that doesn't fit."

"Then I should like to suggest an alternative sequence of events."

Wolfe shot me a sideways look, folded his arms, stretched his legs, and bowed his head as if to say "You have my ear." He made me nervous, because I had no idea what he thought of me or indeed anyone else. In court, his lazy good humor was unwavering whether he was dealing with a wife-beating or petty larceny, but it was impossible to judge his true opinion of either the crimes or their perpetrators. "Wheeler couldn't remember clearly, but he thought that it was Stella who first suggested the picnic," I said. "What if it was she who drove events, and somehow got him to leave her while he went to the pub because she had agreed to an assignation that went horribly wrong?"

Wolfe examined his thumbnail and adjusted a cuticle with his front tooth. "It seems an elaborate ploy. Wheeler was out every weekday. She had acres of time to conduct an affair. And how does that explain the hat?"

"She left in such a hurry—to meet someone—that she forgot her hat. The thing is we know she'd already behaved rashly at least once, when she was out all night that time in April. And if someone acts out of character once, don't you think it's likely they will do so again?"

☙❧

The first witness of the afternoon was the Amersham police officer, who had been awoken by Wheeler early on Sunday morning. The prosecution asked for his account of Wheeler's visit to be read to the court, then asked: "Was there anything about Mr. Wheeler's story, or indeed his demeanor, that struck you as troubling at the time?"

"I was surprised by the fact that he'd gone home at all the previous night. If my wife disappeared all of a sudden, I wouldn't go home. Why didn't he raise the alarm on the actual night she disappeared? That's what I'd have done."

Wainwright got up. "This court is surely not concerned with what the respected police officer might have done in the event of his wife's disappearance."

The objection was upheld.

Then came the dog walker who had discovered Stella's shallow grave, a mousy, soft-featured woman who described her outing early on Monday morning in minute detail and wept as she said: "I was never more shocked . . . I couldn't believe me eyes when he"—a mongrel answering to the name of Caspar—"came out with that shoe, that dainty little shoe, with stains on it. So I thought I must just take a peek, though I was already terrified. The bracken was a little crushed down, so I pushed it aside and there it was, a woman's foot, stockinged . . . "

A clerk from Imperial Insurance, very self-important in a tight celluloid collar, gave interminable evidence about the terms and conditions of the life insurance policy, and the special arrangements that pertained to employees. He confirmed that the policy became invalid in instances of foul play or, as a matter of fact (apologetic glance at the dock), in the event of death by hanging.

By now, a quarter to four, the jury was showing signs of having been cooped up too long in a crowded room, so the judge allowed one final piece of evidence, a letter from Wheeler's regimental CO confirming that it was regrettable but unfortunately not extraordinary that a revolver had not been returned at the end of the war, and that the number on the revolver at the crime scene matched that issued to Corporal Stephen Anthony Wheeler in January 1918.

Thirty-One

That night I woke in the small hours and replayed the trial witness by witness. The sight of Wheeler's defeated bulk in the dock haunted me. Breen had said on our journey home that the jury would not warm to such a passive figure, but I saw him as pitiable. It was as if to retreat like that within his own soft flesh was the only way Wheeler had of defending himself. I imagined him passing night after night during the war similarly motionless, whatever horrors exploded around him.

The next morning saw an even longer queue for the public benches and Breen reported that poor reproductions of Stella and Stephen's wedding photograph were being circulated, tuppence each. The case was a sensation in the press, which had dubbed it the "Shot in the Heart Murder." Breen also said, with chilling pragmatism, that the crowd had caught the whiff of a hanging and would soon be baying for blood. I was dismayed by the fatalism that seemed to have overcome my usually ebullient senior. It felt to me as if Breen & Balcombe was already distancing itself from Wheeler; there was no sign of Wolfe (Breen remarked that the entire firm couldn't suspend its operations for the sake of this trial and Wolfe had other fish to fry). On the other hand, *my* services to the law were obviously expendable. Breen told me he preferred to have me in Aylesbury under his eye and there was always the hope I would learn something.

The first witness was Julie Leamington (née Hobhouse), who was to give evidence about her sister's relations with Stephen. Julie was exquisitely dressed in a navy round-necked dress with a touch of white piping at collar and hip, and more than a hint of a swollen belly. Framed by the dock, she looked fragile, and her little hand rested like a flower on the Bible.

From the defense point of view, Julie's evidence was damning, because it was clear that she'd made up her mind both about Stephen's guilt and about his motive. "He loved her to pieces, anyone could see that. But he watched her all the time. He never believed himself good enough for her. I said to her, Stell, don't marry him. He'll want you always there, under his eye."

"She must have loved him very much to go against such advice."

"The fact is, Your Lordship, Stell was terrified of being left on the shelf. We all were. She thought he was the best she could get. I don't mean to be cruel to Stephen but I know I'm right. He was a good man, had a good job, and she was really very fond of him."

"Your Honor, I must object, this is all speculation . . ."

"Mr. Wainwright, the dead girl is not here to give her own reasons for marriage so we must pay attention to her sister. The jury should understand that in the case of murder where the victim cannot speak for herself, hearsay evidence from those close to her is admissible. Perhaps Mrs. Leamington, however, might be persuaded to give us more detail of the evidence upon which she based her conclusions as to her sister's state of mind."

"Mrs. Leamington, you do not describe the late Mrs. Wheeler, your sister, as being a contented person. What about in more intimate areas of her marriage, did she ever give you cause to think things were not well there?"

Julie shrugged and pouted. "I never had the chance to speak to her after she was wed."

"You say Wheeler was a jealous man."

"I don't want to give you the wrong impression. In some ways I thought he was too good to Stella, overindulged her. He knew she loved dancing. He tormented himself, sometimes, I thought, by watching her dance, but apart from not letting her go to the Trocadero he never stopped her. When she was a girl she had dreamed of becoming a dancer, you know, in shows. Dad paid a fortune for lessons, but it came to nothing. She wanted money for her dancing frocks and such so she started in Lyons. She never saved her money, just spent it on clothes."

"You say Mr. Wheeler didn't like her going to the Trocadero. Did she conform to his wishes?"

"Mostly. Sometimes she went but didn't tell him." She glanced at Wheeler, who sat as usual, eyes downcast, hands clasped.

"So on the one hand you have a husband who loves to watch his wife dance, on the other a man who was perhaps conscious of his own physical deficiencies."

"You are putting words into the witness's mouth," said the judge.

"This is a difficult question for you, Mrs. Leamington, but did your sister ever give her husband real cause to be jealous?"

"If you mean, did Stella have an affair? Of course not. She was a good girl. She didn't have to marry him. If you mean, did she flirt? Yes, she flirted."

"And what form did that flirting take?"

Julie started to weep, rather daintily, and produced a lace handkerchief from her cuff. "If she was noticed by someone she liked the look of, she would become different; more of everything, more smiles, more movement, more spark, you know. She would perform for them, not obviously but so only they and she would know. I've seen her do it a hundred times."

Wainwright, in cross-examination, asked gently: "You say Stella flirted but she never seemed to have been drawn to one man in particular or allowed herself to be carried away. Yet you claim Mr. Wheeler was jealous."

"He would go very quiet sometimes after a night out. Not speak to her for days. He never shouted. Just silence. She hated his silence."

"To your knowledge, was he ever violent toward her?"

"Never. She would have told me."

"So the idea that he might actually have taken her life out of jealousy is, in your mind, absurd."

"Objection," shouted Warren.

He needn't have bothered. Julie was determined to reply to Wainwright's question. "She's dead, isn't she?" was what she said.

ഇൻ

The next prosecution witness was Doctor Reardon, the medical officer who had served with Wheeler in 1917. He was a plump, smart man, more like a naval captain than an army doctor, with a scar on his cheek and another, quite vicious, on the back of his hand.

Once the doctor's report had been read in open court, Warren said: "Dr. Reardon, you wrote: *I would strongly recommend that Wheeler be examined for his psychological fitness to plead. What is acceptable, even convenient in times of war, does not allow a man to survive in more normal circumstances.* You'll be aware that the defense chose not to follow that recommendation. Perhaps you could clarify to the court why you wrote as you did."

"It's exactly as I said in the report. I am not sure that a man's apparent sanity in time of great stress will necessarily hold in later life."

"You think that Wheeler may be suffering from delayed shell shock or some such."

"Possibly."

"But you have not examined him recently, so could not possibly comment on his current state of mind."

"I could not."

"And since the defense is not choosing to call any other experts to give evidence concerning Stephen Wheeler's state of mind at present, or indeed at the time when his wife, Stella, was killed, the court must draw its own conclusions. Now, Dr. Reardon, I have a couple of very simple questions to put to you, concerning army protocol. In your report, you said that Wheeler had formed part of a firing squad. I wonder if you could tell the court the process that was gone through prior to an execution."

"What possible relevance," asked Wainwright, "can this question have to a murder committed in 1924 in Buckinghamshire countryside?"

The judge said irritably: "I'm sure Mr. Warren has his reasons."

"The man in question is given a last meal," said Reardon, "and allowed to pray, and then he is led before his fellows, blindfolded if he wishes."

"And tell us how the men who form the squad are selected."

"Again, it varies from regiment to regiment. Sometimes by lot. Sometimes handpicked. In our case, the former."

"And what was your role, as the doctor?"

"To declare a man dead, obviously."

"Any other function?"

"Sometimes to ensure members of the firing party were fit."

"Anything else?"

Silence. Then Reardon said: "It was my job to place a marker."

"A marker?"

"The men needed a precise target to ensure that the job was done without inflicting unnecessary suffering. We pinned a square of white flannel over the heart of the prisoner, to ensure that he would be quickly and humanely killed."

"So that he would be shot in the heart."

"Precisely."

Wainwright was on his feet. "Your Honor, it's late in the morning and we're all weary but I crave your forgiveness. I repeat, I fail to see the relevance of this line of questioning to the murder of a girl in a wood."

Warren looked pained: "I have finished my questions. I was merely demonstrating to the jury that the defendant, Wheeler, had formed part of a firing squad in which he was ordered to shoot a man through the heart."

Wainwright shuffled his notes and began his cross-examination: "Dr. Reardon, much will hinge, in this trial, on whether Mr. Wheeler was capable of killing his wife in cold blood for some spurious reason to do with money. Give us your impressions of the man."

Warren cried: "Your Honor, this court is surely not interested in *impressions*, particularly impressions formed more than half a dozen years ago."

The judge bowed his head for a moment, as if summoning strength. "Objection upheld, Mr. Warren."

"Tell us more, then," said Wainwright, urbane as ever, "about the case in which Wheeler formed part of the firing squad. You say he knew the man who died."

"It was a regrettable incident in every respect. Wheeler was a member of a firing party that executed a man who I later discovered had been especially dear to him, all the more tragic as Wheeler was not generally known for his ability to form close friendships. This particular boy had been a junior employee at Imperial Insurance and joined up underage, at sixteen and a half, with other members of the firm, then twice ran away and was captured. In my view he was shell-shocked, but another,

more senior doctor dismissed the diagnosis. The first time his sentence
was suspended, the second the court-martial had no option but to recommend he face the firing squad. Fox—the young boy—had not been
alone in trying to escape and when he and his fellow were captured, one
of them turned on the military policeman and shot him in the elbow.
Though Wheeler had attempted to nurture and protect this boy, when
his name was drawn from the hat he did not flinch from forming part
of the firing party, though under the circumstances he would certainly
have been excused. I suspect he took on the work because he knew that
he at least would not miss the mark. I would say this was evidence rather
of a merciful action than otherwise."

I was barely listening. Fox. Yes, there'd been another soldier—a pim-
ply lad—in the only photograph of Wheeler in uniform, kept with its
face to the wall in the spare room of the marital home. I'd assumed that
it was Stella who had set the photograph aside out of indifference but
perhaps after all it was Wheeler who couldn't bear to look at it. I glanced
at Wheeler but he did not show by the flicker of an eyelash that he was
moved by what he'd heard.

"One question in reexamination," said Warren, rising to his feet
again. "As you said in your own report, and I quote: *I have noted that
there are types of personality that survive better in war than in peacetime—
a man like Wheeler thrives on the routine of war and the absolute necessity
to obey orders. The shocks of trench life register less with this type than with
others* . . . Does not this suggest a lack of feeling?"

"No, sir, it suggests that here is a man who has found a mechanism
for dealing with what to others would be unbearable."

☙❧

Over lunch Breen went into conference with Wainwright, so I walked
by myself up and down the little streets of Aylesbury. Nicholas was on

my mind, and the copse on the Chesham hillside. *This bloody war*, he'd said, *it goes on and on, doesn't it?* An invidious link had been made in the jury's minds between Stephen forming part of a firing squad and his wife meeting her death through a shot in the heart.

I passed gabled cottages, grander Georgian houses, cobbled alleys that reminded me of Chesham. It was all so pat, this gradual unraveling of evidence against Wheeler. Each time another witness was called, a new piece was added to the jigsaw. The jury was being led inexorably toward a verdict of guilt, but if it were true, it was almost as if Wheeler had gone out of his way to frame himself. We were all being made to look only in his direction. But if that was the case, what had we turned our backs on? To what had we made ourselves blind?

Don't look at the act, implored my brother from beyond the grave, *look at the cause*. What was the *cause* of Stella's death? And I realized now that what we had not been seeing was the obvious—whoever killed Stella had known everything about her husband: his jealousy, what he'd kept in a tin box in the shed, his love of a lunchtime drink, his war record, every last detail, including that he'd formed part of a firing squad. So what else did they know that had led them to the terrible conclusion that Stella had to be killed? What was the cause?

And more to the point, from whom had they learned all these things? Only two people had such intimate knowledge of Wheeler. The man himself, and his wife.

☙

But I had no opportunity to share these insights. The afternoon was filled with technical evidence concerning the finding of the corpse, a description of Stella's body and its state of decomposition, and testimony from a police examiner to say that she had been killed at close range by a bullet from a Webley service revolver—the same that had been issued to Wheeler during the latter part of the war. In just two more hours, the prosecution had concluded its case. Not one word had been spoken of the possible involvement of any other person, and when Warren sat down, with just the hint of a modestly reflective smile, there cannot have been a person in the courtroom other than Breen (and I couldn't be entirely sure what he believed) and me—and possibly Wheeler's mother—who thought that Wheeler was innocent.

Thirty-two

Meredith had left for her art class by the time I reached home at seven. Not that I was in a condition to notice, because on the hall stand was a letter in a heart-stoppingly identifiable hand. The Gifford habit was to delay gratification; pleasure had to be thoroughly *earned* by self-denial and the thrill of anticipation, so on my way upstairs I called into the drawing room where Edmund sat on the floor at Grandmother's feet, absorbed by a game of bagatelle, ensuring that conversation was accompanied by the whirr of ball bearings on oak.

"Did you see your letter?" said Mother, still trying to placate me. "There is a Manchester postmark. I didn't know you had a friend up there."

"Evelyn no doubt has many clever friends we don't know about," said Prudence.

"Unusual handwriting for a woman," said Mother.

"Oh, I think everyone writes the same these days," I said as calmly as possible.

"Such a shame," said Prudence. "We used to pride ourselves on forming dainty letters. You could always tell a lady's handwriting by its little flourishes."

"I love letters," piped up Grandmother, "reading and writing them.

You never know what a letter might hold. I wonder if Edmund will be a letter writer."

"Letters often bring bad or sad news," said Mother, glancing nervously at me.

Prudence said: "By the way, Evelyn, you perhaps will be interested to learn that I too received a letter this morning. My cottage has been valued at three hundred and fifty pounds. I am surprised it's not worth more, given the location and the beautiful garden, but at least I have taken a definite step."

"What is special about the location?" demanded Mother.

"So convenient for the village and the big house. And the rooms are a good size and have a beautiful view, particularly the front bedroom. The estate agent mentioned that there was plenty of space for expansion, should someone wish to add a conservatory or extra wing. In his letter, however, he states that the house has an air of neglect about it that will not be attractive to a buyer. I shall have to go out there more often to keep it aired while the wretched tenants are away."

I said, almost before I had formed the thought: "I could go, if you like."

It was so unlike me to offer a favor, let alone one of some magnitude, that Prudence was incredulous. "What on earth would you wish to do that for?"

"The trial is in Aylesbury. It is not so far for me to go on from there. If you give me the key I could visit on Friday, perhaps . . ."

I was amazed at myself, the suddenness with which I had formed a plan, the brazenness of the thought that I could be alone with Nicholas in my aunt's cottage. Prudence was rattling off instructions: "You'd have to check and reset the mousetraps, inspect the bedroom ceilings for signs of leaking pipes in the attic, throw open the windows . . ."

"You look so tired, Evelyn," Mother interrupted. "I presume it's this horrible trial. I'm sure it's bad for you, dragging out to Buckinghamshire every day, listening to all that sordid stuff. Do you really want to take on the extra burden of Prudence's cottage?"

༺ༀ༻

The second love letter of my life did not disappoint.

I thought mine was a steady nature and that I was not subject to extremes of emotion. I thought the war had hardened me such that I would never lower my guard fully, or be capable of what I now feel for you. Thank God the case here is straightforward, a plum for me as I am defending the most sympathetic of three, the poor stooge of a bank clerk who has been forced to defraud his unfortunate employer of tens of thousands by a couple of conmen and blackmailers. Thank God, as I said, the case is relatively straightforward because through it all I think of you.

Here are just two of a thousand things you perhaps didn't know about Evelyn Gifford: When the sun is behind you, your hair becomes electric, every strand coiled and burnished and separate in the light. Your hair is like you, Evelyn, it won't conform. Then you have this habit of looking into your teacup or into some distant part of the room and suddenly casting me a glance with such a light in your eye that each time I want to fall at your feet.

I think of you in your ubiquitous hat—never, ever buy a new hat—in some courtroom, gravely attentive, and I want to be with you so much it's all I can do to prevent myself from leaping aboard the first train.

By way of a PS [*I rejoiced in that PS, having been brought up to believe that the use of a PS was downright common*], I hear from my secretary that a prominent member of the board (Good Samaritan Home), Lady Laura Curren, will see you at teatime on Wednesday. Here's the address. This bodes very well for the fate of the Marchant children, I think.

I ate my supper of steak-and-kidney pudding (Rose's menu did not adapt to the seasons) in a daze of love, both his letters pushed firmly into the pocket of my skirt next to James's so that I could touch them from time to time, thankful that Meredith wasn't there to notice my distraction. Meanwhile, Edmund picked the bits of kidney out of his pudding and arranged them on the edge of his plate, like plum pits. Prudence drew breath from time to time as if about to speak, but she'd learned not to battle with him over food, because he always won.

As soon as was possible, I urged him to bed, carrying him all the way upstairs, though it seemed to me he grew heavier each day, and in his room we had a tickling match from which we both emerged gasping with laughter. He demanded one of the crueller fairy stories, "The Handless Maiden," for some mysterious reason a favorite, perhaps because it was rather long or perhaps, Meredith had suggested, because it was about a banished mother and son who are redeemed at last. There was a line that he loved in particular: *So far as the heaven is blue,"* exclaimed the King, *"I will go; and neither will I eat nor drink until I have found again my dear wife and child . . ."*

Then I kissed my nephew's beautiful cheek and whispered in his ear: "So far as the heaven is blue, Edmund, your aunty Evelyn will love you."

These days, he flung his arms around my neck to kiss me in return and ask the inevitable question: "When's Mommy coming home?"

"She'll be late because of the art class, but she's bound to come and kiss you good night."

"I'll be asleep by then so I'll never know for sure that she's kissed me." And his knowing look was so like Meredith's that my heart ached. Why had I never seen it before, the echo of her face in his; the quirk of the head, the compression of the lips, those expressive eyes?

"But you can be sure she will, because she loves you, Edmund."

Even by midnight, what with the Wheeler trial and my love letter, I was still not asleep, so I heard the soft closing of the front door, Meredith's footstep on the stairs, a pause as she looked in on Edmund, then a soft tap at my door. "Are you awake, Evelyn?" She perched on the edge of my bed, reeking of cigarettes and alcohol, having been to the Café Royal, she said, rather expensive but worth it because they'd seen all sorts of famous people there: Augustus John, at last, in a corner, and Lytton Strachey, as identified by Sylvia, and about five different poets all of whom Sylvia recognized, and Sylvia had offered to foot the bill, she was drowning her sorrows while the tall fiancé was away on business, so they'd ordered three bottles of wine and Margot had got horribly drunk and horribly jealous of Sylvia because Hadley was all over her, what with the tall one being absent.

"But listen," Meredith said, "I want to talk to you. I have a plan, unless you're too sleepy to listen."

She sat on my windowsill with the sash pulled up so she could smoke, and I put on my dressing gown and perched beside her. The night air smelled of Mother's garden and soot; traffic still rumbled on a thousand streets. Meredith produced from her art bag a half-empty whiskey bottle, a couple of shot glasses, and a packet of cigarettes, and I wondered whether this late-night visit meant that she had decided we were to be friends. I, who never smoked (Clivedon Hall Gardens deemed smoking fast and unladylike), took tentative little puffs, wishing that Nicholas were here to see me in this un-Evelyn-like pose and that I might be kissing his mouth rather than drawing amateurishly upon a cigarette.

Meredith pushed out her bottom lip as she exhaled. Her head was thrown back so that her short hair ruffled against the wall and my heart beat a little faster, because I had no idea what she would say next.

"The night sky makes me long for home," she said at last. "We have skies there that would take your breath away. Stars so thick you think you must be breathing them in. And there are miles and miles and miles of emptiness between one human being and another."

"You never talk about home."

"You never ask. None of you does."

"Tell me then."

"As a matter of fact I've been thinking of home a lot. I've been thinking I might go back."

Pause. "We would miss you both," I said at last.

"Do you know what? I almost believe you."

"You should believe me."

She laughed suddenly and gave my calf a nudge with her toe. "Look
at you with your knees all uncovered and that old dressing gown half
undone. You have become different. I've noticed that about you. Why?"

"You and Edmund, I suppose. This trial—it's toughening me up."

"Yes, but there's something else, isn't there? Do you know what I
think? I think you have fallen in love." She stared not at me but across
the garden to the high backs of houses in the next street. I said nothing.
From below came a fragrance of roses, just a whiff. "I've seen you go soft
to your core," she said. "Who is it?"

For one moment I was tempted. How intoxicating it would be to
speak his name. But it was of course impossible, given that half an hour
ago Meredith had been with Sylvia Hardynge. Instead I said: "Have you
ever been in love?"

She drew on her cigarette and her painted lips formed a neat little
diamond where the cigarette had been withdrawn. "Aha, that was Miss
Gifford telling me to mind my own business. Well, then I shall. But
I'm not so coy. Yes, I have been in love. I was in love when I entered
the convent, as a matter of fact. You may think that a cliché but it's the
truth. With my whole being I was drawn to love an idea—can you
imagine that? Or no, it was more than an idea, it was a beautiful, breathing, compassionate silence that I loved."

"And my brother, did he end all that for you?"

"Now there's another Gifford remark. It would have to be all down to a Gifford, wouldn't it, that a lifetime's vocation ended? No, not just your brother. There was a falling off, a decline in certainty even before James. I wanted answers: If you love us, why allow the wholesale slaughter of beloved boys? And I found I loved those boys more than I loved my silent and abstract God who I came to see as a heavenly fat boy, too darn lazy to sort things out. I loved your brother. He was so vivid, so keen to seize every last morsel of not being in the war. Oh, I was so tempted to give him everything he wanted."

"And now?" I asked at last.

"And now here I am a little fuzzy with whiskey, and you know what I think? I think, What the hell? I think nothing matters a straw. We must just get through, somehow, anyhow. Maybe do our best. Maybe not. Maybe paint a picture, maybe empty a bedpan. What does it matter?"

She blew smoke, took another swig, and examined her little naked feet with their crimson toenails. "So, in any case," she said, "if you're in love, my girl, does that mean that you won't be interested in my proposal? I have come up with a final plan. If this one doesn't work, I do believe I'll give up and go back to Canada, so it's down to you. I arrived here and disliked you. Then you hit me and I loathed you. Then, I think, we started to soften toward each other. And now I find I am very interested in you. I even think I like you enough to want to live with you permanently. I thought you and I could set up somewhere. Leave the others in this house, get them to take a couple of lady lodgers to compensate for your income. Within a few months they'll scarcely notice anything has changed."

I was so taken aback that I made the first objection that came into my head. "Prudence will notice. Prudence worships you. Didn't you realize?"

"Ah, you've spotted that, have you? Then don't you see that for her sake, if for no other reason, I must move out, and soon?"

"How would we manage? I'd be working . . . there's Edmund."

"I've thought it all out. I will return to nursing, earn some money. Yes, I'll retrain, find my way back. And I shall paint. And you will look after Edmund while I'm out in the evenings or we'll hire Min to come in from time to time. Or he can come back here for his tea. And you and I will have each other and we will be wild and free, a couple of spinster girls. But all this is a pipe dream now because you have this man, whoever he is. Or am I wrong?"

Another surge of blood to the heart. Nicholas.

The sky was now ink-dark except for a sliver of moon. The city was much quieter, as if the night sky was heavy, like pudding, and pressed a hush on the traffic. I said: "But how can you forgive me for James? Won't I remind you of James?"

Her eyes were wide and unblinking. I saw the religious in her, I saw her as an ecstatic who wanted nothing less than to give everything. I felt the spiky complexity of her character and that she was constantly striving to smooth herself out, to find a way of being that would make life bearable. "You do remind me of James. You were a great part of James, did you know? I never told you, did I, that he once said how much he missed you."

"Did he say that?"

"He did. He described this house as pretty dull, I'm afraid, and the future that had been planned for him as one he would sooner get out of. But he described you as his champion, his friend. He said you were much sharper than he. I was interested in you even then."

Did I believe her? Did it matter?

"Anyway, I want to be reminded of James," she said. "I have spent years trying to forget and it doesn't work. Not just what James did to me but the whole show comes back to haunt me. I have only to see a dead tree or a man on a crutch and there I am, probing a foul wound or closing a dead boy's eyes. When I see mud or blood or any kind of ugliness, I am reminded. And each time it's a blow. It makes me shrink because I'm always cowering, waiting for the next. But when I'm with you, however vile you are, I feel better. You are a consequence, a continuum, and not all bad. Do you understand?"

After a long pause, she added: "But listen, Sylvia knows of a flat in Pimlico overlooking the river, quite cheap, she thought no more than fourteen shillings a week each—a friend of hers is renting at the moment but is getting married so it will be vacant from next month. She's arranging for me to go visit on Thursday afternoon. If you won't share with me, I might find someone else, maybe from the art class—not Margot, I can't stand her. Sylvia. Ah. But she's engaged, isn't she? She won't be looking to share a flat with anyone."

Did she know? She couldn't know. For a moment I wondered whether this entire conversation had been staged so that we would reach this point. Her face was turned toward me, eyes huge in the moonlight, little teeth glinting.

It was on the tip of my tongue to say: I couldn't help myself, Meredith, I had to have him. But how could I, to her of all people?

Her parting shot was: "Prudence has agreed to collect Edmund from school the next couple of days because I want to come with you to the trial. Would I get a seat, do you think? After all, I went to all those hospitals with you, I feel as if I have a stake in poor Stella's fate."

The terrible irony was that I tried to dissuade her. I didn't want her there, for the craven reason that *he* might come back early, that his business in Manchester might soon be finished, and I thought then he would come hot-foot to me. But her mind was made up, she would attend the trial except that on Thursday she would leave early to get to Pimlico on time and she would wear her green dress and hat, which she now considered to be her *courtroom* attire.

Thirty-three

Next morning I found Meredith a space high up in the public gallery, then joined Breen in the lawyers' benches and told him Thorne had arranged for me to visit a Lady Curren in relation to the Marchant children. Breen tap-tapped the top of his pen on the bench in front of him. "You spoke to Thorne about the Marchants."

"You know he was involved in Mrs. Marchant's case, sir. He defended her."

"Well, it's good of him to take an interest."

"Are you content for me to go alone to visit Lady Curren?"

"I don't appear to have much choice. It's short notice, Wolfe is busy, I'm needed here. Keep quiet and take notes. Even you should be capable of that."

At that moment, in came the judge swathed in the stifling robes that already, this early in the day, made him sweat. Wainwright stood up, glanced at a watch hanging from a chain stretching from one side of his belly to the other, and said: "I'll call Mr. Wheeler."

It was something of a shock to see Wheeler's legs and highly polished shoes when he was escorted from the dock to the witness box. His posture and heavy gait were bearlike. We had no idea whether or not he would choose to speak and when he was asked to swear on the Bible there was a moment's absolute silence. Then he read the oath in his dismal voice, gripped the edge of the box, and fixed Wainwright with those oddly liquid eyes of his.

Not by a glimmer did Wainwright betray his relief that his chief witness was prepared to talk as he began with soothing questions about Wheeler's name, address, occupation, war service, and finally the date of his marriage.

"That must have been a very happy day for you, Mr. Wheeler."

"I never trusted my luck until that moment." I remembered the wedding photograph, Stella's regular little features, the flash of a false smile; Stella the dancing girl, waitress, fashion-lover. She was there in the courtroom all right, a will-o'-the-wisp to the rest of us but such a real, marvelous girl to dewy-eyed Wheeler.

"Mr. Wheeler, you wrote to your wife constantly during the war, didn't you, and she replied? It's painful for you, I know, but might the court be read some of your letters? If my learned friend is content, I shall read just two from the war, as an example of the others. But then I shall read another, written just before you and Stella were married."

Stella to Stephen, 1917: I think of you often and can't bear it when I hear of all the dead men. All I hope is that you're not one of them and that you will come home, and we'll go for a walk together on the common maybe and you can tell me all about it. I've been at Lyons three weeks today. I like to be in London. I like it when the servicemen come in on leave, but I'm too shy to ask if they know you . . .

Stephen to Stella, 1917: Saw a bit of action. Not much, nothing to be scared of. As usual, before I went up, I took out your photograph and had just a peek. I like to think the last face I shall ever look at will be yours, and it will be. You are smiling but your picture's getting battered in my pocket. Send me another sometime. Don't wear a hat if you have your photograph taken. I want to see your eyes.

Stephen to Stella, two days before their marriage, April 26, 1924: I promise to love you forever. I owe you everything. You have kept my spirits up all these years, my Stella. Without you I would not see the point. You are the point. I will never let you down, I will never make you regret what you're doing for me, not for a single minute. I can't believe we are to be wed and live under the same roof, night and day, that I'll wake up to find you beside me in the morning and when the nightmares come, you'll be there, like you said, to hold me. I will just count my blessings and let it all come about as you want. But Stella, don't forget you can pull out still, I would understand.

"Mr. Wheeler," said Wainwright, "this last letter suggests that you still had your doubts, even on the eve of your wedding, about whether or not Stella wanted to marry you."

The reading of the letters had a profound effect on Wheeler, though neither his posture nor his expression had changed. It was rather as if he had been struck so that even the blood in his veins trembled. There was a long silence while he dragged his attention back to the courtroom. "I still had my doubts about whether I was good enough for her."

Wainwright paused while the jury absorbed this information, then embarked on a different tack. "Mr. Wheeler, the prosecution has been hinting that you retained that Webley service revolver after the war for somewhat sinister reasons. Can you explain its presence in your shed?"

"We all took stuff after the war. The CO wasn't much interested in me—he was on the lookout for the real villains who would try to smuggle anything out and sell it off."

"But why keep the revolver?"

"I thought it might come in useful sometime."

Shocked murmur in the courthouse. "How, Mr. Wheeler? What possible purpose could a revolver have?"

"I thought it might be useful, should I ever want, you know . . . for myself."

"Suicide is a very terrible thought, Mr. Wheeler. Why would you consider such a thing?"

"Why would I not? It was all one to me whether I lived or died, except for Stell. I never told her this, of course, but if she hadn't wanted me, in the end, I would have done it."

"Why would you have chosen to die, Mr. Wheeler, having survived the war?"

"Why would I want to live? I don't want to live among the dead. They are in my head, night and day. I dream about them. It's like I told Stell, even while I was fighting the war it didn't much matter what happened to me except for her letters. Only they counted. She was the one bright thing. Otherwise I knew I'd be better off dead than living with what I'd seen and done."

Wainwright again allowed the silence to extend before he said softly: "We've heard of one incident, related to a friend of yours, to whom you showed great compassion. Would you like to tell the court about the occasion you formed part of a firing squad?"

Silence.

"Why did you not attempt to be excused, Mr. Wheeler, when the lad was a friend of yours?"

Silence. Prolonged. Wheeler, with his head down and his hands gripping the dock, was inexorable.

Eventually, Wainwright changed the subject: "But once you were married, Mr. Wheeler, and you had won your Stella, why keep the revolver, then?"

His head came up. "Habit. And if she ever left me."

"If Stella had left, what would you have done with the revolver?"

No answer.

"You say that you never told your wife that you had these suicidal thoughts. But you told the police that she knew about the revolver."

"Yes. She wanted to see what I'd brought back from the war so I showed her. She held the revolver and said how heavy it was. She wanted to know all about what it felt like to kill a man. She was always asking about the war, I wished she wouldn't. It was horrible to see the revolver in her lap."

"Mr. Wheeler, forgive these intimate questions. You've heard Stella's sister suggest that you were a jealous man. Did you ever have cause to be jealous of Stella?"

"Never. Never. Never."

"She loved dancing. Describe her to me, as she danced."

Wheeler put his head on one side and fixed his eyes on the clerk's desk as if it were a dance floor. "She wore a little dress with silky bows on the hips. They'd play something like 'Tiger Rag,' she loved that, and this look would come into her eye, a faraway look like she was listening for something. And then suddenly she'd be off, grabbing one of her girlfriends, or a partner would tap her shoulder and she'd give him this smile like a yes, yes please, but dancing was serious for her, and once she started her body would free itself and her eyes would shine and her jaw would set, she didn't smile when she was dancing, and those hands and feet would go. Syncopation. You know."

"And that didn't make you jealous?"

"It made me glad. She was so happy when she danced. And then I was sad because however gay she was, she wasn't like that with me."

"It must have grieved you that you couldn't dance together."

"Don't go on about it. I never danced, a great thing like me, even before the war when dancing was different. There was other things we did do together."

"Such as?"

"Such as talk. Plan. Watch each other. Go out." A sudden rueful smile that transformed his sad face. "Go for a picnic."

A note was passed from Breen to Wainwright, who scarcely paused in his questioning. "Ah yes. The picnic. Had you been for many picnics together?"

"No, that was the first. Thing was, her mum had just passed on the basket and Stell wanted to use it. She liked the idea of wrapping things up nice."

"So whose idea was the picnic?"

"Well, hers, at first, because of the basket. But I joined in though I didn't see the point of getting on a train. I thought we could have gone up Harrow Hill."

"Let's get this clear. Not only was it her idea to have a picnic but she chose the location."

"She chose Chesham, yes. She'd been there with her family. And I had as a boy, fishing."

"And then when you were walking up the hill, according to one of the prosecution witnesses, Miss Shearman, you and Stella both looked out of sorts. Had you had an argument?"

"We was often arguing about little things. I wanted to stop near the town so that I could go in for a drink. She wanted to go deeper into the countryside, said there was a field she knew. She kept dithering until she'd found a spot to satisfy her."

"So you ate your picnic. Were you on good terms then?"

"Yes. We didn't say much, just watched the flowers and birds, like you do on picnics. And then she said I might as well go and have a drink since I was so keen on the idea, she would lie in the shade and have a rest."

"So it was her suggestion that you went for a drink."

"That was the plan all along. Picnic. Pub. Home. I was sorry she didn't come with me but I wanted a drink. And anyway, Stell was in a bad mood. Nothing I did was right. So I went down and had a pint, thought she'd be better off on her own."

"You see the prosecution is making the absurd allegation that before you went down for your drink, you bullied or dragged your wife nearly three quarters of a mile and killed her in a fit of jealousy or greed or some such—they seem to have an entire armory of possible motives. What do you say to that suggestion?"

Wheeler smiled sadly, showing his white teeth. "I love her. She is the very last person I would kill. And I'm not killing nobody, ever again. That's the vow I made to myself November 11, 1918. Except myself. If need be. Like I said."

"And when you were in the pub, the other customers said you looked low."

"I was hot. And I was low, yes. I wanted her to come with me. It seemed to me she'd wanted to get rid of me."

"Mr. Wheeler, I want you to think very carefully now. Was she wearing a hat when you left her?"

"She wasn't wearing it, she was holding it. When I left her she was laying down in the shade with her eyes shut and her hat was in her hand, held on her stomach, like this." Silence in court as Wheeler closed his eyes and rested his right hand on his belly. We saw her, his daintily clad wife, lying on the picnic blanket, cropped head flung back, eyes closed against the irritation of her husband's neediness.

"I've nearly finished my questions, Mr. Wheeler, and then my friend will wish to speak to you, but first I must clear up three points. The prosecution will claim that the fact you apparently did nothing to find your wife on the Sunday afternoon and even went into work on Monday is proof that you knew exactly where she was. What do you say to that?"

"I did those things because I didn't know what else to do. I thought she'd gone away and might come back."

"Gone where, Mr. Wheeler?"

Shrug.

"The prosecution will claim that one of the reasons you killed Stella was because you were set to make a great deal of money out of her death."

"You mean the insurance. Everyone knows you can't claim insurance if there's been foul play."

"Thank you. And one more thing. The prosecution has implied that you had become hardened by your experiences in the war, that there is more than coincidence in the fact that your wife was killed by a shot in the heart when you are something of an expert marksman and had been a member of a firing squad."

Wheeler's head went back, so that he might hold the tears against his lids rather than let them fall. "I loved that girl. I would a million times rather kill myself than her. Yes, I shot a man at close range in the war. Many, actually, one way or another. I had to. But that was it. End of story. Do you know what I learned about death?" More animated, he leaned forward and gazed at Wainwright with those relentlessly candid eyes of his. "This is what I learned. It's the loneliest place to be. I seen a man clap another on the shoulder one second, dead the next. I seen that same man's body lowered into the soil. Why would I want my dancing girl in that lonely place?"

Thirty-four

I missed the next part of Wheeler's evidence, because I had to travel back to London and take tea with Nicholas's friend Lady Curren in her house off Eaton Square. Mother would have been gratified to see me climb those marble steps, drag on the bell-pull, and be shown by a butler across a black-and-white-tiled floor, like a chessboard, into a drawing room furnished in highly conventional style, pale greens and creams, including the floral arrangements. Across another acre of polished boards and exquisite rugs, French windows were open to reveal a lawn and beds planted exclusively with white flowers. Even I, with my untutored understanding of art, could tell that the walls were hung with original paintings, including an example of the Impressionist school: water, flowers, a couple of long-haired girls, whose frocks merged with the meadow upon which they lay.

The diminutive Lady Curren, Meredith's height and even slighter, was seated at the edge of what I guessed was an eighteenth-century sofa, next to a tall vase of lilies, whose fragrance weighed heavy in the air. On the same table were arranged a number of framed photographs, in which Lady Curren and a thin gentleman (presumably, her husband) were standing in a line of smiling people or shaking hands with assorted dignitaries; I recognized the Prince of Wales, Lady Astor, Stanley Baldwin.

Lady Curren wore a flowing dress in oyster pink crepe, which provided an unsettling contrast with her hair, cut in a razor-sharp bob that must surely need the attention of a hairdresser at least twice weekly, if not daily, to maintain its incredible shine and symmetry. She was dark-skinned, with a thin but prominent nose and brows that arched up to her straight little bangs. Her mouth was very small, her eyes narrow and heavily outlined with kohl.

Tea was served in what might have been a set for a large doll. Altogether, perched opposite little Lady Curren with that fragment of porcelain balanced on my palm, I felt like Alice in Wonderland after she'd grown or the world had shrunk.

"So you are a lawyer," said Lady Curren, her voice high and creaky as a shed door, the vowels strangulated.

"I am still in training. At present I am an articled clerk."

"How *fas*cinating. Oh, you young things are so fortunate. In my [*maay*] day we gels were expected to sit around and look gorgeous. Full stop."

I smiled dutifully. Mother would have known how to deal with Lady Curren—flattered her by commenting on her *lovely* drawing room, the tea service, the flowers, the *glorious* view to the garden—but I found her immeasurably out of reach, especially having just spent a morning immersed in the Wheeler marriage. The tea was tepid and there was not even a slice of bread and butter, though I was very hungry.

"Now, to business," said Lady Curren, dabbing her lip with a speck of a napkin. "As I expect you're aware, you've caused quite a stir at our home and we can't have that. We are all full of admiration for our dear Miss Buckley who does sterling work for those poor children."

"It was not my intention . . ."

A brow was raised. One did not interrupt Lady C. "You see we spend hours [*ares*] and hours on the board discussing every aspect of the life of the home and this includes regulations for visitors, for children's playtimes, for treats, for meals, all, all are regulated upon the best advice of our doctor and other experts. Be assured, we consult *experts*, Miss Gifford."

That word, *expert*, was intended to annihilate me, as was the infinitesimal flicker of her heavy eyelid. I, in her book, was no more an expert than the women who typed her husband's letters or polished her silver. She continued: "Then I had a letter from dear Nicholas Thorne, whom I adore, and whose judgment I trust absolutely." Her hand made a gesture like a petal opening as she picked up one of the photographs on the side table and handed it to me.

Dear God, there he was, in army uniform, amid a group of people sitting on steps outside French windows, probably the ones that now stood open in this very room. And beside him, gripping a plait of hair that fell across her shoulder, was Sylvia, and behind her another uniformed boy and an older couple. I recognized Sir David Hardynge, mustached and bespectacled. Next to him was his wife, presumably, with her hair coiffed in a prewar cloud of waves and coils.

"He's such a dear friend of the family, engaged to my niece, Sylvia. Sylvia's mother, Margaret, is my sister."

"And the other boy in uniform?"

Her voice tightened. "My nephew, Donald. I'm afraid he suffered tragically in the war."

Nicholas, in the photograph, was not smiling in the way that he smiled at me but still his eyes were warm, head slightly inclined, hands behind his back as if he were a touch diffident about being in the picture. The other boy, Donald, had his sister's exquisitely well-drawn features and dark hair but his expression was stern. "I'm sorry about your nephew," I said.

She flicked her hand as a sign that I had kept the picture too long. We were not, then, to embark on a cozy conversation about the Hardynge family. "I can't deny Nicholas anything. He put it to me that perhaps everyone got a little worked up because this is an exceptional case and one that has attracted a good deal of publicity. We try to protect the children in our care from all this, Miss Gifford. In Nicholas's view, and ours, the mother has brought the whole thing on herself, first by committing a crime which rendered her penniless, then by surrendering the children to the home. Not to mention the kidnapping of poor baby Charles. But we can see that she might have misunderstood the papers she was signing—so many of these women cannot read, it has happened before—and that she expected to take the children back at any time. Nicholas also points out that some mothers, less devoted than Mrs. Marchant, might not have admitted that their children needed care, and that it was an act of self-sacrifice on her part to give them up.

"I don't need to tell you, Miss Gifford, that in all our deliberations parental rights are subordinated to the welfare of the child. However, we think perhaps that in this case the mother has shown sufficient devotion for us to consider releasing her children, under certain conditions."

I was still so startled at seeing Nicholas's face, and Sylvia's, and the rest of the Hardynge clan that I scarcely knew what she had said. Could it really be the case that the Marchant children were to be dropped into my lap like ripe plums? "Thank you so much. Thank you."

"We shall expect twenty pounds to be paid as a token toward the cost of their board and education over the past months; we shall of course inspect the home to which the children will be returning, and our people will pay regular visits thereafter."

"Your people, Lady Curren?"

"We have people trained in making such visits."

"Perhaps you would explain to me what they'll be looking for." Alarm bells were ringing; I saw a terrible danger to poor, sometimes drunken Leah, were she to be subjected to the stranglehold of regular inspections. Thankfully, however, I had learned a little circumspection since my disastrous visit to the Good Samaritan's Home, though I rather despised my own honeyed words. "It's reassuring to know that you have such a care for these children. Mrs. Marchant will welcome such visits. I'm wondering if you have any written guidance about how the inspections are conducted. Presumably a procedure is set down in writing."

"Miss Gifford, I'm afraid I have no time now to embark on a discussion of the organization of our home. The details can be discussed later."

She was reaching for the bell, so I said hastily: "Of course. But there's just one more thing before I go, Lady Curren, I can't help being curious about what would have happened to the children, had we not intervened."

"What on earth do you mean?"

"Would they have stayed in the home, for instance, or been sent elsewhere?"

"The policies of the home are a matter for the board of handpicked individuals, all highly respected members of our society, who give freely of their time and money and who work closely with the Church of England Waifs and Strays Society, an organization with which we have close links—my sister, Lady Hardynge, is one of its most distinguished members—and Doctor Barnado's."

"I believe some homes send children to Canada. Could that have happened to the Marchant children even though their parents are living?"

This time the bell was rung, and I was so terrified that she might, in a fit of pique, withdraw her offer to release the children that I sprang to my feet and said no more. Lady Curren was too well-bred not to extend her fragile little hand when the butler appeared. I crushed her fingers briefly in mine and marched away, though within a hundred yards I was leaning on a wall, clutching my arms about my breast. The children were to be released and that was surely a triumph. But what would happen when Nicholas broke his engagement with Sylvia Hardynge and Lady Curren discovered that her loyalty to him had been misplaced? Would the offer be withdrawn? I had nothing in writing and I had gained nothing for all the other children perhaps destined for the colonies.

I longed to be in the library at Girton, when the due process of law had seemed such a clear and obvious route to follow.

Thirty-five

Perhaps my interview with Lady Curren, which should, on the face of it, have made me triumphant, had instead lowered my spirits irretrievably, perhaps it was the atmosphere in the courthouse, which was that of a death ritual coming to its inevitable conclusion, but as I sat in the advocates' benches on Thursday morning, I wondered why anyone would choose to be a lawyer responsible for a life in jeopardy such as Stephen Wheeler's. Did I really want to spend my days as a party to this process of harrowing through people's lives and turning up the underbelly, the sadness, the weakness, the catastrophic lapses of judgment?

Breen, by contrast, was buoyant, and amused by the account of my conversation with Lady Curren. I think, had we not been in court, he might even have patted my knee. "Brilliant, Miss Gifford. You're shown a shortcut but insist on viewing it with suspicion until you know the price you'll have to pay. A woman after my own heart."

"What should I do next?"

"Once the children are released we'll continue to make a nuisance of ourselves. You were right to raise questions. There could be all kinds of implications in the future should anything befall those unfortunate children."

He told me that Warren, the previous afternoon, had dragged Wheeler through a minute retelling of events surrounding the fateful picnic. Nothing new had emerged and Wheeler had not swerved from his story, which Warren had described as suspiciously consistent with the first time he'd told it to the police. (Warren had been rebuked by the judge for his emotive use of the word *suspiciously*.)

"Did he question Wheeler any further about who planned the picnic? Mr. Breen, I was disappointed that Mr. Wainwright didn't press Wheeler on a couple of points. If Stella had been planning to run away that day, if she had made an arrangement with someone, she would need to be sure that every last detail remained fixed."

"We'll see what comes out today. Listen carefully. If there's more you think needs asking, we'll pass a note to Wainwright."

Warren began Thursday morning on the offensive. The twinkle was gone and his collar so starched that it had already, so early in the day, worn a red line in his fleshy neck. "We learned yesterday that a week or so before her death Mrs. Wheeler suggested the picnic which you described to us in such meticulous detail yesterday. At what stage did you begin to lay your plans, Mr. Wheeler?"

"Plans?"

"Plans, Mr. Wheeler. Plans to journey to Chesham in order to prepare the ground? Plans to take the revolver with you."

"What do you mean, *prepare the ground*?"

"You tell me. Ah, Mr. Wheeler, you seem nettled. It's for you to answer the questions, not to ask them."

"I don't know what you're talking about. *Prepare the ground*."

"All right," said Warren, "you have maintained a silence on these points ever since your arrest, so it would be hoping too much for enlightenment now. Let's look instead at the overall picture of your marriage. I can't be alone in thinking that I've heard two conflicting accounts of your life with Mrs. Wheeler. You tell me that you were devoted to her, but we have all heard how you doubted your good fortune and were anxious about your ability to keep her amused. The victim's sister, Mrs.

Leamington, says you were a jealous man and when displeased you were prone to long silences. I think we've all learned, Mr. Wheeler, that you are an expert on silence. What was going on in your head while you were so quiet?"

"I was just thinking."

"Can you be more specific?"

"Objection," said Wainwright. "Can a man really be expected to list his private thoughts?"

But Wheeler cut in. "I was usually thinking about Stella. About how to make her happier, less restless."

"She showed signs of restlessness even a fortnight into your marriage? Did you find that distressing?"

"It was her nature. She couldn't help it. When I got in from work she wanted to know every last detail of what I'd been doing because she said her own day was so boring. She got angry with me when I had nothing to tell her. I said she must make friends in the street. She said they was all too old. I thought if a baby came . . ."

"Was there any likelihood that there might be a baby, Mr. Wheeler?" Wheeler's head sank.

"Mr. Wheeler, did you and your wife enjoy normal marital relations?" Deathly silence in court.

"Mr. Wheeler," said Warren. "I think we can infer from your silence that your wife may have had cause to be restless. I suggest you thought that you would never satisfy her in any kind of way, including sexually, and that if you couldn't please her, she would be off. After all, the court has heard that you couldn't dance with her and now, thanks to your silence, we may conclude you were unable to satisfy more intimate needs. You were so jealous that you watched her all the time, didn't you? You collected her from work most days during your engagement. You never let her go dancing after you were married, and only reluctantly before. In other words, you kept your eye on her constantly. This paints a portrait of a very jealous man indeed."

Wheeler was silent.

"I put it to you, Mr. Wheeler, that you were eaten up by fear of losing your wife. I wonder who, precisely, you were jealous of."

"What sort of question is that?" interrupted Wainwright.

But Wheeler said, more firmly than he'd spoken before: "There was no one. I trusted Stella."

"Then why did you watch her?"

"Because I loved her."

"So tell me again why you waited so long to marry your wife? Six years. Is it because she was a reluctant bride, perhaps?"

"No, I was the reluctant one. I couldn't believe she'd want me. I didn't dare ask her before."

"All those years you never hinted at marriage?"

"Sometimes we talked about it, joked. But I was saving money until I had something to offer. And then at last I thought, now or never."

"Did you ask her before or after you took out an insurance policy on her life?"

"Before. We needed to be engaged," said Wheeler. "The policy only began on the day of the marriage." Just for a moment I saw Wheeler the insurance man, who must have sat innumerable times behind an oak desk, hands folded, papers neatly arranged before him while he explained to a stream of anxious clients the minutiae of each policy. And they would have listened trustingly (though perhaps not attentively, his voice and demeanor were so lacking in spark), and he would have achieved many sales, because a man with eyes such as his could surely never lie.

"And now, to change the subject, Mr. Wheeler," said Warren, "I'd like to ask about Stella's hat. The defense has made much play of the fact that her hat somehow got separated from her body."

Wheeler's head was well down and he was scarcely audible. "I can't explain it. She would never have left her hat."

"And yet, despite the strangeness of finding the hat and the picnic basket, you still left Chesham and went home without her. Why was that?"

"I've said, I thought she might have been angry and taken the train on her own."

"Without her hat? I travel frequently in trains of all sorts, Mr. Wheeler, and I must say I cannot recall an occasion when I've seen a lady or indeed any woman without her hat. I put it to you that your account of what happened that afternoon is a pack of lies. You planned the picnic meticulously using every convenient detail, including the new picnic basket, which would easily have held a Webley revolver. What actually happened is that after you'd eaten your picnic, you persuaded your wife to walk with you to an isolated copse where you killed her, in cold blood, out of some bizarre mix of tortured jealousy and greed, and that you then went hotfoot into town where you downed a couple of drinks in order to provide yourself with an alibi, before returning to the picnic place, which was of course deserted. I put it to you that you went home that evening because you knew exactly where your wife was, under a few inches of freshly dug soil, so you didn't need to look any further for her."

Silence.

"What do you say to that, Mr. Wheeler?"

Silence.

"I put it to you, Mr. Wheeler, that there could be no other possible explanation for your wife's death. Did she go to the copse and shoot herself, and bury herself and the revolver? Did some mad, invisible person appear from nowhere, lure her, hatless, to a wood, and shoot her with a revolver that happened to be yours? You've insisted in cross-examination that there was no other man in her life. She was a waitress, for heaven's sake. Who would want to kill a former waitress? Who could have killed her with your gun and your gloves, which only you and she knew about, on a trip to Chesham that you and she had planned in private? Mr. Wheeler, everyone's time is being wasted in this court. You killed your wife that day as surely as my name is Michael Warren."

ᕫᔓ

I spent the lunch break with Meredith, who had persuaded Rose to make us sandwiches, which we ate on a bench in the park. She was scathing about Warren's behavior. "Wheeler is condemned by his own actions, there was no need to be so contemptuous of him. Murder, it seems to me, is a terrible but grand crime. A man who could plan and carry out such a thing at least deserves respect."

I laughed. "You amaze me. You, a nurse. Surely the taking of a human life is abhorrent to you."

"So it is. But would Warren have spoken like that to a general who signed the order paper that resulted in thousands of men being killed in half an hour on the Somme? I think not. The difference is that one kind of slaughter is sanctioned by the law, the other isn't. But at least Wheeler gave the matter some considered thought. At least only one person was killed."

ᕫᔓ

The afternoon began with reexamination by Wainwright. "Pay attention, Miss Gifford," murmured Breen, "these are your questions."

"Mr. Wheeler, I want to discuss the arrangements for the picnic one more time. You have told the court that it was your wife who decided the date and the location, and it was she who persuaded you to go for a drink."

"That's right."

"And you've also said you'd have preferred not to travel so far on a Saturday but she insisted. Did you make any further attempt to change your plans?"

"Not really. On the day of the picnic I said I was tired and it was too hot to go on the Metropolitan Line but she said we must go, she had gone to so much trouble."

Trouble? Corned-beef-and-pickle sandwiches made in that joyless little kitchen.

"And after the picnic, she suggested you go for a drink on your own. Were you surprised?"

"Sad. Like I said. She was so keen to get rid of me. I thought I'd irritated her."

"You see the prosecution has said that you used the picnic as a chance to get your wife out of town and, forgive me, kill her. I think in fact the opposite is true. It was Stella who made all the plans and when you tried to alter them, insisted that they went ahead. Is that true?"

Warren of course had the last word. "Mr. Wheeler, do you have any witnesses to the fact that it was your wife who insisted on picnicking in Chesham and then sending you down to the town for a drink?"

Wheeler shook his head.

There followed a succession of defense witnesses, including Wheeler's mother, who spoke of her son's devotion to Stella and the absurdity of the suggestion that he would ever hurt her.

"But, Mrs. Wheeler," said Warren in cross-examination, "I believe the war altered your son's previously gentle nature."

"I wouldn't say so, not much. It made him thoughtful, maybe moody. What did you do in the war, sir, if you don't mind my asking?"

"We are not here to discuss my record, Mrs. Wheeler."

"I think you would not be so ready to judge my son if you'd fought alongside him."

Wheeler's father, though less eloquent, made an emotional defense of his son. "I've heard it suggested that my boy was something of a last resort for Stella. Far from it. There was a queue of girls at our church and elsewhere who would have married our Stephen like a shot, given half the . . ." But at that moment there was such a commotion that Wheeler's potential as a husband was disputed no further. The courtroom door was flung open and Wolfe burst in, perspiring and wheezing, jacket unbuttoned, collar loosened. He held a whispered conversation with Breen, who in turn passed a note to Wainwright, who immediately asked for an adjournment so that he could consult with the judge.

The court was in an uproar as Breen and Wolfe disappeared with the judge and two barristers. Meanwhile, I sat in the lawyers' benches, as bemused as any other spectator, in fact more so because I couldn't for the life of me imagine what Wolfe had been up to or, even more disturbingly, why I hadn't been told about it. Meredith was signaling frantically from the gallery but I merely shrugged, thinking how foolish I must look, claiming to have made inroads into the legal profession but actually excluded at a moment of crisis.

The ten minutes had stretched to forty before the judge returned with his entourage and addressed the court: "Gentlemen—and ladies of the jury, the defense has produced three additional witnesses on very short notice. This is highly irregular, not to say lamentable because one regrets any tendency in one of the parties to spring surprises upon the other. It appears, however, that there has been a degree of confusion on both sides and some failings in the police investigation, which have led me, with my good friend the prosecutor's reluctant permission, to allow this irregularity, especially in view of the fact that we are dealing with a capital offense. I might add that despite the drama with which the defense have introduced these witnesses, it may be that they lead us nowhere. It would be quite wrong of you to read anything into the suddenness with which they've been produced."

Breen refused to meet my eye and I tried to quell my growing frustration. It was as if I were a child again, clamoring for the attention of my father while he quizzed James on what he had learned in school that day. To have been extended the hand of comradeship by Breen and then excluded hurt me.

The next scheduled witness was Carole Mangan, pale and dignified under her dark hat, surely the one she had worn at Stella's wedding, as she gave evidence about Stella's work at Lyons and how she used to be admired by many of the customers. I was a little soothed by the knowledge that Carole had come to court partly at my instigation: she was my witness, I had discovered her.

"You say Miss Hobhouse, as she then was, had plenty of admirers. Did she have any particular followers?"

"There was lots. I made a list and gave it to Miss Gifford. And the police asked me about it too."

"Miss Gifford?"

"The lady lawyer, sitting there." Wainwright smiled benignly at me. The spectators muttered. I met Carole's eye and we exchanged a private smile.

"Despite these several admirers, did you ever have cause to believe that Stella was seeing anyone—I mean, romantically—apart from her fiancé, Stephen Wheeler?"

"No."

"Have you seen any of those admirers since Stella Hobhouse's marriage?"

"One or two pop back to Lyons for a cup of tea from time to time. And I seen one just now outside the court."

In the flurry of excitement that followed this remark, I saw Wheeler's head snap up.

"Miss Mangan. I am about to produce an object—as agreed with the learned judge and the prosecution—that was found in Mrs. Wheeler's childhood bedroom. I wonder if you could tell me whether or not you've ever seen it before?"

Wainwright here opened a cardboard box, about a foot square and four inches deep, of the sort used for transporting shirt collars to and from the laundry, and from it he lifted the bronze dancer. There she stood on the bench before the pallid judge, a tiny foot extended, her hair flung back, and every curve in her slender body sinuous and exposed, poised to run clear off her plinth if only she could.

"I seen it once, when Miss Gifford showed it to me."

"You don't know who gave it to Stella?"

"I told her. No."

"Finally, Miss Mangan, this court has heard the prosecution suggest that the Wheelers' marriage was troubled. Forgive me for being blunt but the suggestion was that Mr. Wheeler could not satisfy his wife, if you understand what I mean. I believe you met her once, after her marriage. Did she give you any indication then that all was not well?"

"No."

When he stood up, Warren pretended to have no interest in the bronze dancer, although his eyes were drawn to her from time to time, as they might have been to the bosom of a woman seated opposite him in an omnibus. In cross-examination, he concentrated on Carole's recollection of the Wheelers' betrothal. "Do you think Stella loved her husband-to-be?"

"Yes. She was very loyal to him and talked about him often, and was always in a hurry when she knew he was going to meet her after work."

"Did she ever show interest in any other man?"

"I've already said. No. None special."

"What does that mean, *none special*?"

Carole fixed him with a cool gaze that made his color rise. "What do you think we girls talk about, when we've got a minute?"

"So you have no cause to think she had any involvement with anyone except Stephen, her husband."

"That's right."

Warren subsided. Wainwright, in response to a note from Breen, had one question in reexamination. "Is there anything, in all your time of working with Stella, eight years in all, that gave you cause to think she was not quite faithful to Stephen?"

"Only the thing I told Miss Gifford." Her pale eyes again met mine. "There was one night she stayed out and come in with her uniform dirty and smelly and mud and grass on her shoes, very tired, red-eyed. I never did find out where she'd been."

Wainwright had no more reexamination but invited Miss Mangan to sit at the back of the court, if she could spare the time. He wiped his brow, folded his hands across his immense chest, and fixed the usher with a benign eye. "I'll call Mr. Smedley."

Mr. Smedley was a diffident, slow-spoken gentleman in a frock-coat, who identified himself as a dealer in fine art, owner of the eponymous Smedley's of Piccadilly.

"Mr. Smedley. I wonder if you would be so kind as to look at this object. Do you recognize it?"

"I do. I bought one of an edition of fifty last year in Paris. Lamourdedieu."

"Could you tell the court where you have been for the last ten days?"

"In Paris."

"For how long had you been planning that trip?"

"I go every three months or so. I plan the next as soon as I've finished the last."

"And what happened early yesterday morning, when you were at your lodgings in Paris?"

"I was told I had a visitor. A lawyer. Mr. Wolfe."

"Mr. Smedley, if you'll forgive me, nothing in your demeanor suggests that you are a man of impulsive habits. What persuaded you to dash back from France to appear in court here today?"

"Mr. Wolfe told me that one of my most trusted employees had suddenly left the business, and that I was needed in his stead to give evidence of a particular sale. I confess that it was largely because I couldn't understand why my man had left in such a hurry that I came back so readily. I still haven't got to the bottom of my employee's desertion but I did search our books for a record of sale. At first I found nothing, but fortunately we make records in triplicate—that is obviously in addition to the receipt we give the customer. I have often been reproached by my wife and sometimes by my senior staff for my insistence on such laborious procedures. The triplicates file is kept locked away in a safe for just such eventualities as this. We deal with very costly and rare items, you see, and it's therefore essential to keep punctilious accounts. At any rate, in the triplicates file I found that the bronze dancer had indeed been bought, on January 18, by one of our regular customers."

"Could you tell the court who that customer was?"

Smedley showed considerable reluctance and had to be prompted. "Sir David Hardynge."

Hardynge. But there was no time to ponder this extraordinary development; Warren was on his feet. "My friend has insinuated that your employee, Mr. Arthur, left under suspicious and irregular circumstances. Do you have any cause to believe this was the case?"

"It is very odd. Mr. Arthur had been in my service more than fifteen years. I would expect him to give adequate notice."

"Odd, you say. Not suspicious."

"Decidedly odd."

"You say you had to look in the triplicates file, again implying, perhaps, that it was irregular not to have found a record of the sale elsewhere."

"It was irregular. But then the files were in a very bad way. I'd been gone more than a week and I'm afraid it showed in the disorganization of the accounts."

I was as transfixed as the most prurient spectator in the back row of the public gallery. Why hadn't I been told about Wolfe's excursion to Paris? After all, it was I who had discovered the bronze dancer and realized her significance. But the next witness, even more astonishing than the rest, had already been called and the courtroom doors swung open to admit Sir David Hardynge.

In he came, Nicholas's prospective father-in-law, somewhat older than in the photograph Lady Curren had handed me yesterday, dressed head to toe in black apart from collar, cuffs, and pocket handkerchief. He was precisely as I remembered from my brief glimpse of him at Wheeler's earlier court hearing: a good-looking gentleman, slim, slightly smiling as if bemused but by no means discomposed at finding himself here.

In clipped tones, he gave his date of birth, March 12, 1868; his address, 18 Belsize Square; his professions—government adviser, parliamentary candidate, entrepreneur, company director, and financier; and his marital status—married, two children, now both grown up.

"Sir David Hardynge," said Wainwright, oily with deference. "Could you tell us, were you acquainted with the dead woman, Stella Wheeler?"

"When I knew her I believe her name was Miss Hobhouse. And yes, I saw her from time to time when I went to Lyons for tea."

"And what did you think of her?"

"I thought she was a very sweet girl."

"Did you ever single her out in any way?"

Hardynge's smile was a touch wistful: "She must have been some thirty years younger than me."

Wainwright smiled too. "Quite so. But perhaps you could answer the question, Sir David."

"Single her out? Rather the other way around, I should say. She was very patient with me. She knew that I couldn't tolerate tea that wasn't piping hot and strong."

"Did you ever see her outside Lyons?"

"Once or twice perhaps. She was the girlfriend of one of my employees, after all. I first met her, I think, at one of our Christmas parties."

"And on that occasion, did a relationship develop?"

Sir David was puzzled. "She and I had a dance. I make a point of dancing with the wives and girlfriends of my employees; they seem to like it and it helps me to get to know them better. She told me she worked at Lyons so I looked in one day when I was passing."

"If you would specifically answer the question."

"Our relationship always kept within the boundaries I have just described: she a waitress, I a customer."

"Did you give her a wedding present?"

There was a long pause. "Why, yes, I believe I did. I made her a present of a little statue. Yes, that one there."

"That statue is worth some fifty pounds."

"Good gracious, is it? I don't remember. I'd bought it some time ago, for my daughter actually, but my wife decided it was inappropriate." He gave a rueful smile as if remembering a painful conversation. "So I gave it to Miss Hobhouse instead, when I heard she was to marry. As a matter of fact I'm surprised to learn she kept it. I thought she would sell it immediately."

"When exactly did you give it to her?"

"I'd say in spring, sometime. I don't recall."

"An extravagant gift for a girl you barely knew."

"I thought it would amuse her. She had looked after me so well."

"A rather suggestive gift, I think."

"Suggestive? I see it as a rather fine work of art."

"Sir David, did you know that the wife of one of your clerks, Stephen Wheeler, had been murdered?"

"Of course I knew."

"And that Wheeler had been arrested?"

"I not only knew about it but I took every possible step to give him my support, financial and otherwise."

"Then perhaps you'd tell the court why you didn't inform the police that you knew the dead girl."

Sir David smiled. "As I recall, I did. I told them it is one of the privileges of my position to meet most of the wives and girlfriends of my employees. I believe my company is admired for its family spirit."

"And did it never occur to you to mention to the police about your gift of the dancer?"

"Forgive me but I had well-nigh forgotten about it. And had I remembered, I would have wondered what possible relevance the dancer might have."

"Sir David, I'm nearly finished, if you'll bear with me. We have heard from a witness that one morning in April not long before her marriage, Stella came to work very late. Do you have any knowledge of why that might have been?"

Sir David blinked twice, as if working through a mental calendar, then shook his head.

"Was that a no, Sir David?"

"It was."

"You were never with Stella Hobhouse, as she then was, other than in Lyons, during an evening in mid-April?"

"I have said: our relationship was within the boundaries I have already described."

"If you would answer the question, Sir David."

"I have no idea what you are talking about."

"Please answer yes or no, Sir David. Did you spend an evening in April with Stella Hobhouse?"

Sir David smiled patiently. "The third time of denial. I did not spend any evening with this Stella Hobhouse."

"Two more questions. Did you ever visit Miss Hobhouse at home, I mean Mrs. Wheeler, after her marriage?"

"I had no idea where Mrs. Wheeler lived."

"Where are your staff records kept, Sir David?"

"In my secretary's office, I think."

"Could you have access to them if you asked?"

He shrugged. "Presumably."

"And just for the record, Sir David, where were you on the day that Stella was murdered, Saturday, May 17, of this year?"

There was a long pause while Hardynge seemed to be counting back across the weeks. "I would have to check with my secretary but I believe I was at home with my wife. Late in the afternoon I would have gone to visit my son, as I do every Saturday. He is in a type of hospital, near Princes Risborough."

"And for the sake of the jury, where is Princes Risborough?"

"I would have thought the jury would know well enough. It's a town in this county of Buckinghamshire."

☙❧

Warren was obsequious. "The jury will forgive me if I am somewhat ill-prepared, but perhaps I could begin by having Sir David Hardynge elaborate a little, by way of background, on an extraordinary career in both business and public service." Hardynge was charmingly modest but after ten minutes it had been established that he served on committees concerned with the financial support of veterans and widows, that during the war his company, Imperial Insurance, had been responsible for a number of charitable endowments to do with refugees, and that having recently been selected as a candidate for a North London constituency regarded as a safe seat for the Conservative Party he was about to embark on what promised to be a distinguished life in politics.

"And now, Sir David, I have to put it to you that my friend, at a very late stage in this trial and for motives that I would suggest are less than commendable—notably to cloud the glaringly obvious—is suggesting that you had an improper relationship with the unfortunate young waitress Stella Wheeler, née Hobhouse. How do you answer that accusation?"

"I'm afraid I find myself so incredulous that I am at a loss how to reply."

"Much has been made of this gift, the dancer in bronze. Yet, from your point of view, it was simply a rather generous wedding present. Could you tell the court what was going through your mind when you gave it to Stella?"

"Obviously not quite enough was going through my mind. It was, in retrospect, an ill-judged gift. But I knew how the girl liked dancing, so I thought she would love the dancer. It also crossed my mind that should she grow tired of the present, she could perhaps sell it for quite a significant sum. For instance, if she should become a mother, I thought she might well need extra funds. You see, her husband, Wheeler, had been an outstanding employee and a gallant soldier. I thought the dancer would be a way of helping them both informally—I did not want to make a precedent of such largesse to all my employees. I'm afraid I simply couldn't afford to make exceptions to the favored few for fear of exciting jealousy."

"Did it occur to you, Sir David, that such a gift might cause Stella embarrassment?"

"I'm afraid not. Perhaps it was thoughtless of me, but, after all, I'm surrounded by ladies, wife, daughter, sisters-in-law, and I can never resist buying beautiful things for beautiful women." Here his nearsighted eyes scanned the women in the galleries, the jury, Carole Mangan, even me in the lawyers' benches. Although there was no flicker of recognition, in the split second that I had his attention I suspected that I was assessed as a possible object of desire and dismissed. "If you came to my house you'd see it is full of artifacts. I have an eye for them and I like to share my pleasure with others. My daughter is an artist and I'm afraid we egg each other on when it comes to buying art." His gaze flickered back to me and his brow contracted with momentary irritation, presumably as he tried to work out what I was doing amid the defense team.

"My friend has tried to suggest that you had some slightly sinister motive in not mentioning the gift of the bronze dancer before now. I wonder if you could again give the court your views on the matter."

"As I said earlier, I had no idea the gift was of any relevance. Good Lord, if I had to appear in court to account for every present I'd given, I'd rarely be at home."

Wainwright got ponderously to his feet. "A few additional questions, Sir David. When did you say you'd given the bronze dancer to Stella?"

"A few days before her wedding, I believe. I can't recollect for sure."

"Isn't it odd that none of the other waitresses noticed you giving her the present and that she didn't show it to any of them?"

"As to the latter question, I can only assume she preferred not to excite jealousy. As to the former, I really can't say."

"And finally, you told my learned friend that you knew that Stella liked dancing. How did you know?"

Another smile. "I expect because she told me so."

"I have no further questions, Your Honor, but I wonder if Sir David might be required to remain in court while we call the next and final witness."

I saw Meredith and Carole leave the court as Mrs. Ball, a pop-eyed, full-chested neighbor of the Wheelers in Byron Street, came in. Presumably, despite the drama in Aylesbury, Meredith could not resist a chance to view the flat in Pimlico and I had no doubt that Lyons had

demanded Carole return to work immediately after her services were no
longer required by the court.

Mrs. Ball was first asked to give her opinion of the Wheeler marriage. "I hardly had time to get to know them," she said. "The young
girl was very quiet. Came in for a cup of tea once but didn't say much.
To be honest, I thought twice about asking her again. Of course had I
known what was about to happen to her, I'd have tooken more trouble."

"Did she receive many visitors, Mrs. Ball?"

"Well, I can't say, obviously, because I spend most of my time in the
back. Her mother came sometimes, I think, and *his* family. And there
was one gentleman caller, I noticed."

"Can you describe this gentleman to us?"

"Not really. I only seen him from the side and back. He was very
smart, I know that."

"I wonder if you could look around the courthouse, Mrs. Ball, and
tell me if you see that gentleman anywhere here."

She cast her eye solemnly over everyone present, even the jury, even
Stephen in the dock. It seemed to me she took a very long time scanning the public benches, perhaps dwelling longest on Sir David, but in
the end shook her head. "I seen the gentleman from the side and back,
not the front. I couldn't say for sure."

"That is very honest of you, Mrs. Ball," said Wainwright, though I
sensed his disappointment. There was no cross-examination.

By now it was four thirty, too late to hear from a succession of character witnesses: fellow soldiers and workmates. The judge, looking
thunderous (on account of his Friday afternoon golf match being
doomed, muttered Breen), thanked Hardynge with unnecessary effu-
sion for bearing witness and announced that the court would reconvene
at ten o'clock sharp tomorrow.

As soon as Wheeler had been taken down and the bench risen,
Hardynge, assuming the demeanor of benefactor and future MP, shook

hands with both defense and prosecution, thanked them for their trouble, told Wolfe he'd been commendably thorough and that it was only
right that the defense should leave no stone unturned in so tricky and
painful a case. Altogether, his attitude was that of a wealthy patron
participating gamely in the fathers' race on sports day.

Afterward, Breen told me I might go home. He had a meeting with
Wolfe and Wainwright and I was not required. So I was left to make
my lonely way to the station, bewildered by this continued ostracism
and thwarted in my need to discuss the sensational events of the day.

Thirty-six

Despite my weariness and confusion, I had a dogged sense that I must fulfill my commitment to Meredith, so from Marylebone I took an omnibus to Pimlico, where I found a narrow street of shabby houses and had to hunt long and hard among a cluster of bells at 11A. After a wait of several minutes, Meredith appeared at the dusty front door, eyes ablaze with excitement. "I was so hoping you'd make it, but that trial was so riveting I thought you probably wouldn't. The girl who lives here has gone out for an hour and left me to get a feel of the place and it's just perfect, you wait and see."

She led me up four flights of stairs until we came to the top landing, which was narrow and had a door on either side, the one on the left ajar. My first impression was that the flat was oppressively small and low-ceilinged, though full of light, being in the roof. Meredith had certainly made herself at home—a gramophone was playing a tune called "Margie" and a kettle was heating on the gas ring. The cubbyhole of a kitchen was far more modern, with its neat little cupboards and enamel surfaces, than the vault of a basement kitchen in Clivedon Hall Gardens; there was a very small room for Edmund and another room with a sloping roof and skylight, which Meredith and I would have to share.

The glory (as Meredith said) of the apartment was the long living room overlooking the street, from which, if one craned one's neck slightly, one could see the Thames through a gap in the buildings opposite. In this room, said Meredith, we would live, eat, and work. She would have an easel at one end and I would have a desk of my own. We might even use screens to give each other a little privacy. And we could hold parties; it would be possible for two dozen people to cram into this room with no difficulty at all.

She made a pot of tea, which we drank from unevenly shaped cups with rough edges and designs that seemed to have been created by spattering them with colored glaze. As she talked, Meredith played "I'm Goin' South" and hopped from side to side, picking up the rhythm. The present tenant, Sylvia Hardynge's friend, was obviously blessed with a bold, artistic nature, because the flat was filled with cushions in brilliant colors, curtains in bottle-green velvet, striped rugs on the bare floors, and on the wall an assortment of paintings, some very primitive indeed.

I playacted admiration but the idea of actually living there seemed too unreal for me to take seriously. The flat occupied less space overall than the servants' floor at Clivedon Hall Gardens; there was no obvious means of heating apart from one oil stove; the bathroom, on the floor below, was shared with three other flats; and all in all it seemed absurd to reduce myself to Leah Marchant–type conditions. Fresh from the humiliation and, as it seemed to me, chaos of the Wheeler trial, my thoughts were all negative: I couldn't possibly work in such a cramped space, we couldn't afford it, we would be bound to fall out, and above all I could not abandon Mother to Clivedon Hall Gardens and the heartbroken Prudence.

"So now," said Meredith, "tell me, what happened after I left? Weren't you just so surprised to see Sylvia's father in the dock? I was. Whatever will poor Sylvia make of it when she finds out? Surely all that stuff with the dancing girl was a bit of a red herring."

"Maybe. But when I found her I thought she was significant. So much didn't quite fit, notably that the dancer was worth a small fortune yet nobody seemed to know how Stella came by her."

"And I don't understand why there was such high drama. Why drag Hardynge in at the last minute, without warning?"

"Because up until today we couldn't connect the dancer with anyone who'd bought her. We tried but . . ."

"It's so unfair. Here we are, scrimping to find a few shillings' rent, there he is, splashing out on bronze dancers. But then he is an extravagant soul, as I well know."

"What do you mean, you *know*?"

"Remember I was in his house only a week or so ago. The place positively reeked of money. And do you know what, when he walked into court this afternoon I recognized him from the war. Like they said, he was a benefactor, fetched up at one of the hospitals from time to time bearing gifts, treats. But we didn't like him. Oh, he had an eye for the young nurses all right. Some men are like that with women in uniforms. And there was something about his son, rumors that he'd bought him out, got him sent home. We didn't like the sound of that either."

"You knew of Hardynge's son, Donald?"

"By reputation only. Through what they said about the father. We were supposed to be grateful to Hardynge, he bought the hospital supplies of medicines when we were very short, and chocolate and cigs for the men, you know. But we couldn't like him. We avoided having to speak to him. There was something calculated about the favors he gave us, as if he were bound to want something in return."

Sylvia's friend came back and I offered to wash the cups while she discussed the flat with Meredith. From the kitchen I glimpsed her, a girl from another world, plucked eyebrows, luminous skin, flitting from room to room as she gushed about the views, the convenience for Victoria Station and shopping, the whole of London, in fact, though she skimmed over the question of how many people actually shared the bathroom and whether the temperature was bearable in winter. Finally, we all shook hands and Meredith and I ran down the steep staircases.

Outside, the skies were gray and there was an untidiness about the streets typical of London on damp and blowy summer evenings. The gutters were full of litter and smoke gusted from chimney pots, hinting at autumn. We had agreed to catch an omnibus, the number 16, which carried us along the side of Hyde Park, and we sat side by side on the top deck, second seat from the front, she with her little green bag on her lap, I with my briefcase.

Meanwhile, beneath all this activity, I was trying to work something out. Surely Meredith had said nothing much of significance? Only that Sir David Hardynge had visited her hospital in France. Well, our post-war world was full of people who'd known each other in that other life. But then, as the omnibus rumbled along the Edgware Road and the familiar nausea of travel sickness set in, I became aware of a weight settling in the pit of my stomach, which had nothing to do with the swaying motion of the top deck, and there was such a ringing in my ears that when Meredith gripped my wrist and spoke to me—something about preparing the ground with Mother—I couldn't attend to what she said. We got off the bus and walked in silence, I stumbling occasionally and even knocking into her. At the door, I pleaded a splitting headache and said I would go straight to bed.

Upstairs, I turned the key in the lock, flung off my skirt and blouse, and lay with my hands clasped on my breast, gazing up at the glass bowl of the light fixture as the evening grew darker.

Hardynge. Bronze dancer. Stella Wheeler. Donald Hardynge's career as a soldier. Connected.

Breen said he mistrusted coincidences and here was an entire parcel of them. A witness in a murder trial, unearthed through a bit of dogged ferreting by the commendably persistent Theo Wolfe, had turned out to be none other than the only suspect's employer and benefactor, who admitted to a passing fondness for Stella Wheeler, former waitress. Was that all?

No. Meredith, a chance spectator to the proceedings, had recognized Hardynge from the war and knew him to have a fondness for young nurses or at least their uniforms, and a reputation for some kind of distasteful dealing to do with his son. Was that all?

No. I had been sent to Lady Curren's house to be offered the release of the Marchant children. And there, on a side table, was a photograph of her close relatives, the Hardynges, and in their midst, Nicholas. Was that all?

Yes, surely.

No. There was something else. What was it? *Why drag Hardynge in at the last minute, without warning?* Meredith had asked. The reason was that the salesman at an exclusive dealer of fine art in Piccadilly, who had promised to connect the bronze dancer with the name of its purchaser, had disappeared. And what day was that?

Last Friday. The day after my tea at Fortnum's with Nicholas. I had told him, as an aside to hide my anguish at his lateness: *There is a statue, a bronze dancer, someone must have bought it . . .*

I got up, strode about the room, seized a pen and paper, and wrote everything down: the date of Stella's murder, the date of Wheeler's arrest, the date that Nicholas came into my life during the Leah Marchant hearing. He had spoken my name on the steps of the court. *Miss Gifford.* He even claimed, during our afternoon on the hill above Chesham, to have heard details of my brother's heroic death.

There was a tentative knock on the door, a testing of the latch. "Evelyn, may I come in?"

I unlocked the door. Mother was very pale and too distraught to notice that her blouse had lost a button and was gaping at the breast. "Evelyn, what is this I've been hearing from Meredith about your sharing a flat together?"

"Oh, it's nothing, Mother. Nothing will come of it."

"That's not what she's saying. Prudence is hysterical. I've never seen her like it. Meredith made her lie down with her feet on a cushion. We had to ring for Min. Meredith says you went to see the flat this evening. Why didn't you mention it? Is this to punish me because I didn't tell you about James's letter?"

"It is nothing of the kind. You know I would not be so cruel. It was very wrong of Meredith to mention it without consulting me first." Or perhaps she had consulted me on the bus and I hadn't been listening. "I really have no intention of falling in with her plans."

"I thought we were getting on so well together. That lunch we had. I told you I was sorry, what else must I do? Oh, Evelyn, I really don't think I could abide it here without you."

"You're always saying I should marry," I said, rallying suddenly. "What's the difference?"

"You know full well that if you were married I would have a second home. Grandchildren. Perhaps, in time, a refuge. And I sometimes thought that if you married, you might choose to live here with your new husband. To save money, you know."

"Mother." I couldn't help laughing.

Her mouth turned down at the corners, a familiar look of hurt disappointment. "I brought you a letter. I always seem to be delivering letters these days, don't I? It's been sitting in the hall all day. Your friend from the north, I believe."

I took the envelope, kissed her, closed the door, and locked it again. This time I waited many minutes before I could bring myself to open the letter.

I have received your note. I'll collect you as you suggest, Friday evening at the corner—I'll be there soon after five. Touch and go whether I can exist that long without you.

Nicholas Thorne

Thirty-seven

I lay *wide-eyed most of the night* and every so often made another jotting in my notebook. The nightmare went on and on. I wanted there to be a flaw, something to call a halt to this speculation. But no. The more I thought, the more plausible it all became.

By five o'clock I had a plan of sorts and at last turned on my side and slept for an hour. Then I dressed, bathed my stinging eyes, went down to the kitchen, and begged a cup of tea from sleepy Rose, who was riddling flame into last night's embers, ate a slice of bread and butter, and told her I would not be back until very late, nobody must wait up for me. Then I crept out of the house and into the early morning, which was already humming with a new day's activity. There was no sign of yesterday's cloud except for a faint pallor in the west, and the streets were skimmed with mist in the early sunshine. I presumed that Wheeler, in his cell, would have no idea whether or not the sun was shining. And I thought of Nicholas, in Manchester, rising from his bed in some rather grand hotel room, dressing in his wonderfully tailored garments, packing his bag, eating a substantial breakfast, thinking perhaps of me.

I had plenty of time, so I took an omnibus to Hyde Park, entered by the Albion Gate, and walked down its eastern end to Hyde Park Corner. As the morning advanced, a breeze got up and a few early fallen leaves rustled along the path and settled at the edge of the lawn. As I passed

the bandstand—deserted, of course—heaped deck chairs, clusters of
trees and shrubs, my head was full of images of the lost. The day after
we'd received news of James's death, I had got up early, like today, and
taken this identical route to the Censorship Office, my feet performing
their regular task of carrying me forward, my heart stone, my mind
refusing to recognize the indelible line that had been drawn beneath my
brother's name. And then there was Stella, who had met her death
among trees, a fearful end for a city girl. Yet she had made a sorrowful
little collection of acorn cups and conker cases. What had she been trying to cling to as she tucked them away at the back of her wardrobe?
The nurse at St. Mary's Hospital emergency department had said that
they regularly received scrapings from the park, an assortment of vagrants, drunks, and prostitutes, some of whom, as I well knew, appeared
in the magistrates' courts each morning. Perhaps Stella had also spent
time in London's green spaces. Alone? With whom? With him?

Next Green Park, St. James's Park, and the long path by the lake.
Every moment London was growing louder. And then I was on Great
George Street, among the significant buildings of Westminster. It was
nearly a quarter to eight.

All but a handful of women had been dismissed from our office after
the war, but I hoped that some men, or rather one in particular, might
have been retained. So I found a bench with a good view of the side
entrance, where we used to bundle in each morning, having wrapped
ourselves deeper in coats and scarves because we knew it would be far
colder inside than out, and watched hopeful pigeons approach my feet,
men in trilby hats, clean collars, and rolled newspapers, the occasional
office girl in her cheap summer frock with its skirt crumpled in the back,
and an older woman in a light green, knitted suit. I saw a brown paper
bag tumble over itself and automobiles, with their hoods up against the
morning chill, a queue of omnibuses, cabs, delivery lorries, a brewer's cart.

Just after eight-thirty, I saw him approach, recognizing him at once though he wasn't in uniform. It was his gait that marked him out, somewhat apologetic, an air of being guarded against the world. Perhaps he had retained his chic little flat behind Harrods where he slept each weekday night, perhaps he even possessed still that startling red bowl. One arm still hung awkwardly and his face had grown thinner. I had pondered for hours how I might approach him; as it was, I simply stood in his path and spoke his name.

He was very puzzled, as well he might be, when his mind had to stretch back more than six years. Perhaps, I thought with a ghostly internal smile, I had made no real impression upon him at all. But finally a light came to his eyes, then clouded as the memories flickered.

"I need your help," I said.

He considered me for a few moments with his thoughtful, rather beautiful eyes, the color of sky just before dawn. Then he instructed me to follow him and we went through the main entrance into the lobby, where the porter whipped off his cap and hurried to summon the elevator. We waited in silence for the doors to open, ascended three floors without speaking (in the old days, the elevator had been out of bounds to girls like me and we had clattered up flights of tiled steps), and came at last to his office, which was very grand with book-lined walls, a silken rug, and south-facing windows. He sat on one side of a vast, empty desk topped with leather, I on the other.

"I took your advice," I said. "I never did tell anyone I could type. So now I am training to be a lawyer."

He put his fingertips together and smiled. I was touched that he seemed after all to have remembered the details of our few conversations. "I have a great favor to ask you. But I also have to be sure that you will treat our discussion in absolute confidence."

He raised an eyebrow. I remembered why I had found him so attractive; the stillness, the air of knowing so much more than he would ever say.

"You ask a great deal."

"A man is on trial for murder. There is a detail missing, a witness who I believe is concealing something, maybe to do with the war, that might shed some light . . ." Could he tell that my lips were trembling?

"Who is the man in question?"

"A businessman and would-be politician, Sir David Hardynge." He nodded as if to say, I know of him. "I want to know about his connections. I want to know if there was anything at all untoward on his record."

He sat for a moment, considering me. I wondered if he remembered the red bowl, the unyielding silence when he had removed it from my hands, the hopelessness with which I received his touch. "I'll see what I can do. It will take a while. Perhaps you could come back sometime next week."

"I don't have any time. The case is being heard at the moment. In fact it may already be too late."

The fingertips tapped together. Then he sighed, told me that he would order someone to bring tea and that he would show me to a room where I could wait.

I was ushered to a lobby, where I sat in a red plush chair with gilt arms like a throne. A young clerk went by, wheeling a trolley stacked with files. After ten minutes, a woman wearing a shapeless gray skirt and with untidy hair escaping from its pins (like yours, Evelyn, I thought drearily) brought me tea in a plain white cup and saucer. A clock somewhere struck nine-thirty, then ten, and I wondered what Breen would say when I didn't turn up at the trial. My life was in the balance, or so it seemed to me. I didn't know what I dreaded most, a report that revealed nothing or a report that somehow gave substance to my gnawing fears.

At about twenty to eleven, another woman appeared, this one very neat in a pale blue dress with a narrow belt, and with well-cut hair. She offered to escort me back to his office.

His desk now had one file upon it.

"I cannot of course let you read the file but I can summarize the documents within it, if you like, and see if any is of interest to you. Hardynge's activities extended far and wide during the war. He served on various committees to do with funding the military. And he seems to have had a benevolent streak, setting up a significantly well-endowed fund for refugees and the wives of prisoners of war. He was trustee of an organization that gives relief to families in which the main breadwinner remains incapacitated by war."

"Is that it?"

"That's it. More or less. There is one thing." And he removed from the file a letter, typed on thin, yellowing paper. "Hardynge seems to have some very prestigious friends. A brief correspondence with General Haig has found its way into the file. In his letter, Hardynge pleads for clemency on behalf of a young officer who, together with his companion, a nineteen-year-old private, was court-martialed for desertion and for firing at the military policeman who attempted to arrest them, both capital offenses as you doubtless know. Hardynge's petition was successful; the officer was sent home and confined to an institution dealing with shell-shocked patients. The other boy was executed. The court-martial accepted the officer's word that it was the young private who had fired the gun."

"What was the name of that boy?" I whispered.

"Fox. Private Fox. The officer in question, by the way, was Captain Donald Hardynge."

೧೪೨

I went back to St. James's Park, where I strode about, sat on a bench, got up. It was midday. What was happening in Aylesbury? Perhaps the closing speeches had already begun. The park was full of people with time on their hands, nannies and toddlers, the wheelchair bound, the limpers, the men in broken boots who sat with their hands hanging between their knees or scouring the columns of a discarded newspaper, ladies in flirty summer dresses, a listless girl making a halfpenny bun last a lunchtime. One of Meredith's favorite songs replayed in my mind: "You must go your way, and I must go mine, But now that our love dreams have ended, What'll I do, when you are far away, And I am blue . . ."

I walked along the other side of the lake, too restless to stay anywhere long. Mostly I kept to paths; sometimes, where permitted, I crossed the new-mown lawns. Stella Wheeler. Mud and grass on her shoes. A pathetic collection of acorn cups and conker cases. Scrapings from the park. I remembered Hardynge's eyes half concealed behind his glasses when asked about Stella's missing night. Blink. Blink. He must surely have been with her, but where? Her clothes had been stained with mud and grass and smelled bad. What had she been up to? Was that the night he'd presented her with the bronze statue? Or—as seemed more likely now—was the statue a reward or recompense for something that happened that night? He was drawn to women in uniforms, said Meredith, and that little waitress, the thwarted dancer Stella Wheeler, would have been easy pickings for a rich gentleman liberal with promises.

Stella had worked in Lyons in Regents Street, so where was the nearest place where a man and woman, intent on a secret meeting, might lose themselves? Green Park. *Hyde Park.* Hyde Park, notorious haunt of those after a quick fumble, a clandestine rendezvous. The newly appointed women police officers were constantly making a nuisance of themselves by plucking from the bushes couples up to no good.

Breen had ordered a search of the police records for the middle of April and uncovered nothing. No matter, I would look again. I was now walking fast and purposefully up Constitution Hill. There were various police stations in or on the fringes of London parks, the most notorious,

Hyde Park, on the slope above the Serpentine, among trees. The last time I'd confronted that innocuous red-brick frontage, I was tagging along after Breen to bail out one of his habitual female clients accused of using foul language to a woman police officer while resisting arrest. Breen treated police stations as if they were his club; genial wave to passing officers, a thumbs-up to the administrative staff, who fell all over themselves to supply him with tea and biscuits.

Wolfe had said, when fingering the cloakroom ticket found in Stella's sponge bag, that he'd seen its type before as his clients redeemed their belongings on release from a police station. We had considered the possibility of Stella spending the night in a police cell—certainly that would explain the smell on her clothes—but found no evidence. Now, though, I knew what I was looking for. I had seen Hardynge, under oath, deny that he had been with her one night in April, but Hardynge was like a boulder buried in sand: the more we cleared away, the more I discovered was obscured from view. And I was driven by the kind of momentum that comes in times of extreme tension, as in the examination hall. I did not consider that I was tired and hungry or that I would face the usual opposition from the male establishment as I pushed through the swing doors and entered the fug of the outer office.

There was, as in every police station I had ever visited, a motley collection of customers awaiting attention. A woman at the head of a languid queue was describing a lost cat to an officer filling out a form. Breen would have marched straight up to the desk, but I bided my time as first the cat woman was dealt with, then a man with a crushed cap who wanted to visit his son who'd been *banged up* for assault, then a gentleman who wished to report a stolen bicycle.

When it was my turn, the interview that followed was predictable. "I am from Breen and Balcombe, solicitors. I wish to consult your records of arrest in April."

The officer was tall, with childish round eyes. "You are from where?"

I produced letters addressed to me at Breen & Balcombe, but he wasn't satisfied. "We don't show our custody records to the public. They're confidential."

"I believe Mr. Breen has already had the records checked. Whoever looked before might have missed something. New evidence has come to light since then."

"Mr. Breen should come back here hisself."

"Mr. Breen is in court in Aylesbury." My control was wafer-thin. "If you want you could ring our office and his secretary will vouch for me."

The officer was torn. He knew Breen, of course, and probably feared his wrath. In the end, he pulled the telephone toward him, asked the operator for the number of Breen & Balcombe (he didn't trust me to give the correct one), and dialed. I prayed to God I no longer believed in that Miss Drake would answer the phone promptly and then cooperate. The policeman's gaze raked up and down my face as he introduced himself to the invisible presence on the end of the line: "It is a matter of verification, madam. Could you confirm for me that a Miss Evelyn Gifford works for your firm of solicitors?"

Long pause before I heard Miss Drake's voice scrape across the wires. "In what capacity?"

A longer pause before the voice began again. I heard the words *junior* and *clerk*. Then the sergeant passed the receiver to me. "She wants to speak to you."

"Miss Gifford," said Miss Drake in her heavily enunciated telephone voice. "Mr. Breen had telephoned me twice this morning to ask whether I know your whereabouts. What am I to inform him if he calls again?"

"That I was delayed."

Pause. "Miss Gifford, do you intend to go to Aylesbury today?"

"I cannot."

A long silence. Then she said something very surprising indeed. "Take care, Miss Gifford."

I was led at last through the back office, down the stairs to the cells, and surrendered up to the custody sergeant, a cozy man so glad of the diversion that he even offered me tea. Someone, possibly the assault case, was hammering rhythmically on a cell door.

"Could I ask about your procedures," I said as he loaded a tin tray with cups and (rather touchingly) a china milk jug patterned with bluebells. "Should a prisoner have valuables of any kind which you wish to confiscate for safekeeping while they are under arrest, what is the process?"

"We writes them down in a book and we issues a ticket. When they leave they show the ticket and we returns their things. Unless of course we want to use something in evidence. We enter the number into the log."

"Could I see the type of tickets you issue?" But I knew already that he would produce a book of mushroom-colored cloakroom tickets.

So I sat in that stuffy little chamber, corridors of cells to the right and left, and the custody sergeant shuffling about with kettle and teapot, and opened the ledger at April 1, 1924. It seemed to me that I must read each entry, one at a time, skipping nothing, or the spell would be broken.

On Tuesday, April 15, I found what I was looking for, inscribed in painstaking copperplate, each column across two double pages filled in. The date. Time: *11:04 in the evening*. Name of the arresting officer. Name of the arrested party: *Julie Fox*. Date of Birth: *March 23, 1902*. Address: *4 Lyons Street, Acton*. Occupation: *Servant*. Charge: *Behavior reasonably likely to offend against public decency*. Legal representative: *None*. Outcome: *Caution*. Released: *9 a.m. morning of Wednesday, April 16*. Chit *437*.

And beneath, another entry. *Miss Fox arrested in association with*: *Name not supplied*. Legal representative: a scrawled signature. *Released without charge*.

I managed to speak, though my index finger would not hold still as I pointed to the entry. "Do you remember that night?"

The sergeant smiled kindly. "I don't, miss. The officer in question has since moved on. I only been here since the beginning of May."

"Isn't it unusual for a name not to be entered in the book?"

He pulled it toward him. "Very. But some hold out until they've tooken legal advice. Looks like this all came to nothing anyway."

I nodded, trembling so hard I couldn't hold my cup steady. The sergeant was talking about his previous posting in Stepney, which he preferred. You get used to the regulars. Here you never know what'll come in next. I nodded again and trembled, and then at last escaped into the daylight.

The name Julie Fox would have meant nothing to a policeman requested by Breen to scan the records for Stella Hobhouse, and the signature of the legal representative was such a scrawl as to be almost indecipherable. But I knew it. Oh, I did. Had I not, in the past couple of weeks, read three letters over and over again, each signed *Nicholas Thorne*?

Thirty-eight

By now it was gone three. I bought a newspaper and ordered tea and toast in a café as my eyes passed over the usual headlines, queues lengthening outside the Labour Exchange, miners rebelling, government failing. On page three there was an update on the "Shot in the Heart Murder," in which Sir David Hardynge, philanthropist and parliamentary candidate, was described as a surprise witness whose generosity in private had led to his unexpected embroilment in a murder trial and whose modest dignity in court was exemplary. At a quarter to five, my feet carried me to Maida Vale and the corner where Nicholas was leaning against the side of his car, arms folded, head to one side, casually dressed, no tie, open waistcoat, blazer.

He flung wide the door, helped me in, and at once the horror faded a little as the truth of Nicholas, the clean lines of his body, the shape of his smile, that upward quirk to the left side of the mouth, soothed my aching heart. He kissed me, studied my face, told me I looked desperately tired, kissed me again, and asked where shall we go.

I said I had the key to Prudence's cottage and we would certainly be private there. Making no comment, he gave me a quick, warm look and turned onto the Harrow Road. I was incapacitated by the shock of being all day so alone and now with him. Here he was, the man I was so in love with, here, the same as when I last saw him outside Fortnum's though perhaps even more impossibly, unreachably Nicholas, his competent hand on the wheel, the intelligent fingers, the contrast of the white cuff with his skin, the changing angle of his thigh as he worked the brake.

At first, he tried to make me talk. What was the outcome of the Wheeler trial? "Not finished yet," I said. "Did you not read about it in the papers?" He'd only glanced at the *Times* in the train and there'd been no mention. What about my interview with Lady Curren? "The children are to be released though it was an uncomfortable half-hour. I wanted to know more about the home's policy on child emigration and Lady Curren thought I was being ungrateful. You obviously exerted quite an influence on her, Nicholas. She spoke of you fondly."

"Well, she's Sylvia's aunt. A formidable woman for her size but her heart's in the right place. Between them, she and her sister, Sylvia's mother, sit on practically every committee in town."

He didn't seem to notice that I rarely spoke after that. Instead he told me about his brief in Manchester and how he'd managed to get his defendant off with two years' penal servitude, a sight better outcome than for the others, who received ten years apiece. "The fact is, though, that the sums involved, more than a hundred thousand pounds stolen from the bank over six months, made it a high-profile case that hit the national press. Others like it perhaps may follow for me. It's all good."

Summer had matured since we walked together in the fields above Chesham. In the luminous late afternoon, there was scarcely a movement among the dense greenery of the woods. I remembered the acute sense of excitement as I traveled out, alone, on the Metropolitan Line, the child in the seat opposite, with the farthing-sized birthmark, the miracle of finding Nicholas awaiting me under the churchyard wall. And now I was with the same man but with the dream, it seemed to me, in ruins.

For the first time I admitted to myself what I had wanted from this evening when I made my offer to Prudence and asked for the keys to her cottage. Him. Yes. All. And now?

Prudence's cottage was in a lane just outside the village of Beaconsfield, a few miles from Uxbridge. It was familiar to me from reluctant childhood visits to the recently orphaned Aunt Prudence, who had sat in rustling black satin and served us meager Sunday teas—agony for James and me until we were released into the garden and allowed to play hide-and-seek among the gooseberry bushes. The cottage, of charmless stucco, was set four-square in its gardens behind a low wall, a quarter of a mile or so from the much grander Georgian house that had once belonged to my grandfather.

Prudence had an eye for function rather than beauty. The garden was rigidly carved up into vegetable patch and fruit bushes, with stepping-stone paths in between and squares of flower bed outside the front and back doors. Inside there was no electricity, the fires were rarely lit, and the furnishings, hastily selected from her dead father's house, the worst of mid-Victorian. On the evening I visited with Nicholas, though the mellow July light was flattering, the angular little house seemed resigned to a future of creeping decay. Leaving me at the gate, he drove off to park in a wider part of the lane. My key gave access to the scullery with its red-tiled floor and dripping tap, where as I child I had been condemned to spend damp half hours with Mrs. Lime, the help, peeling vegetables or washing up.

No wonder the tenants had gone north for the summer. Prudence's furniture was still there, the heavy sideboard and unforgiving chairs at the swept hearth in the parlor. The windows were too small and deep-set to let in much light or any heat. I looked under the sink but found neither ants nor mouse droppings, only an evil-looking but mercifully empty trap, and ran up the steep little staircase to check the two bedrooms, one containing twin beds, the other Prudence's, with a three-foot iron bedstead and pious prints on the walls.

Once, when I was eight, James and I had been sent to stay with Prudence *to keep her company now she's lost Grandfather*, Mother said. James was allocated the spare room, while I had to undergo the torture of sleeping head-to-toe with my aunt, whose sense of decency was outraged when I suggested I share my brother's room. I lay awake with her feet on my hip, swamped by her very distinctive smell. What was it? Coal-tar soap, hair washed once a week, clothes often aired but rarely cleaned, and most pungent of all, the odor of distaste. I regarded Aunt Prudence as an unknowable woman who avoided touch beyond a peck at arrival and departure, whose activities were rigidly regulated and included numerous trips to the village with a basket and a list of dull messages: call in on old Mrs. P to check her feet, visit Mrs. Carstairs (the vicar's wife) to offer a seedcake for the bring-and-buy, deliver a parcel of largesse (rhubarb and a cast-off pair of lisle stockings) to the indigent Lawrence family, buy stamps and postcards so that we children could write home daily.

James, at five, was not expected to participate much in Prudence's life, and a son of the vicar was summoned so that the pair could form a reluctant bond. They were even given an old sheet to make a wigwam. I, on the other hand, was to be Prudence's little helper as she paid her calls, fussed with church matters, sewed, or worked in the garden. By the end of two days, I was near screaming with boredom. Next morning I took James for a long walk in the enticing country lanes. I remember his hot, rough little hand in mine, the ache of responsibility as we ventured farther and farther from the cottage, his questions: Where are we going? How much longer? What's a baby bat called? We ate blackberries and stopped to look at everything, a foal rubbing its ear on a gate, a scattering of feathers betokening some dreadful death, a well with a little pitched roof. We got lost, had to ask the way back, and arrived at the cottage with berry-stained mouths and filthy hands. Prudence slapped our legs and refused us jam at teatime. James obligingly howled all evening and far into the night until at last I was allowed to sleep with him, his delicious, fruit-scented, salt cheek pressed against mine. The next day we were collected by Min and brought home to Maida Vale by cart, train, and omnibus.

I stood in Prudence's bedroom window, facing the front, and watched Nicholas, who leaned on the wall by the gate in a stance that was already wrenchingly familiar, arms folded, head down, legs crossed at the ankle. Bathed in that steady golden light, he seemed to me the image of irrepressible manhood, on the brink of greatness, of an entirely different world to mine.

Where had my dream of a happy ending come from? Happy endings of the fairy-tale variety had not been part of the plan since war was declared, since the toasting fork clattered onto the hearth, since I listened to that fateful lecture in Girton. What a fool I had been to think that a man so beautiful, so full of promise, so sweetly inclined to fall in love, should actually have been destined for me. He, after all, like most other eligible men over twenty-four in Europe, was deeply, fatally snared by the past.

I stood at the window a little longer, making up my mind, then I went down to him.

"What is it?" he said. "What kept you so long?"

"I want you to do something for me."

I led him inside, closed the scullery door behind us, passed through the kitchen with its blue gingham frills on cupboards and windows, and climbed the little staircase leading to Prudence's bedroom, where the net curtain at the window was still thrust to one side.

"What is it?" he asked again.

I still held his hand, which I lifted to my breast. "I want you to give me this, only this."

He took a little indrawn breath but shook his head. His fingers pressed momentarily, promisingly, on my flesh, then withdrew. "Evelyn, we'll have a lifetime."

"So much could happen. I want to take this now."

"My very, very dear girl." Stunned, wrong-footed, he took a step backward. "Do you know what you are doing?"

I sat on the edge of the bed, hands in my lap, waiting.

"Evelyn."

"You said you wanted to be with me." I pulled the pins from my hair and placed them on the quilt, then undid the top button of my blouse. His back was to the light. I thought, if he refuses me, I shall die.

At last he pulled me up so that we stood one on either side of the window, looking half through the lattice, half through net to the overgrown fruit bushes now in deep shadow. Sighing, he reached out his other hand, lifted my hair, held the back of my neck, and brought my face close to his. I was weeping so hard that I had to take long, indrawn breaths as he kissed my mouth.

Everything broke apart, the pink-and-brown-trellis pattern on the wallpaper, the greens of the garden, the darkness of Nicholas. I kept my eyes open because I wanted to know what happened to the world when lovemaking was involved. I heard my own stunned cries as his kisses deepened, my hands tore at his clothes, my flesh shivered under the shock of his touch as he slid his hand inside the neck of my blouse and stroked my breast.

He whispered: "Are you sure?"

I drew him back until I felt the side of the bed against my knees. When we lay down, I guided his hand onto my thigh. He watched me for a moment then tucked me under his arm so that we lay clasped together as he undid the buttons on my blouse and pushed the fabric aside.

"You're so perfect," he whispered. "You don't know. My head has

been full, all these years, of images of men who have been most obscenely broken. I don't know how I shall bear it, the beauty of you."

"All. Not just men. All of us broken." Our kisses deepened and I laid
his hand on the fastening of my skirt. I had time to wonder, in those
kisses, about other women, Sylvia. And then I gave in.

Pay attention, Evelyn. Don't miss a thing. I followed his hand as it
cupped my knee and swept my inner thigh. My flesh shuddered at the
impossible intimacy of his tentative fingers. I loved the conjunction of
our bodies, the beat of his stomach and thighs so that the pain in my
heart at last was crushed to a distant echo. My fists clenched, ankles
flexed, neck arched until I didn't recognize my own body. How would
I, when it had been shrouded for a lifetime in shapeless garments, but
was now unwrapped at last, and being made love to by this man and no
other? I wept to see Nicholas exposed, connected, revealing a face not
as it was in public but absolutely stripped of any defense, soft-mouthed,
soft-skinned, blurred with love.

This was the opposite of all the rules I had grown up with; cover up,
avoid touch, treat your body merely as an inconvenient, suffering vessel
for the soul. What a lie to pretend the body wasn't packed with sensation and desire, capable of embracing and opening itself up to be filled
with a new light, a new freedom to be Evelyn Gifford, alive, alive.

But afterward, as I lay in his arms, even as I marveled at the touch
of his warm moist skin against mine, they came back, softly at first,
mouths whispering against the window, a million dead mouths, among
them James, the shadowy Private Fox, and Stella Wheeler with her
bronze dancer and her false smile.

I shut them out again and for a while longer spun on the pivot of
our brief time together while he covered my neck and breast with kisses.

I couldn't believe that he didn't love me.

The shape and contents of the room emerged again: a print of a child
kneeling at prayer, blond curls, shut eyes; a spider, legs thin as hairs,

twirling from the picture rail. Nicholas's face, close up, was full of movement, the flutter of his eyelid, a momentary tick at the side of his mouth,
the adjustment of his lips as if the muscles were relaxing in preparation
for sleep. With one arm he held me, the other hand rested on my stomach. I heard a car in the lane, remembered the gooseberry bushes and
how their thorns used to tear at my hair when I hid among them as a
little girl.

He opened his eyes and smiled. Was that love, the softness and heat
in his gaze, or was that how all men looked after sex? I stroked his face,
waiting. It's not too late, Evelyn, to say nothing. He caught my finger
between his lips and kissed it, leaned over me and kissed me again.

The last thing I did, before I spoke, was to trace the shape and texture of him from chin to navel, the slight roughness of his throat, the
muscular breast, the soft, tender skin of his stomach. Then a voice I
scarcely recognized as my own said: "You know that Wheeler will hang."

He tightened his arms about me. "I fear so."

"Despite the fact that right at the last moment Wolfe found a new
witness, an admirer of Stella's who'd bought her that bronze dancer I
mentioned to you."

"How clever of Wolfe. But it made no difference?"

"Nicholas, you'd know the answer to that because the gentleman was
Sir David Hardynge."

His muscles became rigid. "Hardynge."

"He met Stella at a Christmas party, so he says, dropped into Lyons
on a whim, bought the bronze dancer as a wedding present. We could
pin nothing else on him, even were it plausible that he wanted her dead.
He has an alibi for the day of the murder, at home with his wife over
lunchtime, then visiting Donald."

He said again: "Hardynge."

"Yes. I don't expect you're entirely surprised."

"You're mistaken. I'm shocked to the core."

I lay for a moment longer in his arms, inhaling his scent, then jolted upright and knelt above him, my hair tumbling onto his chest and my arms crossed to cover my naked breasts. "Tell me the truth. Please. I need to hear it. Tell me you are not somehow bound up with Stella's murder."

He put his hands behind his head and stared at me. I saw the shadow of a defiant boy in him, a tightening of the lips, eyes voided of expression. Already we were so far from what we had been minutes ago. "I can only tell you what I believe to be true."

"Tell me. Tell me. Nicholas, don't you understand? Wheeler will hang. Who is protecting whom? What's going on? You can't let a man die, Nicholas."

"I didn't know that Hardynge had bought her the bronze dancer."

"I wish I could believe you."

"When Wheeler was arrested Hardynge telephoned my chambers and asked me to keep an eye on the proceedings which concerned a loyal employee—one for whom he had a particular affection and respect, especially bearing in mind Wheeler's wartime service—and if possible to protect the good name of Imperial Insurance. He said he was worried for poor Wheeler and wanted him to have the best possible defense. He wanted to be kept abreast of developments. That was all."

"No. It wasn't all. You deliberately befriended me. You approached me after the Marchant case not because you admired me, but because you wanted to keep your eye on Breen and Balcombe and I was the easiest way in."

"You knew that, I told you so in the café near Toynbee. You were utterly incensed, as I recall. But I was hooked after that. Believe me."

"You looked up my brother's war record so that you would form a bond with me."

The briefest of pauses before he answered: "That was before I knew you. Once I'd met you everything changed."

"I told you we were going for a fitness-to-plead argument. You dissuaded us after consulting with Hardynge, who I now realize would have been most unhappy if there had been excessive probing into what had happened to Wheeler during the war. And then the bronze dancer. Whom did you tell about the bronze dancer after I mentioned her to you during our tea at Fortnum's?"

"I might have said to Hardynge . . ."

"And he somehow got to the salesman who disappeared, heaven knows where, we still haven't tracked him down, though apparently Wolfe has discovered he has family in Devon, so the whole thing came to light too late for us to stop the trial. There are too many connections and too many things that don't fit. And I haven't told you the most significant thing of all. Do you remember an incident late at night on Tuesday, April 15, when you were called to Hyde Park police station?"

All this time he had lain with his hands behind his head, watching me. Now he raised himself on one elbow. Even in the last of twilight, I saw his sudden pallor. "Possibly."

"Your name is on the records in the case of a Julie Fox and an unnamed other party. Julie Fox was Stella, I'm sure. Julie came to mind because it's her sister's name, and Fox . . . I'll tell you later why she chose Fox because I think it could have been that use of a false name, on a whim, that got her murdered. Who was the man you bailed out, Nicholas?"

He lay on his back with his palms crushed to his eyes. "Christ."

"Nicholas."

He sprang from the bed and began to dress. After a moment I did the same, though it seemed a dreadful thing to be struggling with buttons and hooks, arming myself against him. We didn't look at each other. Now that I had wrenched myself apart from him, the process of dressing was cumbersome and shameful. Nicholas stood at the window once more, head bent in the low-ceilinged room, holding his elbows.

"Tuesday evening," he said at last. "Mid-April. About eleven o'clock.

I was telephoned from Hyde Park police station. A gentleman wished to speak to me. Hardynge. He sounded flustered, for him. In a spot of bother, he said. Come down to the station, Nicholas, I need your help. Turned out he'd been caught among the trees in Hyde Park embracing a girl, rather more than embracing. The pair had been arrested. Hardynge was agitated, didn't want it to come to court, didn't want his wife to find out, was obviously terrified lest it spoil his chances of being selected by his constituency. I had to use all my powers of persuasion, summoned the inspector who fortunately was of the opinion that women police officers were forever bringing time-wasting cases back to the police station. I made a few promises, alluded to a few influential people, and managed to get Hardynge out."

"And the girl?"

"I knew nothing about the girl."

"Not even her name?"

"I wasn't told her name. I never saw her. Simply got the police agreement that a caution for her was the most convenient resolution for all. The thing was, Evelyn, I wasn't surprised when I got the call from Hardynge that evening. It was an inconvenience to me rather than a shock. I'd known that he had a weakness for young girls—I suspect even his wife has an inkling—because I'd bailed him out before."

"And when Stella was murdered, it never occurred to you that she might have been another of his dalliances?"

"It did not. I trusted him. As I trusted you." It was too dark now to read his eyes as he said, very low, very cold, "I never thought to be used by a woman as you have used me. You knew all this, you believe me to be implicated in whatever it is that Hardynge has done, you were determined to confront me with all kinds of accusations and yet you asked me to make love to you first."

"Was that using you? Perhaps. I love you so, Nicholas, you have no idea how much or how sure I am that it will be the only time for me. For once I took a risk and asked for what I wanted. But it's hopeless because you are in Hardynge's pocket. He whistles, you jump. A woman is dead and her husband will hang for a crime he almost certainly didn't commit because you couldn't resist doing another seedy little favor. Can't you see what happened after Stella was released that night? She had a hold on him, or thought she did. Perhaps he assumed he could buy her off with the bronze dancer. I'll bet she tried to pester him into providing her with some other kind of life than that little terrace with Stephen Wheeler."

He was a stranger, face averted. And still I loved him and wanted to take the step that would bring me back to his arms, surely, soften the steely perfection of his profile, restore his kisses. He said: "Doesn't this give Stephen the motive we've been looking for, if he got wind of the fact that Stella was having an affair?"

"Wheeler didn't kill Stella. You know he didn't. My God, what that man could teach us all about love. At first, when I was at the police station today, I thought: probably Stella tried to blackmail Hardynge after that night by threatening to tell the press about the sordid outing to Hyde Park. But even I know that a man like Hardynge could buy off any number of newspaper editors or pushy little waitresses." (I thought, but didn't say: After all, Nicholas, he appears to have bought off you.) "Unless Stella threatened to tell a much more significant truth, one he couldn't bear even to speak about. Nicholas, do you know what your friend Donald Hardynge got up to in the war?"

At last he faced me and grasped my shoulder. "Jesus Christ. Jesus. Jesus." Thrusting me aside, he clattered down the narrow stairs and through the kitchen, where I heard him fumbling with the bolt on the scullery door. By the time I'd caught up with him, he was outside at the gate, white-faced, trapped within the low walls of the little garden.

"Can't you see," he said, "have you any idea how this hurts? Donald. If I'd known Hardynge had bought the bronze dancer . . . I might have known . . ."

But the next moment he laughed, as if in rueful surrender to the fates that had so perversely brought him to Prudence's cottage, looked about him at the darkly shadowed garden where the unruly gooseberry bushes extended vicious spikes, then returned to the house and sank down against the wall under the parlor window, hands loosely locked about his knees. "Don't tell me, the other boy was called Fox. Is that where Stella got the name? I was never told it, though I knew Don liked boys, of course I did. He always had. And I knew that he'd run off with someone and that one of them had fired a shot. I knew that Hardynge had got Don home, even though he was the officer and older, and therefore far more culpable."

"Did you never probe what happened? How Hardynge managed it?"

He sank his head into his arms. "I owed him too much to ask questions. My life, probably. A month or two later he had me moved to a safer posting behind the lines. I wasn't given a reason at the time, just thanked my lucky stars. Later, after the war, Hardynge told me he'd had a word in someone's ear; he'd lost one son, he said, couldn't bear to lose another."

We sat shoulder to shoulder against Prudence's cottage, just where James and I used to crouch safely out of sight. The stucco at our backs was still warm. "Stella knew all about it," I said, and as I dropped words into the soft air, they became nuggets of truth, diamond-hard. "She'd have drawn the story out of Wheeler; how he formed part of a firing squad and all the details of the young boy's crime, including the name of his accomplice, or rather leader, I should say, because he couldn't deny her anything. Perhaps he even hoped she would comfort him. There was a photograph of Fox in their house. That's why she used his name at the police station, as just a hint to Hardynge that she had a hold on him.

Imagine if Stella had told the world not just about her little fling but that Hardynge had sacrificed the life of a frightened young boy for the sake of his son, who was, incidentally, a coward and a liar. Do you really imagine it was the boy Fox who shot at the policeman?

"Hardynge killed her, or had her killed—he has an alibi for the afternoon of the murder—because she was a liability. The gift of the bronze dancer wasn't enough to satisfy her, so he visited her at home and perhaps promised her a tryst, an elopement even. I think he planned every detail so that we'd all focus on Wheeler. It was only the bronze dancer that betrayed him; a matter of pure arrogance to overlook the value of something that to him was a trifle. And it would have been simple for him to get hold of the gun and gloves, kept in an unlocked shed, once he'd persuaded Stella to tell him about any souvenirs Stephen had kept from the war. After all, he was a dab hand at using scapegoats. Like father, like son."

The garden was warm and full of moths, and though ill-kept, some flowers had struggled up through their weedy beds so that I could smell the sweet, dusty perfume of perennial sweet peas. Still, in some drowning part of me, I hoped we might soon come to a resolution that would extract us from this dreadful place. Nicholas was bound to say something to save us.

"What will you do with all this speculation?" he said.

"I don't know. Tell Breen. As you say, it's only speculation. But perhaps there's enough to convince the judge that to convict Wheeler would be unsafe. Perhaps it will buy us time."

There was a long silence. "You know it will destroy me," Nicholas said, "if it comes out that I put undue pressure on the police at Hyde Park; especially if Hardynge is brought back to court and has to admit to being with her that night."

That was the worst. Until then I had thought that he might not be culpable. After all, my lips were still swollen, my body thrumming and overturned by our lovemaking. And yet there he sat murmuring of the damage this would do his career.

I went to the back of the cottage and locked the scullery door. Then I walked to the gate and waited. At last he too got up, brushed himself down, and followed me out of the garden. When I closed the gate behind us, I listened for the snick of the latch, remembering the flash of joy as James and I had been led away by Min, in such disgrace that Prudence couldn't bring herself so much as to shake our hands or wave from the window; how the gate had snapped fast behind us and how we had pranced off one on either side of Min, who was in great good spirits due to the fun of an unexpected excursion to bring us home. Leaving the cottage, I had felt triumphant. By the time I reached home, I had been overwhelmed by guilt.

It was now quite dark in the surrounding woods, and through the trees I saw a gleam of orange; low sunlight reflected on a windowpane. The inside of the automobile was quite cool and steeped in that unforgettable scent of leather and oil. Nicholas's hands gripped the wheel but he made no attempt to start the engine.

"I want to take you somewhere, Evelyn, that might make it easier for you to understand."

I said nothing.

"Will you come and meet Donald?"

I drew a long breath. "What difference would it make?"

"Perhaps none, I don't know. At least you'd have the full picture."

"You want me to keep quiet. This is just an attempt to win my sympathy."

"Think that if you must. But perhaps it will give you more evidence. After all, wouldn't it help to check the records at the nursing home and find out what time Hardynge visited on the day of Stella Wheeler's murder?"

Of course I couldn't object after that. Besides, anywhere in Nicholas's company still seemed to me the only bearable place to be. It was well past eight o'clock and the lanes were dusky, though the sky in open countryside was luminous. I sat very neatly, not allowing my elbow to touch his as I watched the occasional flicker of light of an oil lamp in a cottage window, a passing car, a cluster of houses.

Thirty-nine

The Grove, to the north of Princes Risborough, was reached by a narrow lane and our way was eventually blocked by wrought-iron gates. Nicholas had to knock at the door of the lodge until a bent little man in an oversized cap and jacket emerged.

"It's late to come visiting," he said, but having recognized Nicholas, let us in. Beyond, because shrubs and trees were in full leaf, the house, a rather beautiful, white-painted mansion with a colonnaded porch, only came into view when we were a few hundred feet away. As I got out of the car at the foot of a short flight of curved steps, I stumbled, unable for a moment to remember what I was doing there.

The door was opened by a nurse, Sister Phelan, who wore a flowing white apron and complicated headdress and was as surprised as the gate-keeper to see us. "We never usually allow visitors so late in the evening. It's too disruptive. Our men are nearly ready to go to bed." She had a strong, southern Irish accent, and eyes made staring by the fierceness with which her hair was dragged back from her forehead. However, she too remembered Nicholas, shook him by the hand, and exclaimed: "Don't tell me there's bad news in the family."

"We were in the area on business," Nicholas said. "Miss Gifford is also a lawyer. We thought we'd call on the off chance that Donald was still up. He won't want to see me, I'm sure, but I thought he might appreciate a young lady visitor."

"It's true he has a softness for the girls. Are you a family friend, Miss Gifford?"

"An acquaintance, rather."

"My goodness, but you look all in," said Sister Phelan. "I can't imagine what possesses you to come calling so late. Shall I be getting you a cup of tea? Shame on you, Mr. Thorne, for asking so much of your young lady friend." But she asked no further questions as she bustled away to order tea. Meanwhile, Nicholas and I avoided each other's eye as he picked up the visitors' book from an occasional table, leafed through, and found the entry for Saturday, May 17, with Sir David's name and signature. Hardynge had arrived at four thirty, left just after six.

In my trancelike state, I thought, how easily the world molds itself for Nicholas. Everything he wants, he gets. Even me.

"Does Donald Hardynge have many visitors?" he asked Sister Phelan when she was pouring the tea.

"Just the family. His father is a wonderful man, never misses a Saturday, though he must be in such demand elsewhere. And as you say, Sylvia is a very popular visitor here, with all our men."

A few sips of tea revived me a little, and afterward Sister Phelan led me through room after room along one highly polished set of floorboards after another, deeper into the house. Glass doors divided the old house with its elaborate plasterwork and graciously proportioned rooms from a much newer wing consisting of long, low corridors with closed doors on either side. Turkish rugs dotted the floor, semicircular tables held floral displays, and the walls were adorned with photographs of the staff arranged in blurred ranks so that I could scarcely make out their faces, and delicately tinted prints of botanical specimens. The house, said Sister Phelan, had until the war belonged to a private family and was not ideally suited to its present function; food had to be carried too far and the rooms in the old house were not secure and therefore good for little except meetings and staff accommodation. Occasionally, we passed a deferential nurse who fell back against the wall, but we never saw a patient, and I watched the floating wings on our guide's headdress, heard the rustle of her starched uniform, and wondered at the profundity of the silence beyond.

Donald Hardynge was seated on an upright ladder-back chair in a glassed-in veranda overlooking a garden graced by a cedar and S-shaped flower beds, exactly as Nicholas had once described him. Perfect lawns were edged by shrubs and crossed by gravel paths. A couple of other men, young and crisply turned out, with sleeked-down hair and spotless shirt collars, sat tranquilly reading their newspapers. Donald Hardynge, who was not doing anything, was also dressed smartly in a buttoned-up waistcoat over his shirt and tie, well-pressed trousers, and gleaming shoes, as if he were about to stride off and meet a client.

All three men leaped to their feet and I was introduced to each as a friend of Sylvia Hardynge. One had a dreadful facial wound, across which skin had been grafted, but the corner of his mouth and eye were dragged down and his right ear gone. Donald's grip was firm but cursory. He was very thin with a tick at the hinge of his jaw and had the looks of a fashion plate: high cheekbones, cleft chin, lightly curling hair. I saw the echo of his father and sister in the shape of his bones; I saw nothing in his eye.

Once we were both seated, we stared at the garden and he drummed his fingers on the arm of his chair. Sister Phelan said she would return in ten minutes. At the far end of the veranda, a nurse was knitting a garment in pale blue wool.

"It's getting dark," I said, sensing that the banal words seeped into

Donald's mind as if it were a sponge spreading and spreading them out until they didn't fit together at all.

After a pause, his cultured voice, like his father's, said: "I have not been out all day." The next moment he got up and offered me his arm.

The young nurse in the corner set aside her knitting. "He wants you to go out with him. He always wants to go out. But he won't stay long, just a few minutes."

She slid open the glass door, and Donald Hardynge and I stepped first onto a gravel path, then a lawn. His arm was rigid under my hand. I tried to imagine him in another, prewar life; the tennis-playing schoolboy with his future mapped out by an ambitious father; and later as a young man bolting across a desolate French landscape in the company of a frightened boy soldier. Meanwhile, I was being guided in a very straight line across the lawn, under the cedar and beyond, toward the shrubbery.

At the edge of the lawn, Donald stopped. From here we could see both the front of the house and the bedroom block with its glassed-in verandas, where his two companions sat exactly as we had left them. "Have we walked far enough?" asked Donald.

"I should say so." The last of the sun had sunk away and the shrubbery was very dark. We did not go back across the lawn but walked on around its edge in what I assumed was a well-worn ritual. I glanced up into Donald's face but he was staring straight ahead and did not acknowledge me at all.

So this was why Stella had died, this long-dead boy. I leaned on his unyielding arm and thought how fruitless it had all been, Donald's attempt to escape the war, his father's efforts to save him. And as we circled the lawn, I could not help giving thanks that it was Donald Hardynge's and not James's arm that lay under my hand, Sylvia's brother and not mine, who marched sightlessly along the gravel paths leading one to another in the garden of an old mansion.

Nicholas and I drove back to London in near silence. Occasionally, his fingers drummed the wheel or he sighed deeply and shifted his weight on the seat. When we reached the corner of Clivedon Hall Gardens, I moved to open the door, and for the first time in over an hour he spoke. "Evelyn, I've been thinking. There's something else you should know. I remember the weekend of the murder very clearly because of course on the Tuesday of the following week, I met you. That Saturday I played tennis as usual with Sylvia in the garden of her house. You say Hardynge's alibi is that he was at home. I saw him at twelve when I first arrived, he greeted me very effusively, but I didn't see him again."

"He could have been anywhere in the house, surely."

"I don't think so. Lady Margaret was there with a luncheon party— they were having a committee meeting or some such and in the early afternoon they all came spilling down the garden to watch us. There was no sign of Sir David."

I couldn't take in either the implications of what he said or the fact that he seemed to be offering this information as a kind of plea, or pledge.

He said, "Can you forgive me?"

But you are a stranger, I thought. What I knew of him was that if I lifted his hand to my lips, his wrist would smell of soap and, very faintly, the leather of his watch strap, and that if I were to lean my head on his shoulder, I would see the pulse in his throat and how the soft hair above his ear sprang a little sparsely so that I might actually have counted the follicles, one by one. I would try again to puzzle out what it was about his face, his mouth, his eyes that quickened my pulse, why I found so beautiful the fall of a lock of hair on his brow and the sweep of his fingers thrusting it aside. But the inside of him, what enthused and inspired or disgusted and deadened him, what kept him awake at night, I did not know at all.

"How can I forgive you," I said, "when I have no idea now whose side you are on?"

I got out of the automobile and was about to close the door behind me when I thought I heard him say: "Yours. I love you."

A light was burning in the hall where Edmund's little blazer was hung carelessly on the stand, his satchel tossed alongside. My brother's hat, I noticed, had been shuffled to a less prominent hook. Perhaps soon someone would take it upstairs and put it away.

I crept to the kitchen, fumbled for the light switch, went to the scullery for bread. But I could not escape Meredith, who came pattering down in pale green silk pajamas. "Evelyn. For heaven's sake, where were you? You missed everything that happened in court today. Your Mr. Breen was so concerned he kept looking at the doors hoping you'd come in. He says you're to telephone him when you get back, no matter how late it is. But in the Lord's name, what are you doing with that knife? Give it to me."

The knife clattered off the board and onto the floor. She pushed me into a chair and held my cold hands as a tidal wave of exhaustion overcame me. When the wrenching sobs came, she held my face against her stomach, stroked my hair, and would not let me go.

Later she revived the fire in the range, boiled an egg, heated milk. She talked about the trial, how the defense had done his best to persuade the jury that Wheeler should not be found guilty; there was too much doubt, evidence of another man in Stella's life, evidence that she had planned the picnic, above all overwhelming evidence that Wheeler loved her so much that the idea he might have killed her was quite absurd.

Mr. Breen (*your* Mr. Breen, as Meredith said) was pessimistic, however.

She watched me eat, nudging the plate closer, as she did with Edmund, to remind me to take another mouthful, then went to telephone Breen and tell him I was safe home and would speak in the morning.

Not once did she ask what had happened, though she must have longed to know. Instead she switched off the lights and urged me upstairs, where she turned back the quilt of my bed and plumped the pillow.

And I discovered, as I lay down at last, that beneath the pain there was a spark of hope, because this time, when I'd lost my love, I'd been given a hand to hold.

Forty

ext morning Breen and I sat on either side of his desk in the Arbery Street office, and he rocked back in his chair, twiddled his thumbs, and gazed at the ceiling while I recounted events of the previous day, though not, of course, the detail of what had happened between Thorne and me.

"There's no need to be so woeful and melodramatic about all this," said Breen, fixing me with his blackbird eye. "I'm not a complete fool, I knew most of it. The moment we got back to London last night Wolfe and I visited Hyde Park police station to see what you'd been up to. I found the entry in the ledger, same as you did. And we were well aware that you had developed feelings for Thorne and, incidentally, he for you. Why do you think I excluded you from our investigations? You should not reproach yourself. As you well know, the world is oiled by people making connections with each other."

"I let my feelings interfere with my . . ."

But he'd had enough of this talk of feelings. "None of us is made of stone, Miss Gifford. And if we become stone, we should give up criminal law at once and stick to conveyancing. It's simply a matter of watching one's tongue and keeping confidences where appropriate. I'd say, on the whole, feelings aside, that you have done rather well." He was, I realized, concealing considerable excitement by shuffling papers, adjusting the knot in his tie and the handkerchief in his pocket, and seizing his hat. "I really do believe, Miss Gifford, that with all this new information, we shall be able to save Stephen Wheeler."

Next we took a cab to Wormwood Scrubs, where an officer friend of Breen granted us an interview with Wheeler, who received us as if we were paying a social call and expressed amazement that we had troubled ourselves to visit on a Saturday. Altogether, he was a different man from the one who had been confined each day to the dock. His beard and hair had been trimmed and he looked more comfortable in his laundered prison shirt than in the cheap suit he wore in court. We brought him the gift of half a fruitcake, the remains of one of Miss Drake's offerings to Breen, for which he was touchingly grateful. Then I took out pen and paper and placed it neatly on the table, and Breen and I sat facing Wheeler, my hands gripped tight in my lap and my heart beating very fast in anticipation of his reaction to our news.

Breen wrapped his hands around his knee, cocked his head on one side, and looked Wheeler in the eye. "Stephen, we are here because more evidence has come to light about Hardynge's involvement with Stella. I always counsel caution, I would advise you not to raise your hopes too far, but we think we have enough to suggest that there should be further investigations. Even his alibi for the afternoon of Stella's murder is now questionable. And if the judge won't allow us to suspend proceedings at this stage, we definitely have grounds for appeal."

Wheeler's reaction was not at all as I'd anticipated; in fact, it was the opposite of hope. The genial light went from his face and he adopted the same posture as in the dock, slumped, head bowed.

"You served with Hardynge's son, Donald?" Breen said.

The slightest nod. "What has that to do with my Stella?"

"Stephen, you have asked us to defend you, but I think that you have been less than helpful in telling us what you know. You have kept quiet when you might have given us information that would have saved a lot of time. So now that we have found everything out, I hope you're going to cooperate with us."

Wheeler sat more upright, but would not look at Breen. "Go on, then. Ask me what you like."

"What happened between your friend Paul Fox and Donald Hardynge, Stephen?"

This time, Wheeler did not seem in the least surprised by the question but nodded as if we had confirmed something in his mind. "The Hardynge boy got off, the young lad was sentenced to be shot. I'd known Fox since he was twelve—he used to be a messenger at work. Knew him to be a soft sort of boy." He glanced at me. "Forgive me, Miss Gifford, he was a bit of a honey trap for men who took their pleasures that way. I kept my eye on him as far as I could but there was always someone else wanting to offer him a different type of protection."

"Did you find it surprising that Hardynge was sent home while the boy was left to face a firing squad?"

"Neither of them should have died. They were too scared, not right for the war. I saw them when they were brought back to camp. Both crying."

"Did you know which of them shot the military policeman?"

There may even have been a glimmer of humor in Wheeler's eye. "Well, it couldn't have been the boy, now, could it? Everyone knows that common soldiers aren't issued with revolvers."

"Weren't you angry, then, that Fox was shot?"

"'Course I was angry. But it wasn't the Hardynge boy's fault. It was the way things were bound to turn out given who each of them was."

"Did Stella know this story?"

"I told Stella everything."

Breen said: "You've heard already how Sir David made Stella a gift of the bronze dancer. And now we discover that there was a night in April that they were caught red-handed, Stella and Hardynge . . ."

Wheeler leaned forward. "What are you saying?"

"We think that Hardynge committed perjury last week in court or came damn close to it—I suspect he chose his words very carefully, I'll have to look at a transcript. He knew exactly where Stella was on April 15, because he was with her. We think that afterward Stella tried to blackmail him by threatening to make public the story of Donald and Private Fox, and that's why he killed her."

Breen had spoken in the soft tones normally reserved for soothing distraught female clients, but Wheeler was stricken. I saw dawning comprehension in his eyes, then a kind of horror. Next he sprang to his feet so abruptly that his chair scraped back, teetered, and clattered to the floor. "If you bring this up in court on Monday, I'll change my plea to guilty."

"Stephen, you've said all along you're not guilty. It is quite wrong to plead otherwise if you're innocent."

"Then don't make me. I'm not having my girl's name dragged through the mud. I don't want to know any more about it, if she was connected to him."

"Stella will not come out of this badly. Hardynge is the seducer, the manipulator. She was just a girl. Stephen, you cannot let a guilty man go unpunished."

"I'm not interested in what happens to him. I'm interested in my girl and what people will say about her."

"You'll hang, Stephen. I cannot let an innocent man hang."

"It's not your choice. I want my Stella to myself. I'll change my plea to guilty if you bring this up in court. For all you know I am guilty. For all you know I knew about Hardynge and Stella all along and killed her because I couldn't bear that she had an affair with my boss. That's what they've been saying in court or something like. Maybe it's true. What do you think of that?"

"Then why have you pleaded not guilty all this time, if you suspected Stella of having an affair and didn't want it to come to light? Why did you put yourself through a trial?"

Wheeler's smile illuminated his face and gave a glimpse of an utterly different man. "I'm not such a fool as you all think me. I didn't know what had happened to my Stella. Before they found her body I thought she'd met up with someone after I left her at that picnic place. Soon as I saw her hat I knew she'd gone off in a tearing hurry. Eloped, I thought. I'd known for months, before we was married, there was someone else on the scene though I'd never have believed it was him—that was a bad shock, to see Sir David in the dock and think it might have been him. He is a gentleman who always has been very good to me. But he was old and Stella . . ." He looked away and bit his lip, squeezed hard on the chair back. "I could tell by her eyes, the way she seemed to be listening to a voice in her head sometimes, that she was distracted. Even on our wedding day she was waiting for something else to happen. Then, when she was dead, of course I wanted to know who'd got hold of my revolver and killed her. Mr. Breen, you was just the man, I thought, to find out for me. And you have. I'm satisfied. I've got what I wanted, thank you."

Breen said: "Well, I suppose that's the greatest compliment I've ever been paid. But now Hardynge must be charged with murder and we can only achieve that with your cooperation."

"As I said, I don't choose to say anything more about this. Stella is my dear girl. I won't have her name publicly linked with his again."

"But, Mr. Wheeler," I cried, "we are sure Sir David Hardynge is guilty. All we are trying to do is bring him to justice. You can't mean that you are prepared to hang instead of the man who seduced . . ."

"Now you just listen to me, Miss Gifford," Wheeler held fast to the back of his chair and fixed me with suddenly fiery eyes, "in my book, this has nothing to do with the kind of justice you're talking about. In my book, I have the right to be given what I want, and what I want is to save my Stella's name. Her name is the one thing, the *one* thing, Miss Gifford, that has kept me alive for the last ten years, that name, Stella, and all that it means to me. Oh, I'm not saying I'm different from anyone else, I daresay you have your own terrible story of the war, and Breen here, I know, was out driving ambulances. I might have guessed," and he grinned at Breen, "that my old school fellow Daniel Breen would be close to the thick of things, running about, getting people organized. But I, I took one look at that war and thought, I am done for, Stephen Wheeler cannot survive this. When I was a young man, before the war, these hands were good hands, Miss Gifford, they did good things. They held a pen and filled out insurance forms that made people feel safer, God help me. They made things about the house and served others in small ways. In the war they was required to be killing hands. But there was nothing in me that could find justification—or should I use your word, *justice*—for what we were doing. There was not a scrap of sense that I could see in living like insects, killing men we had no reason to hate except they was the mirror image of ourselves. So I died to myself, I did what was required and I did it as best I could.

"Haven't you asked yourselves, how I could have formed part of a firing squad, taken a rifle, and pointed it at the heart of a boy who was very dear to me? I see him now, every hour of every day, that scrawny, sniveling lad, sniffing and sobbing, unable to stand upright so he had to be tied to a post, unable to control his bowels. I killed him as I would a rabid dog. It had to be done and it had to be done well. But what kind of a world was I in, that made the killing of that boy the kindest thing I had done in three years?

"And do you know why I'm here still, why I never pulled back my shoulders and walked into the teeth of machine-gun fire, it was the thought of a little girl who wrote to me every week and signed her letter, *Love, Stella*. In those nights when there's no sleep because there's rats and lice and mud and icy rain instead of a bed, there she was, light as air, this good, soft, rushing thing, this girl who had nothing whatever to do with the war, but who wrote me letters because she remembered the old Stephen who used to carry her on his shoulders and admire her dancing. Oh, I knew I would lose her in the end, she was always just out of reach, but she gave me all the joy I have ever known, and I won't barter her good name for the sake of a life that means less than nothing to me."

For a long time after he'd finished speaking, we were still. Breen's chin rested on his palm as he stared at Wheeler, I looked at the blank sheet of paper before me. "So," said Wheeler, as if both to recover himself and to stir us into action. With the hint of a conspiratorial smile, he held out his good hand to Breen.

We gathered up our things. Breen clapped Wheeler on the shoulder, gripped his upper arm, and said: "At least let me be there."

Wheeler nodded and clasped first Breen's hand then mine, smiling, to comfort me. At the door, I looked back to where he sat, very upright, hands resting on the table edge, like an obedient schoolboy. He was already far away from us and the look in his eye was achingly familiar. Hadn't I seen the same in a thousand nightmares as I floundered across no-man's-land, trying to reach my dying brother? And hadn't Donald Hardynge sat just so in the elegant conservatory at the Grove; nowhere to go, nothing to do but attend to unquiet ghosts?

So on Monday morning we went back to the court in Aylesbury to witness the inexorable process of Stephen Anthony Wheeler being sentenced to death.

With remorseless precision, Judge Weir punched out advice to the jury. "Defense case . . . Wheeler devoted to his wife . . . no plausible motive for killing her . . . much play put on spurious bits of evidence such as a hat left with the picnic blanket. Although there is some evidence that Mrs. Wheeler had other admirers, one of whom was generous enough to buy her an expensive wedding gift, there is no evidence at all that anyone else with sinister intent was on the hill that day or had access to Wheeler's gun.

"The evidence we've heard of Wheeler's war record is that he fought bravely and was respected by his fellows. He was certainly an able marksman. But you should not be swayed by either of these considerations. We are dealing with events that took place nearly six years after the war ended.

"The prosecution has told you that Wheeler was the owner of both gun and gloves. They have told you that Mrs. Wheeler's life was insured. You might agree with the defense, however, that it is far-fetched to suppose that a man with Wheeler's experience in insurance could believe that he might profit from his wife's death at his own hands. However, he seems to have been a jealous man, a rigid man, and one who would probably take no small exception to the idea of his wife's having admirers other than himself. And poor little Stella Wheeler seems to have attracted a good deal of attention while on the dance floor and indeed as a waitress.

"However, when all is said and done it is not for you to be certain of Wheeler's motive, but it is your task to be sure that he and none other murdered Stella Wheeler."

At the end of just two hours, the jury returned a unanimous verdict. The judge pronounced that Wheeler had cold-bloodedly, and with malice aforethought, murdered his wife of less than one month by shooting her through the heart with his own service revolver and in these circumstances the only possible punishment was death by hanging.

Wheeler's head went up. As he was led from the courtroom, he smiled lovingly at his mother, who sobbed, a handkerchief pressed to her mouth in a tight ball, as if it wasn't polite to show so much feeling in so public a place.

Forty-one

In the days between the end of Wheeler's trial and the date of his execution, set for Friday, August 15 (the day after my birthday), I found that everything had changed.

In the first place, I could not tolerate the prospect of living indefinitely in Clivedon Hall Gardens. Perhaps the outcome of Wheeler's trial was in some way connected with this decision: the fact that he had not allowed us to save him made me all the more determined to save myself. Besides, in the brief spell—the week between tea at Fortnum's with Nicholas and discovering his signature in Hyde Park police station—when I had tried to envisage myself as the wife of a rich and successful man, one image I had particularly relished was the leaving of Clivedon Hall Gardens. In my mind's eye, I saw myself close the front door, run down the white steps, and walk away. So I told Mother that I would move in with Meredith and Edmund for a trial period, in Pimlico, and in the meantime I would help her find a lodger or two. To my great surprise (and slight mortification), she didn't put up any further fight— I suspect she was relieved that thus punished she had done sufficient penance for concealing James's letter from me.

We heard, through Meredith, who met Sylvia at art class, that Sir David Hardynge was reconsidering his decision to stand for Parliament. He was drawn, said Sylvia, to more philanthropic activities and thought that politics might be a distraction. If this was the only price he was prepared to pay for what he'd done it seemed inadequate, and I was sickened by the knowledge he might yet elude retribution. But for the time being, I was distracted by Sylvia's other news, from my point of view even more sensational. Her engagement to *the tall one* (as Meredith insisted on describing Nicholas) was over. Sylvia said that he had disappointed her, kept her waiting too long, and she'd called it off. So heartbroken was Thorne, according to Sylvia, that he intended to leave London altogether and return to his hometown of Reading. Death to his career.

A fortnight later, a letter duly arrived, postmarked Reading. I burned it. Wheeler was to hang and I wanted nothing to do with Hardynge or Nicholas, who had been his creature. Then I spent fruitless minutes trying to rescue the letter from the flames, but when at last I'd salvaged a few scraps, I thrust them back: Hardynge's influence was so far-reaching, so insidious, I told myself, I could never trust Nicholas again. In fact, at Breen & Balcombe, we thought it expedient to get the Marchant children out of the clutches of the Good Samaritan's as soon as possible, in case Hardynge took it into his head to wreak his revenge on us for bringing him to court by the devious means of having those little girls migrated to Canada. But after a flurry of letters, payments from the *Daily Mail* fund, and a cursory visit by Miss Hands, assistant matron, to Caractacus Court, we received notification that the children would be released. A qualified lawyer was required to be present. Breen sent me.

Leah and I met outside the gates of the home at a quarter to two on a blustery Thursday afternoon, a week before Wheeler's execution. She was looking very trim in a neat gray coat (cast off, she told me, from one of her new ladies, who she charred for) and her best hat with cherries. When I offered to shake hands, she ignored me but I told myself it was not so much that she was choosing to slight me as that her whole being yearned toward the release of her children, and she would allow herself no distraction. As we crossed the yard, I noticed that she avoided treading on the painted squares of hopscotch.

The door was answered by the ubiquitous Miss Hands, who informed us apologetically that there were yet more papers to sign before the children could be released. Miss Buckley had not chosen to be present (she was out on charitable business, according to Miss Hands), so we were shown into a cubbyhole of an office (bare walls, presumably to ensure that I was not tempted to steal information from them), where I read out loud a document stating that Mrs. Marchant was a fit parent and would bring the children up in a moral Christian environment, and Leah put her cross on the dotted line.

Miss Hands glanced at me so often from under untrimmed eyebrows that I suspected she had been given dire warnings by her superior. Or perhaps she remembered the horror of our last visit when she had attempted to tear the children from their mother's arms; perhaps she wanted to speak but didn't have the courage. As we left the office, I gave her Breen & Balcombe's card, which she scrunched in her hand and thrust into a pocket. Then we were directed to a row of hard chairs in the hall and told to wait while Miss Hands disappeared upstairs. A clock ticked on a wall to the right, and beyond was the institutional mutter of a hundred children and their female teachers.

Leah was supernaturally still, her spine tilted toward the stairs, and I realized that this was the first time I had troubled myself to regard her as a woman worthy of respect rather than as a weak and reluctant client. She, after all, in the face of overwhelming odds, had remained unswerving in her devotion to her children. To her mind, sheer force of will would prevail in the end.

A door opened and then came the sound of feet on a corridor above. First to appear on the landing were the little girls with their tightly bound hair, hands clasped, dressed not in uniform this time but in summer frocks, long outgrown. Each wore new shoes, courtesy of the *Daily Mail*, and carried a small parcel. Next came Miss Hands; then a woman in a nurse's uniform, who clutched a fat baby.

For a moment, the group paused. Then Miss Hands gave the youngest girl a gentle prod with her knee and she moved down a step. Leah stood up. The children came slowly, one step at a time, their eyes fixed on their mother. When they reached the bottom, they waited as she crossed the space between them. Even when she held them they didn't respond, but I noticed the youngest had taken a fistful of her mother's skirt and wound it around her wrist.

The baby, when passed to Leah, cried lustily and arched his back. I tucked my briefcase under my arm and held the little girls' hands. At the gates of the home, mother and children were photographed and Leah made an incoherent speech of gratitude to the reporter, and then we bundled into a waiting taxicab. The baby, plump after weeks with an indulgent foster parent, and with a dazzling crop of blond curls, hurled himself about in his mother's arms while the girls sat one on either side of her and fixed me with unblinking eyes. They did not smile or respond to their mother's questions. The youngest, Cathy, had not released hold of Leah's skirt. Meanwhile, I pointed out sights along the way, the trees of Regents Park, and look, behind this road is Arbery Street where I work, and there's St. Pancras Station. The children swiveled their eyes obediently but didn't comment. Leah struggled with the baby and from time to time squeezed the shoulder of one or other of her daughters.

At Caractacus Court, Mrs. Sanders had laid on a substantial tea. Her spotless overall was removed when the kettle was boiled and she wore a brooch of tiny mosaic pieces pinned to her collar, which Cathy could not resist touching. I admired Mrs. Sanders for her thoroughness, the absolute commitment she gave to a task even as mundane as filling a teapot. She gave me the impression that her life consisted of a series of unwieldy packages, each of which had to be dealt with and dispatched

before another was opened. It was reassuring to believe that the Marchant family was her latest package.

The children's eyes were full of wonder as they took in the jam, the
fairy cakes, the lemonade. Sometimes they looked at each other, sometimes at Mrs. Sanders, sometimes at their mother, who dandled her
baby on her lap and pressed bread and jam into his mouth.

I drank a cup of tea, ate a slice of bread and butter, and became aware
that my status had changed from officious intruder to honored guest, and
that a speech had been prepared. "We 'ope you will call again anytime,
Miss Gifford," said Mrs. Sanders, "to see 'ow we are all getting on. It's a
rare thing to find someone who doesn't give up on people like us."

These words, which should have been a balm to my soul, were salt
on a wound. To my mind, the fact that Leah had been reunited with her
children was inextricably linked to Wheeler's fate: the Hardynge machine and its instrument, Nicholas, had sprung to the assistance of
Breen & Balcombe in the Marchant case because it suited them to do
so. By another flick of his fingers, Hardynge might have ordained an
entirely different outcome.

Afterward, they all crowded into the courtyard to wave me good-
bye. I produced chocolate for the girls and kissed Charlie, whose cheek
left a sticky smudge on my lip. When I stooped to embrace her, the
oldest child, Ellen, suddenly put her thin arms around my neck and
squeezed hard.

Forty-two

My *birthday, on August 14,* coincided with our next meeting of women lawyers. As the Law Society restaurant did not run to birthday cake, my friends clubbed together and bought me a pink concoction from the ABC tearooms. Altogether, the day promised to be far more festive than usual. That night in Clivedon Hall Gardens, there was to be a party, arranged by Meredith, to include the new lodger, Miss Griffiths, who had been recommended by an acquaintance at church, taught the piano (the prospect of music in the house delighted Grandmother), was overwhelmingly grateful to be offered a room, and on all three counts was therefore considered to be *ideal* by Mother. Prudence made no comment but cast wounded glances at Meredith and bit her lip to prevent unaccustomed tears falling. At the weekend, Meredith, Edmund, and I were to move out but in between these two dates—my birthday and the new flat—was the horrifying fact of Wheeler's execution.

At our meeting of lady lawyers, I was not the only person with news. All had been busy. While I had allowed myself to be distracted by murder trial and love affair, the others had forged ahead. Maud was halfway through writing a book titled *Women Under English Law,* and Carrie had been working on a divorce case that she herself would conduct under the Poor Persons Rules and thereby be the first woman ever to handle the breakdown of a marriage. For my own part, I told them that we had failed to save Wheeler, that I was about to move out of Clivedon Hall Gardens, and that I had rescued Leah Marchant's children from the threat of emigration by reaching an out-of-court agreement.

"You did *what*?" said Carrie. "Well, that's not going to get the law changed. I was hoping your Marchants might be a test case to raise the issues of child migration."

"These are real children. We could not use them as legal pawns. We had a chance and we took it."

"You should have gone through the courts. That way you could have brought to the public attention the sometimes barbaric way destitute children are treated."

"And what if we'd lost? The mother is known to be fond of the bottle, the father is absent. We risked her losing the children altogether."

"Oh, you would have had plenty of time to get it right. Canada is putting its foot down about accepting unaccompanied children under fourteen. All the British charities which ship them out there are terribly worried. After we spoke last time I got hold of these minutes of the Church of England Waifs and Strays Society. You can take them away with you if you like. And you know Mrs. Bondfied is conducting an inquiry on behalf of the government. There'll be a rush to emigrate children this year and next but then there'll be a tightening up of the rules, I hope."

"Perhaps we can find another way to expose the policy of migrating young children."

"We are not social reformers, first and foremost, we are lawyers. That's why it's a pity you missed your chance."

"You're wrong. I took my chance. And there'll always be other opportunities, surely, to see justice done."

❧

Breen & Balcombe had rustled up a birthday card, bought out of petty cash by Miss Drake, who had selected a picture of a white puppy with a blue ribbon tied to its ear. I was also instructed by Breen to go home early, since "you women like to have such a fuss made of you when it comes to birthdays."

It was odd how, when I reached Clivedon Hall Gardens, I already felt like a visitor. For once I was back earlier than Meredith and Edmund so that only women's hats and scarves adorned the hooks on the stand, though it still held a collection of massive black umbrellas. ("If there was to be an intruder," said Prudence, "he would note the male umbrellas and be deterred.") On a tray under the mirror were a few cards addressed to me, including one in a hand that still took my breath away, with that same Reading postmark. Raised voices came from the drawing room, one more high-pitched than the others, presumably Miss Griffiths, who, I thought guiltily, was bound to get on someone's nerves before too long.

I picked up Nicholas's card as if it might scorch my fingers, slipped it into my briefcase, and crept upstairs. The rest I would open later, in front of the family.

On the second floor, confusion reigned. Meredith's room was strewn with so many boxes and trunks that they had spilled onto the landing and even into James's room. My own clothes were draped over chair, bed, and bookshelves, my books stowed into cardboard boxes, my shoes (three pairs), lined up in a suitcase. Unlike Meredith's, my packing would take only an evening.

I was drawn to my brother's room by its relative tranquillity. James's slippers had been put away and the surfaces were clear, but Mother had told Edmund that he might choose from his father's books and toys anything that he wanted. He had taken the kaleidoscope and (perhaps to please her) a turgid-looking *Encyclopedia for Boys*, which used to fascinate me with its tips on deer-stalking and lighting fires without matches.

I sat for a while on the bed, enjoying the heat of afternoon sunlight on my neck. And inevitably, I thought of Wheeler, for whom color and sunshine were already only memories. Or perhaps it did not occur to him to grieve for such things, given that the one thing he'd ever really wanted was Stella, his dancing girl.

Nicholas had said: *You know it will destroy me if it comes out that I put undue pressure* . . . Yet I couldn't help lifting my briefcase onto the bed and opening the envelope from Reading. Inside was a birthday card (how on earth had he known the date?) with a picture of a cottage among trees, inscribed with the words: *For Evelyn Gifford, on her birthday. From Nicholas Thorne.*

I read it a dozen times, closed it, looked at the picture, opened it up, and read it again. I told myself his words meant nothing, they were cold, and in any case what had I to do with Nicholas Thorne? Then, infuriated by my own excitement and remembering again, with a surge of dread, that Wheeler was to die in the morning, I adjusted the files in my briefcase so that I could push the card far down among Carrie's papers, which I determined to read and act upon tomorrow.

From below came a sharp knock on the door, a pause, Min's ponderous footsteps. Then I heard Meredith's voice, and Edmund's. "Is Aunty Evelyn home yet? Where is she?"

Ah, James. I touched the mound of his pillow, warm from the sun.

The sound of running feet on the stairs, Edmund shouting: "Aunty Evelyn. Where are you? It's your *birthday*."

I got up. I laughed. I didn't look back. "I'm coming, Edmund, here I am."